MYSTERY IN

HARARE

Mystery in Harare

Published by
M. J. Simms-Maddox, Inc. ~ P.O. Box 1966 ~ Salisbury, NC US
https://www.novelsbymj.com

ISBN: 978-0-578-19519-3

Printed in the United States of America

Book Cover Design by Authors Hike

M. J. Simms-Maddox

MYSTERY IN HARARE

Priscilla's Journey into Southern Africa

Revised Edition

M. J. Simms-Maddox, Inc.

To the loving memory of my eldest sister,
Sharon K. Dixon Dewberry.

CONTENTS

Preface
"The Making of the Priscilla Series"

Not all of us grow up yearning to become authors; for some, becoming an author happens. When I began writing creatively in the late 1990s, I had no idea I would write a novel series. For the record, I am self-taught. My background is in the social sciences. I had to learn how to craft fiction. After publishing my first book, *Priscilla Engaging in the Game of Politics*, I thought I was done, but more ideas emerged. By 2021, I had published five novels and a creative writing and self-publishing handbook, with more in progress.

Meanwhile, much had changed in my life. My mother—my family's first published author—and my spouse died. I retired as a professor of political science. The COVID-19 pandemic happened, and more.

During the COVID pandemic, I edited the original five books, redesigned the covers to reflect a series of novels, and wrote six more manuscripts in succession. I also hired another editor to enhance my writing and provide a fresh perspective.

The Priscilla series began with a recurring dream about a conversation I'd had with my father, a great storyteller. He shared precious thoughts about his love and hopes for me. I told a friend (Ada Taylor) about that dream, and she said, "MJ, the next time you have that dream, write it down." As I began penning that dream, I reflected that I had served as a legislative aide in the Ohio Senate in the early 1980s and more.

At the time, in the late 1990s, I knew little about the publishing industry. I sent an unsolicited voluminous manuscript to a publisher in Berkeley, California, and he responded with a kind rejection letter complimenting my writing style. He also provided contact information for an editor, ending his correspondence with, "You have three books in one." Thus began my journey as a fiction writer.

It took me almost one year to extract my first book from those "three books in one." Then, I spent a decade receiving "critiques" from the Berkeley editor mentioned earlier. As it happened, I learned the difference between critique and substantial editing the hard way.

Then, I researched, interviewed, and ended up retaining three editors. Lee Titus Elliott is excellent at substantial copyediting and helps with restructuring. Laurie Devine is excellent at developmental editing and has enlightened me about character development. It sometimes takes more than one editor to work on a book, especially the lengthy ones I write.

The other editor, Alice McVeigh—based in Britain—recommended that I work with the two American editors because, at the time, the pound sterling was valued at twice the American dollar. But Alice also enlightened me about the significance of my work—that American literature is virtually void of stories about contemporary professional Black women, specifically, about Black women with agency.

Next, I searched for a literary agent. I must have written hundreds—well, maybe not hundreds—but many query letters for almost three years. Then, in the fall of 2015, my sister-in-law, Clintina Cooper Simms, suggested that I contact Linda Ellis Eastman of the Professional Woman Network (PWN). Linda performed the final editing of *Priscilla Engaging in the Game of Politics* (2016), a political thriller. She then turned the manuscript over to her team— Professional Woman Publishing, LLC (PWP LLC)—who designed the cover, converted the document into digital format, published the book in my name, and turned the finished product—and all publishing rights—back over to me. That marked the beginning of my desire to publish my work myself.

My second novel, *Mystery in Harare: Priscilla's Journey into Southern Africa* (2017), stems from travel stories. For several years, my family, mainly my mother and I, would pick a place to visit. We toured the West Indies, Britain, France, Italy, Greece, Zimbabwe, Ghana, Senegal, and many other places, which I chronicled in a journal. Then I wrote about our travels.

The more I edited the travel stories, the more they seemed flat. Frustrated, I told a friend, Michael D. Connor, about my situation. He suggested I keep writing about *Priscilla* and give her "something juicy!" So, I wrote a love scene with Priscilla and the man she once shared a passionate love affair with.

Later, I wondered what had happened on the world stage in the middle 1980s. Terrorists were bombing airports and densely populated places. I remembered visiting one of my sisters and her family, who lived near an air force base outside Croton in the United Kingdom. When I arrived at Heathrow Airport, crowds anxiously awaited their loved ones. That was when I learned about the Islamic militants who had hijacked a TWA passenger jetliner en route from Athens to Rome. At the time, I, like many Americans, thought terrorism was "something that happens elsewhere." So I researched terrorist activities on the CIA website and drew upon my experiences during a six-week visit to Zimbabwe.

As a political scientist, I knew about the cultures and politics of Zimbabwe and South Africa, particularly the apartheid system. I was also familiar with the mineral-rich African continent. So I made up a conglomerate of mine owners and distributors of the diamonds, gold, and platinum, and named it the "Executive Committee of the South African Nationalists Movement" (the SANM). Then I created an enforcement arm called "Patrol Guard" (the PG).

At the time, the world's eyes were on the growing terrorist activities of Middle Easterners. And even though the situation in the Middle East was devastating and remains so today, little attention was given to the plight of the Black people in Zimbabwe and South Africa. Sure, news stories covered those two countries, particularly the corrupt regime of Robert Mugabe and the brazen apartheid regime in South Africa, not to mention Nelson Mandela's imprisonment. Still, it seemed to me that there was much benign neglect of the plight of Black people—the majority population—in those two countries. So the material in those travel stories proved to be useful, after all.

After writing the story, Linda Ellis Eastman and the PWP LLC published *Mystery in Harare* in my name and turned the final product—and all the publishing rights—back over to me.

Mystery in Harare: Priscilla's Journey into Southern Africa (2017) is a fast-paced, action-packed thriller. Its genre is African historical fiction, terrorism thriller, and travel adventure.

Writing is easy when one is onto a good story and in a suitable writing mood. *Three Metal Pellets* came about after talking to fans and colleagues about the presidency of Barack Obama. But there already existed a wealth of information about President Obama. Even so, I wanted to write a novel about the first president, who happened to be a Black American. So I did.

Initially, I wondered why some people still held unfounded stereotypes about Black people. Black people come from all walks of life and socioeconomic backgrounds—even billionaires. So I started by creating a fictional presidential hopeful from a family similar to the Kennedys, Rockefellers, Roosevelts, and Vanderbilts. I focused on the family's quest to build its legacy—a universal idea that anyone, regardless of race, ethnicity, or social class, can relate to. Ah, heck, it's "the American Dream."

This story begins after *Priscilla* returns from her harrowing experience in southern Africa, where, in her home office, she waits and waits for something of substance to cross her desk. About a year later, in 1987, she receives a handwritten request to head the marketing efforts of a relatively unknown presidential candidate. The story then unfolds from there.

The political scientist in me threaded a presidential election campaign through the General Election.

I brought back the terrorists who did not get Priscilla during her first time in southern Africa, which turned the book into a terrorism thriller.

Additionally, I show more of Priscilla's personal life, her family, and the family of the man with whom she had once shared a passionate love affair.

Unlike my first two books, I entirely published *Three Metal Pellets* (2018). My earlier experiences with the PWN team had prepared me for that moment, and I have been an indie author ever since.

When I completed the trilogy, I thought I'd finished writing about *Priscilla.* But I had another idea. *Special Envoy: Priscilla Journeys into Arab Islamic Territory* (2019), the fourth installment in the series, is an example of how, when an author thinks she has exhausted all that she can do with a character, more comes to mind. Its genres are Middle Eastern historical fiction, terrorism thriller, and travel adventure.

Set around 1990, most Americans are still unaware of terrorism. And for sure, most are oblivious to behind-the-scenes and off-camera work involving the brave men and women in the diplomatic and intelligence communities, whose job is to promote peace among nations.

If you have read the series' second book, some intelligence officers approach *Priscilla* about entering their realm. Her façade is that of an ordinary woman who "makes good." She resumes her PR business. But it is not until this fourth novel that I portray her as an intelligence agent. This book involved lots of research and took me about one year to compose.

Since much of the narrative deals with Arab Islamic cultures, I once again called upon my political scientist instincts to craft scenes depicting American foreign policy and do so as not to put anyone to sleep.

Approaching retirement and with the pendulum of my life moving from side to side too rapidly, I wanted at least one classic to my credit. So I published *Special Envoy* (2019) in the classic format: gold lettering on red linen hardcover, Smyth-sewn, crème-color paper stock, and a dust jacket, available only on my website or wherever I exhibit my books.

Then I published a case-bound version entitled *Special Envoy 1* (2020) and revised the title because, as it turns out, this is the first of more novels portraying Priscilla "in service to her country."

In the next novel, I wanted to show more of *Priscilla's* personal life and her romantic side. I thought about a plot involving art, notably the Metropolitan Museum of Art—hence, *The Mysterious Affair at the Met* (2021). Although the Met board of trustees retains *Priscilla* for her public relations expertise, they have no way of knowing that she will use her intelligence-gathering prowess to avert some of the deceit, fraud, and skullduggery that could quickly become the scandal of the decade if not the century. Its genres are a mishmash of art, historical fiction, mystery, romance, and travel.

Much to my surprise, I received an offer from a hybrid publisher for *The Mysterious Affair at the Met.* So, another version will be published in all formats, including a Spanish translation, in the future.

Next, *Priscilla* surprises everyone when she travels to the South of France with her six-month-old son and three household staff, where she attempts her hand at writing and unexpectedly resumes her work as a secret agent.

It's early 1992, and *Priscilla* heads into the volatile Yugoslav region, where her mission coincides with the outbreak of the Bosnian War. As it happens, *Special Envoy 2: In Service to Her Country*—the sixth novel—depicts the genocide endured by some societies as they transitioned into democracies.

There you have it, but there is more coming in 'The Priscilla Series'.

M. J. Simms-Maddox, Ph.D.

FOREWORD

Authors have always written fiction to tell the truth. Accordingly, there is proof that the only effective way to tell the story of Black Women in the political arena is, therefore, by way of writing fiction, as this area is often neglected and sidelined for obvious reasons.

The proof is manifest in some of the books that I have read, such as Stone Virgins, Yvonne Vera (2002), Negras, Yolanda Arroyo Pizarro (2012), Woman at Point Zero, Nawal El Saadawi (1975), On the Road Again, Freedom Nyamubaya (1986), and Living in the Light, Zoe Wicomb (2006). Having had the privilege and the opportunity to read the manuscript of Mystery in Harare before it was sent for publishing in 2017, I have no doubt that this book, which is part of the Priscilla Trilogy, has broken new ground.

Professor M. J. Simms-Maddox is a courageous and talented author. She deserves to be congratulated for this sterling piece of work. I have been a witness to the subject matter since I was a little girl, and I now realize that my presentation, "Silent Liberators – The Sex Workers of the 1970s," at the 2016 African Literature Association Conference in Atlanta, was not a mistake after all, as it has connected me to this great book.

Mystery in Harare is a thriller that demonstrates the wit and skill that Professor Simms-Maddox carefully crafts, reflecting Priscilla's leading role in what could best be described as a mission impossible, since the issue of Apartheid South Africa has always been sensitive. Because of the natural resources in diamonds and gold, the system could not let go.

This book cuts across cultures and nations, reflecting that the question of kith and kin cannot be underestimated, as clearly shown by the sacrifices and the commitment made by Priscilla and her abductors to bust an apartheid assassin's network thousands of miles away from home.

ALSO BY SCOTT DENNIS PARKER

Mysteries

Wading Into War

The Phantom Automobiles

Ulterior Objectives

All Chickens Must Die

Calvin Carter

Empty Coffins

Hell Dragon

The Aztec Sword

Cash Laramie and the Sundown Express

Westerns

Mosaic Law

A Father's Justice

The Killing of Lars Fulton

The Box Maker

The Agony of Love

The Naked Con

Hancock walked a short distance to his right to get a better view. After he cleared the shrubs and rocks, he saw them: two bodies. Even from this distance, Hancock could tell that the bodies were floaters. The three officers around the bodies had their hands over their noses, trying to keep the stench under control. A sudden gust of wind brought the smell up the embankment. Truman and Hancock just grimaced. McLeod gagged and brought out his handkerchief.

Truman pointed down to the bodies with his chin. "That what I think it is, Carl?"

"Certainly looks like it," Hancock replied and started down the embankment. Truman followed close behind. Starting to get queasy, McLeod hesitated, but followed.

"What do you think it is?" McLeod's voice sounded small. Neither of the two men answered but, as McLeod got closer to the scene, he didn't need anyone to tell him. Both bodies were wearing khaki shirts and fishing vests. On the chests of both bodies were large dark blood stains.

Hancock was half way down the slope when the officer with the notepad noticed the newcomers. He excused himself and plotted an intercept course.

"Hold on a minute," the officer said. He limped over the uneven terrain. "Duncan" was stitched on his uniform. "Just where do you think you're going?"

Hancock tipped his hat to Duncan. "Howdy. We were just driving by and thought we'd stop and see if you boys needed any help."

Duncan, a young man whose uniform seemed to just hang on his slight frame, outwardly bristled at the comment. "This is official police business, sir. We do not need any civilian assistance."

"Well, I'm a civilian now," Hancock replied, easing his hand inside his coat pocket, "but I used to be..."

Duncan's right hand went to his service revolver, gripped the handle, and pulled the gun halfway out of its holster. His left hand, still holding the notebook, extended straight out in Hancock's direction. The Texan froze, his hand still in his coat. Truman had seen the aggressive move by the officer and stopped cold. McLeod, still staring at the dead bodies, ran into the back of the senator.

"What the...," McLeod started to say but was overwhelmed by Duncan's shout.

"Freeze right there!" Duncan's voice cracked. " Sheriff!"

Priscilla's abduction—having been a question of a protective ploy to keep her safe from an assassin who blew her groom's brains out at the altar instead of an intended anti-apartheid associate—leaves her frightened and confused. Yet, despite the trauma resulting from the foiled assassination, abduction, and other odds, she wins the battle.

Her sole crime for being hunted down was having been a witness.

First, the battle exposes the evil and hypocrisy of the Anglican Cathedral of the Diocese in Harare and its hierarchy for being the nerve center for the pro-apartheid assassins' network.

Odder still, the real battle to liberate South Africa so that the majority Black population could be free is fought at the Anglican Cathedral, without sophisticated weaponry, where—thrown into the deep end—Priscilla's resilience helps her win the silent battle in unarmed combat supported by duck and dive tactics. Ironically, the battle takes place in the environs of the Parliament building, banks, hotels, and newsrooms. Still, no one is aware, including the security forces, who are always on the lookout for trouble.

With the apartheid commandos out of the way, Priscilla and her abductors, who are, in fact, her comrades in arms, march on to South Africa for the final push, despite baptism of fire from more assassins on the way and in South Africa itself.

In the end, Priscilla is the heroine in the liberation of a nation.

Fictional histories, futures, and current affairs of Black Women in the political arena must continue to be written by women themselves in all corners of the world. The struggle continues.

VIRGINIA PHIRI

Ms. Phiri is a founding member of Zimbabwe Women Writers, active in the African Literature Association, and an orchid expert. She has published over fifty articles in orchid journals and four novels: Desperate (2002), Destiny (2006), Highway Queen (2010), and Grey Angels (2017).

MYSTERY IN
HARARE

1

Everything Went Black for the Bride

Columbus, Ohio
June 28, 1986

Priscilla J. Austin floated through the handsomely carved wooden double doors from the vestibule of her First AME Zion Church. Ever conscious of the power of an entrance, she paused on the threshold for all those who mattered most to her to catch sight of her in this ivory gown and tiara. She had always vowed she would never marry, yet here she was, resplendent in her glorious face-framing veil, her bridal bouquet demurely held in her hands. *Incredible, just incredible,* she thought.

Moments earlier, she had gazed in a mirror as her ever-meticulous mother adjusted her tiara and train; the train rolled out seemingly forever. Her elegant gown was laced with fine pearl beads on its collar and across the bodice and shoulders. The broad-gauged satin skirt was embroidered with the old English artwork that her sister Camille, who was one of her bridesmaids, had incorporated into the design of the wedding invitations. Priscilla was aware that she did not look at all like herself—a take-charge executive of a Columbus, Ohio-based PR firm—who dressed in tailored business suits and, on occasion, in earth-tones that complemented her pale "red-bone" complexion. But here she was playing out the part of a storybook bride, and she was not so sure she liked it.

Savor the moment, she told herself. She was determined to make a success of this, like every other role she had taken on. *Besides, everyone says this will be the happiest day of my life.*

Tremulously Priscilla smiled as she scanned the congregation and spotted her four sisters and sole brother, her aunts and uncles, and her cousins galore from both sides of the family. There were three hundred guests, including so many politicians from all over Ohio that they might have been able to declare a quorum and vote on some important legislation right here in the church. Of course, once she had decided to do this, there had been no question of an elopement or a small city hall ceremony. She was not only a preacher's daughter but was also about to marry her pastor. So it had been unthinkable not to have a church wedding. Yet, as accustomed as she was to coordinating state-wide special events, even she had been unable to control the scale of her own wedding. There were even a dozen in the wedding party!

As she gazed down the long aisle at her bridegroom waiting for her at the altar, a cold chill shot through her, and her smile froze on her lips.

Jonathan, she thought, and almost she cried out his name.

Sometime later, she was to wonder if she had been experiencing a premonition of what was to come.

But, at the time, she shook off her foreboding.

It's only grief again, she thought. And then: *If only Daddy were here!* She was so conscious that he was not right there beside her, preparing to give her away. She had lost Nelson five years ago, and mostly she had learned to live with the muddled waves of unexpected grief. But seldom had that loss hurt as much as it did just now, on her wedding day.

Beside her, her ten-year-old nephew Germane tugged at her hand. "Aunt Priscilla, do we march down the aisle now? Is this when I give you away?"

Their eyes met, and again she was smiling as slightly she shook her head, waiting for the organist to strike up the wedding march.

Priscilla felt a sharp, sudden rush of energy coming at her from the sanctuary. Her gaze centered on the man she was about to marry. Fondly, she smiled. Nelson—she had often called her parents by their given names; since her teenage years, it had been Nelson and Liza—would have loved Jonathan. The two men—both ordained Methodist ministers—were cut from the same clerical cloth. They were kind, ethical, good men. Jonathan was only slightly lighter-complexioned and shorter than Nelson, perhaps a little slimmer of build, but serious like Nelson. Stalwart. Older, as her father had been older than her mother. Then Priscilla recalled what she had once said to her best friend Julia, who radiated this afternoon in her maid of honor finery. If she ever married, Priscilla had told her that what she wanted most of all was not grand passion but simply someone who accepted her as she was and who would treat her kindly. Jonathan fitted the bill.

"I suppose you know how proud your father would have been to see you marry Jonathan," Liza had said to her just moments ago in the dressing room adjacent to the sanctuary.

Priscilla had nodded and wondered again why it was—her mom's nagging tone or maybe even her habit of always stating the obvious—that, compared to her adored father, Liza had so often been a source of irritation. Nelson had always been relatively easy to please, but Liza more often had been critical. Take her choice of husband, for example. Not only her mother but her sisters and her friends had made it their business to share their deep reservations about whether she loved Jonathon enough to marry him. Even her father—in the last real words they had shared before cancer took over and he slipped away and died—had confided that he wanted her to make her own choices and live her own life to please herself and not—as so often had been her penchant—to please him. "Be happy," he had told her.

Steadily she returned Jonathan's smile. Priscilla was not one for reflection and second-guessing. But, with this marriage, was she following her father's advice to be happy? She had most certainly known passion, but she believed a good marriage could be built on other factors like compatibility and shared values. Yet her thoughts trailed to that one day with that one man—that delectable surprise of a man she had known *that way* only once and then put out of her life. Better not think of *him*. This was her wedding day. *Jonathan, concentrate on Jonathan.* In time, her love for him would grow. They would have a fine life together. She nodded to herself in finality.

Priscilla had thought everyone was in place and that, any second, she would be walking down the aisle.

But no. Ohio state Senator Daniel P. Callahan was taking what seemed to Priscilla to be carefully measured steps escorting her mom down the aisle to her front-row seat. Priscilla's smile widened at the sight of the senator and Liza together. The senator had long since been Priscilla's mentor and friend, but for years before that, he had also been her lover. But, on this, her wedding day, she was pleased seeing him in the role of a member of her extended family.

She had to admit that her mom was aglow in a bright floral-print dress against a black silk gown that complemented her sparkling, prematurely salt-and-pepper hair. It was easy to understand why Nelson used to call her "my little angel."

As the senator escorted Liza down the aisle, they both nodded regally at the many familiar and happy faces because they both relished being the focus of attention.

Ah, Priscilla sighed when she saw her mom sit down. But then, for some unknown reason—maybe, Priscilla thought later, the gesture was simply the automatic habit of the politician always to shake hands—he swiftly stepped toward the altar. Then, just as the organist struck up the wedding march, the senator extended his right hand to the groom, the Reverend Jonathan Morgan. That single gesture alone seemed to unleash a bolt of rumbling thunder.

A piercing cracking flash hurled across the sanctuary. An uninvited guest—an unknown implacable god—entered into the midst.

Priscilla watched in horror as a massive portion of Jonathan's head erupted. She raised her hands and covered her mouth, for she could not believe her eyes. Her pulse quickened. Her heart pounded. Her eyes glazed over and widened. She saw dark-red blood and clumps of dreary grey matter drenching his morning suit and spilling down to the white runner covering the red carpet. Then she saw him fall to the floor beside the white linen-draped altar rail.

Priscilla heard another clap like thunder hurling from overhead.

"No!" She clutched Germane's hand. *Surely, this isn't happening! No, this can't be real!*

The second jaded bolt ripped through the holy arena, striking the senator's right temple. When he reached up and tried to touch his bloody head, he slumped and fell unconscious onto the floor. Red liquid splattered his face and the white robe of the bishop, who was one of the concelebrants. The bishop dropped his *Book of Discipline* and froze in place.

The mother of the bride stood up abruptly, speechless and confounded.

The guests nearest the altar sat aghast. Those seated from the midsection to the rear of the sanctuary turned around and faced what they seemed to think was the direction of the flash, where, at the top of the inclined aisle beneath the balcony, stood the bewildered bride and her young nephew.

Unlike almost all others in attendance, who were focusing on her, instinctively, Priscilla was looking up in the direction of the stairwell.

Just as she was pulling her nephew back through the massive wooden double doors, she caught a clear look at the face of a man with a black leather satchel descending the stairs and sprinting through the vestibule and out one of the side doors.

That face! I know that face! Although Priscilla could not remember when or where she had seen that man, she knew she had seen him somewhere before.

She had just enough time to glance down at Germane and to see that he, too, must have seen what had to have been the assassin when someone grabbed her from behind and, with phenomenal precision, covered her nose and mouth with a damp cloth. As she inhaled the strong toxic substance, she had one clear thought. *Chloroform.*

And then everything went black for the bride.

2

Stranger Things Have Happened

Germane sprang into action. He lunged at the mysterious man, kicking and beating his long legs, and screaming, "Who are you? Why are you doing this to my Aunt Priscilla?"

The mysterious man who had grabbed Priscilla and sedated her was accompanied by another man—dark-haired, well-groomed, and dressed in a black Armani suit. But before he and the other man could take Priscilla away from the church, they had to contend with her nephew.

The mysterious man stumbled, but he quickly regained his composure. "Germane—" He held up his hand in a nonthreatening way, palm facing outward.

"How," the child asked, still holding onto the man's legs, "do you know my name?"

"Young man, please, we're the good guys," the mysterious man said, as he gestured to the other man. Then, still holding Priscilla's small limp body, he spoke more intensely, "No harm will come to your aunt. But we need to get her out of here for her own protection. Now, run down front and comfort your grandmother. Be strong for your aunt *and* your grandmother."

There was something infinitely reassuring in the man's tone of voice. But before Germane could yield and do what he had been told to do, he welled up: "Don't you hurt her." His voice broke. "And… and …You give me something to hold onto until you bring her back."

The mysterious man gently removed Priscilla's tiara and her veil. He handed them to Germane.

Germane could smell the chloroform, yet he kissed his aunt's cheek, anyway. "See you soon, Aunt Priscilla." Then, as if holding the mysterious man in check, he looked back up at him. "Soon," he repeated, and wept.

The mysterious man picked Priscilla up in his arms. Then, the other man, who had kept still and quiet, looped the long train of her gown around her body and opened the colossal wooden door leading to the outside. Then together, the two men raced out of the church, the one with Priscilla in his arms.

Germane watched as the two men carried his aunt away. He wiped away his tears and runny nose. Then he walked back inside the sanctuary.

Just inside the wooden double doors, he stood staring at the pandemonium inside the immense Gothic space. The glory of the jewel-toned stained glass and polished mahogany pews and pulpits for once were overwhelmed by the panic of the terrified wedding guests, some of them stampeding toward the side doors, many others gravitating toward the center of the sanctuary where, under the massive dome, yet others—not just the women, but men, too—sat in their pews, screaming and hollering.

Germane lurched forward, down the inclined aisle, where—a mere three minutes ago—he had anticipated escorting his favorite aunt to her waiting bridegroom, with all eyes upon them.

He had been thrilled when Priscilla asked him to give her away, although his mother had cautioned him a few days later that some of his great uncles on Grandpa Nelson's side of the family had been hurt, even angry, that none of them had been singled out as the rightful stand-in. But his Aunt Priscilla had stood firm. Germane had been her choice, and she had personally chosen the boy-sized black tuxedo that he wore with such pride.

He made slow progress down the long aisle. At times he had to cling to the pews so that he was not knocked down and trampled. He saw long-stem red and yellow roses everywhere, even on the shoulders of the pews, where they were entwined in yellow ribbons.

Germane staggered onward, the tiara and veil held in his hands. Dimly he noted that the chancel showcased white floral floor-model vases filled with bunches of red and yellow roses. The deaconesses had covered the altar and the other sacred objects in white-laced linens. Yet in the super-charged atmosphere of the sanctuary, the long-stem red and yellow roses seemed to droop, and the white altar clothes, now splattered with blood, seemed anything but holy.

At last, he reached the crowd closest to the altar, where, in his peripheral vision, he sensed his grandmother was still sitting in the front row pew. He hesitated. He wanted the comfort—and safety, too—of either her arms or those of his mother. But he could not see his mother, Helen, anywhere.

Yet he could not resist the pull of whatever was the center of interest on the floor beside the altar rail.

Germane was small for his age, so it was easy to insinuate himself between the legs of the big people. So many of them seemed too frightened to move. Ahead he glimpsed something on the floor. He recoiled at the memory of the flash of the gunfire, and the two men falling.

Finally! Germane stopped dead at the sight of the two bodies on the floor. Blood and brain matter splattered all about them. There was blood everywhere. He could not see the faces, but he was never to forget that blood and that gore.

A middle-aged woman kneeled next to the senator, sobbing. "Daniel! Oh, my Daniel!" Senator Callahan and his wife were in their late fifties, the same age as Liza. As Germane watched, he saw another woman put her arms around the first one, and together they sobbed.

One of the concelebrants finally regained his composure. He knelt and felt the senator's throat for a pulse and then nodded. "Still breathing," he whispered. But he shook his head as he stared at what was left of the bridegroom's head. He prayed aloud for the living and the dead, and the people said, almost in a whisper, "Amen."

Germane reached over and, in a tender gesture for one so young, covered Jonathan's head with the veil of the bride. But he held onto the tiara. For a moment, though, he stood there, wondering if he should be doing something else. Finally, he tore his eyes away from the blood and the gore.

Quickly then, he stepped back and ran over to his grandmother's waiting arms, where he nestled in her bosom and wept like the child that he was. When he told her what had happened to Priscilla, his grandmother recoiled in horror. Then, true to her lifetime as a preacher's wife, she, too, prayed aloud.

Gradually now, Germane could sort out words from the screaming crowd.

"Someone, call an ambulance!"

"Call the police!"

While Germane was telling Liza what had happened to Priscilla, his eldest aunt, Ellen, leaned over from her pew behind them and asked, "Where's Priscilla, Germane?"

But it was Liza who responded, saying, over her shoulder, "Ellen, Priscilla's gone. Germane said, 'a mysterious man took her away from all this.'"

"No!" Ellen covered her mouth with her hands, and then she cried, "Oh, no!"

Just then another voice drowned out the others. "Clear the way! Security!"

Two burly, middle-aged men shouldered toward the crowd closest to the altar rail.

"Who's in charge here? We're the security." Doug, one of the security guards, said and then asked, "What's happened in here?"

Julia, Priscilla's best friend and maid of honor, detached from the crowd. Her once-lovely melon tea-length silk dress was splattered all over with blood. During the pandemonium she had been kneeling beside the two bodies, for the entire bottom of her skirt now drenched in blood.

"I'm here, Doug," she said. "And you, Mitch, come here." Always master of every detail, Julia remembered the names of the security detail, and, as usual, she took charge and deftly guided the two men away from the throng. "I'm sorry to tell you this, but someone shot Senator Callahan *and* the groom, Reverend Morgan." The guards both stood in disbelief as Julia described the gruesome chain of events that had occurred inside the church while they had been stationed outside.

"Holy cow," Doug breathed. He and his partner had thought they were providing minimal security, as it were, for this church wedding. Charged with patrolling the exterior of the site, mostly they had lounged around and loaded the numerous wedding gifts onto vans for transport to the parsonage. "Has anyone called for an ambulance?"

"I did." Julia nodded. "They're on their way. The police as well. There's a phone in the sacristy. I asked for two ambulances. I'm afraid it's too late for the groom. But the senator is still breathing. I think—"

Doug broke in. "But the bride! I think there's been a kidnapping, too!"

Julia staggered, but Doug caught her before she could fall. "Priscilla?" She sank down in a nearby pew. She and Priscilla were more than best friends. Since they had teamed up a few years ago—when Priscilla was a legislative aide in the Ohio Senate—Julia's attachment to her friend had grown and grown. Whenever Priscilla was rash or demanding, Julia was the one who smoothed things over in the end. She looked over at the two bodies on the floor. What would Priscilla do if she were facing a similar fate? Julia could hear herself breathing hard, almost panting. With an effort, she mastered her rising panic. "What happened? Tell me everything! Every detail…."

Tersely the guard reported that, moments ago, he had seen a man dressed in a black suit, carrying the bride in his arms, out of a side door of the church. "She looked unconscious to me. There was a white cloth covering her face. That guy and another one with him put her into a silver Land Rover that seemed to be waiting at the curb with the motor running. And then it sped away! That's why we came running in here!"

Julia pulled herself together. She stood up in her blood-drenched dress. Priscilla needed her. She would be here for her now, as she always was. Already she had done what had to be done to get the emergency crew and police here to cope with what had happened to the groom and the senator. But now she would have to do whatever she could to help her Priscilla. She narrowed her eyes as she looked toward the rear of the inclined sanctuary. *Why would anyone kill the groom and kidnap the bride?* Then she looked back at the floor near the altar rail. *And Senator Callahan? What was his role in all of this? Who had been the actual target, the politician or the preacher? What lethal enemies would a pastor have? The senator,* she thought. *It had to have been aimed at the politician.* Her mind raced. *Of course Callahan had enemies. Every politician does. But Ohio was not Beirut. And his foes might have the tongues of a serpent, but surely they weren't assassins. Was this a professional hit? If so, what could he possibly have done to trigger such retaliation?*

Mitch, the other security guard, pulled his radio from its holster and called the police. There was static, some quick responses. The others heard him say, "Yes, two down. Yes, gunshots. One may still make it. The other may be DOA." He paused and listened. Then he nodded. "OK. Got it. 'Nobody leaves.'" Grimly he signed off and replaced his radio in its holster before turning back to face Julia. "You're right, lady. They already knew. Ambulances should be here at any minute. But it's anybody's guess who will get here first, the cops or the EMS."

Doug broke in. "You forgot to tell 'em about the kidnapping."

"First things first. The two who took the bullets take priority." Mitch bellowed to the congregation at large. "Has anybody else been hurt or shot?" There was no response. He raised his voice even louder. "I'm sorry, folks, for the apparent tragedy, but I just talked to the police. They are asking—no, *ordering*—no one leaves the premises until the authorities arrive. It could be a long day, or they might just get your contact information. But for now, everybody remains, just as you are. Please cooperate, folks...."

There was a collective intake of breath, and then the wedding guests withdrew from the section nearest the altar rail. Many sat back down in the pews, and they remained there, as though too afraid to move too far away. Besides, no one knew whether the shooter or his possible accomplices were still on the premises.

As the guests were settling back down in their seats, a dark-complexioned, portly figure approached Julia and the security detail. "I saw something before the shooting started," he began. "Or rather *someone*...."

Julia wheeled. *"'Someone?'"*

"I was over by the side door," the man continued. "The bridesmaids were coming down the aisle when I noticed a tall, white man with a strange accent elbowing his way toward the door. 'Excuse,' he kept saying. 'Excuse!' He had this funny foreign kind of accent. I heard him say that he left his wedding gift in his car. So out the door he went, and it wasn't long—all those pretty bridesmaids were still in the aisle—when he returned carrying an elongated black leather satchel. For all I knew it was just an unusual wedding gift."

"And then?" Julia asked. "Did he return to his seat?"

The informant shook his head. "No. He never did. But I kept looking for him, and I think I saw him going upstairs to the balcony."

Mitch whistled. "Where he'd have a perfect line of fire to the altar."

Julia and the security guards were still staring up at the balcony when there was a commotion at the church's main entrance. A trim white man in a dark suit, flanked by two policemen—one black, one white—strode down the aisle. Another, carrying a camera, hurried behind.

At the altar rail, the police detective lost no time directing the photographer to record the presumed murder scene.

"They're trying to get the pictures before the ambulances arrive," murmured Mitch.

"Where *are* those ambulances?" Julia wrung her hands and shook her head. "Every minute makes it less likely the senator is going to make it."

As she spoke, they all heard the sirens, and in a moment the emergency crew was wheeling a gurney down the aisle. One of them shouted, "Make way! C'mon, people, let us through!"

It seemed only seconds later that Senator Callahan—evidently still alive but unconscious—was loaded onto the gurney and wheeled back up the inclined aisle, his wife clinging to the arm of one of the emergency crew. The first responders loaded the senator into the ambulance and helped his wife inside as well, then they slammed the doors and sped away with their sirens blaring. The siren's wail receded as the senator was rushed to the hospital.

A second crew took its time with the remains of the groom. As the bridegroom's twin brother conferred with the police and the EMS crew, the police photographer took more photographs. Then the remains of the bridegroom were lifted onto the gurney and wheeled back along the inclined aisle to the waiting ambulance. The bridegroom's brother rode in the back of the ambulance. When he was out of earshot, a first responder said that he expected the bridegroom would be declared dead by the doctor at the emergency room.

The Columbus Police detective, a sandy-haired fellow in early middle age, had meanwhile been talking to the guests. Before long he approached Julia and the security guards. "You're Julia, Ma'am? The maid of honor?" When she nodded, he flashed his police badge and stuck out his hand. "Detective David Stoudemeir." He gestured to the floor in front of the altar rail where the slain bridegroom had fallen. "Sorry for your loss, Miss."

Julia and the security guards told him what they knew, including the portly eyewitness reporting his suspicions about a guest having re-entered the church with a rifle-sized package. But then the detective's thick eyebrows rose at the mention of the bride's abduction.

"Details?" he asked. "This man in black, whom you think abducted the bride. What did he look like?"

As Mitch gave him a vague description, the police detective shook his head. "Surely someone else saw the guy?"

To everyone's astonishment, Liza stood up from her front row pew. Shoulders squared, head held high—still in mother-of-the-bride mode. She would not lose her composure, not in public. There would be time enough to break down and cry, but not here, not now. She stood proudly amid the groundcover of her four other daughters and Nelson, Jr., snuggly buffering her and Germane. Onlookers could not help noticing the distinct cheekbones framing each of their faces, their overarching eyebrows, their alluring, though reddened, weeping eyes, and the natural radiance of their skin tones ranging from Harriet's Nubian to Helen's ostensibly pale complexion. At once the siblings' spirits lifted as all eyes fell upon their matriarch. For surely someone would tell *her* why the two men had been shot and where and why her beloved Priscilla had been abducted. For the Austin tribe had come to Columbus not only for a wedding but for an equally auspicious occasion, a family reunion, but not for this, whatever this was.

"My grandson Germane," Liza said with a stoic air, "he was with Priscilla when the men took her away." She beckoned her grandson to stand. Then she dabbed her uncontrollable flow of mucous with a Kleenex tissue. "Go ahead, Germane," she prodded him. "Tell the officer what that man said to you."

Perhaps Liza's comportment caught Detective Stoudemeir off his guard. Or perhaps he was more than a little surprised that he was about to get an eyewitness account of one of the alleged crimes, from a youngster! His eyes shifted from Liza to the young man's shimmering, dark, almost ebony, freckled skin and alluring dark eyes, and, even when he was trying to stand still, a kinetic kind of energy. *A handsome little fellow*, he thought, *but probably not much use in a murder investigation.* "So, you saw the bad guy, did you?"

Liza was not pleased with the detective's seeming condescension to whatever it was that her grandson was about to say. "Ahem—" But Germane had already begun talking.

"First, he called me by my name," Germane said. Then, word for word, he repeated what else the man had said, adding: "Then I did what he said. I came down here to be with Grandma. I've been living with her in Sills Creek, Illinois."

"Such a brave young man," Detective Stoudemeir said. "Now, Son, did you have any reason to be afraid of that man? Did it appear as if he carried a weapon?"

"No, Officer, I can honestly say I wasn't afraid of him. And no, Officer, he didn't seem to be carrying a gun."

The detective nodded at the boy and then looked around the church and frowned.

Germane sat back down.

Then Detective Stoudemeir said, "We've got a situation here, folks. Either the shooter and the kidnappers were a team, or the gunman acted alone—and the other men really did rescue Ms. Austin from the scene."

Whichever seemed more likely to him, Detective Stoudemeir did not share any more speculation, at least not about the abduction. Instead, he turned to the question of why something that seemed like a professional hit would have happened in the middle of a church wedding—at a black church in the vicinity of the Ohio Capitol, at that.

His look now encompassed Julia, the grandmother, the boy, and the security guards. "I'm wondering about motive," he began. "Any of you have any thoughts about why something like this happened here?"

Julia bit her lip and then spoke her mind. "I don't want to sound crazy," she began. "But I've been thinking and thinking about that very question. There could be a link with something that's been happening in the Ohio Senate." As the detective looked incredulously at her, she elaborated. "I mean, there've been a lot of headlines about Senator Callahan—he's the one who was just taken to the hospital with the head wound—speaking out about South Africa."

"'South Africa?'" The detective repeated the unlikely locale.

"It's a big controversy," Julia continued. "Very political. The South African Divestiture Bill is all about racism, apartheid and, at its heart, all about money. Diamonds! Gold! Platinum! You name it! And it's one that Senator Callahan has been in the thick of. It's been all over the news. Not just local but national. International, in fact."

"You're serious?" The detective stared closely at Julia—a tall, commanding woman with a radiant Nubian complexion, short hair, and take-charge demeanor. *A woman to be taken seriously.* He thought fast. He had indeed seen reports in the newspapers and on television about Ohio politicians sounding off about South Africa. He had shrugged that off as just more publicity-seeking politicians whom he thought should be spending their time on bread-and-butter Ohio issues, anyway. *Africa.* But maybe, just maybe, this woman in the blood-drenched maid-of-honor dress was on to something. His

30

first insight at the crime scene had been that the range of the shooting and the damage to the two men had seemed consistent with a professional hit job. One of the men was the intended target, but which one and why had puzzled him. *Had the senator been the target, and the bridegroom only collateral damage?*

Julia seemed to be able to read his thoughts. "Stranger things have happened," she said.

The detective squinted even more closely at her. *OK, so she has credibility. But surely this isn't a case of international terrorism? In Columbus? At a wedding in a black church?* He sighed. *These days, one couldn't be too careful. There would be hell to pay if this woman in the bloody dress turned out to be right. I'd better cover myself and call in the big guns. Besides, just in case she is right, it'll be a feather in my cap to make this call right away, on the scene. Maybe even a promotion if I played this right.*

"Nobody moves," the Columbus Police detective eventually said.

Columbus Police Detective David Stoudemeir then excused himself and walked outside to his vehicle. From there, he made a series of calls at various lengths to his captain at the station, and then, at his superior's direction, to the local office of the Federal Bureau of Investigation. Once on the line with the FBI, the detective was shuttled from agent to agent, and there were delays and hemming and hawing. But at last, he shambled back into the church.

"What's happening?" Julia asked Detective Stoudemeir.

"We wait," said the Columbus Police detective. "The FBI is on the way."

3

The Makeover & Missing Videotapes

While the FBI agents made their way to the First AME Zion Church, called "First Church" by its members and friends, the men who had abducted Priscilla had all but made their way to the Port Columbus International Airport, where they quickly boarded a private jetliner. The plane took off at seemingly warp speed.

Several hours later, the passengers disembarked at Charles de Gaulle International Airport, taking a diversionary course from their destination. Effective and efficient at such a tour de force, the relief team of the clandestine American-based Collective Force (the CF) had already arranged a layover at the Château Cheverny, an exquisite, though inconspicuous safehouse situated in the Loire Valley.

With international terrorism on the rise, the team had many choices for rendering a new look for their ward. The men thought that Priscilla's physical characteristics resembled, for the most part, those of many of the people in Ethiopia, Jordan, Israel, Lebanon, Egypt, and a few other North African and Middle Eastern cultures. But just in case her headdress—a tan, lightly woven rayon turban—was removed, they cut her hair short so that, if necessary, she might pass as a young man.

The next morning, around 9:00 a.m. GMT, the CF relief team and their singular passenger boarded another private jetliner. This time they were heading to the Harare International Airport in the recently independent nation of Zimbabwe.

Back in the American Midwest in Columbus, Ohio—after what seemed like only a few minutes but could have been a half hour or longer—the FBI team arrived at First Church.

FBI Agent Marvin Rothschild—tall, pensive, cool, with a full head of thick, dark hair—stepped confidently down the aisle to meet the Columbus Police detective. The two officers walked off to the side and talked in low voices while the wedding guests, who still had not been allowed to leave the church, watched as raptly as though they were at home watching a police investigation on television.

When the two lawmen returned to the scene of the crimes at the altar, Agent Rothschild stared down at the tape markings where the two bodies had fallen. He shook his head. "A wedding. Something like this, and at a wedding." He looked around at the staring congregation. "So they all saw it. But what did they really see, Dave?" Already the two officers were on a first-name basis. It was Agent Rothschild's opinion that too much energy was lost when different government agencies worked at odds with each other. "From the people you've questioned so far, who do I need to talk to?"

Detective Stoudemeir pointed to Germane. "The kid may have seen the shooter. And for sure, Marv, he saw the one who abducted the bride."

But first, he beckoned to the portly figure. The man rose from his seat and walked to the two lawmen. After he repeated almost verbatim what he had said earlier about the white man with the strange accent, FBI Agent Rothschild said, "Hmm." *Rarely*, he was thinking, *does an assassin behave so boldly*. Then, "Thank you, Sir." After that, the portly figure turned to go back to his seat, but not before the FBI agent told him, "We need you to provide a description of the 'white man with the strange accent' to a sketch artist."

Then, Detective Stoudemeir beckoned to the youngster.

Eager to do something, anything, to see his Aunt Priscilla again and to find out who had killed his Uncle Jonathan and shot the senator and why, Germane proudly stepped forward. "Glad to help," he said. "You're going to show me your FBI badge? Like on TV?"

The agent smiled, nodded, and produced his identification. He took an immediate liking to the kid. He had a boy about this one's age.

Sagely Germane examined the credentials and then grinned. Without being prompted, he repeated his story. But this time, he added the information that his aunt's abductor had given him the bride's tiara and her veil. He held out the tiara, which he had been holding in his hands all this time.

"You didn't tell me all that," said the Columbus Police detective.

"You never asked," Germane said.

"Is there anything *else* you haven't told me about your conversation with the man who took your Aunt Priscilla?" the detective asked.

"No, Officer. All I know is that the man was kind to me, and he gave me Aunt Priscilla's headpiece. Aside from what else I've already told you, there's nothing more."

After that exchange, Agent Rothschild ramped up his queries of the young man: "Do you think, Germane, that you can sit with a sketch artist and describe the man who took your aunt? And by the way, did you happen to get a look at anybody else in the vicinity of the vestibule during or after the shooting?"

"Yes, and yes. I remember the face of the man who took my Aunt Priscilla very well, and yes, I caught a side glimpse of a man running out of the church. He had a long, black canvas or leather bag. It wasn't exactly as big as a military duffel like my father used to have, but it was as narrow and long."

As Germane described what he had seen, FBI Agent Rothschild said, "Hmm." He was thinking, *Just received corroboration of the statement by the overweight figure.* But Detective Stoudemeir was flabbergasted, for as it turned out, Germane was a key eyewitness to critical elements in not one but all three of the crimes.

Germane whispered to his grandmother, "Agent Rothschild seems to appreciate me, you know. He talks to me as if I can think." Germane seemed to grow taller with the role of "man of the house."

His Grandma Liza basked in an aura of absolute pride. She also liked to think that she had just received the blessed assurance that, come what may, she would see her daughter again.

Agent Rothschild called over to the police photographer, who was still lingering on the scene. Together he and the detective studied the images framed in the camera's memory.

"I got plenty of photos of both men before the paramedics took them away," said the police photographer.

Agent Rothschild nodded at the detective. "Looks to me, too, like a professional hit."

Agent Rothschild then asked the other policemen if they had collected ample evidence to gauge the trajectory of the shot, and they nodded and explained. Just then, it seemed readily apparent to both the Columbus Police detective and to the FBI agent that the senator was the target and that, for some unknown reason, Jonathan had entered into the line of fire.

But Agent Rothschild was not yet prepared to share any of his preliminary findings. Next, he asked Detective Stoudemeir if he had gathered enough information from the other guests regarding what they had observed, and he said that he had.

Agent Rothschild then immediately turned to the congregation and said, "Is there anyone here who knows of anyone who'd want to harm Senator Callahan, Reverend Morgan, or Ms. Austin? I'm providing my contact information for you in the event you find the courage to share your thoughts with me in person or anonymously. Whatever, we *will* get to the bottom of this tragedy. Meanwhile, although many of you might be from out of town, please do not attempt to leave the vicinity. And please, people, help us in any way you can. A state lawmaker has been shot, a minister has been killed, and a young woman has been abducted, kidnapped, or otherwise taken against her will. All total, we're looking at a pile of federal offenses. We realize all this is strange to most of you; however, in order to solve these crimes, we need everyone to think about everything you know about the victims, *everything*, and share that information with us. Only then will we be able to bring the perpetrator or perpetrators to justice. For now, however, we needn't hold you any longer. Try to resume your lives as best you can. And call us with anything you remember about today's tragedy or about the senator, the Reverend, or Ms. Austin."

He turned and faced Detective Stoudemeir and asked, "Detective Stoudemeir, is there anything you wish to add?"

"No, Agent Rothschild, not at this time."

The FBI agent's attention shifted. "Where's the maid of honor?" His eyes scanned the myriad of troubled faces across the immense inclined sanctuary. "And what about the best man?"

Even as Detective Stoudemeir beckoned to Julia to join him and Agent Rothschild, he explained to the FBI agent that the best man was the twin brother of the dead bridegroom and that he had, understandably, ridden in the ambulance to the hospital. He added that he had doubted the brother could have provided any useful information because he was wholly outside the loop of Jonathan's work in the church and was apparently not even remotely political.

The FBI agent nodded and said that someone could take a statement from the brother later. Julia, however, became the subject of the agent's undivided attention.

Agent Rothschild quickly learned that Julia, as Priscilla's longtime executive assistant, was intimately familiar with both the personal and professional aspects of the missing bride's life, especially with her work in the political arena. Julia also spoke candidly about Priscilla's concern for the senator's safety as it pertained to the debate in the Ohio Senate over the South African Divestiture (SAD) Bill. His eyes brightened when Julia mentioned how Priscilla, as part of her work as a political public relations consultant, had overseen the videotaping of the bill.

"As I remember it, Priscilla was very uncomfortable on the day of that taping," Julia recalled. "She said something about having seen some strange-looking characters in the gallery."

"'Strange looking characters?'" The FBI agent had become even more attentive.

Julia nodded. "She said something about them looking 'like soldiers out of their uniforms.' It generally takes a lot to get Priscilla upset. But she said that 'those guys made my skin crawl.' She actually said that she feared they might do something bad to the senator."

The FBI agent and the Columbus Police detective looked at each other.

"You know much about this South African thing?" asked the detective.

"Some," answered the FBI agent. "But I think we're going to be finding out lots more." Briefly, he told Detective Stoudemeir that the FBI was already putting together a special team and that a series of briefings for the two of them would be scheduled soon.

Glumly the detective nodded. Promotion or not, this was more than he'd bargained for.

Agent Rothschild turned back to Julia. His superiors had made it clear that he was responsible for running down whatever leads emerged from the crime scene. "You wouldn't happen to know, Miss, where she keeps those tapes from that Senate hearing on South Africa?"

"If you take me to her place, I could give it a good search," Julia offered. "Priscilla is a very organized person. She even labels the food in her refrigerator. But just in case I can't find her copy of that Senate session, I know the firm that taped it—Wiseman's on North High Street."

"Now we're getting somewhere." The FBI agent was smiling. "Now we're really getting somewhere."

At that point, Julia looked over at the empty pew where Liza and Germane had been sitting. She jumped to a conclusion. "Protective custody?" When the FBI agent did not answer, Julia took a deep breath. She could not worry about everything and everyone. She would have to assume that Priscilla's mother and nephew were in good hands. Her priority now had to be to help the authorities get Priscilla back as quickly as possible—and unharmed. To her way of thinking, the key to unlocking her whereabouts could turn on those tapes.

When the FBI agent and the Columbus Police detective asked her to take them to Priscilla's West Third Street home office, she agreed.

Julia inserted her house key into Priscilla's front door. She led the agent and the detective into the first-floor apartment of the stately Victorian home, which served as both an upscale residence and a trendy workplace. She opened the French doors from the reception area to the office space and pointed to filing cabinets heaped with stacks of videotapes.

Detective Stoudemeir walked in first and headed over to Priscilla's desk. Then he pressed the message button on her telephone recorder. Hurriedly he listened. Most of the messages related to the wedding, but he packed the recorder's tape to take away as part of the evidence, anyway. "It's worth another listen," he said. "Might find something useful on this."

Agent Rothschild searched through some of the videotapes, but he did not find anything labeled SAD. When he sat down at Priscilla's desk, the detective asked, "What ails you, Marv?"

"Could she have labeled the tapes under another name," Agent Rothschild asked, "in case something like this incident might've occurred? Obviously, she was suspicious of something. So where exactly would you hide something that you didn't want someone else to find?"

"Is it possible she didn't label the outside of the box?" the detective replied. "Try that angle."

Just then, Julia suggested: "Okay, fellas, why not allow me to take all these tapes down and open them up, one by one? And remember," she reminded them, "if we're unsuccessful, we can always call Wiseman's, the company that did the videoing."

"Go ahead," said Agent Rothschild, "For now, however, I need to check in with headquarters."

Julia opened some of the boxes that contained the videotapes. Detective Stoudemeir continued searching the office for anything he thought might be useful. Agent Rothschild talked on the telephone to his superiors about what he called "the shooting incident at First Church in Columbus." He nodded as he listened to the voice on the other end. Then he said, "We're almost certain the ballistics report will confirm a professional hit. But get a load of this: it's beginning to look like we're dealing with a hitman from South Africa. Yeah, I'm thinking it might be the PG. If that pans out, you know the next call we need to make."

After Agent Rothschild completed his call, he turned around in his seat and looked directly at Julia. "You know you're going to be out of contact with your friend, the bride, for a while?" Then he watched the detective finish his call on his cellular phone. "Come to think of it, Dave, maybe we'd better consider attaching a security detail to Ms. Julia here, too. If we connected you to Ms. Austin, surely the other side will."

Julia shrugged. Her attention was more engaged in getting Priscilla back, safe and sound. "But listen," she said, "I'm not getting anywhere with these tapes. You might want to get somebody to play each one of them to see what's on them. Otherwise, there's still Wiseman's."

"We've already got that covered." Agent Rothschild turned to Detective Stoudemeir. "What have your men come up with?"

"I'm afraid," the detective answered, "that when our fellas arrived at Wiseman's Studio, it had already been ransacked. Somebody else is looking for a copy of that tape. As we speak, our men are in touch with Herbert Wiseman.

Seems he's on a yacht somewhere up on Lake Erie but has agreed to cut his outing short. He was completely shocked at the news about the shooting, not to mention the condition of his shop."

Julia needed to do something to take her mind off her new predicament, so she went into one of the back rooms searching for more files. When she returned, she packed the videotapes. She was not exactly pleased with the reality of the impending situation. She knew nothing about this "PG" the FBI agent had just mentioned. But to her mind, even the organization's name sounded bad. Yet it seemed obvious to her that those videotapes must have contained information important enough for Wiseman's studio to be ransacked. Still, what mattered to her was that the person who mattered most to her in this world had been abducted, her bridegroom had been murdered at the altar, and Senator Callahan looked like he, too, was at death's door. The realization swept over her that her friend was in a dangerous predicament. And an instant later, another wave struck her: she herself, according to what Agent Rothschild had just said, was also in danger.

But she mastered her anxiety as she held up a file folder labeled "SAD tape distribution." It listed several legislative offices and a corresponding number of copies for the distribution of the tapes. Also on the list were the names "PJ Austin" and "Daniel P. Callahan."

Detective Stoudemeir wondered aloud if any of those tapes had actually been delivered. He asked, "Is the Senate Clerk's office on that list?"

Julia nodded. "It's the first one listed."

"Okay, folks," Agent Rothschild said, "I'm sure we can get into the clerk's office right away. Meanwhile, let's keep searching for Priscilla's copy. It's quite possible that the one released to the public has been edited, so we need to get our hands on the copy that was produced for Priscilla and the senator. And lest we forget that debate was also covered by the area television stations." His last statement was another not-so-subtle directive to Detective Stoudemeir to dispatch his men accordingly. Then he had a question for Julia. "Does Priscilla have a safe deposit box?" When Julia smiled, the agent asked where she might have hidden the key.

"My Priscilla is old school," Julia said. "Pull out some of those desk drawers and run your hand underneath the ledge between each drawer."

The FBI agent did as she suggested and, in a moment, was grinning. "Gotcha." He felt a small packet that was taped underneath the ledge between one of the drawers. Sure enough, the packet contained a safe deposit box key. Although there was no information about which financial institution the key belonged to, the FBI was expert at completing that part of the puzzle. Agent Rothschild held the key firmly in his hand. "Now we're getting somewhere."

Agent Rothschild took up lodging at the nearby Sheraton Hotel downtown, where he scheduled a meeting with his counterpart from the Central Intelligence Agency for six o'clock that evening. Shortly after the other agent arrived, the two men shared a meal.

However, his counterpart's arrival created a bit of intrigue among some of the diners. They thought they were looking at a "Lieutenant Colombo" impersonator, yes, the television star. But they were not. Anyway, CIA Agent James Froley wore a receding hairline, a crumpled old suit, an unmatched polyester necktie, and brown Oxford shoes, minus the raincoat. Otherwise, he could easily have been the television character. But he was not, but rather an esteemed intelligence agent, whom his FBI agent colleague knew well.

After FBI Agent Rothschild filled him in with all that he had gleaned from the preliminary data about the case, the CIA agent responded accordingly.

"When you raised the possible involvement of the PG, we immediately dispatched additional security for Senator Callahan at the hospital," the CIA agent said. "He now has another medical specialist and a male nurse. Our people, along with your officers and the local blue suits, ought to provide ample security for him. On the other hand, however, protecting a ten-year-old eyewitness, and to some extent, Ms. Julia, might prove a tad more challenging. I mean, my God, man, do Ms. Austin's family and friends have a clue about the nature of circles she seems now to be playing in?"

"I tried to broach the subject with Julia, but I'm not sure she even wants to know," Agent Rothschild said. "And although she's our primary resource for 'all things PJ Austin,' I doubt she's even aware of the significance of what that means." Then he produced the key that he had discovered in Priscilla's desk. "And here's the safe deposit box key. Do you want to check it out tonight or later? We can also get a copy of the tape from the Senate Clerk's office—that is, if the tapes were even delivered. And we might have some luck with the local television stations, too."

"Hold off on that a while, Marvin," Agent Froley said. "First, I want to see those sketches of the profile of the alleged shooter, not to mention the sketch of the two men who abducted Ms. Austin. Only then will we have something solid to cross-reference any images on the videotape. Now, why is it that my stomach is churning? I mean, I'm having an awful feeling that we both know something about the abductors. Am I right, ole boy?"

The two intelligence officers smiled conspiratorially at each other.

But unbeknownst to the two intelligence agents, they were a distant third in the race to find the missing videotape. Both Priscilla's abductors—who also were, in fact, her rescuers—and the shooter had already gotten hold of copies of the tape, and from the same source. Bartholomew Jordan—a high-powered lobbyist for construction contractors in Ohio and New York and a member of the clandestine CF—had picked up a copy of the unedited version of the tape from Herbert Wiseman immediately after the Senate session had concluded; and later, that same weekend, Claus Fokker, a high-powered Washington, D.C.-based South African lobbyist—and a member of the PG— had broken into Wiseman's office and destroyed what he thought were the only copies of the videotapes.

But what PG Claus Fokker did not know was that two copies of the SAD tape were unaccounted for.

Additionally, as things stood at the time of Priscilla's abduction, there existed an Executive Order that prohibited activity by the CIA on American soil. The basis for that order stemmed back to the foiled assassination attempt of Fidel Castro and the Bay of Pigs fiasco, and to President Richard M. Nixon's abuse of power during the Watergate Scandal. But Priscilla had no way of knowing that—apart from the collaboration between the FBI and the CIA to track down the SANM Patrol Guard, the CIA had not quite cleaned up its act. More plainly put, the CF unit of the CIA had yet to cease its activity on American soil. But Priscilla was wholly unaware of any of that either.

4

The Closest to Her Most Fervent Prayer

Priscilla almost but not quite came to. She was at the first of what would be three safehouses, as it were. But as to the actual location of this first one, she would not know for a while.

Better, she thought, *much better*. She was sinking into unconsciousness again when she heard a voice—a loud masculine voice, in an accent she had heard before—talking not far away.

Again her eyelids fluttered. Again she was glad to shut them.

But the part of her mind that was conscious followed the familiar voice. *Tommy Wozniah? Nah. That couldn't be him. What's he doing here, wherever this is?* she thought. That Tommy was a high-powered Ohio lobbyist was about all that she knew about him, someone she had met back during her tenure in the Ohio Senate.

Her eyelids felt so heavy. Halfway open. Shades of light. Groggy. She let her eyelids fall shut again.

She was lucid enough to realize that she had been drugged, but for whatever reason, she was not afraid. She did not know why she was not afraid, only that she was not.

Then, she thought she heard Tommy's voice again. But he was not talking to her. She felt alone. The voice sounded distant to her. The voice would talk awhile, then fall silent before speaking again. The long pauses made it easier to follow at least one side of what had to be a conversation. The voice seemed to Priscilla to be reciting what sounded like an itinerary. Then there was silence.

Then she thought she overheard Tommy say something like "the cathedral in Ha-rah-eh."

Another voice—which she did not recognize—said, "Salisbury?"

"No, man. Today it's called Hoorah-eh or Ha-rare-ry. Whatever," It sounded to Priscilla as if Tommy was trying to correct the other man.

Confused. She blanked out again.

Priscilla did not know whether she had drifted back into unconsciousness for a while, but the next thing she remembered was having asked herself what had happened and where she was. Was Jonathan really dead, or had she experienced a bad dream? Did the perpetrator mean to shoot Jonathan, or had his target been the senator? Had she really seen Tommy Wozniah and Carlton Bernhardt? If so, where was that? Were her mom and other family members and friends safe? Did anybody even know why the assassin had chosen the occasion of her wedding? Did her family know where she was and why she had been abducted? Was that stupid South African Divestiture Bill worth someone's life? She repeated her questions to herself over and over, but no answers were forthcoming. Nor did any of her abductors come into her midst and talk to her. She felt so alone.

Satisfied they had secured the safest haven for their ward—Priscilla— what she had overheard had been a telephone conversation between Tommy Wozniah, a member of the CF relief team—which she was unaware of—and his contact informing him that they had accomplished the first part of their mission.

"Yeah, man," Charlie (Tommy's manservant)—the other voice that she did not recognize—the contact at the safehouse, had said in his intentionally encrypted report: "Missy's snuggled in like a gnat in a rug. By the way, she's not gonna like it when she realizes this is home for a while." Then there was a pause. "So … how's it going on your end? And the senator?" By this time, he was briefing Tommy about Priscilla's situation. So Priscilla had, in fact, heard two different voices and bits and pieces of two different conversations at that.

Another pause.

"Hmm."

Then, "Too bad about the bridegroom. He seemed like a pretty good fella. He was just in the wrong place at the wrong time. I guess our girl's going to take it really hard. But I'm sure she already knows he's dead," the manservant had said with finality. "Oh, yeah," he continued, "she's been talking out of her head. Sounds like she thinks she saw you and the other fella at the château. You know who? So, how's it going on your end?"

Then there was another pause in the conversation.

"Her makeover? Excellent," almost laughing, the manservant had said. "Damn, we're good at this job. You'd hardly recognize her."

The voice that sounded like Tommy's then moved on with the conversation. "We're pretty sure our guy is back on his home turf," adding, "Is the messenger system set up? Besides, when our girl *fully* regains consciousness, we're going to have to answer her questions before too long." Then Priscilla heard what sounded like the end of the conversation. She would never know for certain that it had been Tommy who had come and gone so quietly and quickly.

As Priscilla regained consciousness, to a greater degree of clarity than at any time before, she happened to raise her hand to her head. She rubbed both hands around her head. *Where's my hair?* Her worst fear was confirmed. The parts of the conversation that she had overheard about some makeover had been about her.

While her rescuers were in the kitchen continuing their discussion about their situation, Priscilla chanced to get up from what she observed to be a tattered sofa in a stifling, strange, drab-colored room that contained, at first sight, none of the modern conveniences that she was accustomed to. Somewhat sluggish, she stumbled. She stared out one of the windows and noticed that the dwelling in which she and the masculine voices she had overheard in the next room were situated in the central part of a large compound walled around with bricks and cement. She did not see a telephone in the room. She continued milling about and noticed antiquated plumbing; odd-shaped pipes protruded from a washbasin and a bathtub in what must have been a bathroom. She returned to the living space and saw a ceiling fan, but no air conditioning units.

Man alive, is it hot! But at least her clothes were comfortable. *These certainly are not my clothes*, she thought as she examined the loose-fitting, long-sleeved, blue, black-and-white-striped shift over baggy linen pants and leather sandals that she wore. Instinctively she continued to rub her head, feeling for her hair that had been cut off at the French château.

No ropes. No shackles. No armed guards standing over her. *Plainly*, she thought, *I'm not much of a threat to anybody*. Not yet fully recovered, she kept stumbling about, lightheaded, but much more lucid than before.

Priscilla chanced a walk outside. That was when she realized that no one was alarmed enough to stand guard over her or to curtail her movements about the place. So she decided that she must have been among friendly forces. Once she stepped outside, she felt the heat of the sun overhead. *I'm certainly not in Ohio*. She saw a couple of stray dogs, goats, and chickens. She saw a smidgen of grass, some exotic succulents and trees, and the tops of a few other dwellings nearby. She saw a dirt roadway and that the other dwellings resembled the mud or clay huts usually found in countries where poverty runs rampant.

"Where the devil have they ditched me anyway?" she whispered to herself.

At first, she thought she was somewhere in the Caribbean, but off the beaten path of tourists. But she had never seen clay huts in Trinidad and Tobago or in the Bahamas, so maybe she was stashed someplace else.

That's it. I'm in North Africa, she thought, *somewhere like Morocco*. Then she decided, *Nah, this can't be Africa. I mean, it can't be*. At the least, she hoped that she had not been that far from home. As if her situation could not get any worse, she remembered the absence of telephones in the house, at least from what she had seen. Indeed, Priscilla was wholly isolated from most of the conveniences and the people whom she knew.

Suddenly, terrible images flooded her mind. Again, over and over, she saw Jonathan's head exploding, falling, his blood splattered everywhere. She hid her eyes with her hands as though that would stop her memory.

No, she told herself. *Not now. Don't think about that now. Just now, it's too much ...*

It took all her considerable inner strength to shut off her memory and master her grief. Later, probably for the rest of her life, she would have to deal with the reality of her bridegroom's death. Yet her even more pressing concern was having been whisked away to the hinterlands of God only knows where.

"Tomorrow," she whispered. "Maybe tomorrow and after tomorrow, I can think of all that ...."

Just then, she concentrated on the gratitude that she had escaped physical harm and death. Her limbs gave way beneath her, and there, on the ground, she knelt, cupped her face, and prayed. As it so happened, her behavior showed a remarkable likeness to what her rescuers—who were watching her from the windows inside the house—had hoped that she would manifest; they had wanted Priscilla to shield herself from all things American.

Kneeling, she thanked God for her life and for the men who had rescued her. She asked God to keep her family and friends safe from further harm. She told God she was not ready to talk about Jonathan or the man who had killed him. Last, she said, "Bear with me, O Lord, and give me the strength and the wherewithal to cope with whatever lies ahead. Amen." As she knelt, it came to her that this was only the second time in her life she had felt such depth in her prayer. She was a preacher's daughter, but it was not until the night her beloved father died that her faith was so affirmed by the grace and presence of her loving God. And again now, here, as she mourned the man who had almost, yet not quite, become her husband, she felt the deep comfort of her faith. Oblivious to her surroundings, she rose and began strolling about as if her new situation were normal.

As she began to find a way to cope with a situation she somehow knew was not turning out to her advantage, she was aware that, apart from her faith and her strong will, nothing could prepare her for the events that lay ahead— nothing. Even so, in her customary way, she began to figure out how she had come not to this physical space but to this mental space in which she now found herself.

She spotted a big tree stump under the shade of what looked to her like a spreading banyan tree. She walked over and settled herself on this natural bench. "What I need now," she told herself, "is some time with Jonathan." She settled in for a long, restorative visit with happier, more serene and ultimately more innocent times.

The first time they met, she remembered, she did not have an inkling of how important he would be to her.

Priscilla had just returned from a Bahamas and European excursion. In fact, she was actually unpacking when the phone rang and Willa Mae Robinson—an elderly deaconess friend from her church—launched into a rendition of everything that had happened during Priscilla's "whirlwind vacation," as she called it. The two of them, despite their age difference, were fairly close, with their occasional lunch outings and teas together. But apart from their relationship, Priscilla remained distant from most other members of the church. Because Mrs. Robinson was also Priscilla's class leader, part of her responsibility was to inquire about her members' well-being, their family situation and more. Sometimes she asked Priscilla, "How fares your soul?" Because First Church had an unusually large membership, association with one's class leader was one way to maintain communications. It made the members feel a part of the large church.

Soon Mrs. Robinson got to the point of her call. "Miss Lady," she said, "get some rest and come out to church tomorrow. I want you to meet our new pastor. He's single and unattached, as far as I can see."

Priscilla was glad the woman could not see her grimace. "Mrs. Robinson, you know how I feel about preachers." But Priscilla also knew how churches were. After all, she had grown up inside of one. "See you in the morning."

A little later, when Julia came to call, Priscilla invited her to come along.

"Sure, why not?" Julia laughed. "Besides, when was the last time you went to church, anyway? I wouldn't want to miss a rare appearance." Priscilla laughed along with her.

Looking back, knowing what was to come, Priscilla smiled.

Sunday was a beautiful sunny day. The First AME Zion Church was an impressive stone Gothic Revival structure with tall stained-glass windows. It had been acquired from the United Methodists in the mid-1960s when the demographics of the neighborhood had begun changing. Those years were part of the Civil Rights era, back when Black families began moving into the neighborhoods that many white families had fled to the suburbs. The church was situated in the midst of the stateliest of Victorian properties and off a main thoroughfare. Not only that, but her place of worship was not far from the Ohio Capitol, which was just dandy for Priscilla.

The two young women arrived shortly after the processional and sat in Priscilla's usual pew, about five rows from the chancel. Mrs. Robinson and a host of other elderly women sat in the front two rows; they were the deaconesses, the women who attended to the pastor and the other clergy. Nun like, the deaconesses were all dressed in white uniforms, shoes and stockings; even the dainty caps atop their heads were white. There were six or seven clergy at First Church, but only three of them were seated in the chancel that day.

As they were settling in the pew, Mrs. Robinson turned around in her seat to see whether Priscilla and Julia had graced them with their presence. Satisfied that they had, she nodded and smiled at them. However, she would have been perturbed if she had heard Priscilla's whispered words to Julia.

"Pitiful, just plain pitiful," Priscilla said quietly to Julia, referring to the deaconesses. "Why do they serve in such subservient roles, always tagging along behind those men, catering to their every whim?"

Priscilla knew that deaconesses represented "women who are beyond reproach," sexually, that is. Presumably, they could be in the presence of male clergy without temptation flowing either way, and they were righteous. The deaconesses prepared refreshments and conveniently placed the full platter near the pulpit. They also cleaned the ecclesiastical linens and stoles, and they dressed the altar and other sacred objects in the chancel for special occasions such as the Eucharist (or Holy Communion), baptisms, weddings, and funerals.

To Priscilla's way of thinking, most of those women had already spent a lifetime catering to men who had taken them for granted. But now—older, single or widowed—she was puzzled why they continued such service in the name of the church.

"Do they really believe they're going to heaven 'cause they bend and bow to those men?" she continued whispering to Julia. Such a subservient role grated against Priscilla's grain. "I'm not saying we shouldn't be considerate of the clergy. But get a grip on it, folks. We're so good at projecting sexism, and we do it with such tacit humility."

Julia reflected on how dogmatic Priscilla could be, and at the most inopportune times. But she herself was Baptist, so none of what she observed at First Church that day mattered much to her. She smiled at her friend but remained quiet.

Priscilla and Julia then tried to figure out which of the several clergy was the new pastor. It turned out that he was the one in the white cassock, "looking," as Priscilla said, "all pious, as if you'd touch him, he'd crumble." She was not impressed.

Following the service, the new pastor greeted the parishioners at the rear of the sanctuary. As Priscilla approached him, he reached for her hand and gripped it firmly.

At that point, the Reverend Charlie Strathmore made the introductions.

"Reverend Morgan, you may not remember her, but this is Priscilla Austin, 'PJ', as her friends call her, and she attended Livingstone College around the same time as you."

By then, however, Reverend Morgan was already lost in Priscilla's grace. As he was to tell her sometime later, he was wholly enraptured by her straightforward, though elegant, demeanor. He gripped her hand as though he might never let it go.

"Ms. Austin," said Reverend Strathmore, "this is our new pastor, the Reverend Jonathan Morgan."

Priscilla smiled. She had grown up with church etiquette. She managed to look the good reverend over without appearing to be doing so. He was of average height and weight and light brown in complexion. He had close-cut hair and a well-trimmed moustache and beard. *Not bad for a preacher, if you like that type,* she thought.

Then she said to the enraptured Reverend Morgan, "Why are you still holding my hand?"

Standing somewhat off to the side, Julia immediately observed that her friend was in trouble. Later she was to tell her, "It's all over now, Priscilla. That man likes you. That's why he was 'still holding' your hand." As she had regarded the pastor still clinging to Priscilla's hand, she would have liked to grab Priscilla and hustle her away while she could.

Priscilla seemed somewhat embarrassed because some other members had also noticed the new pastor's apparent interest in her.

Then, as the young women left the sanctuary and entered the vestibule, Jonathan whispered to his friend Charlie, "Make sure to invite Ms. PJ to my welcome reception."

Outside, Julia turned to Priscilla and said she feared she would soon be lost to the new pastor.

"Don't be ridiculous," Priscilla snapped, unaware that she had already been caught up in a situation the likes of which she had never before experienced.

Yet, Priscilla had a secret that she had not even confided in Julia.

Priscilla sighed as she sat on the stump of what she decided was a banyan tree at the safehouse somewhere in Africa, where she was not yet aware, remembering how it had been in those first days and weeks after she had met

Jonathan. Even then, she was acutely aware of a "special someone" with whom she was more than fond; however, she had vowed to push that secret way down deep into her being and leave it there. Sometime later, much later, but not now, her secret would reveal itself. As it turned out, she had willed herself to do exactly what her father had cautioned her against; Priscilla was still living to please someone other than herself.

Then, she recalled that her public relations business had slackened—or was it that her interests had changed? For reasons she could not account for, she had found herself taking on different kinds of projects and clients, which had been a continuation of contacts from her work in the Ohio Senate: construction contractors, architects, engineers, lobbyists, businesspersons and several public officials. Priscilla had made it her business to land projects that paid the highest retainers.

However, something had changed. But Priscilla was not yet cognizant of what it was.

She did remember, however, agreeing to work with the new pastor in renovating First Church. No one could recall the last time the church had undergone any major renovations. The church was recognized for its spectacular stained-glass windows and Gothic arch, but those features were so badly marred that it was difficult to make out the many images and natural colors. The once-remarkable stone structure required cleaning, electrical upgrading, and new fixtures for the kitchen and bathroom, painting, point-n-tuck repairs, and plumbing.

Priscilla's skills had been perfect, and she had set out to pull the project together from behind the scenes. She advised the new pastor on ways to interview contractors. The pastor had been easily persuaded by her knowledge of the contracting process.

She had worked with the church secretary in preparing the invitations for competitive bidding, at which—given her experience in the state's contracting process—Priscilla was masterful. Then she set up the meetings for the presentations by the architects and engineers, one firm for which she had conducted an open house just prior to her trip to the Bahamas and Western Europe. Simultaneously with her efforts, the pastor and other officers at the church met with representatives of financial institutions and began putting their part of the plan into action. Priscilla had done all this work pro bono because, she remembered saying, "It's the church."

At the same time, she also took on a few other projects because, she said, "I need to pay my rent."

One such project involved the national premiere of the documentary film *Mandela*, a project that she took on with considerable interest. Priscilla not only produced the PR for the project but also assisted in its fundraising. She discovered how expensive it was to produce a film of such magnitude and then to distribute it nationwide. Once again, she'd made use of her political contacts, which included Senator Callahan. She set up the Ohio Mandela Premiere Committee. She even recruited its members: Governor and Mrs. Antonio Scalise (Democrats), Mayor and Mrs. Dan Witherspoon (Republicans), Senator Callahan (Democrat), the Director of International Trade for the State of Ohio, Peter Cox, and the Director of the Administrative Services Agency for the State of Ohio, William Sorenson. She also recruited a bipartisan group of four state representatives and senators, a television station manager, and the Executive Director of the National Black Programming Consortium, Inc. (NBPC), Marlene Hannah.

When Priscilla first met Marlene, she did not know whether to feel sorry for the woman. Marlene bore a striking resemblance to a young Angela Davis. But Marlene's garb was ostensibly African attire, nothing like Davis's military camouflage. Like some directors of nonprofit programs, Marlene spoke of lofty ideas, some of which Priscilla thought were 1960s-oriented.

"Here sits a Black woman in my age range with a vision the likes I've never seen," Priscilla had said to herself. Perhaps what drew Priscilla was her similarity with Marlene's race and age, not her doubts about Marlene's vision.

For Priscilla, "producing the PR for the documentary *Mandela* is earthy," not what she'd once described to someone as "some stuck-in-the-mud clamor for Black folks." She took pride in performing work of substance and significant purpose. Priscilla could touch and feel something different about this project. Before this, never once had she imagined that she would lend her name and expertise to petitioning for the release of South African activist Nelson Mandela, who had been in prison for over twenty years for demanding reforms in the South African apartheid system.

She grinned as she remembered having thought, *Wait until my folks get a load of this!*

The evening came when Reverend Morgan, who always insisted that his friends call him Jonathan, called Priscilla and asked her to go for a drive."

But in response, she had sharply said: "Are you serious?"

Caught completely unawares by her response, Jonathan stuttered. "Why—yes, Ms. Austin. I *am* serious. Have I offended you or something?"

After realizing he had misunderstood what she had intended to say, she said, "Oh, that's just a figure of speech. I was wondering whether you were really serious about asking me to 'go for a drive.'"

The upshot was that the two agreed "to go for a short ride." Jonathan drove a little red Plymouth Horizon, which Priscilla liked because, as she said, "It looks so cute."

They drove southeast of Columbus on an unfamiliar highway when, after a while, Priscilla spotted a diner and asked Jonathan to pull over. They went inside, and Priscilla ordered a cup of coffee, smoked cigarettes and talked endlessly—mostly about her "Daddy," the late Reverend James Nelson Austin.

At one point in their conversation, Jonathan interrupted her: "Why is it that you talk about your father in the present tense? I thought you said he had passed?"

Priscilla shrugged him off. "So what if I talk about my daddy that way. It works for me."

Jonathan—unabashedly enamored but shrewd—had quickly decided to oblige the woman whom he so admired.

It was not long before Priscilla repaid the favor and invited Jonathan to lunch at Chelsie's, a fine dining establishment across from the Statehouse. There she knew she would encounter political acquaintances to whom she could show off her new friend. When the drinks waiter arrived, Priscilla chose red wine to go with her meal.

But her action annoyed Jonathan. She'd had no idea that he neither drank nor condoned the habit. *My goodness! This man isn't a Puritan or something, is he?*

Even so, she asked what the problem was, and Jonathan told her a story about his father's alcoholism and the church's policy on alcohol, as if she were ignorant of both matters.

But neither reason meant much to Priscilla. Her father, Nelson, used to stock wine and liquor at their home in Prendergast, which the family drank on special occasions, especially on New Year's Day. In fact, drinking was a normal habit among the Austin clan, and with Liza's family, too. Many of Liza's brothers were habitual drinkers, even alcoholics. Those who fought in the European and Korean theaters of war seemed to need something to take the edge off the memories of their horrible experiences. One of her uncles had often deposited a pint bottle in the back pocket of his trousers. Priscilla had also routinely been exposed to alcohol at the political fundraisers and receptions that she attended. And so it was that Priscilla still could not altogether understand Jonathan's stance.

After taking a couple of sips of her wine, she knocked over her glass and apologized to the waiter for having stained the tablecloth. When the waiter offered to replenish her drink, she politely refused. She did, however, think her new friend a tad sanctimonious. Plain-spoken, too. And always meticulously turned out.

After they left Chelsie's, Priscilla escorted Jonathan across the street to meet Senator Callahan and a few of his colleagues. As they walked to the Statehouse, Jonathan admitted that he had never before visited the Ohio Capitol and that he was impressed with its grandeur.

Shortly after their introductions, Senator Callahan asked, "Do you have political aspirations, Reverend? Your predecessor ran for state rep against the incumbent from your district. I mean, he was a formidable contender." Since the former pastor at First Church had been a political activist, Senator Callahan was pleasantly relieved to learn that Jonathan was hardly interested in seeking public office. Weeks later, he invited Jonathan to deliver the invocation for one of the opening sessions of the Ohio Senate.

One evening near Thanksgiving, when Priscilla visited Jonathan at the parsonage, he asked her to come with him into the living room. Then he knelt down on one knee and held onto her hand and said, "Priscilla, there's something important I need to discuss with you. Priscilla, I'm in love with you, and I want to spend the rest of my life with you. Will you marry me?"

He also said that he realized theirs had been a short acquaintance, but that still he loved her.

"I'm also," he added, "the pastor of First Church, and I can't be seen about town dating one of my members. That can cause friction, and it might not be good for your reputation, either."

There now: he had presented his case.

Completely off-kilter, Priscilla said, matter-of-factly, "Sure, Jonathan, I'll marry you. Why not?" But Priscilla was aware that she was not in love with him and that he was equally aware of her lack of feelings for him. But she also knew that Jonathan Morgan was as close to the answer to her most fervent prayer as she would most probably get: her prayer for "someone who accepts me the way I am and who treats me good," or so she had thought at the time. And yet something told her that Jonathan was right for her.

Priscilla waited a few days before she called Liza, but their telephone conversation was about everything but Jonathan's marriage proposal. She told her mom that she would visit with her for Thanksgiving.

Meanwhile, she confided in Julia about Jonathan's marriage proposal: she called her and asked her to come over.

As soon as Julia arrived, she said, "I expected this would happen. I just knew you were having too much fun. But I'm happy for you, Priscilla. 'Cause I can tell that you want to marry him, too. You do, don't you?"

"Yeah, I do. Don't know why, but something tells me he's right for me. Listen. Let's talk about something else. Want to see the pictures from my trips?" Nearly five months had passed since Priscilla's "whirlwind vacation" —less time than she had known Jonathan Morgan—and only now was she ready to examine her photographs. So the two friends looked through the many pictures and drank plenty of coffee, while Priscilla smoked umpteen cigarettes.

Priscilla sighed, got up from the stump, pulled a twig from the tree and continued reflecting on the events that had brought her to this walled-in compound, wherever this was. But she wished that her family—especially her mother—had been more affirming of her choice of Jonathan.

She supposed in her heart she must have known that Liza would not approve, because she'd waited a whole week after accepting Jonathan's proposal even to telephone her mom. And even then, she had not mentioned it.

It was Thanksgiving Day when Priscilla broached the subject as the two of them were working on the stuffing for the turkey. Without any preliminaries, Priscilla said, "Well, Momma, I met this man. His name is Jonathan Morgan, and he's the pastor of our church in Columbus."

Liza set down her knife, sank into a kitchen chair and shook her head. She shut her eyes and said prayerfully, "Lord, Lord …." Then she complained, "What is it with my daughters and their men? They never seem to have the foggiest idea about what they're getting into." She opened her eyes wide. "Oh no, Priscilla! You're not *expecting* or anything? You don't *have* to get married, do you?"

Piqued, Priscilla shook her head. "Oh, Momma, no. It's not at all like that."

"But you can't have known this fella for very long. I've never heard you mention him. Who are his people? Besides, I mean, didn't you just return from Europe? When have you had time to get to know him?"

"Well," Priscilla continued, completely ignoring most of Liza's questions, "he's been married before, and he has three children, grown children with children, so I don't have to worry about having any children of my own."

Each revelation completely took Liza aback. She clasped her hands over her mouth as Priscilla continued describing the circumstances surrounding her fiancé: "I haven't met his family yet. All I know is how he treats me. He treats me good, Momma."

"Good Lord. Listen to me, Child. That man is much farther down the road than you are. Your head's in the clouds. You're acting as if you have to *settle* for whatever you can get. You can do better, much better, Priscilla. I know you can."

Priscilla did not argue with her mom because she had half-expected some disagreement. But she was stunned that Liza was so adamantly opposed to her decision to get married. In fact, she found her mother's reaction somewhat strange because she and so many other relatives and acquaintances had routinely hassled her to "leave something for the man in your life to do" and "find a husband and have children." Yet now that she had begun the process, their first reaction was not good at all.

When Priscilla returned to Columbus—unshaken in her conviction that Jonathan would be her husband—she was equally distressed over reactions from others about her plans to marry Jonathan. Some folks called her and said, "Girl, I heard the news. Tell me it isn't true." "How can you marry an older man, and someone who's already been married with grown children, of all things?" "PJ, I thought you had eyes for so-n-so. What gives?" The unwelcome reactions seemed endless and so strange to her, especially since most of the people who called her were themselves unhappily married or divorced.

The situation worsened when her older sister, Harriet, whom she had just visited in Europe, called and reminded Priscilla of their conversation during her visit earlier in the summer.

"Yes, Harriet, I know what 'rebound' means. So be it," Priscilla had said in a simple retort. "But at least when I talked to Ellen, she wished me happiness. That's all I want from anybody, but not this. Besides, Harriet, I never met either of your husbands before you married. In fact, all of you guys just jumped the broom, and then you brought your husbands home to meet the family. So why're you so upset now that it's my turn?"

At the end of her tether, she asked Jonathan in a telephone conversation, "Do you have a criminal record or something you're not telling me about? Have you committed some god–awful deed that everybody else but me knows about? Surely, something's wrong with you, or else so many people wouldn't object so strongly to your marriage proposal."

Jonathan had realized there was little he could say in his defense because he had not done anything wrong, so he suggested, "Perhaps you should consider the source. Apart from your mother's earnest concern, who are these other people questioning your decision? And how, if at all, do they fit into your life?"

For whatever reason, Priscilla then remembered the recent deaths in her family: Nelson died in 1981; Grandma Lilly died in 1983; and Uncle Maxwell died shortly before her whirlwind excursion in the late spring of 1985. So in her simplistic way of reasoning, she thought, *Surely my folks are ready for something good to happen.* Eventually, she realized how naïve she had been in thinking that her good news would generate an element of cheer in other people's lives because, more often than not, the people she knew preferred that she wallow in her misery and that her misery would become their joy. Nevertheless, Priscilla ultimately resolved, "I've agreed to marry Jonathan, and that's in fact what I will do."

Yet, she reflected, not all the signs had been so bad with respect to her wedding.

First, she remembered how meticulously she had planned her wedding. In fact, Julia and Priscilla's office assistant had commented that she was planning her wedding as if she were producing a major public relations campaign. That was not meant to be a compliment. By Christmas, she had decided who she would ask to perform each role in the ceremony, as well as the setting for each part of the wedding. She booked the Sheraton Hotel Downtown Columbus as the official lodging for her guests and the rehearsal dinner. She also contracted the hotel's caterers to conduct a reception on the lawn of the parsonage.

Jonathan took care of contacting his father-in-the-ministry, the Reverend Dr. Elijah Edmonds Rushe, to serve as the chief celebrant. Still, Dr. Rushe advised him to extend the courtesy instead to the Right Reverend Joseph Pascal Logan. Bishop Logan was the episcopate for the Ohio Conference of their church; Methodist Church protocol was at play. In order that her own family was represented properly, Priscilla contacted the Right Reverend William Josiah Walls, who presided over the Western New York Conference, where her father, Nelson, had last served. Bishop Walls had also performed the eulogy for her father's funeral and had officiated the wedding ceremony for one of her cousins in Sills Creek.

Then, quite unexpectedly, a major disagreement had developed over her wedding dress.

In early May, Priscilla had purchased a pale powder-blue tea-length wedding dress. It was overlaid with lace and was a perfect match for her rainbow-hued bridesmaids' dresses. At nearly thirty-four years of age and certainly not a virgin, Priscilla was about to marry a middle-aged man with three grown children and who himself had been previously married. So she had surmised that the last thing she needed was a flowing white gown.

To her surprise, however, that was exactly what Jonathan had wanted.

When finally she told him about her powder-blue tea-length dress, he had shaken his head decisively. "You've never been married before, Priscilla. It's in perfect order for you to wear *a white wedding gown*," Jonathan had insisted.

After trying—and failing—to rally support from family and friends, Priscilla had given in and made a begrudging trip to the Lazarus Department Store in downtown Columbus. To her surprise, she had fallen in love with an ivory bridal gown that had been special ordered by another bride who later had decided she could not use it.

Priscilla had gazed at herself in the mirror, all aglow in the storybook bridal gown that met her childhood dreams, not her dreams as a more mature woman. And so it was that she had let go of what she knew was the more age-appropriate attire—that pale powder-blue tea-length dress—and settled on the broad-gauged satin storybook bridal gown, and tiara!

Remembering how she'd looked not only that day in the department store but then at the church—the church where Jonathan and so many dreams had died—for a moment, Priscilla wondered what had happened to her wedding gown.

But then she remembered something else.

As the date of her wedding approached, she was blown away when she received an unexpected note in the mail with a poem written on the back of an envelope. It was a poem—or was it really a prayer? —written for her wedding day by her mother:

Entwine

This is the most important day of our lives,

Other than the day we received Christ.

Dear God, guide us, help us lest we falter

As we stand here before the altar.

There's so much that lies before us,

The known, the unknown, yet we go on.

We stand here as two before You,

Making our vows, we become one.

Like an eagle spreading its wings,

Flying off into the unseen.

–Liza Austin
MOTHER OF THE BRIDE ©1986

A world away in remote southern Africa—which she still did not know for a certainty—Priscilla wept and kept wiping her streaming tears. She had committed her mom's poem to memory. For her, what it represented was her mother's long-awaited approval.

Priscilla thanked God for that reminder.

Here and now, it gave her the grace to go on.

As it turned out, she let go of at least this wave of grief and resumed strolling about the walled enclosure as if her new situation were normal. Purged and centered, she was now acutely aware that nothing could prepare her for whatever lay ahead. But she had her faith, her intelligence and her strong will. She walked the grounds of her African hideaway with purpose.

5

A Crash Course in South African Politics

Back in the American Midwest—two days after the carnage at First Church and the abduction of the bride—FBI Agent Marvin Rothschild and Columbus Police Detective David Stoudemeir sat in a small conference room in a federal office building downtown Columbus where two academicians were presenting them with a crash course in South African politics and its economy, which, as it turned out, was much more than either of the two law enforcement officers had bargained for.

The clock on the wall of the windowless conference room read 9:00 p.m.

Yawning and stretching his long limbs, Agent Rothschild could not contain his fatigue. But this was his agency, and these two academicians had direct access to his superiors. The last thing he wanted was for one of them to make some offhand comments about his not paying attention or about his complaining about the intellectual components of the two cases. Already he had drunk four coffees since they began four hours ago, and at the next break he would have another.

Seated next to him at the conference table, his pale skin—greenish under the fluorescent lights—Detective Stoudemeir was comparatively attentive. At *The* Ohio State University (OSU), he had been a history major. He once dreamed of becoming a teacher, maybe even a college professor, after going to graduate school and getting an advanced degree. Instead, he had married his pregnant high school sweetheart more than a year before he finished his bachelor's degree. Working nights, he had managed to complete his B.A., but a higher degree had been out of his reach. His father-in-law had been a police officer, and before long, he, too, had become a man in blue. Unlike his FBI colleague, Detective Stoudemeir was enjoying this part of the FBI briefing as "it all relates to the two cases stemming from the shootings at the Black church," one of the professors kept saying.

Their first presenter had been an OSU history professor; he gave them a condensed version of the modern sweep of African history. Next, there would be a presentation on the geopolitics of South Africa. And finally, an FBI agent flown in from Washington, D.C., would help them apply the information presented to them this evening to the Priscilla J. Austin case and to the foiled assassination of Ohio state Senator Daniel P. Callahan.

The disinterested FBI agent mainly stared at the two professors throughout their lectures. At the same time, the police detective had taken copious notes with the diligence of the undergraduate he had once been. In a flash, whenever a short break was announced, the FBI agent was out in the hallway on his way to the coffee machine in the staff lounge.

However, Detective Stoudemeir examined his notes. Much of the first lecture about modern South Africa had centered on Nelson Rolihlahla Mandela, who could trace his royal lineage across twenty generations. He came from the Thembu tribe of the Xhosa nation in the territorial division of Transkei, located several hundred miles east of Cape Town and 500 miles south of Johannesburg. Like the biblical Israelites, Mandela's family worshipped the god of their fathers, Qamata. His family practiced rituals similar to those of the Israelites: they slaughtered animals and conducted traditional rites for planting and harvesting, as well as for births, marriages and circumcision. "Hmm," the Columbus Police detective said to himself.

Detective Stoudemeir remembered from his own college courses that the advent of colonialism changed the indigenous power structures on the African continent. The professor had agreed, saying that, "The historical record for most African nations was, in fact, chronicled from the advent of European exploration and invasions. That most of the African continent was already inhabited by tribes like those of Mandela's—tribes that traced their family lineage back for centuries—had been regarded as having little significance. Yet in South Africa, the Bushmen and the Hottentots were in their tribal regions long before Bartolomeu Dias and Vasco da Gama 'discovered' the Cape of Good Hope in the late 1400s and charted a shorter route to India."

Then in the late 1800s, gold and diamonds—the hallmark of the South African economy—were discovered. "As it so happened," the professor noted, "the Dutch, the French, the Afrikaners and the Boers, the Germans, the African tribes, and the British all fought among themselves to control the mineral-rich territory." Chief among the Boers was Paul Kruger, who was elected to lead the territory of Transvaal for several consecutive terms. Kruger was also known for his belief that the discovery of the minerals would bring bloodshed to the territory, which it did. Yet because of his leadership of the new territory, his face is shown on the obverse of the Krugerrand; Kruger National Park is named in his honor; and a museum in Pretoria recognizes his contributions to South African history.

Detective Stoudemeir leafed through several more pages of his notes. *All of this is interesting*, he thought, then frowned, *but where are the stories about the indigenous people?*

The professor continued. He told his two students that the Nationalist Party had advocated Boer supremacy and secession from the British Commonwealth, policy positions that remained in force up through the establishment of the Union of South Africa in 1910. "But by the middle of the 20th century," he emphasized, "apartheid was the order of the day; and, as long as the ruling party paid homage to the Crown, the British government maintained a laissez-faire attitude toward the apartheid-ruled regime."

But most disturbingly for the Columbus Police detective had been the onslaught of colonialism—and apartheid—which had led to prohibitions against Black South Africans from owning land in their own country; the denial of Black political participation, especially in the franchise; prohibitions against Blacks from marrying outside their own tribe and race; and prohibitions against Blacks from traveling without identity cards. The detective was, however, aware that such prohibitions were much like the policies of segregation that had existed in America, such as legally sanctioned racial segregation of public facilities in the transit systems and in other public accommodations.

The police detective blurted out: "And so the whites (Afrikaners) control *all* the industry, the land and the minerals, which includes the diamonds, gold and platinum, and the means of their production, *too!* Essentially, then, Afrikaner domination means that the Black South Africans are persona non grata in their own land. My God, man. That's crazy."

Agent Rothschild struggled not to yawn for the umpteenth time. For much of what he had heard up to this point was truly to him a crash *review* course. But he had no idea that Detective Stoudemeir had been this unfamiliar with the situation in South Africa.

The professor remained quiet while his two students shared a moment.

"Now that my classmate is catching up with the rest of the class," Agent Rothschild said unapologetically, "perhaps he now sees the *significance* of the South African Divestiture Bill that Senator Callahan sponsored last spring."

Detective Stoudemeir disregarded his colleague's needling. He wanted to know more. So he looked at the professor with eager anticipation on his face. "Please continue, Professor."

The professor told his two students that it was into such a world that Nelson Mandela was born.[1] He was born on July 18, 1918, and having accepted the faith of the Methodist missionaries, his mother arranged for his baptism in the Wesleyan tradition. Also, like many youngsters who grew up in such dire circumstances, a young Nelson once aspired to great wealth. However, while studying at the University College of Fort Hare, he faced an unexpected philosophical challenge: would he stand on principle or on that which was expedient for his own self-interest? He chose the former and was expelled from the University for demonstrating against racism.

"As Mandela reached his twenties," the professor pointed out, "the world was consumed with World War II, and so it paid little attention to events on the African continent, especially in South Africa." Then, when Mandela enrolled in law school at the University of Witwatersrand in Johannesburg in 1943, he was the only African (meaning Black person) in his class. Later, he would write that his worldview expanded tremendously and that in law school, he made lasting, influential acquaintances with such activists as Joe Slovo and Ruth First, George Bizos and Bram Fishcher, Tony O'Dowd, Harold Wolpe, Jules Browde, Ismail Meer and J. J. Singh.

"Finally," Detective Stoudemeir noted, the professor had come to Mandela's affiliation with the African National Congress (ANC), which led to

---

[1] Mandela, Nelson. *Long Walk to Freedom*, 1994.

the leader's imprisonment and the fulfillment of his political party's agenda. The oldest national African political organization in the country, the ANC sought full citizenship for Black South Africans and the denunciation of "racialism." Then, in 1950, Mandela was appointed to the ANC's executive committee and later became a deputy president.

"I didn't know about any of *this* stuff," Detective Stoudemeir said. This time, it was Agent Rothschild who did not react.

"Then, in one of his first significant acts," the professor intimated that he was about to say something more profound: "Mandela wrote a letter to Prime Minister Daniel Francois Malan, a South African Nationalist, and demanded that the prime minister repeal the six 'unjust laws,' denounce white supremacy, and call for equality of all citizens and for the establishment of a democracy. Those demands carried an ultimatum: 'Or else we will take extra-constitutional action,' which made the ANC leadership outlaws because such actions were treasonous offenses."

As if their demands of the prime minister were not enough, the ANC also conducted the Defiance Campaign, a six-month nationwide demonstration of civil disobedience for which Mandela and 155 other ANC members were indicted and incarcerated in Johannesburg in December 1956. Their time in court, which later became known as "the Treason Trial," lasted five years.

The professor then told them that apartheid even prohibited prisoners of different races, ethnic groups and tribes from sharing the same cells. That meant that Black South Africans, the mixed-race "Coloureds," the Indians and the whites were segregated from one another. They even wore different types of clothing, ate different cuisines, and experienced tacit intimidation.

Detective Stoudemeir was engrossed with the part about the prison conditions. However, the sarcastic Agent Rothschild was bemused by the fact that there were no windows in the small room where he and his colleague had sat since 5:00 that evening. "Imprisoned," he said to himself. "Imagine that."

"When the inmates protested those conditions," the professor went on saying, "the authorities caved in and allowed the male prisoners—regardless of race and ethnicity—to share the same cells. The female inmates, however, continued to be incarcerated in separate cells. Once the male ANC members were grouped together, it was easier for them to continue the work of the Defiance Campaign. They also enjoyed the support of scores of sympathizers outside the prison walls, who were relentless in calling for the men's release."

When the trial proceeded, the judge released large numbers of the defendants, group by group, until only thirty were left. Those thirty men, of whom Mandela was the primary target, constituted the executive committee of the ANC, the organization's backbone.

Shortly, however, other unexpected events unfurled. British Prime Minister Harold McMillan made his highly acclaimed "Winds of Change in Africa" speech, acknowledging that "nation by nation the shackles of European colonialism were dismantling."

Despite all that had happened, Mandela and his fellow inmates were granted passes to go home periodically. During one of his leaves, on June 14, 1958, he married Winnie Madikizela. The couple's life together began during Mandela's imprisonment, and *it was Winnie who was in charge of the ANC throughout her husband's incarceration.*

The professor rolled on.

"Tragically, the world watched as another incident occurred, precipitating further action by the ANC." According to Mandela's rendition in *Long Walk to Freedom*, police shot into a crowd of demonstrators in Sharpeville on March 21, 1960. Sixty-nine Black South Africans were killed, and over four hundred were wounded. The ANC had issued a statement from prison calling on Black South Africans to burn their identity passes, which they did in front of scores of international media. Media coverage, once modest, spontaneously increased the international broadcasts of the Sharpeville Massacre and the ongoing Treason Trial.

Then, the professor brought his lecture to its logical conclusion: "On March 29, 1961, the thirty remaining ANC prisoners were exonerated, but Mandela's story did not end there. By this point, he had decided to continue the fight to reform the apartheid system, so he went underground. Soon, the world watched as the ANC abandoned its nonviolent protest tactics because Nelson Mandela was elevated to the rank of first military commander."

"Then, in 1964," the professor said with finality, "Mandela was imprisoned again; only this time, he received what might best be described as a life sentence at Robben Island, where so far he has already spent over twenty years of his life."

What a hero! Detective Stoudemeir thought. He looked up from his copious notes as Agent Rothschild, who had slipped out during the part of the lecture about the prison conditions, returned with two mugs of thick, bitter, black coffee.

"This stuff is fascinating," the Columbus Police detective said as he looked over at his colleague.

"Yeah." The FBI agent—who had a greater worldview than did his colleague—tried to smile. Point in fact, Agent Rothschild held a master's degree in political philosophy. He was an avid reader, and he certainly knew more about global affairs than his humble colleague, who seemed to hang onto every word that the two academicians had uttered. "But next up is one of our guys from D.C. I sure hope *he* can provide us with the kind of information we need to solve these two cases. Then maybe, just maybe," the FBI agent said, "we'll get down to brass tacks."

The "guy" from Washington turned out to be a "gal" from New York, and she *was* able to fulfill Agent Rothschild's expectation for the background data necessary to connect the dots—from the foiled assassination attempt of Senator Callahan and Priscilla's abduction—with the seething politics of South Africa.

FBI Agent Bonnie Gibbons was young, slim and authoritative. Briskly she cut to the chase.

"We're thinking that the catalyst for the carnage at First Church may have been those hearings in the Ohio Senate on the South African Divestiture Bill, called 'the SAD Bill.' None other than Senator Daniel P. Callahan was the chairman of that committee. Those hearings attracted international media."

"And," Agent Gibbons noted, "Priscilla J PJ Austin, a former aide to Callahan, may have brought the mess in South Africa to the attention of Ohio politicians and other interested observers with the premier last March here in Ohio, of all places, of that documentary on Nelson Mandela. It was *her* PR firm that spearheaded the Ohio Mandela Premiere Committee."

This time, it was Agent Rothschild who blurted out. "So that connects the dots."

Agent Gibbons nodded. "This *is* our working hypothesis."

She then told the two law enforcement officers that President Ronald Reagan and his foreign policy advisers had adopted a policy of "constructive engagement" with South Africa, fostering cultural, economic, and other exchanges. At the same time, the diplomats sought to influence a change in the political regime. As it turned out, although the president's policy aligned with that of British Prime Minister Margaret Thatcher, a strong American ally, the U.S. Congress had opposed the president's approach, overrode his veto, and enacted an economic sanctions bill against South Africa.

"Marvin, David," Agent Gibbons pointedly said, "as I am sure you're both aware, an increasingly large number of prominent individuals, organizations and nations the world over—which includes the Ohio Senate and the Ohio Mandela Premier Committee—are joining with the Black South Africans in their quest for freedom. Several American states have already enacted laws encouraging corporations doing business with South African-based corporations and the South African government to divest and to dispossess property, authority, and titles. Not only that, but calls for the removal of South Africa from the United Nations have reached epic proportions. South African dissidents and religious leaders such as Anglican Bishop Desmond Tutu are accessing American media and illuminating the situation in their country even further. Therefore, as it turns out, Nelson Mandela, the ANC, and the Black South Africans are no longer acting in isolation."

Her pace slowed, and her pitch lowered, even saddened, when she said: "But not everyone supports the call for reform of the South African society. Some of America's most reputable colleges and universities, as well as corporations, now find themselves in the midst of the controversy. Many others are contriving ways to comply. The State of Ohio and *The* Ohio State University have millions of dollars invested in South African corporations and the Republic of South Africa. Plenty of money is at stake."

Tersely she explained that—when Senator Callahan and members of the Black Elected Democrats of Ohio (BEDO) and their supporters linked their petition for the release of imprisoned ANC activist Nelson Mandela to their call for support of the SAD Bill—the Afrikaners and their sympathizers began a vigilant counterattack.

"Enter the bad guys," whispered the FBI agent to the Columbus Police detective.

"And maybe enter our perpetrators," agreed the Columbus Police detective.

Agent Gibbons said that the most powerful of all these were the diamond and gold magnates who were the muscle behind the South African Nationalists Movement (SANM), and that, although the SANM's leadership did not seek public office, they determined who could.

She paused. "OK, guys, hear me now. What we think might have happened then was that when the magnates learned about the SAD Bill in the Ohio General Assembly, they dispatched their forces."

Proficient at laundering money and promoting their cause, the SANM's funding floated from corporation to corporation and from financial institution to financial institution, until it eventually reached the most high-powered lobbyists in the U.S. Congress and most American state legislatures, including the Ohio General Assembly. They targeted lawmakers who faced difficult reelection campaigns, lawmakers who needed financial support in one way or another, and weak members, such as those with problems with alcoholism or difficulties in their marriages. The SANM lobbyists offered something for whatever ailed the 132 Ohio lawmakers, well, except for Senator Callahan.

"But the thing is," Agent Gibbons then noted, "the political fallout from the SANM's lobbying activities met with mixed reviews." She opened a file and read from it. One newspaper headline read, "SANM Meets with Lukewarm Reception by Ohio Lawmakers." Another headline read, "Black Lawmakers Reject Calls from SANM Lobbyists." Yet another read, "Growing Resentment by South African Sympathizers over SANM's Overt Lobby."

She nodded. "So, we're thinking that Senator Callahan is fighting for his life in an ICU because he was quoted in the press expressing disdain for 'the utter gall of those white racists! #*!#? coming up here in our house, trying to buy our silence and consent. Well, they can take their blood money back with them to wherever it is they came from.'"

Now Agent Rothschild was as rapt as Detective Stoudemeir.

"As it all happened," Agent Gibbons pointed out, "The senator was quite concerned that some of his own Black colleagues might yield to the temptation of the generous gifts of the SANM, so he admonished all of his colleagues in the Ohio General Assembly—particularly those in BEDO—who had met with the SANM lobbyists, and then he vowed to 'call them out.' For how effective would he be if the BEDO membership broke ranks and accepted the gifts from the very group they fought against?"

Then, the "gal" from New York opened another file folder and tossed a copy of the stapled report to both of her students.

"Read it and weep," she said.

The two law enforcement officers were silent as they did what they had been told to do.

The report said that "With such open defiance by many in the Ohio General Assembly, the SANM's leadership soon unleashed another element that is more lethal than their lobbyists":

> Just in case the Ohio lawmakers do not fully grasp the meaning of the phrase, 'Don't mess with our money,' they will soon come to terms with how the SANM deals with the opposition. The other element of the SANM is likened to a terrorist organization whose operations could be called into action at a moment's notice. It is comprised of male Afrikaners who are trained to do that which is necessary to maintain the order of the day—apartheid—and to protect the organization's vested interests in the diamond, gold and platinum industries. This element is known throughout South African society and neighboring countries as the SANM's Patrol Guard, the "PG" or "Guardsmen" for short.
>
> The PG is part of the Afrikaner elite, the sons, the nephews and the grandsons. They are highly educated and cosmopolitan and, in addition to Afrikaans and English, they are fluent in at least three other languages. They undergo intense indoctrination and psychological training that includes brainwashing, resulting in a trained cadre of believers that their kind, the Afrikaners, are superior and the only ones fit to govern the country. They hate all nonwhite people and any white sympathizers to the cause of the likes of Nelson Mandela. They not only approve of Mandela's imprisonment, but they also want his head.
>
> Known primarily for their hideous torture techniques, the PG specializes in dreaded practices such as putting a Black person inside a stack of rubber tires that reach up high to the person's neck; then they set the tires aflame. Since the PG believes that Black

South Africans are not human beings, they practice this ritual with the burning tires as sport.

They are also expert marksmen, and they possess the training and the weaponry to fulfill their kills effortlessly and with undeniable precision.

The report concluded: "The SANM has unleashed the vicious PG, and their target is Ohio state Senator Daniel P. Callahan."

As the two law enforcement officers finished reading the report, Agent Gibbons nodded again and said, "We believe that Senator Callahan was unaware of the PG's intentions. And that even if he were, he would not have cared anyway."

The FBI agent and the Columbus Police detective nodded in unison, and then both men began to speak at once.

Agent Gibbons held up her hand, palm facing outward. "You first," she said pointing to the Columbus Police detective.

"I get it. The SANM Patrol Guardsman who came to the church intended to assassinate Senator Callahan, but for some strange reason, he killed the groom who happened to be in the wrong place at the wrong time. But—"

The FBI agent cut in. "But what about the abduction of the bride? Wouldn't the assassin be out to get her as much as the senator?"

"My question precisely," said Detective Stoudemeir.

This time, Agent Gibbons smiled and said, "Right on. That, in a nutshell, is our question. And what I'm suggesting as an operating premise is that there are not one but possibly two assailants …." Smiling at the detective, she then said, "Two different assailants are indeed at work here. One shot the senator. Another took the bride. What we need to find out is who the good guys are."

"Any guesses?" Agent Rothschild asked because he was not about to let her leave without picking her brain.

"That's for you to find out."

At that, FBI Agent Bonnie Gibbons decisively closed her folders and packed her briefcase.

6

More Ruminations, the CF Relief Team & Raised Antennas

Priscilla still did not know for a certainty that she was in Zimbabwe, and that her rescuers had intentionally taken her there as they prepared to deal with her assailants, head–on and on their home turf in neighboring South Africa. Nor did she know that it would be quite some time before she would see her family and friends again, and that her life would never be as it once was, serene and simple and sheltered. Priscilla had no way of knowing it, but she was in for the adventure of a lifetime.

She may have been coming out of her drug-induced state.

She already knew she was not alone because she had overheard someone talking, and now, she felt someone watching her as she moved about the grounds. But she did not know that three-armed men were guarding the walled-in compound, and that they moved about such that she could not see them. These CF mercenaries were also waiting for three more members of the relief team to join the others inside.

Meanwhile, Priscilla continued staring at the smidgen of grass and the exotic-looking trees and succulents. She could hear a few feral mutts barking on the other side of the wall surrounding the house.

Then she remembered, sort of; her drug-induced haze still blurred her mind, but Priscilla thought, for a moment, that she knew something about Africa. She sighed. If what she had overheard in that distant conversation was correct, she was in the vicinity of Harare, *wherever the devil that is*. Priscilla was in the village of Prospect, a suburb of the capital of Zimbabwe, about an hour's drive from downtown Harare, which she would soon know for a certainty.

She supposed she knew as much as most people did about Africa, if not a little more than most. Some of what she knew was from her graduate studies in political science at *The* Ohio State University, and that had been refreshed and augmented by the research she had done before the premiere of the documentary on Nelson Mandela not long ago at home in Columbus, Ohio.

Just six years earlier, Harare had been called "Salisbury, Southern Rhodesia." Priscilla's familiarity with the name was reinforced by the fact that she had attended Livingstone College in Salisbury, North Carolina. But here she was in the midst of southern Africa in a place which—prior to British exploration and occupation—had originally been called "Harare," hence its current name. The city was situated 600-odd miles north of Johannesburg, South Africa, the final destination of Priscilla's trek. But she was not yet aware of that not-so-small detail, either.

Priscilla knew that Zimbabwe and South Africa were similar in more ways than geography. She already knew that British colonialism once prevailed in the two countries and that many of the people in both countries spoke English and enjoyed fairly well-developed educational systems. She also knew about Cecil Rhodes, the son of a British clergyman, who discovered and opened the Kimberley diamond fields and formed the De Beers Mining Company in South Africa. And later, she would learn from reading books in a library in Harare, that Rhodes' ultimate ambition had been to acquire all of Africa—from Cairo to the Cape of Good Hope—in the name of the British Crown and of his success in founding Salisbury and in eventually establishing Southern Rhodesia— which derived from his name—as a self-governing British colony. Last, she would learn of Rhodes's failed plot to overthrow the South African government and to force Paul Kruger out of power, and that Rhodes himself was then forced to resign from the National Assembly there. The only other fact she had already known about the man was that he had bequeathed much of his fortune to public service for young "civilized men" from the colonies, the United States and Germany in a scholarship which bore his name.

But Priscilla understood that Rhodes was a colonialist and a supporter of the Boers, far from an advocate for racial equality.

Cecil Rhodes was a racist. Pure and simple, she surmised, with distaste, as once again she looked around the bleak yard where she felt so confined. She peered at the top of the surrounding wall and, for the first time, noticed the barbed wire. She gritted her teeth. Her legs and arms still felt a little heavy. But she was thinking much more clearly now.

She went back to her ruminations about Africa.

In addition to Cecil Rhodes, Priscilla knew the name Ian Smith and about his role in subjugating the Black people of Southern Rhodesia. She knew him mostly from having seen his face on black-and-white television news shows. She detested the man because he had refused to grant civil liberties to the Blacks. Watching his face and listening to his voice would make her uncomfortable because he conjured up images of U.S. Southern governors who had fought against the federal government's efforts to desegregate public accommodations, and especially its efforts to allow Black students admission to public universities. She hated that Ian Smith's voice sounded so much like the voices of those Southern governors.

Priscilla was uncertain whether she was in the exact territory of someone whom she hated so much, and where most whites who remained here still believed they were inherently superior to Black people. Her rescuers had reason to be concerned about her reaction when she would learn that she was, in fact, situated in the next-to-last bastion of legally sanctioned racist regimes, the last being South Africa itself and its apartheid regime.

But by the time of Priscilla's predicament here, the British government had already granted the colony its independence, and the nation had reverted to its original name, Zimbabwe. The Zimbabwe African National Union (ZANU), led by Robert Mugabe, had prevailed against the Zimbabwe African People's Union (ZAPU) in the parliamentary elections of July 1985, so Mugabe had become Zimbabwe's prime minister. Yet the civil war between the military forces allied with the ZANU and those allied with the ZAPU still raged, so Priscilla's rescuers made use of that war.

More Ruminations, the CF Relief Team and Raised Antennas

Priscilla was nearly fully conscious yet wholly unaware that she was in a country where people viewed her as neither black nor white. Like so many so-called "Black" Americans, she had ancestors who were also white and Indian. But here in this part of the world, she—a racially mixed person—would be considered an outcast, *an unwanted*. If her abductors had taken her south of the border into South Africa, she would have been treated as an outlaw. So at the end of June 1986, the date of Jonathan's murder, Priscilla's rescuers first took her to this village in Prospect, Zimbabwe, and took up residence in this compound as they prepared to engage the SANM Patrol Guard head–on and on their own turf.

She sank down on the trunk extending from the banyan tree. Vaguely she remembered sitting here before. She was suddenly so tired. She leaned back against the tree, closed her eyes and dozed off into an uneasy sleep.

While Priscilla slept off the remaining effects of those sedatives that the CF relief team had given her, the three mercenaries—Eduardo, Onslow, and Terrence—continued patrolling inconspicuously outside the compound. Given the politically contentious environment, these white and Hispanic Americans could not parade around in plain sight. Later, Priscilla would interact with them, especially CF Lieutenant Onslow, who sported bushy, sandy-brown hair, black horn-rimmed, thick lenses and hilariously high-water, saggy trousers—held up by a rope, of all things. But all three men wore their shirt sleeves turned up displaying the same tattoos on their shoulders and necks—snakes and tigers crawling up the trunks of oak trees. They also carried heavy weaponry: machine guns, hand grenades, and several big knives.

Priscilla did not know the men who were guarding her. But she was familiar with two of the three men inside the house at the center of the compound: Angelo Delgato (called Angel) and Bartholomew Jordan (called Jordy). She later learned that the third man, Charlie (the manservant) was called only by his first name and that he was, in fact, the manservant of Tommy Wozniah, whom she also knew. (But Tommy was not there.)

Soon, the three mercenaries guarding the Prospect compound heard the sound of an approaching jeep. Cautiously they moved toward the driveway. Then they relaxed as they saw who was in the jeep. They opened the gate and allowed the jeep to enter the compound. They greeted the white driver and his two white passengers and escorted them inside the rustic dwelling.

Quickly, the guards brought the newcomers up to speed. Priscilla was still napping outside. Between her time inside on the tattered sofa and outside by the banyan tree, she had slept nearly around the clock. Even though her rescuers had stopped medicating her, they rightly expected she was still experiencing the lingering side effects.

"Let her sleep for a bit longer," said CF Agent Delgato, one of the men who had already been inside the kitchen. "We need to talk."

CF Agent Jordan nodded to the third member of their team, the manservant, and said, "I think we'd like some coffee."

As they waited for the coffee to brew, the trio sat at the table in the modest kitchen of the safehouse and tried to plan precisely what they would say to Priscilla, who knew Angel and Jordy as high-powered lobbyists from her time in the Ohio Senate. She also knew Jordy from her high school years in their hometown of Prendergast, New York. She had not yet met the manservant.

"I wish our guys hadn't been so crazy with the tranquilizers," the manservant said. "The boss told us to talk to her about what happened. You know, let her get it out of her system. I don't know how we can do that if she's so zonked out."

"My God," Jordy agreed, as he openly pondered, "I still don't know what I'll say when she asks me why I drugged her and then dragged her off in her wedding gown." It was he who had grabbed Priscilla from behind at the church and covered her face with the chloroform-filled cloth. It was he who had spoken to her nephew, Germane. It was he who had been in charge of the CF relief team at the safehouse in France and who had insisted that Carlton Elliott Bernhardt, another member of their elite squad, not travel with the entourage to Zimbabwe. After all, it was he who had done that which was most expedient to save Priscilla's life. Ironically, however, only Jordy had known about the paradox of the situation: namely, that Carlton was not only a member of the Collective Force, but also Priscilla's former, albeit one-time, lover.

What a mess, he thought, *what a mess*. Most of all, Jordy knew that, even partially sedated, there would be hell to pay when Priscilla realized who had abducted her and why.

"But, man, you had little choice," the manservant insisted. "My God, she'd just seen her bridegroom and the senator get gunned down at the altar. You couldn't risk the likelihood of her doing something rash, now, could you?"

Angel chimed in hurriedly: "Besides, Jordy, she likes you. She'll be okay once all the facts are revealed. You'll see."

"The facts," Jordy shook his head and said, "Take it from me, fellas, Miss Prissy is not going to be happy when she hears *all* the facts."

But the manservant, with little regard for what Agent Jordan had just said, continued: "So after those preliminaries, we'll get right down to it. We have to find out whether she even saw the face of the shooter. And if so, can she identify him on the tape from that Senate debate?"

They were all well aware of that fateful tape that Jordy had managed to procure from Herbert Wiseman's office back in Columbus.

"Once she confirms what we already suspect," the manservant concluded, "then we'll tell her about our plan of action. And we'll deal with how to handle the other mess later."

"The other mess" that the manservant and Jordy referred to had, in fact, been two different situations. The situation that Jordy referred to was his undisclosed knowledge that Priscilla and Carlton were former lovers. In contrast, the situation that the manservant had referred to was the team's need to devise a strategy to get Priscilla safely to Johannesburg.

But just then, the coffee was ready.

"Everybody good to go?" the manservant asked.

"Give a guy a minute to think," Jordy said.

While the three of them blew on the hot brew and then sipped in silence, Jordy was alone with his thoughts. He had known Priscilla since high school, where their classmates had called him Bart. But now, some sixteen years later, Jordy was a powerful lobbyist for union contractors in Ohio and New York. His associate, Angel, represented his family's highway construction business, Delgato Construction Contractors. Their third comrade, Tommy Wozniah, was the chairman and chief executive officer for the Chesterfield Bank of Cleveland and a prominent political operative—primarily for Democratic Party concerns. They had all met Priscilla during her tenure as legislative aide to Senator Callahan, when she had gotten caught up in, and actually straightened out, a political scandal that had attracted national attention. In the end, Priscilla had not only survived but triumphed, and they made her a lucrative offer to join their ranks, an offer she refused. Around the time of her refusal, she decided instead to operate her PR consultancy full-time. Although Jordy and his CF associates had seen little of her after that episode, they had all remained in good standing.

After draining his coffee, Jordy stood. "OK, let's do this thing."

But just as they were about to go outside, Priscilla filled the doorway. She rubbed her eyes. "Am I seeing things?" She looked from Jordy to Angel. "I should have guessed the two of you would be here. Tommy was here yesterday. And I guess you can't have one of you without the others."

She did not smile. Those same three men had just reappeared in Priscilla's life, but this time she had already figured out there was more to them than their so-called day jobs. *Otherwise, how the hell did they know an assassin would show up at my wedding? These suckers are no ordinary lobbyists*, and right she was. In only two days, Priscilla's life had been transformed from political intrigue on the state and local level to a worldwide epic.

With more confidence than she felt, Priscilla walked to the table, took a seat and helped herself to a mug of coffee.

"All right now, fellas, give me your party line, and then tell me how you plan to get me the hell out of here, wherever the hell *this* is. Make it good now."

In a slightly bungled attempt to start the conversation, Jordy said, "Miss Prissy, it's good to see you're back at yourself." Immediately he regretted what he had said. Words spoken, he could not take them back; however, those very words were necessary to ignite the anger inside her. When Jordy reached the end of the tragic story, Priscilla turned around to face him, who helplessly watched as she seemed to swell with anger.

"Was it you, Jordy? Was it you who grabbed me and forced me to inhale that ghastly chloroform? And why'd you do that, pray tell? Did you dare to do that to me just seconds after I saw my bridegroom's head burst open? And why'd you kidnap me, Jordy? Why?" Priscilla spoke so loud that her own head ached.

"Priscilla, I'm sorry," he said hurriedly. "But I had little choice. Under the circumstances, we had precious little time to act." Jordy had practiced his lines well. "You see, Priscilla, we weren't sure if the perp would come after you next, sort of a revenge killing since he'd been unsuccessful in killing the senator." He paused. "You do know that Senator Callahan, well, at least, is still alive? He was the *real* target. Your bridegroom was shot ... by mistake."

Priscilla snapped. "Just now, I don't give two wooden nickels about the senator. My Jonathan is dead. He can never come back to me." Her eyes were desolate, but after a moment, she amended what she had just said. "But that is good to hear about the senator. I'm glad they didn't get him." She heaved a great sigh. "But what about my mom, my nephew Germane, and my other family members and friends? And my goodness, what about Julia? Where and how is Julia?"

Jordy tried to explain, "Priscilla," he began, "we're all very sorry about the death of your fiancé. Honest, we are. But we're not going to lie to you. We now know the bullet that killed Jonathan was intended for the senator. This whole mess is related to the SAD Bill. But first things first. Charlie here will bring you up to date on the whereabouts of your family and friend, Julia." Then Jordy moved out of her line of fire.

The manservant spoke succinctly. Priscilla's family had been taken to an undisclosed place and provided with security. But the manservant could not reveal to her the exact location because her family's security depended partially on her not knowing those details.

Priscilla would learn later that Liza and Germane were taken to Hueston Woods, a resort area in southwestern Ohio, which was ironic because that was the site for her planned honeymoon.

Intentionally left out of the manservant's briefing also were the words "federal witness protection program."

But soon Priscilla would figure out the meaning of those words on her own.

"As for Julia," the manservant continued, "the feds felt it best that she carry on life as usual, but with a security detail."

Angel chimed back in, saying, "They're all OK. Take it from us, everyone else is A-OK." As Angel tried to convince Priscilla that he spoke the truth, he noticed something he had not seen in her before.

Jordy cut in smoothly while Angel mulled over his thoughts about Priscilla's changed demeanor.

"We hear from the most reliable sources that there is extra security for Senator Callahan at the hospital. He now has another medical specialist and a male nurse. And we're told he is stable at this time."

Although Jordy paused, Priscilla said nothing.

She was no longer interested in the senator's security, but rather that of her friend Julia. "But isn't that taking unnecessary risks with Julia's life?" Priscilla cried out. "I mean, it seems to me you're using her as bait. My God, is there no limit you fools will go to get what you want? Julia's a damn good friend, trustworthy, dependable and all that stuff. Why are you using her?"

Then she turned her attention to the man who had spoken the least. "Gee whiz, Angel, no tales about sunbathing in the Caymans?" But Angel knew better than to respond.

Priscilla was angry. But the others knew she needed to vent. The more she carried on, the more likely she'd eventually reveal tidbits of useful information.

After they let her rave on for a while, Angel finally broke in again, saying, "Priscilla, we need to know if you saw the face or caught a glimpse of the man who shot Jonathan. Can you help us out? You see, in order for us to catch the people who did this horrible thing, we need to know exactly what you remember before Jordy drugged you. Take your time."

Priscilla went silent and considered. She sipped the cooled coffee.

"I can tell you for certain that I saw his face," she finally said.

Talk about raised antennas! All three of the men leaned closer to her.

"He even stared at me as he descended the stairwell. He knows I saw his damn face. But he was in such a hurry to get out of there, I figured he thought he could take care of me later. Is that what you wanted to know?" Her lips curled. "And another thing, fellas. I've seen that man before."

That was precisely the information they needed to confirm the identity of the assailant. As storybook as their mission might seem, it had just changed course from "Hide Priscilla" to "Hide Priscilla and Seek the Perp." Theirs had been a hide-and-seek mission all along, which was what they had wanted it to be in the first place.

"One of Wiseman's cameramen pointed him out to me when we taped the SAD debate," Priscilla said, as she became more and more animated. "Yes, I'd recognize that Nazi-like figure anywhere. I see him in my dreams. I see him when I walk around this god–awful place. I've choked him to death in my dreams. I've hung him by his private parts, by his fingers—"

Just as Jordy reached out to comfort her, Priscilla folded her arms across her breast. "I know, Priscilla," he said softly and wrapped his arms around her. Then he patted her shoulders. "That's okay, let it out. Just let go of it all." Then quickly, he pulled away from her. For even he knew that Priscilla did not like people touching her, of which she made no secret and often said as much to most people's surprise.

Part of Priscilla's discomfort with being touched was attributed to her upbringing. During her youth, Nelson and Liza used to caution her and her siblings against allowing people outside their close-knit circle to touch them "affectionately or any other way." However, Priscilla took their instructions to heart and had since suffered intimacy and relationship problems.

She was also claustrophobic and suffered from positional vertigo—the latter of which she contracted from a car accident during her time as a professor in Tallahassee, Florida; and she suffered from a few other phobias, such as acrophobia, which, as it so happens, not even Jordy knew about. But her "special someone" knew, but he was not here. Even so, Priscilla's phobias were going to be problematic for the duration of her time in Africa.

Not thinking much about what had just happened between Jordy and Priscilla, the other men looked at each other in triumph. As far as they could discern, they had just succeeded in getting Priscilla to release what they assumed was much of her anger, and they had. Now they needed to prime her. They had to give her a new game face: a poker face, as it were.

Then, unexpectedly, Priscilla looked Jordy in his eyes and said, "You know something else, Jordy, I'm certain I heard Carlton's voice. But for the life of me, I can't remember when or where that was. But I know I heard his voice."

7

The Mandela Premiere

Later, Priscilla could not remember what was said after she asked about Carlton; she thought that maybe they all ate together at the table and talked a little more. However, she did remember eating something that tasted like bland mashed potatoes and a piece of bread, and that she mostly moved her food around her plate because she did not like her meal. Priscilla had eaten sadza, a maize- or cornmeal-based staple, the national dish of Zimbabwe. But the time would come when she would look forward to eating the "bland" local cuisine, which included avocados, beans, butternut squash, cucumbers, peanut butter stew, dried fish (kapenta), and strips of sun-dried salted meats (biltong) like kudu, ostrich, springbok, and warthog. Or else, she would starve.

As she regained full consciousness, she felt that whatever drugs they had fed her earlier had *finally* worn off.

She remembered that Jordy, the manservant, and Angel had told her that Jonathan had not been the intended assassination target, that the shooter had been after Senator Callahan, and that the reason had been the senator's outspoken support of the South African Divestiture Bill. *Now if I could only remember that darn Senate debate, maybe,* she thought, *I can help Jordy and the others to identify the assassin.*

Another thought struck her. The South African Divestiture Bill might have been the final straw for whoever it was who had killed her Jonathan. But what had led to that showdown in the Ohio Senate had, in fact, been the premier of the *Nelson Mandela* documentary.

Ah, yes, she decided: It *was* the Ohio premiere of the documentary *Nelson Mandela*. But, just then, a foul odor disturbed her concentration. *What's that awful smell?* Since there was no central air conditioning, whatever foul odors there were—and there were many—permeated the atmosphere like dense cloud cover; and, when the ceiling fan was functioning, it merely moved the stifling odors throughout the rustic dwelling.

Priscilla learned not to linger in the backyard, either, because whoever had stayed in the house before them had used the backyard as a dump. There were no dumpsters like back in the States, no municipal sanitation department for waste removal, at least none that Priscilla saw. So whatever the chickens, dogs and goats did not consume remained on the ground and attracted flies, rodents, and even vultures. Mostly, the garbage and other debris had created foul odors.

As Priscilla continued reminiscing, before she knew it, the date of the *Mandela* documentary premiere, Friday, March 24, 1986, had come closer to her wedding date (June 28) than she had realized. Because both events had required so much coordination and planning, and many of the deadlines had fallen at the same time, she was simultaneously ordering bridesmaid dresses and wedding invitations and hurriedly filing her news stories and placing ads to generate interest and ticket sales for the premiere. Priscilla had known that public awareness and education were essential to the event's success. So she'd set up radio interviews for Marlene and even made some presentations herself to small groups that included First Church. She recalled how some of the behind-the-scenes work for *Mandela* involved an excessive amount of her time: writing letters, soliciting funds and following up the letters and the solicitations with telephone calls. She compiled invitation lists for the private reception before the premiere and added an educational component to attract schoolchildren. Since most of the guests were unfamiliar with Nelson Mandela's life, the primary goal of the event was to heighten people's awareness of the man: "Who is Nelson Mandela, and why should anybody care about his predicament?"

Priscilla had been charged by the Ohio Mandela Premier Committee with finding a way to explain who Mandela was and why it was vital that he be released from prison. So, another daunting task was to show that *all people* could acquire Mandela's great qualities if they only knew about the man. As she set out to do her homework on Nelson Mandela and the Republic of South Africa, she read news clips and microfilm, talked to people familiar with global political issues, compiled her "talking points," devised a brief profile of the man and widened the scope of her research to include modern South African history.

But she had felt her own anger building as she read about the history of the country and its political system. She had forgotten much of what she had learned in college and graduate school, when, like many students, she remembered only what she needed to pass an exam. At this point in her life, however, she noticed—just as FBI Agent Rothschild and Columbus Police Detective Stoudemeir had, that the historical record for most African nations was chronicled from the advent of European exploration and invasions; and, that most of the African continent was already inhabited by tribes like those of Mandela's—tribes that traced their family lineage back for centuries—was regarded as of little significance.

Also, by that time, some of the more curious church members had learned more about her, too. They had been surprised to learn that their new pastor's fiancée had a family connection to the church and that Priscilla herself was the daughter of a Methodist minister. The more they learned about her, the more acceptable she became to them. But Priscilla was hardly impressed with their newfound interest in her.

Since several of the members already knew about her association with Senator Callahan—and a few others, about her PR business—they immediately signed on to her request for sponsorship of the *Mandela* premiere.

That wasn't a hard sale, not at all, she had thought.

Besides, by then almost everybody had come to terms with the eventuality of the wedding, especially the Austin clan. In fact, Liza, Helen and Germane even came to Columbus to attend the *Mandela* premiere. During that visit, they observed firsthand Priscilla and Jonathan together and realized that Jonathan was head over heels, but Priscilla was still herself.

Young Germane found much amusement in the couple's relationship. He even said, "Uncle Reverend Morgan is always staring at Aunt Priscilla like she's a doll or something. And Aunt Priscilla moves all over the place and tells

82

everybody what to do, while he runs up after her, asking if he can help with anything." Germane had begun calling Jonathan "Uncle" even before the wedding took place.

The private reception for the *Mandela* premiere was held at the newly renovated Ohio Theatre, located immediately south of the Ohio Statehouse. The event attracted an impressive gathering of the city's social and political elite and overshadowed any other public event in the capital that evening. The theatre filled quickly.

From the moment the curtains were raised to the airing of the sixty-minute documentary itself, the audience was enthralled. Then, as the finale neared, the audience rose to its feet and applauded for a long time. Part of the documentary's success came from its billing as "a national event premiering in Columbus, Ohio." Showing the personal dimensions of Nelson and Winnie Mandela as portrayed through the eyes and voice of Winnie was very effective in capturing the attention of the audience, not to mention the guest appearance by one of the Mandela daughters. The documentary portrayed Nelson Mandela as a noble and courageous man who, except for three months of marriage in freedom, had been imprisoned for most of his adult life. Simultaneously and succinctly, it effectively described the oppressive system of apartheid that was the order of the day in South Africa.

Along with the proceedings of the Ohio Mandela Premiere Committee, Senator Callahan and his colleagues during this same time period were preparing to conduct hearings on the South African Divestiture Bill. When the Ohio Senate reconvened in January 1986, the Commerce and Labor Committee received the SAD Bill from the House of Representatives. After the bill passed out of the committee, it was scheduled for a floor vote in June.

8

Senate Bill 71
&
The SANM Executive Committee

Priscilla was now standing in front of one of the windows next to that tattered sofa inside that rustic safehouse, shaking her head in disbelief that she was even in Africa. She found it even harder fathoming Harare, so she just continued staring out the window at the bleak landscape and at the few feral mutts and goats and chickens traipsing about the grounds of the walled-in compound. She sensed that she had been here before, not in this space but in this mental state. She remembered what happened when she wrote an open letter to Ohio state Senator Theopholus Madison, when, following his defection to the Republican Caucus after the 1982 elections, she encouraged him—lambasted him was more like it—to return to the Senate Democratic Caucus. She remembered that Statehouse observers called the incident "the political scandal of the decade." In an effort to get her some relief, Senator Callahan had invited her to join him on a political junket to Hilton Head Island, South Carolina, and it was there that she found herself staring out a window as she tried to figure out "the ramifications of her own action." Only now, at this particular juncture, she found herself once again trying to figure out what had created her current seemingly unbearable circumstance.

To Priscilla's discernment, her recollections about the *Mandela* premiere produced no notable results. But then she recalled receiving an unexpected telephone call nearly four weeks before her wedding.

Without any greeting, the familiar voice of the caller said, "Priscilla, the SAD Bill is scheduled for a Senate floor vote in less than two weeks. I need you to cover that event for me."

"But Senator—"

"I've already secured clearance for your camera crew to set up in the Senate chamber."

"Senator, listen to me—"

"And by the way, Sweetheart, I'm fully aware that this job comes on the eve of your wedding. But you didn't get this far on your looks." Senator Callahan chuckled. "Lord knows, if anyone can handle this type of assignment, you can. Thanks, Kiddo."

"But, Senator, surely you know that this is a tall order for such a short timeline. And you want me to subject a camera crew from the commercial marketing arena to a mad-dog fight among some of the most aggressive media moguls out there and during Senate deliberations on one of the most controversial issues in the nation? Why, that's a recipe for catastrophe!"

"I've taken care of that, too. You see, young lady, your cameramen have been cleared to set up *inside* the banister. You'll be directly on the Senate floor. What else do you need?"

Priscilla remembered how livid she was and that she had snapped. "My goodness, Senator, is there anything you *won't* do to get what you want? I've not exactly been oblivious to the presence of those South African lobbyists at the Statehouse. And those bastards are vicious. Do you hear me, Senator? This time you've rubbed a lot of folks the wrong way, so back at you."

"Yes, yes, you're absolutely correct again, young lady. But that's why I'm the senator, and you're the PR girl."

"Let me finish, because I might not get this chance again." Priscilla was no longer the senator's legislative aide, and she was far from the naïve graduate student whom he had first met. She spoke with much resolve: "Senator, those folks blow people like you and me out of their noses. We're talking about gazillion-dollar global interests. Besides, hasn't the case already been made? Is it really necessary to enact another state law at this stage of the game?"

As it turned out, almost one month before the day of her wedding, Priscilla had felt that something bad was in the offing. Only, at the time, she had no way of knowing how bad and that whatever it was would eventually involve her, because—even though she had heard about such bad people as the SANM PG, she, like many others at the time, hardly envisioned herself caught up in any terrorist activity. And she certainly never imagined an assassin showing up at her wedding or herself being abducted and taken as far away as Zimbabwe and eventually into the bile of apartheid-ruled South Africa itself.

As angry as she had been at the time, she distinctly remembered the senator had had the last word: "Priscilla, I've listened to you. Now, allow me to say that I've heard arguments from everyone who matters to me. Just do what you're good at doing and leave the rest to me. And call me when you've worked things out."

Then Priscilla remembered that it had been on Tuesday, June 11, around 1:45 in the afternoon when the Ohio Senate had conducted final deliberations on the SAD Bill, officially called Senate Bill 71. An atmosphere of anxiety permeated the chamber. Daniel P. Callahan and two of his colleagues had already withstood a tidal wave of opposition from the thirty other senators. In fact, it was widely believed that the bill was dead on arrival, but the senator had heard that type of hyperbole before—the reality of politics, Ohio politics.

Priscilla's recollections became increasingly complex; the closer the events led up to her wedding day, the less she wanted to remember them. So her mind drifted from one minor incident to another, such as the time that she and Julia finalized the menu for the reception at the parsonage, or when they finalized the lodging for the guests at the Columbus Downtown Sheraton Hotel, or when they counted the incredibly large number of confirmations to attend the wedding, or when they placed the order for the long-stem red and yellow roses to decorate the massive sanctuary at First Church, or when she and Julia discussed the rift that occurred between her and Jonathan over her wedding dress.

She remembered that in early May, she purchased a pale powder-blue tea-length wedding dress, a perfect match for her bridesmaids' dresses. With the purchase of that dress, she thought that she had completed one more of her "things to do."

Then she remembered she thought it somewhat strange that Jonathan kept nagging her: "Let me see your wedding gown. What color is it?" (During the time they had spent together, he still had no idea of her avowed feminism or of her social conservatism.)

Then, she vividly remembered going to the bridal shop and trying on the wedding gown and discovering that the garment was a little big on her. So the attendant immediately called for a seamstress who pulled, lifted and pinned the gown for a snugger fit on her; and then she and the attendant both agreed that, since the skirt was flared, "No one will even notice it's a little long on you."

Priscilla had just incurred an expense that she had not anticipated, all to satisfy Jonathan.

It was following her fitting that she went to the Sheraton Hotel, where she was surprised to learn that her account executive had reserved the bridal suite for her and Jonathan. A short time later, in a conversation with Julia, she was equally shocked that her invitation list had surpassed the limit of 300.

Oddly, Priscilla still did not visualize herself as the bride.

"Priscilla, this isn't one of your business projects," Julia had said. "This is your wedding. So, why all the emphasis on Jonathan? My God, you even bought a gown to please him. This is your territory, not his. And besides, everybody knows 'the wedding belongs to the bride;' that's you, Priscilla, not Jonathan. This is your day to shine."

At that point, Julia recognized that her friend was hardly prepared to play out her role as the bride at her own wedding.

Fast forward to that "eerie" day in June when the Ohio Senate debated and voted on Senate Bill 71, and when what Priscilla—and others in her camp— later learned, but did not know at the time, had been happening in a well-appointed boardroom in Johannesburg, South Africa.

SANM CEO Simeon Johannes and his twelve Executive Committee members met in their penthouse suite in one of Johannesburg's most opulent office buildings. The thirteen angry men—all Afrikaners—watched television as the Ohio Senate prepared to vote on Senate Bill 71, the SAD bill. The stately suite featured a huge table at its center. Alcoholic beverages and hors d'oeuvres abounded. Most noticeable, however, before each committee member was a thick, leather pouch that resembled a bulky place setting with an African motif like a leopard hiding out in the bush. Indeed, they were pouches filled with dossiers: photos, biographical sketches, and voting histories of each of Ohio's thirty-three state senators. Thickest among the batch was the dossier on Senator Callahan.

As the television camera lenses zoomed in on the senator, one of the thirteen angry men shouted, "I want that damn bastard's head—and yesterday! Do you hear me?" Otherwise, the exclusive executive suite grew quiet in anticipation of the debate and the eventual vote.

Across the Atlantic, in the Ohio General Assembly, the Senate president called for the third reading of Senate Bill 71, after which he said, "The Chair recognizes the distinguished gentleman from Cincinnati, Senator Callahan."

"Thank you, Mr. President," Senator Callahan said. "The whole world waits with great anticipation for the state of Ohio to act. Will we divest Ohio's holdings in corporations doing business with corporations that conduct business in and with South Africa? And although many of my own colleagues in this august chamber disagree fervently on the means, we all agree that the time is now. Plainly, apartheid has long since played out its hand. Men of reasonable conscience no longer find favor with such blatant disregard for humanity as practiced by the South African Nationalists Movement. Yes, I dare call out the name of the official organization that has poured tons of blood money into this very chamber and into America's highest legislative body, the U.S. Congress. The SANM hopes to hold onto any lingering affirmation, but 'the winds of change' have already passed them by."

While Senator Callahan spoke, Priscilla's camera crew panned the room for reaction. Marlene Hannah, who had produced the *Mandela* documentary, applauded along with some of her staff at every interval in the senator's speech. The cameras captured several members of BEDO sitting quietly in the gallery. Also captured on tape were three men from Washington, D.C. They were not American citizens, but high-powered SANM lobbyists, one of whom was also a member of its PG. Expressionless, they stood together at attention in the rear of the chamber. Later, it was that very demeanor that captured the attention of observers. The only discernible difference between those three men and images of the Nazis was the absence of those hideous black uniforms and tall, black leather boots. Otherwise, they resembled military men garbed in expensive executive attire.

Senator Callahan continued speaking: "After nearly a century and a half, the British government has still failed to act, even in the face of a dramatically changed world. Nonetheless, a short while ago, the state of Ohio demonstrated integrity and hosted the national premiere of the documentary *Mandela*. We called for the abolition of apartheid and for the release of Nelson Mandela."

The senator rolled on: "So you see, we're not calling for the ruination or for the dismantling of the diamond, gold and platinum industries, but for the dismantling of the political system wreaking havoc on the majority population in South Africa. We are demanding that the South African government recognize the civil liberties of the people comprising over 80 percent of its population. Provide the original people, the Black South Africans, with their citizenship rights. Restore their property rights. After all, it's their land. Restore their voting rights. Restore their marital rights. Restore their right to travel freely on the public transit system *without* identification cards. Restore their right to lodge in public accommodations. Rid South Africa of the very vestiges of discrimination that we Black Americans have only recently overcome ourselves. This year, not far from the dawn of the 21st century, show forth South Africa in a way that will make the world proud. Grant freedom, equality, and dignity to all the races, ethnic groups, and tribes."

The senator then sat down.

"Does the distinguished gentleman from Cincinnati yield?"

Senator Callahan nodded and said, "I yield."

"The Chair recognizes the distinguished gentleman from Toledo, Senator Sandusky."

"Mr. President and members of the Senate, I rise in absolute opposition to Senate Bill 71."

The volume of ecstasy in the boardroom of the SANM Executive Committee's penthouse office suite in Johannesburg escalated exponentially. The thirteen angry men screamed: "Now we're getting somewhere!"

Meanwhile, back in the Ohio Senate, Senator Sandusky bellowed: "Ladies and gentlemen of the Senate, what my colleague is asking for is outrageous.

He's essentially blackmailing the South African government. He's asking the South African government to provide civil rights to its Black citizens in *exchange* for our side withdrawing economic sanctions. Well, I, for one, will not stand for it. I oppose Senate Bill 71 and encourage the rest of you to do likewise." Then he sat down.

"Does the distinguished gentleman from Toledo yield?"

Senator Sandusky nodded and said, "I yield, Mr. President."

"The Chair recognizes the distinguished gentleman from Columbus, Senator Chamberlain."

"Thank you, Mr. President. I, too, rise in opposition to Senate Bill 71. If the distinguished senator from Cincinnati wishes to make a public statement against apartheid, he ought to draft a resolution. This legislative body drafts laws, but a law isn't necessary for his proposal. Besides, Ohio cannot tell South Africa, a country, how to govern. Nor can Ohio tell private corporations how to conduct their operations in other countries. Ohio cannot do what is embodied in Senate Bill 71."

Once again, there was thunderous glee in that penthouse office suite across the way in Johannesburg.

Yet there was little reaction inside the Ohio Senate chamber, where nerves frayed, and everybody simply yearned for the issue to be put to rest. Earlier, the SANM lobbyists and others retained by them had—except for Senator Callahan—approached every one of the other 131 lawmakers in the Ohio General Assembly. But their most extraordinary efforts had been concentrated in the thirty-three-member Senate. Although none of the senators had spoken publicly of the lobbyists, both the Senate Democrats and the Republicans had resented their strong-arm tactics. Because of their resentment, the two typically opposing Senate caucuses had come together and contrived a scheme, the linchpin of which was Senator Callahan.

Senator Chamberlain continued: "Though I empathize with my Senate colleague's concerns for racial equality and justice, I submit to you that passing Senate Bill 71 is not the way to achieve such. Therefore, I cannot condone the dismantling of whole industries to the effect of untold economic devastation the world over. I simply cannot support this measure, and so I ask for your opposition to Senate Bill 71."

After Senator Chamberlain spoke, the Executive Committee of the SANM felt that their lobbying efforts in the Ohio General Assembly had effectively killed Senate Bill 71. Several of them even began small talk and ignored the rest of the Senate debate. Meanwhile, the debate in the Ohio Senate continued.

The Senate president was asking Senator Chamberlain whether he yielded the floor. "Does the distinguished gentleman from Columbus yield?"

"I yield," Senator Chamberlain said and took his seat.

"The Chair recognizes the distinguished gentleman from Marietta, Senator Trexler."

"Thank you, Mr. President," Senator Trexler said. "I join my colleagues from Toledo and Columbus in opposition to Senate Bill 71. This bill is unconstitutional and unrelated to the general welfare of Ohio citizens. A state government in one country cannot prescribe a law for a sovereign entity elsewhere. Nor has the distinguished senator from Cincinnati shown forth the connection between the general welfare of the people of the great state of Ohio and that of the people in South Africa. This measure is a travesty to the rule of law. I urge my colleagues to vote 'no,'" Senator Trexler ended and sat down.

"Does the distinguished gentleman from Marietta yield?"

"I yield."

"The Chair recognizes the distinguished gentleman from Cincinnati, Senator Callahan."

"Mr. President, I've listened attentively to the opposition to Senate Bill 71, much of which has been unconvincing. There aren't any threats, intimidation, or conflicts in law, nor is there any blackmail in Senate Bill 71. Rather, the bill contains mere statements of fact and proposed courses of action. Governments the world over, the United Nations, our own U.S. Congress, and several American states have already called for no less than what is outlined in the bill before you. In fact, it's common knowledge that we in Ohio wish to be counted among those on 'the right side of history.' Let us face it: change is imminent in South Africa."

On that note, Priscilla had walked up to one of the cameramen. "Finally," she said, "he's made his point. Now let's capture some close-ups for reaction."

As the cameraman zoomed in on the faces of several people in the gallery, something else caught Priscilla's attention.

"Those guys standing over there out front? I've never seen them before. Focus on them for a while, and then for any reaction to the voting."

She walked over to the other cameraman and selected several senators for him to cover as they voted. As far as Priscilla was concerned, she was simply doing her job.

Meanwhile, it was the first cameraman who noticed something peculiar about the three men Priscilla had asked him to cover. At first, he thought they were members of the governor's security team. He sensed a strong element of discipline. Then again, he reckoned, "It could have been the mood of anxiety in the room," as he later told Priscilla.

At the same time, Senator Callahan concluded: "The question before us, therefore, is not *whether* to support Senate Bill 71 but *when* will Ohio join forces with right-minded peoples of the world? With that question, I urge your support of Senate Bill 71." The senator yielded the floor for the last time.

The Senate president then ordered, "The clerk will call the roll."

In sync, alphabetically, the first three senators cast their votes in line with the prearranged scheme. One by one, each man echoed the others, "No," "No," "No."

Shortly, however, there was murmuring throughout the chamber because of the sound of a different word.

"Aye," "Aye," "Aye" resounded quietly and rhythmically.

By the time the roll call ended, the Ohio Senate had voted thirty to three in favor of Senate Bill 71. Even more noteworthy, contrary to their debate positions, Senators Sandusky, Chamberlain and Trexler all voted in favor of the bill. Their speeches had been mere distractions from three of their colleagues, who found it necessary to vote in opposition to the bill. Those other three men also had last names that came early in the roll call, so they did not want to draw any attention their way—hence, the sideshow.

"The bill has passed," the president said to a subdued Senate chamber. There were no cheers of triumph, rather concern for possible fallout, for it was generally understood that the SANM exacted retribution on anyone who opposed their operations. Yet the action by the Ohio Senate that day manifested a rare act of courage, bipartisanship and the brazenness of Ohio politics.

Back over in Johannesburg, with their hopes wholly dashed, the SANM Executive Committee was beyond outrage. Because it was Senator Callahan who had championed the bill's passage, it was he whom the SANM targeted.

The Executive Committee members drew lots. The man with the shortest twig was privileged to dispatch his Patrol Guardsman to eliminate the target. The other twelve men tossed their dossiers of the senator into an open flame in a large bowl, indicating, in effect, they had just issued his death warrant.

Back in the Ohio Senate chamber, as the camera crew packed up their equipment, one of the men said he would have something for Priscilla in a couple of days. He also said there was something interesting he wanted to share with her, but he kept forgetting what it was.

Satisfied they had completed their work, Priscilla and the camera crew congratulated Senator Callahan and left the Statehouse. But as they walked through the Senate parking lot, they talked about the "eerie atmosphere that permeated the Senate chamber."

"Oh well," said one of the cameramen. Then he and the others bade Priscilla farewell and offered their congratulations on her upcoming wedding.

At the safehouse in Prospect, Zimbabwe, Priscilla abruptly turned and walked away from the window where she had been reminiscing and staring out disbelievingly. *Gotcha,* she said to herself.

"Jordy," she called out. "Have I got something for you!"

In an instant, he was at her side. But he could not help noticing how calm and in control she seemed to be. She no longer looked half-dazed or troubled, but rather relaxed and self-assured.

"Priscilla," he said to her, "my, my, Girlfriend, how you've come alive. Now, what have you got for me?"

Priscilla told Jordy exactly what she remembered from the Senate debate. "If you have that tape, and I think you do, take a close look at the scenes in the background, particularly in the gallery right after Senator Callahan sat down for the last time," she stressed, "right before the roll call. You'll see three noticeably disciplined, well-dressed Nazi-like figures standing together, one of whom is our guy. You find me that footage, and I'll show you the shooter."

But no sooner than she told him what she remembered, Priscilla welled up. Yet she did not seem to mind that Jordy could see her beginning to weep. She had just fingered, as it were, the man who had shot Jonathan, the man who had shot the senator and for all she knew, the man who was after her as well. The occasion called for a hug, a slap on the back, or some other display of affection. Still, Jordy, keenly aware of Priscilla's dislike of being touched, quickly, but affectionately, grabbed hold of her shoulders and planted a kiss on her cheek. Then he noticed a slight smile on her face. This time, as she and Jordy relished in her recollection about when and where she had first seen the Guardsman who had shot her Jonathan and the senator, she never minded his touching her.

Shortly afterwards, Jordy, the manservant, and Angel, together with Priscilla, reviewed the tape. They recognized the three Nazi-like figures and the one who fit the description that Priscilla had just given them. There he was. His name was Claus Fokker. The CF relief team knew the names and faces of their adversaries, particularly in such groups as the SANM PG.

At this point, however, even Jordy, Angel, and the manservant all noticed that that single incident alone had been a bit much for Priscilla. Then they watched in silence as she walked away from them back outside, where she perched up against that banyan tree, where she was about to relive those last painful memories of her ill-fated wedding day.

9

The Ill-fated Wedding Day

Once she realized that closing her eyes would not make the memories disappear, Priscilla decided to let what one might call a movie reel play itself out. She remembered that amid all the commotion by family and friends to do something for her wedding, there were several offers for bridal showers. Which ones should she accept—and when and where? The situation got a little testy at the church, for some members had decided to host a bridal shower *and* a reception. Jonathan's family also hosted a bridal shower, as did one of Priscilla's other acquaintances in Columbus. Priscilla learned quickly that she was not only a well-recognized businesswoman but also the fiancée of the pastor of a reputable church. She did not like the attention that surrounded her personal life, not in the least.

At last, she remembered the day of her wedding, June 28, 1986; it was beautiful, mild and sunny. She had almost finished dressing when Liza offered to help with her tiara.

"Suppose you know how proud your father would've been to see you marry Jonathan," Liza said.

Apart from her heartfelt poem, that statement was as close to offering another blessing for her daughter as Liza could have made.

Priscilla also remembered how proud both she and Liza were of Germane. They agreed that he was "a dashing young man." In fact, all the Austin men envied the youngster because they had assumed that Priscilla would ask one of them to be her escort. But the thought had never crossed her mind.

Most of the guests arrived at the church well in advance of the 1:30 p.m. ceremony. Customarily, some of them sat on the side of the bride, others on the side of the groom. Given Priscilla's association with public officials and businesspersons, no one was surprised at the extent of their presence. So the ushers were not alarmed when a relatively tall Caucasian male "with a strange accent" excused himself on the pretense, "I left their wedding gift in my car," when, in fact, he had gone to his car and gotten an elongated black leather satchel. For all the ushers and the security guards knew, it was merely an unusual gift.

Priscilla did not want to recall the ride to the church, but it unfolded before her anyway. She envisioned the white stretch limousine arriving for her, Germane and Liza. During the ride to the church, she noticed how attractive her mom was. She absolutely loved Liza's premature salt-and-pepper hair. "So that's what I have to look forward to someday," Priscilla remembered saying to her mom. Quickly, however, she grew anxious as she remembered the limousine driving through the neighborhood in the vicinity of the church. She remembered several people on the streets stopping and gazing at the impressive vehicle. Then she remembered how uncomfortable she had felt when she did not see anybody standing outside the church.

"Priscilla, don't you know?" Liza said in her matter-of-fact way. "They're all inside waiting on you."

It had been at that moment that Priscilla finally understood, "The wedding really does belong to the bride."

The sanctuary was adorned with single, long-stem red and yellow roses that were entwined in yellow ribbons and affixed to the shoulders of each pew. The chancel showcased a pair of huge white porcelain vases overflowing with red and yellow roses. The deaconesses had covered the altar and the other sacred objects in white-laced linens.

The bridal party was aligned according to gender against the rear wall, where, upon cue from the maid of honor, each male would step into the center aisle and reach for the arm of his companion. The color-coordinated dresses of the bridesmaids were eye-catching. The first bridesmaid wore a melon-colored tea-length silk dress, gathered at the hip, and she carried a long-stemmed red rose. Her earrings were pearl drops, a gift from Priscilla. The second woman wore a lemon-colored tea-length silk dress and carried a long-stemmed yellow rose; the rest of the bridesmaids were just as eye-catching.

First in line were lifelong friends Amber from Prendergast and Cathy from Livingstone College; both claimed bragging rights among the bridesmaids. The men wore black tuxedos with the corresponding boutonniere of the kind of rose that was carried by each woman they escorted. The twelve men and women of the bridal party awaited their cue from Julia.

Senator Callahan prepared to escort Liza down the aisle; his wife sat on one of the front pews on the groom's side. The congregation thought they were awestruck with the decorum, but then the senator and Liza walked down the aisle. The couple radiated, but for different reasons. Senator Callahan was proud to finally be accepted as a family friend by the Austin clan, and Liza was proud to finally play an integral role in the marriage of one of her daughters.

As her conscious state neared the finale of that awful day, Priscilla wanted to stop remembering it, but something would not let her. She tried to close her eyes again, but then she realized that the images would be etched behind her eyelids. Then she tried to stop thinking about how the day had ended, but the story refused to be contained.

She started to well up. Her nasal passages drained mucous. Priscilla vividly remembered what transpired in those next few minutes. She and Germane quietly entered the handsomely hand-carved wooden double doors from the vestibule to sneak a peep of the processional from behind the bridal party. Like clockwork, they watched as the senator and Liza reached the end of the long, inclined aisle. They saw the first couple of the bridal party step into place at the top of the aisle. They saw the senator helping Liza settle in her front row seat; then, they saw the senator reaching across the aisle for Jonathan's hand, but for whatever reason, Priscilla never knew. That simple gesture alone seemed to have ignited the loud, sharp thunder of gunfire that had been hurled from overhead.

She remembered pulling Germane back through the massive wooden double doors, instinctively peering up the stairwell, and then seeing the assailant fleeing out of the church.

Priscilla could feel herself about to have a major cry, something she had not done since her father died, as she now knew that Jordy and Angel had done that which was necessary to save her life as they sedated her and whisked her away from the church.

Now she also realized that she was not only the next primary target for the SANM PG assassins, but that the CF relief team now knew that she had seen the face of the shooter and that he had seen her as she watched him flee the scene of his foiled assassination attempt of Senator Callahan. Now she and her rescuers also knew that her nephew Germane had seen the face of the perp, too. More importantly, the CF relief team now knew that Priscilla and her nephew and maybe even her friend Julia were suddenly and unwittingly the new targets of one of the most vicious terrorist groups in the world.

"Problem is, where do I go from here?" Priscilla asked herself, rising from her makeshift seat on that banyan tree. "What a mess I've caused, what a mess." As she considered her next move, she fell into a state of deep depression. She felt tremendous guilt for Jonathan's death. She regretted the psychological impact of that horrific, bloody scene at First Church on her young nephew. Her mind raced as she called out the names of several other loved ones: "Momma, Camille, Helen, Harriet, Ellen, Nelson, Jr., Julia, Cathy, and Amber, even Mrs. Robinson . . .. What have I done?"

She thought about what her parents used to say about some of her actions: "Child, you live too close to the edge."

She thought that now her lifestyle had directly contributed to another person's death, possibly two people's deaths.

For the first time since the horrific tragedy at First Church in Columbus, Ohio, Priscilla wept uncontrollably and aloud.

10

The Patrol Guard & Partial Payment

Contrary to the CF relief team's thinking that PG Claus Fokker had returned to his home turf in Johannesburg, he was holed up in a boarding house in Amsterdam, where he placed a call to his supervisor on the Executive Committee in Joburg, the nickname its familiars used for the capital city.

"Yes, it's me. Ran into a spot of trouble. Killed the wrong man and critically wounded the target. But I've got this, Boss. I just need a little more time to fin—"

"Idiot!" Hans Evekink snapped. "How could you have missed the damn target? These guys will have *your* head if you don't fix this. The international media and intelligence community are all over this story. Word is 'they suspect *we* had something to do with it.' It's not safe to re-enter the country. You've got to fix this mess and hurry. Do you hear me?" Then Hans Evekink hung up the telephone.

Of Dutch descent, both Claus Fokker and Hans Evekink had much at stake. But Claus was new at this particular job. He had no kills to his credit. As for Hans, well, he needed to prove that his guy could conduct a campaign to the advantage of the Executive Committee.

Each Executive Committee member had three Patrol Guards under his supervision. Like government intelligence operatives, PGs, though privileged, had a relatively short life expectancy. If a PG were captured or killed, or even imprisoned, the Executive Committee would disavow any knowledge of the man. So apart from dying either on the spot or in prison, the only way out of the service was to reach middle age and retire—or to be invited to membership on the committee, an invitation that rarely happened, because executive committee membership was deemed largely a birthright. Almost every member was either a son, grandson, or nephew of one of the charter members, all of whom were magnates of the diamond, gold, and platinum industries in southern Africa. The likes of Cecil Rhodes and Ian Smith paled by comparison to these thirteen men, who, in a dramatically changed world, were more brazenly protective of their inheritance.

Claus dialed the number again, and Hans answered the phone almost immediately.

"Listen to me," Claus said. "Don't drop on me. The bride saw my face. I'm not sure about the kid, though. And, if my picture is posted, well— Meanwhile, they've got that Ohio senator in a miniature medical Fort Knox of sorts."

Again, Hans snapped. "If you don't produce at least one head by the week's end, you take up residence someplace else, perm-a-nent-ly."

"I need more time, and you know it. That's three targets scattered about, maybe four if you count the maid of honor."

"Whatever! Now, Claus, lose this number until you have something worth reporting." Frustrated, both men hung up their telephones.

Claus's head really did ache. His stomach had become unsettled, too. *Why didn't I just tell him all the bad news?* He held in his hand a copy of the videotape distribution list he had stolen from Herbert Wiseman's office. Although he had destroyed most of the packages that were slated for delivery, two of the tapes were still missing—the ones designated for PJ Austin and Daniel P. Callahan. *Where are those damn tapes?* Claus had no way of knowing.

On Monday, following the horrific events at the altar of First Church, the Executive Committee gathered in their usual meeting place, the office suite in the penthouse of the lavish Johannesburg Hilton. Red-faced, the lot of them took turns cursing the unnamed Guardsman who had brought on the catastrophe.

"My goodness, this was supposed to be a simple assignment," Jonah said. "Makes no sense to me. How did this happen?"

As a general rule, the names of the Guardsmen were not known beyond their respective supervisors. So the other committee members knew only that the PG was one of Hans's; they did not know the man's identity.

Between his chewing and spitting tobacco into a handheld tin can, a raunchy Moses Cameron bragged, "My boys can take out those coons blindfolded." The man's clothing was rumpled. He smelled of musk and stale cigarettes, and he was constantly scratching his hairy body. The grandson of a charter member, Moses was also the only former PG on the committee. Many of the other members detested him because his comportment was way out of line with the social mores and status afforded to him as a birthright. Yet his hardcore nationalism—just like theirs—had offset his weaknesses.

"Moses, give him a chance," Hans said resolutely. "Besides, how many of you can honestly say that your men were successful their first time out? How many of your guys ever even had a job in some Midwestern city in the U.S.? I tell you, you've got to give him at least one more chance. I've given him one week before reassignment."

Unlike Moses, Hans was in the organization for the money. He had no desire to kill Black people—or anybody else, for that matter. In fact, like Hans, most of the other committee members had reached a point in their lives where they wanted to take the money and start anew as far away from South Africa as possible. They no longer relished assigning Guardsmen to kill people who disagreed with their way of doing business and their politics, both of which, for them, meant the same thing. A few of them had already secretly decided to live out their last days with the wind at their back, not in their face. But would they even get the chance to do so?

"Hans," Joseph Sabato said, "is it true? Are we now looking at four targets: the senator, the bride, her nephew *and* her maid of honor? My God, man, this is *crazy*."

Simeon Johannes interrupted to issue the rule of law. "One week, Hans, and one week only. And if there's no good news by then, be prepared to shell out a quarter of a B per week until the matter is settled." In this group, "B" was short for "billion."

"But, Simeon, that'll deplete my emergency fund."

As if Hans had deliberately provoked him, Simeon let out a thunderous roar. Like an angry lion, he shouted, "Who do you think *we* are, socialists or something? Shit, no! We're the world's greatest profit-yielding capitalists—that's who we are."

"But Simeon!" Hans' face was red.

Simeon ignored Hans and instead continued his tirade: "Some clown on American TV called us 'a cartel.' And what of it? What exactly was his point, anyway? He also said that we deal in 'blood diamonds.' Mother#*! #%^!"

"Oh damn," Hans said under his breath. The less-than-admirable performance by his Guardsman had brought out the worst in Simeon. So all Hans could do was sit there and take the hits.

Simeon roared on: "And if this shit sticks, our investments will take a devastating blow. Right Heinreik? (Heinreik was the finance officer.) Yeah, yeah, I know I'm right. I don't even want to think about the market, so somebody's gonna cover our damn losses. That would be you, Hans. Yes, you!"

Simeon had completed the point of his outrage. Yet it was always difficult for the others to really read him. As soon as they thought he was the cold-blooded bastard that he pretended to be, he might do something to the contrary. On the other hand, there was never any doubt about Simeon's love of money, because if there was one certainty, it was that Simeon never had enough money. So despite "the winds of change," Simeon Johannes would die grasping for one more dollar, one more pound, one more rand—whatever.

"I'm not so sure if I'm pissed off over our financial losses or from our having lost face from a botched assassination," Simeon said. "My God, guys, we're the laughingstock of the whole wide world. Go figure. The SANM PG can't kill a nigger."

A few men let out hearty laughter, while others remained indifferent. As for the latter, money mattered more than any recognition for killing Black people. So much for high-stakes gaming among the SANM tycoons.

"Say Heinreik, what gives?" Simeon asked Heinreik. "You've been out of sorts since we watched that damn Ohio Senate debate on the SAD Bill the other week," Simeon said as if he had not just shafted Hans.

"Oh, Simeon, man, I'm fine," Heinreik said. "Might need a holiday or something, though. You know how it is sometimes."

But Heinreik (Bernhardt) Lipponeg was a troubled man. Some weeks earlier, on the day of the Ohio Senate debate, he had been astounded at the sight of a familiar face on the television screen—but it was not the face of one of the SANM lobbyists. "Nah, that can't be him," he'd said to himself. "It just couldn't be."

Unlike the other members on the SANM Executive Committee, Heinreik was not of South African ancestry, nor did he have any family connections there. Of Lebanese descent, Heinreik's family had farmed and exported olives, olive oil, figs and dates for nearly a century. Later, the capital-rich family acquired significant holdings in Lebanon's leading financial institutions and then ventured into banking. But when Heinreik approached adulthood, he had an unsettling row with his father, asked for his inheritance, and—unbeknownst to his family—relocated to South Africa, where he took on a new identity. Once he settled, he used his inheritance to invest in the diamond industry, after which he ventured into a familiar occupation, banking. It was then that the SANM executives first observed the finesse of the young, top-notch banker and broker and invited him into their inner sanctum. But none of them ever knew that "Lipponeg" had been an adopted name.

By the spring of 1986, Heinreik Lipponeg was the number-one man for the financial affairs of the SANM Executive Committee's multibillion-dollar global conglomerate. Chief among its latest, most profitable investments was high technology, particularly sophisticated electronics for governments and industries, including military operations. Now in his sixties, for the first time in his life, Heinreik feared that the actions of someone from his own family—that familiar face in that faraway American state legislative chamber—would be in direct conflict with the well-endowed lifestyle that he had built for himself here in South Africa.

Back in the American Midwest, Detective Stoudemeir sat at his desk at the Columbus Police Department and listened carefully to the tape that he had taken from Priscilla's telephone recorder. He heard several thumps, clicks and obvious hang-ups—all of which led him to check for a possible wiretap. Once his suspicions were confirmed, he called the Ohio Bell Telephone Company for a printout of all calls to and from Priscilla's number over the previous four months. After receiving the printout, he studied it. He observed a pattern of calls centering on two events: the Ohio premiere of the documentary *Mandela* and the Senate debate on the SAD Bill. A batch of those calls revealed communication between Priscilla and the staff in the Congressional Black Caucus (CBC) in Washington, D.C., almost all of which corresponded with the Senate session on the SAD Bill. In fact, it was the CBC staff who had provided Priscilla with information about the SANM lobbyists in the first place. But several other calls had originated from a South African lobbying firm in that same D.C. area code from which the FBI later corroborated Detective Stoudemeir's suspicion that the wiretap was directly connected to the telephone number for that D.C. lobbying firm.

"Damn, man," Detective Stoudemeir later said to FBI Agent Rothschild, "those guys are good. I wonder if Ms. Austin even knows her line is bugged."

On his way back to the United States, PG Claus Fokker used an Australian passport and reentered as a tourist. After all, he could not very well use his South African visa. He knew the Americans were preparing to celebrate the Fourth of July, so plenty of tourists would distract the attention of law enforcement away from him. Once through security and customs at the Chicago O'Hare International Airport, he took Amtrak to Columbus. He waited until evening; then he made his way to Priscilla's West Third Street home-office in Victorian Village.

Claus's plan was simple. He intended to find Priscilla's copy of the videotape and then to locate and kill each of his targets. He easily picked the lock to the front door. Once inside the home-office of P. J. Austin and Associates, Inc., he kicked furniture about and rummaged through some of whatever he touched. He went into Priscilla's bedroom, lifted the mattress, and ripped it open. He opened the cedar chest and pulled clothing off the racks. He tossed open shoe boxes and pulled out dresser drawers. He even went into the bathroom and opened the tank to the toilet and felt for anything behind it.

"Nothing," he said to himself. "I was sure it would be here."

He walked to the kitchen and looked through the racks and compartments in the refrigerator and the freezer. He tossed food on the floor.

He stood still for a moment and noticed a door off to the side. When he opened it, he could see that it led to the basement. But just as he opened the

104

door to descend the stairwell, he immediately felt a sharp object impaling deep into his chest. Claus tumbled down the stairs and then lay on the cold cement floor and cried out, "Oh, dear God, no, not like this." An assassin like Claus, who sustained a wound like this, would have a very good idea about what would come next. So, if he prayed at all, he would pray for a quick death.

But unfortunately for PG Claus Fokker, his assailant—a tall but otherwise nondescript man with a knotted brown ponytail—had another plan. He clamped a muzzle over his victim's mouth and methodically proceeded to prick and dig holes in his face. Then, after he disfigured Claus's face, he hacked off his right hand and bagged it—all while Claus was still alive.

The tall man leaned over Claus and whispered, "And this is for all the hurt and pain you've caused." He raised a heavy sledgehammer and slammed it down on the victim's knees, instantly crushing them.

Muzzled, delirious and pain-stricken, Claus struggled to speak but could not. "No, please, no more. Just shoot me," he mumbled. Evil men who inflict great pain on others can be so pitiful when the same pain is inflicted on them. Even the tall but otherwise nondescript man had known that the humane thing to do would be to shoot his victim to end his misery. But the tall man, like PG Claus Fokker, knew the game. Both men were well-trained paramilitary special operatives. They knew their primary responsibility was always to disable or to eliminate their target. As for torture, well, torture was a discretionary tactic often imposed to exact revenge for some previous act, such as the attempted assassination of Senator Callahan, or for some act perpetrated against another, more helpless victim—for instance, Jonathan Morgan.

Like the Nazi regime's Gestapo, the training for the SANM PGs involved practicing their torture techniques on the lesser elements in society, namely the Black South Africans, whom they treated as game. The PGs hunted them down, tortured and killed them for mere sport. Yet the torture and killing of PG Claus Fokker reflected more personal issues.

The tall man, Tommy Wozniah, was a commander in the covert American-based Collective Force—one of those clandestine units within the Central Intelligence Agency that did not officially exist. He was the very same operative whom Priscilla had overheard talking in the kitchen in the safehouse in Prospect. Like SANM PG, the CIA's CF agents were trained to conduct paramilitary operations anywhere in the world. Among some of America's most accomplished special operatives and secret agents were attorneys, bankers, construction contractors, lobbyists, medical doctors, and even college professors. When their supervisors contacted them, they suited up and went into game mode. Like the PG, the CF agents were aptly described as international terrorists, for they killed anybody who interfered with their business, political or otherwise. Priscilla actually knew four CF agents, but she knew them only as high-powered lobbyists. Soon she would learn of their wide-ranging résumés.

On the tragic day of Priscilla's wedding, Columbus Police Detective Stoudemeir, FBI Agent Rothschild, and Julia had searched her home for her copy of the videotape. But Tommy Wozniah had come there first and beaten them to it. He had holed up in the basement while the authorities conducted their investigation upstairs. But he'd been surprised that PG Fokker had not come around that same day. Yet he knew that he would come, eventually. So he used his time wisely and soon discovered a package underneath the clothes dryer—Priscilla's copy of the SAD videotape.

The videotape secured, CF Commander Wozniah had made a lightning trip to the safehouse in Prospect, Zimbabwe, and then returned and waited in Priscilla's basement for the South African agent. As he crouched in that dim, drab, poorly ventilated cellar, he'd planned his revenge. He wanted PG Fokker to feel the pain that Priscilla had felt as she watched her fiancé being gunned down at the altar. He also wanted the SANM to know the gravity of their "mistake," so he took pictures at each interval of his torturous assault. Then he packed some of Claus's body parts on dry ice and wrote a note to the Executive Committee labeled "Partial Payment," its destination: the Johannesburg Hilton. After he determined his victim was dead, the CF commander disappeared from the scene as quietly and stealthily as he had repeatedly entered.

A short time later, Columbus Police Detective Stoudemeir and FBI Agent Rothschild discovered Senator Callahan's copy of the videotape in a brown paper bag underneath a spare tire in his car. As they had anticipated, the image on the tape matched the artist's sketches of the partial profile of the man whom Germane had seen running out of the church, as well as that of the man with the strange accent whom the overweight figure had described. Together they stared at the face of Claus Fokker, that is, before it had been disfigured.

Around the same time that the authorities validated the likeness of the partial profile of the assassin, they received a phone call about "a body of a man with an Australian passport in the basement of the woman who had been abducted." Off to Priscilla's West Third Street home-office, the Columbus Police detective and the FBI agent went.

Since the police photographs of PG Fokker's tortured and partially mutilated body were too gruesome for public display, they chose instead to release his Australian passport photo.

11

A Mission of Retribution

Priscilla and the CF relief team adjusted to but did not quite settle into their Prospect safe house. For instance, Jordy, Angel, and the manservant took turns filling pails with water from a pump or cistern out back; Priscilla was never sure which it was. They used the water to brush their teeth, to flush the toilet, to shower themselves after lathering up outside, and to fill the tub indoors for Priscilla to bathe in. They also boiled water for their coffee and to clean kitchen utensils, because there was limited plumbing in the kitchen, too. As for cooking, the manservant made do because of the unpredictability of the electrical power, which was rationed a few hours each day. No sooner than the sun went down, so too did the power. So the manservant lighted the house with candles. In fact, by early evening, save for a lighted candle here and there, the entire village of Prospect was pitch black.

On July 6th, shortly after midnight, Zimbabwean time, what Priscilla had begun to think of as "the good guys" were informed that the PGs knew of their involvement and their whereabouts and that the SANM Executive Committee had authorized Hans Evekink to dispatch another PG to complete the failed assignment previously given to Claus Fokker: to track down and kill Senator Callahan, Priscilla, and any other pertinent survivors of the church massacre.

But direst of all, the men who had rescued Priscilla knew immediately that someone close to them had leaked information about their whereabouts. No longer able to rely on their contacts with the ZANU, the CF relief team prepared to leave what was no longer a safehouse in Prospect. They had to get out immediately, in the middle of the night.

Their exit "Plan A" involved a relatively straightforward trek, by air, to Tel Aviv, across territory mostly in the same time zone as Harare.

"Under our new circumstances, however," the manservant told the others, "we can't take the direct path. Besides, the PG already suspects we have the support of the Mossad."

If exit "Plan A" were implemented, the CF relief team, which now included Priscilla, would fly from Harare to Tel Aviv by way of Amman. Once in the presumably safe territory of Israel, Priscilla would be placed into "protective custody" with the Mossad, after which the CF unit, led by CF Commander Tommy Wozniah, would venture into the throes of South Africa to engage the PG head–on.

"So much for our flight outta' here," CF Agent Jordan said with a grin. "Looks like we're roughing it after all."

The men leaned over a map as the manservant refreshed their memory on the many conditions and unknowns that exit "Plan B" entailed.

This second way out meant that they would have to travel on foot and in jeeps over 200 miles southwest to Bulawayo. This trek would give the PG the impression that the CF was heading toward their territory, South Africa. Once in the vicinity of Bulawayo, however, the CF would either charter a jet to Cairo or they would continue "roughing it" like tourists on grand safaris and then beeline back up-country toward Hwange Park and Victoria Falls. But that part of the trip covered over 360 miles of extremely treacherous terrain. In fact, this itinerary included all sorts of tactics to distract the PG from what was the CF agents' ultimate goal: to storm into Johannesburg and fight the PG head–on.

Also, most of exit "Plan B" required immense physical endurance. Road conditions were poor: most were unpaved, and some led nowhere. With poorly constructed roads, bridges, tunnels, and poorly functioning power grids, and only a shell of telecommunications, Zimbabwe lacked adequate infrastructure. Nor were the country's grocery stores stocked with staples and fresh meats. Pharmacies were all but shams, not to mention the rarity of another convenience that Westerners take for granted—service stations to replenish gas or to repair vehicles. Besides, most of the inhabitants were poor—very poor, and countless unsavory types could be bought for a pittance. But the CF had one advantage: most educated Zimbabweans spoke English.

Exit "Plan B" was further complicated because even if the CF agents made it to Victoria Falls, they would have to charter a boat and travel another 300 miles north on Lake Kariba. That treacherous body of water was home to creatures that fed on humans. Then, if they survived the lake, they would have to cross the northwestern border into Zambia and then charter yet another jet from Lusaka to Cairo. That part of the trip alone covered more than 900 miles.

"Ludicrous," Agent Jordan said. But he was still grinning as though he relished the very thought of it.

That particular plan was also wrought with uncertainties about the trustworthiness of the pilots of the jets and the captains of the boats—and, of course, with uncertainties about Priscilla's behavior. Everyone in that room was aware of her reputation for unpredictability. With Priscilla in tow, what would, or could, the CF agents do if they encountered the PG? Otherwise, for fear of being overheard, they did not openly discuss how they would protect her. Then, as if answering what was to them the obvious unspoken question, they looked across the table into one another's eyes and said in unison, "We do what we must."

"Okay, guys," Agent Delgato said, "who's gonna break the news of our departure to Miss Prissy?" (Whenever Priscilla behaved beyond herself, her family and close friends called her "Prissy" or "Missy.")

Agent Jordan sighed. "I know my role."

In the late afternoon of that same day, a package arrived at the Johannesburg Hilton, addressed to: "Simeon Johannes, CEO, SANM Executive Committee." Only Simeon, Hans, Heinreik, and a couple of staffers were in the office. As she opened the package, the receptionist hollered a shrill, frightening sound. Her voice reverberated throughout the luxurious space.

Hans and Heinreik ran out of their offices into the reception area and found the receptionist backed up against the wall behind her station. There on her desk was an oddly shaped open package with a heap of even odder objects protruding from it.

The two men walked over to examine the contents of the package and noticed immediately that atop the heap was a handwritten note pinned to an

110

index finger severed from what appeared to be a human right hand. The note contained the words that CF Commander Wozniah had written: "Partial payment—retribution was more like it—for crimes against humanity. Substantial balance due."

Hans and Heinreik looked at each other. Plainly, this was a formal declaration that the CF intended to bring the fight directly to the PG, and now the Executive Committee knew it.

Gingerly, Hans examined the other contents of the package: a left hand with its fingers intact, a tongue, and an eyeball rolling around loose on the bottom of the package. There were other pieces of flesh and organs, too, which once had been part of the man known as Claus Fokker.

Heinreik shuddered. Soon the PG would retaliate, and its retaliation would be extreme. But what most concerned Heinreik was that it was only a matter of time before his associates would learn of his relationship to a member of the American-based CF. But as his eyes returned to the gore in this terrible package, he wondered whether his nephew had done this awful mutilation of that other man's body. *My God*, he asked himself silently, *is he even capable of such heinousness?*

Early in the morning of that same day, Columbus Police Detective Stoudemeir and FBI Agent Rothschild had driven two hours southwest to the Hueston Woods Lodge and Conference Center in College Corner, just inside the Ohio border to Indiana. Apart from its' out-of-the-way location, the FBI had thought it a suitable safehouse for Liza and her grandson, primarily because of the activities and points of interest for their ten-year-old ward: an impressive lake, golfing, fishing, horseback riding, and nature preserves.

On their ride to the resort, the two law enforcement officers thought it best not to bear bad news, and they certainly wanted to conceal the news about the most recent episode in the chain of events. So, as they neared the resort, they decided not to tell Priscilla's mother and her nephew about the grisly basement mutilation and murder at her West Third Street home-office in Columbus. Besides, there were no televisions in the bungalows, so Liza and Germane were outside the mainstream anyway.

Instead, as they checked in with Liza and Germane, the two law enforcement officers did their best to assure them that all was well. In this, they had their work cut out for them. Both Liza and Germane were ultra-conscious that they themselves were at risk from those whom Germane thought of as "those bad guys," and both were scared, and neither wanted to die.

But Agent Rothschild and Detective Stoudemeir were surprised by how upbeat Priscilla's relatives were. What seemed to console them the most was their confidence in Priscilla and how she might be handling her situation—wherever she was.

"There's no telling what Priscilla will do when she gets her hands on the men responsible for Jonathan's death," Liza had just said.

"Yeah, I'm betting on my Aunt Priscilla," Germane answered.

They knew of Priscilla's propensity to compartmentalize her feelings and to call them up unpredictably—to the disadvantage of whoever was after her. "Priscilla," they told each other, "was nobody's victim." Indeed, when it came to Priscilla, the CF, the PG, and all those other government agents would soon learn that they had much with which to contend.

Liza leaned forward and raised her eyebrows. "But what about Julia?" she asked. "We were hoping you might be bringing her here to be with us. Isn't she in danger, too?"

The FBI agent shook his head. "We offered, but she declined."

"We can't make people accept protective detail." The detective nodded.

As it so happened, Julia—Priscilla's best friend in the world and her maid of honor—was home alone, save for the two federal agents who stood guard outside. She had grown overwrought when the FBI had offered to put her in protective custody, and she had flat-out refused to leave her home. Priscilla meant the world to her, and she was beside herself with worry. *Where the devil is she anyway? Why won't they let us talk? Is she even alive?* Julia's worst fear was that her friend would be sexually assaulted before some madman killed her. An avid reader, Julia eventually took to reading novels to take her mind off her fears.

"And what of Senator Callahan?" Liza leaned closer to hear the news.

"He's in critical, but stable, condition at an undisclosed location," said the FBI agent.

"We can assure you, Ma'am," added the detective, "that his injuries are being tended to by the best medical care available, along with a large security detail."

Finally, Liza said, "Let us pray." She bowed her head. When she and Germane linked hands and held out their hands to the officers, the two men took those hands and bowed their heads as Liza prayed.

Late that same night, CF Commander Wozniah and CF Agent Carlton Elliott Bernhardt boarded a gigantic military aircraft at Langley Air Force Base, Virginia. The men were on a mission of retribution. A lethal interloper from another culture and another country had come to America to assassinate a lawmaker but had failed to do so. That same assassin had killed another man who had nothing to do with the matter in the first place, and the man he killed happened to have been betrothed to a woman for whom the CF agents had some time ago promised a favor, for which she was wholly unaware. That same woman had also earned the protection of the CF because of her intimate ties to one of them, but she was not aware of that, either.

On the flight from Langley, CIA Agent James Froley sat down between CF Commander Wozniah and CF Agent Bernhardt. He opened a gray file folder and showed them photos of several SANM Patrol Guardsmen.

"Pay particular attention to these two fellows," Agent Froley said. "They're the other monsters under Hans Evekink's supervision."

First, Agent Froley showed them a color photo of a tall, handsome man with long, sandy-brown hair pulled back in a ponytail. "This is Alistair Longworth," he said. "He has a habit of playing with his ponytail right before he tortures his victim. And when he's satisfied his torture's done its job, he pulls strains of his ponytail through his teeth—and smiles!"

Next, he showed the two CF agents a color photo of a tall, close-shaven, muscular man with red hair combed military-style. "This," he said, "is Leonard Genn. He's known to loathe women's bodies and to use electric cattle prods to torture their private parts. Mostly, he's notorious for the way he tortures Black people: he dismembers them first and then burns them until only their charred skeletons are left."

Agent Froley directed his next comment to the CF commander. "And remember, Tommy, they're both in heat over that little Claus package you sent to their boss in Joburg."

Commander Wozniah listened attentively. Perhaps the quietest and most nondescript and unassuming member of the CF unit, he nonetheless had earned the reputation for being able to remove a man's body parts effortlessly, swiftly and without emotion. In his civilian life, he was an accomplished banker, a political mastermind and a high-powered lobbyist. In his current role, however, he waited for specific instructions from his superior—and no more than that.

As for Agent Bernhardt, he was not yet aware of his estranged uncle's role as a kingpin in the South African enemy cartel. Carlton's familiarity with his uncle derived primarily from his uncle's reputation as a formidable banker. He knew his uncle had changed his name. He knew he was a successful broker. He even knew of his uncle's role in the diamond business. But he did not know that his uncle had become one of the enemies he was about to pursue to their death. For now, his primary responsibility was to secure the return of Priscilla, his former lover.

He looked closely at the photos of Alistair Longworth and Leonard Genn. "Apart from what I'm guessing are their many façades … any identifiable marks or idiosyncrasies?" he asked Agent Froley. Then he added, "Do any of them pick their noses, scratch their balls, or have a preference for men? Give me something concrete to go on, man."

"First off, Carlton," Agent Froley said, calling the agent by his given name, "All these guys get their jollies off killing people. Seasoned killers. Not upstarts like Claus Fokker. I mean, this one, Alistair Longworth, ejaculates on his victims and prefers to burn them at the stake. But they all enjoy watching their victims suffer. They lead their victims to believe that they will help them out of their predicament or that they will use a less torturous technique, 'if only you do this or that for me.' These guys are vicious, downright brutal, nasty pieces of work."

But Commander Wozniah had other interests: "Is it true, Jim?"

"Is what true?"

"You know what I mean," the CF commander insisted. "Is it true that the big dogs are only interested in the safe return of Miss Prissy? And that we only possess 'unauthorized authorization' to escort her to friendly territory? Full stop."

The CF commander seemed to be seeking further confirmation for his 'unauthorized' mission: "And another thing, Jim. I'm guessing that whatever else happens, we're pretty much on our own. No official U.S. government involvement? And, of course, any engaging with the boys down south is between my team and me?"

"Sorry, Tommy," Agent Froley said, shaking his head. "But right now, the U.S. government doesn't much care to project unfriendly terms with the South Africans. And even though our Congress blasted them with that divestiture stuff, our president wants to maintain fairly positive diplomatic relations with Cape Town."

But by then, the CIA agent wore a smirk on his face as he dropped his voice to a whisper. "Uh, but, you can understand, however, that we'd be hard-pressed to fly a commando right smack onto their front lawn, blow up their lavish Joburg headquarters and then fart in their faces with images of all of us white boys and Miss Prissy at bay. You do comprehend the reality of our situation? Don't you, fellas?"

"Good speech, Jim," the CF commander said. "Okay, now, Carlton and I'll take it from here."

In fact, what Agent Froley had just transmitted was an unauthorized "authorization" to the CF. If the raid were successful, the U.S. government would disavow any knowledge of its involvement in the incident. If the raid failed, the U.S. government would disavow any knowledge of the CF forces—an organization that they could, in fact, deny even existed. What might appear as a no-win situation for the CF agents was, in reality, how such special "unauthorized operatives" actually function.

After authorizing the CF to undertake yet another "unauthorized" mission, CIA Agent Froley disappeared as stealthily as he'd appeared.

Armed with their ultimate game plan, CF Commander Wozniah and CF Agent Bernhardt worked out the details of the endgame without any input or interference from CIA Agent James Froley, or anybody else for that matter, who was not on the flight, anyway, as it were.

12

The Unwanted & Calls for Reinforcements

Back at the Prospect compound, CF Agents Jordan and Delgato had their heads together working out their final plans before departing. As they reviewed their tactics to divert the PG, they constantly disagreed about "what to do with Priscilla."

At issue—at least for Angel—was their plan to hide Priscilla in the Anglican Cathedral in Harare, which was the seat of the Archdiocese of Zimbabwe. "I'm still uncomfortable leaving her at that place," Agent Delgato said, frowning.

"Yeah, well, Angel, we have no choice," Jordy said. They had already agreed that Onslow, one of their best men, would be looking out for her there, along with a few other previously tested members of their team. "Our boys know what to do. She'll be alright with them. You'll see."

"But a cathedral—and a girls' school!" At once, the thickness of Angel's Italian accent pounded Jordy's ears. Then, more forcefully: "My God, man!" As the only Catholic among the four friends and CF associates, Angel liked to think he had a greater understanding of the Anglican Church. He could not fathom Priscilla fitting into the culture of an African Anglican all-girls' boarding school, something his superiors had presumed to be a logical fit,

116

mostly because she closely resembled the physical characteristics of the pupils in the school.

"Oh, come on, Angel. We've gone over this for the umpteenth time. She'll fit in perfectly with those other girls. That part of the plan is damn near perfect. Simply brilliant, it is. Those PG goons will never guess she's there." Jordy laughed, yet Angel still did not seem in the least convinced.

As it turned out, the men had told Priscilla only about the "need to move on," not where she actually was or where she would be stashed next.

Then the manservant, who was primarily responsible for fulfilling his team's part of the plan, came back into the kitchen and gave the order to abandon the Prospect site. Shortly after they set out on foot, the men discovered they had been correct about Priscilla not being "road tested." Accordingly, they began to pace themselves more slowly.

It was abysmally dark, and although they walked through a so-called suburban neighborhood, it could easily be classified as rural by American standards. The streets were not paved. There were no streetlights, and the men also quickly realized that the utilities really were rationed to the point that there was little or no electricity, and none at night. Worse, petroleum was so scarce that most homes were, in fact, lit by candles. Thank goodness the CF unit was equipped with battery-operated flashlights. At different intervals, Eduardo, Onslow, and Terrence were aided in their roles as bodyguards by local recruits, who guided them through the myriad roadways. Since they did not have electronic devices to help keep them on course, such as a GPS, the entourage was pretty much at the mercy of the local guides. And although the bodyguards were readily visible, periodically they would disappear into the darkness as an added precaution. But before long, the entourage could hear the bodyguards as they caught back up with them from the rear. Over the course of the laborious trek, Jordy and Angel did not talk much—mainly because of Angel's apprehension about the next safehouse for Priscilla, not to mention the men's fear of being overheard by strangers, especially by the PG. And by his very nature, the manservant remained silent and on high alert.

After the entourage had walked a little over two miles, Priscilla observed the strangest scene. Her group met with two other groups practically identical to them in appearance. She thought she saw doubles, and she did. She even caught a glimpse of her own twin, and maybe even a third look–alike. The exchange happened so quickly that, if she herself had not been the genuine PJ

Austin, she might not have been able to tell for sure which the authentic Priscilla was. The only thing she later remembered with any certainty was being hoisted onto a huge vehicle that sat high off the ground. Like clockwork, the other two groups, with their Priscilla look–alikes, simultaneously dispersed back into the darkness from whence they had come.

When Priscilla attempted to figure out what had just happened, someone pushed her down onto the cold floor of the vehicle. It was then that the absence of waste removal was ever as apparent to her as when she rode into downtown Harare on that cold floor of that high-riding vehicle. She had to cradle her stomach to stop from throwing up. She was not sure, but she thought that she smelled human waste. Or was that an animal carcass?

She pulled herself together and then looked up at the man who had pushed her there. "Say, fella," she said, "do you suppose you could give me one of those guns or knives? Besides, what exactly am I supposed to do if someone attacks me? Kick 'im or something?"

Totally oblivious to the situation, she assumed that Jordy, Angel, and the manservant were still with her. But the diversionary plan called for Agents Jordan and Delgato, and the manservant, to continue separate from Priscilla and the others.

As she taunted the men in her vehicle, Eduardo and Terrence ignored her. But Onslow blurted out, "Damn it all, lady, stop talking. Remember, you're the American everybody's looking for. Be quiet, and do what we tell ya. Above all, please stop talking."

The entourage drove along a rugged, pothole-covered dirt road in silence for nearly an hour; then they turned onto a smoother surface, on which they traveled only briefly. Then the driver slowed the vehicle and stopped in a parking lot adjacent to a cathedral compound. They were either in downtown Harare or in uptown Harare—they were not sure.

The men jumped out of the high-riding vehicle, pulled Priscilla out and carried her across the parking lot to a single-story oblong-shaped building nearby. Eduardo rushed up to the monstrous wooden front door. He banged on it; it unlatched from the inside. Onslow and Priscilla entered the dimly lit foyer and waited.

Still unsettled, Priscilla said, "Anybody got a cigarette and a cup of café au lait or something?" She still did not know for certain where she was, and she knew even less about what was going on.

At once, a man wearing a gray flannel nightgown and rubbing his eyes appeared before them. He was inconspicuous and noticeably shorter than the men accompanying Priscilla. He was also the first and only Black man Priscilla had seen since her time there.

"Evening, folks. What have we here?" He spoke as if he'd half-expected the visitors.

"Evening, Father. This here's your pesky new client," Onslow said, as he shoved Priscilla toward the priest. "Now remember, Missy," Onslow stressed, "no more talking."

Then Onslow turned around abruptly and walked back out into the darkness, where Eduardo and Terrence were keeping watch. All three then walked back to their vehicle and drove out of sight, yet they remained close by. They were Priscilla's bodyguards for the duration of her stay at the cathedral compound.

Inside, Priscilla remained absolutely confounded with her presumably temporary circumstance. She turned to the man that her bodyguard had called a priest. "What the devil is this place anyway? An African version of a convent or something? Please tell me I'm not in a convent."

"No, young lady, this is not 'a convent or something.' But I am Father Jacob Mbuwayesango. I am indeed a priest, only I am not Catholic. Welcome to the Archdiocese of Zimbabwe. We're Angli—"

"Wait a minute, Bubba. This is *where?*"

"The Anglican Dioc—"

"Not that part—the part about Zimbabwe." This was the first time that Priscilla received confirmation of her precise whereabouts. "Why, the bloody bastards!" she said of the men who had abducted her halfway around the world.

The priest had no idea that Priscilla had only just learned for a fact where she was, so he continued playing out his part in the plan that the CF had commissioned. When the manservant first made arrangements for Priscilla to be stashed in the cathedral, he had said the woman he would be bringing was not only much older than she looked but also older than the girls in the cathedral boarding school. He had also suggested that the priest give her some work to do. "Try the kind of work 'the unwanted' do. Maybe cooking and cleaning. We'll pick her up shortly."

"Won't you come with me, please?" the priest said to Priscilla.

This particular cathedral compound, she would learn later, was situated in the Diocese of Harare and was one of five administrative sites for the Anglican Archdiocese of Zimbabwe. Each diocese had its own bishop. But the Bishop of Harare was not currently in residence, nor was he privy to the transaction that involved Priscilla. So it was left to Father Mbuwayesango to facilitate Priscilla's safekeeping for the CF. As it turned out, in addition to her presumably "logical fit," the CF commander and the relief team had deemed the site suitable for Priscilla's cover because the cathedral of the Diocese of Harare provided housing, education, and other services for orphans.

"Oh, so I sleep over here, and then we head out to where—"

The priest quickly covered Priscilla's mouth. "Whatever you do, do not ever speak in terms of movement. This is your new home. So you must forget about those other men. I'm the only person here that you know. Are we clear, young lady?"

"Uh-huh," Priscilla murmured. She now also realized the priest was not all he pretended to be. *But how does he fit into the greater scheme of things? Ah, heck, is he even a real priest?*

For the rest of what she was unsure about was whether it was that night or early that morning, Priscilla slept on a cot in the corner of a drafty room at the end of the corridor. The only window was too high for her to reach. There were no mirrors, and there was a piece of furniture that seemed to function as a chest of drawers. As she prepared for bed, she noticed that the light switch on the wall had a strange knob and that the fixture in the ceiling was also incredibly odd. *Is that an upside-down lantern, a gas light or what? What exactly is this place anyway?*

Later that morning, she awoke depressed. She could not remember the last time that she felt so alone. She missed her family and her life in the States. She missed amenities such as American cuisine, hot water and electricity. She still found it hard to believe that Jonathan had been shot and killed at the altar on the day of their wedding. She could not reconcile herself to her ignorance of almost everything about the part of the world where she was stashed. Except for Jordy, Angel, and the manservant, she did not know anybody here in Africa. And not one of those three was with her now.

But Priscilla did know what was universally known: Ian Smith had been the most ruthless ruler of the racially segregated regime of Southern Rhodesia.

Yet she did not know much about Robert Mugabe, the new leader, who, as it turned out, was not much different from his predecessor—and just as hurtful to his own people. So, aside from the priest, she had not yet met anyone in whatever this new, presumably "safehouse" was. She did not even know if anyone aside from the priest spoke English.

As Priscilla prepared to entertain herself at her own pity party, the door to her room opened, and in walked Father Mbuwayesango. He stepped over to the chest and took out some items. He handed her a plain oversized blue-black-and-white smock, a pair of used men's pants, a pair of brown leather high-top boots and a dingy cotton handkerchief.

"These should fit you," he said. "There's a washroom down the corridor. After you freshen, come back, and I'll brief you on the rules of the house."

"May I speak? I mean—"

"From now on, you're called Megan," the priest said. "You're the abandoned child of a Rhodesian farmer and a Zimbabwean mother, but you never met them. You were orphaned at birth."

"You've got to be kidding me."

He gestured toward the washroom. "Go freshen and meet me back here."

With that emphatic directive, Priscilla took her new clothes and headed down the hallway.

First, she grumbled to herself, *they make me out to be Middle Eastern. Now I'm a castaway of mixed blood in Rhodesia, or Zimbabwe, wherever the hell this is. When will this nightmare end?*

Along the corridor, she pushed open several doors until she opened one and spotted a crude bathroom: cracked linoleum covered a cement floor, crude knobs attached to a rusty pipe protruded from the wall, and a makeshift washtub for a sink. As for the toilet, well, suffice it to say that Priscilla would probably never sit on it.

"Oh crap!" She vomited.

When she returned to her room, the priest handed her a piece of paper that contained a list of her chores. "Each day you rise at six o'clock, freshen and then breakfast in the dining hall with the others. In silence, of course."

"Oh? There are others?"

"Like you, Megan, the other girls are the offspring of white farmers and Zimbabwean or South African mothers. But you live separately from them."

"Okay, but do they have a chores list?"

The priest ignored her constant antics. "We are the church of the diocese and provide shelter for the likes of you. Some of our clients finance the education of their children, whereas others provide a modest stipend to keep their unwanted children. You, Megan, are an 'unwanted.' And so you, Megan, must perform chores for your sustenance."

"Well, I'll be a—"

"And now for the good news. As an unwanted, you have limited privileges, among them being speech. You may only speak when spoken to. Besides, you don't know anyone here. And you don't want to know anyone here. You don't even know where you came from. Any wrong move by you compromises your security. Do you understand me now?"

"Alright, we're clear. Where's my darn mop and duster?"

"First, breakfast, and once everyone else has finished theirs, place the chairs on the tables, sweep the floor, and then mop. After that, continue with the other chores on your list. Then, shortly before noon, report to the kitchen staff," he concluded.

Under her breath, Priscilla cursed Jordy and the other guys. But that day, as she indeed worked her way through the long list of chores, she spent each moment contriving ways to get back at them, the *lot* of them. *Surely they could've ditched me somewhere better than this. The sleazy bastards!*

Priscilla had no way of knowing it, but she now resided amid the corridors of power that the colonialists had erected. Situated between the Parliament and the Standard Bank buildings, the Anglican Cathedral was directly across from Cecil Square, the downtown park, which was later named Africa Unity Square. Directly opposite the park was the Salisbury Club, later named Harare Club, a country club of sorts that only admitted Rhodesian and South African men and operated much like a hotel. Across the park on the other side, facing the cathedral, was Meikles Hotel, one of the first grand hotels constructed during the era of those grand buildings.

While Priscilla settled into her new situation at the Anglican boarding school in Harare, PG Commander Alistair Longworth arrived at the Prospect compound only to find it abandoned. As he searched for clues about the CF's next move, he spotted a notepad on the kitchen table. "This is too easy," he said to himself, "just too damn easy."

Then, to his disappointment, there was no writing on the notepad. But he perked up when he saw indentations on the top sheet. So he scratched a pencil point across it, and its markings revealed a drawing that pointed to Victoria Falls and Lusaka to the north and to Bulawayo and Johannesburg to the south.

He sat down and examined the drawing for other possible clues. In an instant, he experienced an exhilarating rush. The CF had laid a trap. The CF agents were no longer playing the role of the prey; they were now the hunters. They'd left that easily discernible drawing to alert their adversaries that they intended to bring the fight directly to the PG's home turf in Johannesburg. In so doing, the CF agents were possibly trying to divert the PG's attention from its growing list of targets—PJ Austin, her friend Julia, her nephew Germane and, of course, its primary target, Senator Callahan—and instead were luring them into battle on their home turf in Johannesburg.

Talk about all-out warfare! PG Commander Longworth unbuckled his cell phone from its holster and entered the telephone number of his supervisor.

Hans answered on the second ring. "Yes, Alistair? Why call in so early?"

"The Americans are apparently bringing the fight home to us in Joburg," the PG commander said. "There were five or six of them here, and I'm fairly certain they're bringing in an equal number of reinforcements. I wager they've split up, though, some headed south by way of Bulawayo and some north to Lusaka by way of Vic Falls. Have no clue about their overall game plan, but it's gonna be heavy. That's for damn sure."

"Good boy, Alistair, good boy," Hans said. "I'll inform the others about our new situation. Oh, yeah, I sent Leonard to America to take care of those other loose ends. I'll contact you after my meeting." Hans smiled as he disconnected the call. From then on, Hans made sure the PG focused most of its attention on the impending battles with the CF on their home turf.

Sure enough, the PG switched most of its attention to the impending battles with the CF. PG reinforcements arrived at Harare International Airport within thirty-six hours aboard a flight filled with hunters eager to begin safaris and big game hunting. At the time, it was easy to take advantage of the relaxed gaming regulations in Zimbabwe because its government had yet to nationalize many of its wildlife preserves. Because the nation was still fresh in the throes of transitioning from colonial status to democratic and Black majority rule, hunters—amateurs and professionals alike—traveled from the world over to Zimbabwe and to the open, unmonitored expanses of other African countries, where they were free to stalk the so-called big five game: elephants, lions, rhinoceros, leopards, and African buffalo.

Mainly on board that flight, however, were mercenaries disguised in camouflage as hunters. Some had come to Harare to join up with the PG, while others had come to aid the Rhodesian farmers, who were fighting to keep their property from seizure by the Mugabe regime.

The PG's priority was to fight to preserve a society that time had eclipsed—a reality which the SANM had not admitted even to itself. In this, the PG possessed several key advantages over their CF adversaries: they knew the customs and beliefs of the local inhabitants; they knew the territory; they knew the rugged terrain off the beaten path; and they were expert at tracking their prey, whether human or animal, in the wild.

Soon, thirteen mercenaries sympathetic to the cause of the PG were assembled at the abandoned Prospect compound. PG Commander Longworth briefed the men about their situation. Then he dispatched six of them north to Lusaka by way of Victoria Falls and the other six, south to Bulawayo. As for the PG commander himself, he decided to stay in the vicinity of Harare. His instincts suggested he had overlooked someone, or something, of importance. *If I could just put my finger on it*, he thought. After all, Alistair Longworth had not survived so many years of assignments like this for want of wit.

13

Enter the CF and Its Recruits

The Collective Force also issued a call for recruits.

CF Commander Wozniah and Agent Bernhardt completed their business in Tel Aviv and were en route to Lusaka. First, they flew into Nairobi, Kenya, to rendezvous with their first group of recruits at a site just outside the capital.

Priscilla would learn shortly—from her reading at the cathedral boarding school library—that Kenya was among the first African nations to secure independence from European rule. Its first president, Jomo Kenyatta, was elected to that position in 1963. Upon Kenyatta's death in August 1978, Vice President Daniel arap Moi assumed the presidency. In October 1978, Moi himself was elected president. Like other newly elected leaders, Moi pushed through legislation to make his country a one-party state and—to the disadvantage of the Europeans—instituted land reform. But many other new rulers were known for corruption—and even cruelty to their own people.

The Kenyan government, having given the CF the status of an internationally recognized military unit, welcomed their presence. There, on the periphery of the capital, the CF openly assembled its magnificent military unit. Then the leaders briefed their recruits on their mission, after which the whole military unit prepared to move south into enemy territory.

Like the PG, the CF leadership and recruits also wore camouflage, but theirs was of a slightly different color and design. Their uniforms blended in with the animals, mostly the black- and brown-colored zebras, whereas the PG uniforms matched the moss green and tan colors of the forest. Otherwise, all the men looked like the paramilitary special ops that they were.

CF Commander Wozniah and Agent Bernhardt and their other agents, soldiers, and mercenaries rode in three high-riding military-model open jeeps, trailed by a few canvas-covered trucks, tanks and a stream of army jeeps. They drove full tilt across the open territory.

The likes of Carlton Elliott Bernhardt and Tommy Wozniah welcomed the battles before them.

"Okay, Carlton, what're you thinking?" the CF commander asked.

"I swear to you, Tommy, man, the PG should all still know this is about the senator, not the girl. I sure as hell hope those crazy fools know the difference and the real priorities. Otherwise, we could be here 'til Labor Day."

"And I'm hoping that meantime, 'the girl' never figures any of this out," the CF commander agreed, saying, "I mean, my goodness, Carlton, both sides are using her as bait. But maybe you remember even the senator telling us once that Priscilla is 'a quick study.'"

Both men let out hearty laughs, although it was unclear if they shared the exact reasons for their mirth.

But Tommy was unaware of the intimate relationship that Carlton and Priscilla had once shared. Nor did he know about Carlton's long-lost family member in the enemy camp. And Tommy's dirty little secret really was not so hidden after all. As CEO of the Chesterfield Bank of Cleveland in Ohio, his bank's holdings were a matter of public record but not general knowledge. His own bank held more than a few billion dollars in endowments and trust funds that had been generated from investments in South African-based corporations and financial institutions, particularly corporations in the diamond industry. Such was the complexity of the rift behind the enactment of the Ohio SAD Bill. Virtually no entity was immune to, or exempt from, the call for divestiture. From the U.S. government to its fifty state governments to major colleges and universities, corporations and foundations, retirement and pension funds, and individual investment portfolios—all sorts of investments were tied up in other investments connected to South Africa.

"Charlie checked in yet?" Carlton asked.

"Yeah, man," Tommy said, referring to his manservant, adding, "He sure left enough clues for Longworth and his boys."

Carlton wore a big grin as he pushed his ponytail off his shoulder and said, "Man, this is going to be an incredible adventure. Opportunities like this come only once in a lifetime, if at all." Although his primary goal was to help rescue the woman with whom he once shared a secret love affair, Carlton, like his comrades, relished the impending fight with the South African terrorists.

"Plus, we got our little bait all comfy in her little cathedral trap," Tommy said as he swung his right leg over the side of the door of his high-riding jeep. "Now all we need to do is dangle enough cheese to lure the rascals in."

At this point, one might wonder how important rescuing Priscilla was. These two leaders of the American clandestine special operatives had no compunction about expressing their desire to engage the enemy in what might best be described as war. Indeed, it seemed that rescuing Priscilla was secondary. Or was her abduction the excuse they needed to engage the enemy in the first place?

Like a flagship, the CF caravan snaked across the majestic East African landscape at remarkable speed—a myriad of jeeps, tanks and trucks stretching back as far as one's eyes could see. The CF had successfully called up a massive number of international mercenaries to create their own little militia, and they carried enough ammunition, fuel and food to fight a small war for days.

For a while, the pair fell silent as they drank in the beauty and splendor of the terrain.

They were both aware from previous briefings—as was Priscilla from her reading in the cathedral boarding school library—that Tanzania, another country they'd pass through, like most African nations, had been pillaged by European and Asian exploitation much earlier in its history. Yet the country still possessed tremendous resources, including oil, diamonds, gold, cattle, coffee, cotton, and cashew nuts. In April 1964, Tanganyika and Zanzibar formed a republic named Tanzania, with Julius Nyerere as its first president. Although a member of the Commonwealth in East Africa, the country suffered immensely from internal conflict, war with neighboring Uganda's Idi Amin, and a secessionist movement in Zanzibar.

Moreover, Tanzania had been plagued by catastrophes such as an influx of refugees, as well as by civil war and drought. Some of the affected refugee populations immigrated from as far north as Sudan near the Nile basin, while others immigrated from nearby Rwanda and Burundi. Moreover, those refugees brought with them their own customs, and especially their faiths—which were neither Christian nor Muslim—religions indigenous to their tribes and sects for centuries.

In preparation for the next leg of their trip, the CF caravan headed southwest into the Serengeti Plain, approximately 100 miles southwest of the Kenyan capital. If they took the southeastern route, they would face the mountainous terrain of Kilimanjaro, which comprised two snow-capped peaks, the highest in Africa.

As appealing as that route might have been, the commander reminded his men, "This is a military mission, fellas, not a safari or a bucket list."

A key component of the CF caravan was its local guides, mostly men of European descent and a few Black men from the countries the CF would later pass through. The guides were an essential asset for the CF because, unlike the PG, a disproportionate share of the CF was from outside the African continent. The guides helped explain the customs and beliefs of the people with whom they would come into contact, and they knew the terrain and the wildlife. Like the PG, the local guides tended to be bilingual, even multilingual. As circumstances changed, the CF's international military unit's diversity would lend a tremendous advantage to their side.

While Priscilla settled begrudgingly into her new hideaway in Harare, the men of the CF caravan continued to experience the splendor of Africa's easternmost region. As they passed through the Shinyanga territory, they met with rich images of tropical wildlife and forests—perhaps because of the recent rainy season; otherwise, the area was riddled with parched, cracked Earth.

Soon they drove across the equally mesmerizing Iwembere Steppe and came upon a group of nomads. Unlike the native Bantu, the young women in the group wore multiple gold bracelets around their extended necks, arms, and ankles. They regarded gold for its aesthetic value, not as a measure of currency. Several servants trailed behind the young women, behaving like teenagers as they pranced playfully about the camp. Tall, slender and graceful, the young women were remarkably unblemished and alluring. The men of the small community shepherded a herd of cattle that grazed nearby. Their community was an offshoot of the Sudanese who had migrated into Tanzania from the north. Over the course of many years, they had found a new and more promising life in Shinyanga, but they remained Nubian.

A few of the men, allured by such beauty, had already decided to ignore the warnings of the local guides, who had cautioned them to steer clear of such temptation. One guide had told them: "This community places a high premium on its young women. Their clothing and especially their jewelry symbolize their high value. Do not touch them." As the caravan passed the camp, some of the men spray-painted a pathway that would lead them back to it.

That evening, after everyone else went to sleep, the men snuck out and followed the path back to the Nubian camp. The men woke up the young women. Because the young women had never seen white men before, they assumed they were gods who had come to deliver the much-needed fertilizer for their crops. In fact, they had never before known a man in the biblical sense. So they had unwittingly succumbed to the men.

But their sexual indiscretion was soon discovered. Unfortunately for the offenders, those young women had been betrothed to the local chief. Their tribal function, as well as their purpose in life, was to marry him and thus consummate a pure offering to the gods—not to have sexual intercourse with impure strangers.

Early the next morning, the tribal chief learned of what had happened in the night. Almost immediately, he summoned the CF commander to meet with him. Restitution for the apparent wrongdoing was in order. No longer suitable for marriage to the chief, the once highly valued young women were suddenly outcasts; although they were spared death, they still faced a miserable future.

CF Commander Wozniah was aware that one way to acquire allies in unknown territory was to respect the customs and beliefs of its inhabitants. According to the tribe's mores, money and material items were unacceptable terms for retribution; only public castration or harsh whipping were suitable punishments for the offenders. CF Commander Wozniah deferred to the general practices of the community. The males in the Nubian camp tied the offenders to a post and whipped them mercilessly in plain sight of the other nomads and the mercenaries.

Shortly after the public flagellating of the soldiers, the caravan resumed its mission.

But they were barely out of the Iwembere Steppe before they encountered another obstacle in the form of crossing over a main thoroughfare at Tabora.

That key crossing stretched from the westernmost border of Tanzania at Kigoma, off Lake Tanganyika, across the width of the country to its easternmost border at the capital, Dar es Salaam, at the Indian Ocean. But the Taboran authorities allowed only a few vehicles to cross the highway at a time. Permitting the long caravan unimpeded passage would have created a terrific traffic jam in both directions on one of the country's busiest highways. So, to buy time to consider how to handle this, the local authorities searched several of the vehicles intermittently and demanded, "Papers and passports, please."

Meantime, aware of the time being wasted, CF Commander Wozniah and Agent Bernhardt fumed. Plainly, someone had failed to transmit the memo about the international military unit to the Taboran authorities. This delay at the Taboran thoroughfare was an incident that the CF forces had not anticipated.

But the CF did know that the PG had spies and supporters all over the continent. The presence of such a large military contingent at this crossing would surely be reported to the SANM headquarters in Johannesburg.

But in this, the CF were lucky. By the time the report reached the SANM Executive Committee, it was dismissed as "movements of UN and international peacekeeping forces." At this point, the SANM PG still had no inkling of the CF's exact strategy.

Yet the regrettable incident with the Nubian tribe and the delay at the highway crossing in Tabora did have an impact on the CF adventure. From then on, their trek became grueling, all but for the beautiful scenery and occasional hunting of some of the wild animals.

But as the caravan finally reached the southernmost tip of Tanzania at Mbeya, the men's spirits lifted. They could feel the trip was shortening. Since they were almost in Zambia, they readied themselves to cross the border and head southwest to Kasama.

Then, for no ostensible reason, the snakelike caravan began slowing down again. It came to a sudden halt. Radios beeped, and all became silent. One by one, the guides jumped out of their vehicles and put their heads to the ground. To the person, they shouted out loudly, "Elephant stampede! Elephant stampede!" With remarkable precision, the many vehicles formed tight-knit clusters with nearly half-mile breaks between them. The men strained to turn some of the jeeps on their sides. Canvas-covered trucks and ambulances were protected inside the clusters, and the tanks were used as buffers. The men needed to create the image of something impenetrable. But the breaks between

130

the clusters were created to allow the huge mammals easy passage, because it was futile to try to outrun them.

Within minutes, the massive herd appeared. Hundreds of elephants swept across the terrain at remarkable speed. Sure enough, the nearer they approached, the more the herd veered away from the clusters of vehicles. Throughout the stampede, the men hovered together underneath and behind their vehicles and prayed not to be trampled. By the time the elephants passed, they'd left enough dirt and dust to create another Depression-era dustbowl, but no one was hurt—a remarkable blessing in itself.

"Well, Carlton," Tommy asked sarcastically, coughing up dust to clear his throat. "How's that for an incredible adventure? Damn, that was close."

"Hell, yeah, Bro. Hell, yeah."

The men turned the vehicles back upright, and the caravan resumed its trek into Zambia—the destination for its next camp, Kasama. There, the CF agents and recruits would get ready for the tumultuous trek through the valley of the Muching Mountains. Much closer now to enemy territory, they opted to hug a path close by the mountains to avoid being ambushed by the PG in open territory. At this point in their trek, however, the CF did not know that the PG had assumed them to be precisely what their game plan defined them to be, an internationally sanctioned military force, more precisely, a peacekeeping force.

They stopped about twenty miles north of Kasama and set up camp. Now, nearly 400 miles from their final destination, the CF commander and his agents ratcheted up their plan of action. With fewer than three days to reach Lusaka, they needed to cover at least 150 miles per day. The trip was already complicated enough. There was no electricity along the path they traveled, and there were few highways, many poorly paved roads, and sometimes pathways instead of roads. There were no amenities. The men relieved themselves in the open fields and covered their waste with chemicals. Or they dug holes and covered their waste with tree branches. Occasionally, they drenched themselves in lakes and ponds or under waterfalls, but most of the time, they simply stank. For these men, such conditions were all part of the thrill of such an adventure.

Then, one night, just outside of Kasama, a family of mountain lions pounced upon some of the men while they slept. One man was so severely mauled that he begged for mercy, so his mate shot him to death to relieve his intense pain. A couple of other men required major surgery. The medics performed the minimum medical treatment and transported the wounded men to the airport nearby for the next flight into Lusaka. The wounded men's careers as special paramilitary operatives were effectively ended.

But there were still over 120 men in this unit of the CF force. The game plan had taken into account the likelihood of the loss of life and other incidents that might reduce their numbers. Yet the trek from Nairobi into northern Zambia had only strengthened the men's resolve. They were geared up for the ensuing battles with the PG. As the caravan passed through each country, it was greeted or even escorted by each country's army. Having earlier acquired the consent of the governments of Kenya, Tanzania, Zambia, Zimbabwe, Botswana, and eventually South Africa, the fictitious international military unit—affiliated originally with the United Nations and now with the African Union—was almost in position for war.

The CF's game plan also involved setting up three stations or outposts: one in Nairobi, which had been established earlier; one in Lusaka, which they were about to establish; and the third in Gaborone, which was being established under the direction of Agents Jordan, Delgato, and Charlie. Unfortunately for the PG, however, that part of the game plan was missing from that scrap of paper that had been left on the kitchen table at the CF's abandoned Prospect compound.

Nonetheless, the PG had a few tricks of their own.

14

The Anglican Cathedral Boarding School

Back at the Anglican cathedral boarding school in Harare, after nearly three days of the same routine, Priscilla became bored with the tedium of manual labor and silence.

Then, one time, while dusting the bookshelves in the library, she noticed a section on the history of several African nations. Little did she know it, but those books would be her companions for the weeks ahead. Priscilla had always read with tremendous vigor, and now she appreciated the opportunity to learn more about the African peoples' quest for self-rule, self-determination, and independence.

She had begun with the understanding that Nelson Mandela was the preeminent figure in modern African history. But she quickly developed an appreciation for others, many of whom had appeared long before Mandela had come onto the world stage, particularly Maqoma, the most renowned Xhosa chief of South Africa's 19th-century Cape-Xhosa Wars. Maqoma was a successful resistance leader during the colonial period. As such, he was eventually captured and imprisoned on Robben Island long before Mandela.

Priscilla also admired Julius Nyerere of Tanzania and Kwame Nkrumah of Ghana. She learned about the economic impact of the resource-rich continent, and now fully understood the concept of "the winds of change." She knew that although it was a native of Britain who had coined the phrase, it was the Africans themselves who were bringing the concept to fruition. Ultimately, before her African adventure would end, she would know that—among the last bastions of European colonialism—the likes of the SANM would soon be swept off the world stage. That change, she understood, was merely a matter of time.

Meanwhile, when Father Mbuwayesango learned of Priscilla's interest in the books, he urged her to take them to her room to read.

"You mustn't allow the others to see you reading, especially not these types of books," the priest told her. "You must not even let them know that you are so well-educated. Instead, try to practice being slightly illiterate and ignorant. And never ask anyone about themselves or this country. And above all, for heaven's sake, conceal your American ways."

On the few occasions when Priscilla missed breakfast, the priest correctly suspected that she was in the library. Sure enough, when he would go there looking for her, she would be slumped over a pile of books at one of the tables, fast asleep.

"Pick up your duster, Megan," he would say if he feared some of the other girls were close enough to see Priscilla with those books. After one or two close calls, he even began delivering the books to Priscilla's room himself. "Can't be too careful," he would say to her.

On yet other occasions—when she became bored with the tedium of manual labor and silence—Priscilla would venture into the garden, where she almost always was followed by the priest, who tried his best to keep a close watch on her. On one particular day, she noticed similar foul odors as she had during her stay at the Prospect safehouse, which was puzzling to her because she assumed there would be fresh scents of the flowers and the trees in the garden. But the priest told her that the foul odors had floated over to the cathedral grounds from the spoiled produce that the vendors sold in the open markets on the neighboring streets. He told her that "Fresh food, especially meat and seafood, is a precious commodity" for the inhabitants of landlocked Zimbabwe, and that due to the scarcity of such commodities, many vendors sold the produce, even after it had spoiled. He told her that there was little electricity to keep food fresh or frozen, and that even if it were more readily available, most people could not afford to buy it or the iceboxes (refrigerators) in which to store the food. It was then that the priest realized that Priscilla had not the foggiest idea of what it was he had not said, "That many Zimbabweans were impoverished, that even if the electricity operated around the clock, the people could neither afford it, nor the iceboxes, for that matter."

"Typically," the priest expounded, "Meat is sun-dried and salted in springtime for consumption in the winter." (It was winter during Priscilla's time there.) But if improperly dried or salted in the first place, the meat spoiled, hence the foul odors that Priscilla kept smelling.

Notwithstanding, she now understood that many Zimbabweans were malnourished and that many were therefore underdeveloped and suffered many maladies, such as stunted growth, as was the case with the priest, who himself was barely five feet tall. But Priscilla realized something more. She now understood that all that she had learned about modernization and development in the African nations in her academic studies was relative, so to speak, and that no amount of cash infusion would create change in societies such as Zimbabwe, for a long time. It takes much time and effort to change a people's way of life, but first, the people must desire change.

As he became acquainted with Priscilla, the priest had his own curiosities about the woman whom he supposed was more mature and sophisticated than the one the televised media kept showing in that storybook get-up of a bridal gown and tiara. So Priscilla told him, that day in the garden, that her father had been a clergyman and that her family were Methodists, that she had a college degree in political science, and that she worked in public relations. But that was all that she told him. Even so, the priest had observed something peculiar about this apparently mixed-blood young woman who did not seem at all the stereotypical image of the Black people portrayed in the news media and the reruns of *Good Times* and *Sanford and Son* that he sometimes watched on Zimbabwean television: This woman, whom he called "Megan," had a distinct comportment about herself. She seemed wholly unfamiliar with the circumstances of poor people. *This is no ordinary Black American woman, college-educated or not*, he thought. *So who is she?* Even so, each time that he thought of her as a plant to infiltrate the boarding school, he let it go.

As it turned out, Priscilla had not given any thought to the image that she portrayed in her ivory, pearl-laced, broad-gauged, satin bridal gown and rose-covered tiara. She looked so innocent and much younger than her thirty-four years. But what Father Mbuwayesango saw in Megan was an assertive, carefree and resourceful woman. Why, even CF Agent Delgato had discerned that much as he stared at her back at that safehouse in Prospect. So, people the world over who watched those televised images of her in her bridal gown and tiara saw an inaccurate view of Priscilla. Yet, it would be that inaccurate view of her that would engender empathy and sympathy for Priscilla throughout her time in southern Africa.

It was not long before Priscilla began to understand that things were not what they appeared to be with the "other girls" in the cathedral of the Diocese of Harare, either.

She would soon discover—an overheard word here, a whispered innuendo there, and through her assertive and enterprising nature—the mystery behind the other girls which dated back to the early 20th century, just after apartheid had been subsumed into the South African political landscape, back when wealthy European men from Johannesburg, Pretoria, and Cape Town began sending their mixed-blood children to an orphanage in the nation that was later renamed Zimbabwe.

During another of her garden conversations with the priest, he filled in the gaps in her curiosity about Zimbabwean history and about the boarding school itself. As she pretended to be folding some laundry, she asked the questions that had plagued her from the start: "What was your country like before the white man came? And how is it that a Black man such as yourself came to be headmaster over all these privileged white girls?"

First, Father Mbuwayesango reminded Priscilla that, "The man called Onslow told me to watch you, not to engage you in conversation, and to keep you separate from the other girls." But the priest was a proud man, and he sensed something special in this peculiar Black American woman, especially since she had said that she was once a professor and that "My father was a clergyman like yourself." After Priscilla had pleaded her case for him to tell her about the Zimbabwean people, the priest agreed, though reluctantly, to tell her what she wanted to know.

Mostly, he wanted her to know that she was "in the midst of a society whose people were proud and who knew who and whose they were, that we have a rich history, even before the white man came." The priest talked succinctly and fast, for he did not wish to be overheard talking so intelligently to the housekeeper, whom he was not supposed to be engaging in the first place.

He told her that Zimbabwe meant "House of Stone," named by the Shona people over 800 years ago, and that, although gold and the valuable farm land were discovered by 1300, the Shona and Ndebele had held onto power alternately until the Europeans arrived in the 1850s. Priscilla was already aware that the latter period of explorations had included David Livingstone's, whose colossal bronze statue overlooked Victoria Falls, which he named honoring Britain's Queen Victoria in 1855, and for whom her alma mater in North Carolina was so named. Then, after that came the likes of Cecil Rhodes, who paved the way for the eventual takeover of the resource-rich territory by the British government.

But it was when the priest told her that—as the European explorations continued, some of them fathered children with the Shona women—that Priscilla's curiosity piqued. "Since the explorers did not wish to engage in mass genocide," he said, "they set up orphanages such as this one, operated by the Anglican Diocese of Harare," which was in the cathedral of the diocese—the one in which Priscilla was stashed.

Later still, she would come to understand that, nearly 100 years later, during several meetings of the SANM Executive Committee, the shrewd capitalists had decided to convert the orphanage into a boarding school. The Anglican Diocese of Harare would operate it, and it would admit only the mixed-blood daughters of the leading capitalists. And although the priest talked about the "mixed-blood girls," he omitted the part about the Executive Committee in his rendition of the boarding school's history.

As Father Mbuwayesango concluded, he noted that, over the course of time, the facility was transformed from an orphanage for underprivileged and outcast Zimbabwean children to a sort of boarding school for the so-called "unwanted" female children of white Southern Rhodesians, and later, white men from neighboring countries, primarily the Afrikaners of South Africa.

"And since I was already here, I was made the new headmaster," Father Mbuwayesango said with a slight smirk. Yet even he knew that Priscilla was hardly convinced by such a shallow explanation for his role as headmaster of an all-white boarding school for such privileged youngsters in the heart of the second-to-last bastion of apartheid-era regimes in Africa. Nor did he ever mention what happened to the mixed-blood boys!

But Priscilla learned firsthand, from pretending to wipe the walls and mop the floors around the classrooms during the priest's lectures, that, after graduation, the mixed-blood young women would be introduced into European society, where they would carry out the SANM's two primary missions. First, they would espouse the views of the South African regime—namely, that apartheid and white supremacy, as well as unfettered free-market capitalism, were necessary to the betterment of society. Second, they would promote the financial interests of their fathers—namely, that the work of their fathers in the SANM conglomerate, which operated the diamond, gold and platinum industries throughout South Africa—would be protected and allowed to flourish at all costs.

Three of the girls—Camilla, Joyce, and Anna—formed a special bond. They were not the children of ordinary Rhodesian farmers or Afrikaner miners; they had come from the socially and politically prominent. Their acceptance to college in Great Britain or Switzerland was virtually guaranteed, and their fathers would introduce them into European society, where they would meet, interact with, and eventually marry European men of distinction.

But what did the fathers stand to gain from such an arrangement? They already controlled the diamond, gold and platinum industries. But these were avid capitalists; they desired to control the whole global marketplace. They also desired to preserve white rule within all major governments and industries. The "coterie of the privileged," these three daughters of Rhodesian and Afrikaner capitalists, knew who they were, and they played that particular card for all it could generate.

And yet the boarding school scheme, which was initially planned as merely a way for the SANM executives to advocate their own brands of capitalism and nationalism, soon evolved into a darker and more sinister purpose.

For Simeon Johannes and his immediate predecessors had created a secret society of female assassins called "the Judges." It was a well-kept secret. Except for Simeon and Moses Cameron, no other members of the current Executive Committee knew about it.

Additionally, after the first headmaster died, Simeon had recruited a young, ambitious Anglican priest—Jacob Mbuwayesango—to replace him. It was a role Jacob would play for nearly forty years.

And so it was that—because Priscilla resembled a person of mixed blood—the manservant, at the behest of the CF commander, had authorized that she be placed in the cathedral at the Anglican Diocese of Harare. But at the time, neither man had any knowledge of the secret society of the Judges.

The sleeping quarters for the young women were situated at the extreme far left of the oblong edifice of the cathedral compound and contained twenty bunk beds and a dozen twin beds. A corridor separated the shower stalls and the toilets from the sleeping quarters and allowed the young women access to the dining hall, which was adjacent to the kitchen. At the extreme far right of the oblong edifice lay the library, which faced the front yard of the cathedral.

The main entrance to the facility was approximately two-thirds of the way down the façade. But one could also enter the facility by walking directly out of the dining area, turning right, and then walking up the main corridor to the front door. A left turn led to the rear exit, which, in turn, led into the garden.

At the opposite end of the facility were the administrative offices, the classrooms and the private quarters. Priscilla occupied the private quarters in the extreme right wing. Across from her room was the headmaster's—Father Mbuwayesango's. There were two more private spaces next to his. There was neither an attic nor a basement.

During Priscilla's stay at the cathedral compound, she had more than enough time to observe, with some admiration, the young women's routine. She was not the only one to rise at six o'clock in the morning. After breakfast, the young women—who ranged in ages from ten or eleven to perhaps eighteen or so—attended devotions in the cathedral. They marched in lockstep from the dining hall, down the corridor, out the rear of the boarding school building, into the garden and then over to the chapel for worship services.

Although socially, the girls tended to associate based on their age, there were, of course, a couple of cliques. One comprised the three young women who were fortunate to know their fathers. None of the girls knew their mothers, who were predominantly South African or Zimbabwean (Southern Rhodesian). For the girls who knew their fathers, those fathers had visiting rights. Who knew that an orphanage operated as if it were a boarding school? The Anglican Diocese of Harare operated the orphanage in just that fashion.

The longer Priscilla stayed in the cathedral boarding school hideaway, the more fascinated she became with every curious aspect of it. She learned that the girls mainly behaved according to the British tradition. They wore fine

European clothing, which included specially designed blazers and skirts. With remarkable fluency, they spoke the King's English—*or was that the Queen's English?* Priscilla thought. They also recited facts about European history, literature and society as if they themselves were already members of the aristocracy.

A few times, as she passed by an open classroom door or the door to the chapel, she witnessed some of the religion classes and the chapel services in which they participated. Once, she heard Father Mbuwayesango say, "Open your prayer books," to begin the formal devotions. He read several passages, and then the young women recited their responses. But whenever he read from the *New Testament*, he stepped out of the chancel onto the main floor, and the young women stood up and listened. At the end of his reading, he said, "Thus ends the reading of His holy word."

In unison, the students all said, "Amen."

Priscilla also noticed whenever the priest said, "Let us pray," the pupils, like little hobbits, pulled out their prayer pads, knelt and prayed, or at least they pretended to do so.

So, too, when the priest began to celebrate the Holy Eucharist, Priscilla observed a kind of caste system among the girls. Camilla, Joyce, and Anna— the three young women who knew their fathers—always led the way to receive the holy sacrament.

Priscilla was most fascinated with three gifted young women whose voices soared above all the others in song. They sang with such ease and grace that even the coterie who knew their fathers yielded to their magnificence. A cappella, their rich voices resonated throughout the sanctuary.

Priscilla was not supposed to attend the worship services, but she often sat on a pew at the back of the sanctuary. Having been deemed a commoner, she ranked least among the lot. And although, occasionally, the priest had seen her break the rules by sneaking into the chapel, he still allowed her that small privilege, despite Onslow's strict orders that she be kept separate from the other girls.

One day, while Priscilla was wiping down the walls of the hallway, she happened to pass the room where the oldest girls were in session. When the pupils attended their classes, they were grouped by age.

"Now, to resume our lesson on the biblical text for the day," the priest was saying. "Remember, young ladies, those judges didn't just sit in judgment of others with respect to the law. They also ruled over the nation of Israel. They used military might to lead their people. They instructed the military generals and captains on strategy. They were judges because the Lord and Master had called them to lead His people. In leading His people, they fought battles against evildoers such as King Jabin of Canaan at the behest of the Lord."

Priscilla stopped wiping the walls and dropped her rag beside her feet. As she peered into the classroom, she noticed the young women sat at old-fashioned wooden desks, the ones with lids that could be raised. Their textbooks and writing utensils, which seemed to include what looked like a manual, were inside the pouch, or the boot, as the Europeans termed it.

By squinting hard enough, she was able to see that the manual was entitled, *The Book of the Judges*.

But only later, much later, did she discover that the manual was not the King James Version or the New Revised Standard Version or any other version of the bible, for that matter, but rather a manual with explicit instructions on military leadership, strategy and tactical maneuvers.

On the day that Priscilla had lingered outside that classroom, she heard the priest say, "Please turn to the section on the role of the female judges. Some of you will rise to become judges, heroic leaders of your people. Like Deborah, the prophetess, you will follow the orders of your Lord and Master. Yet others of you will be like Jael; you will eradicate the Earth of its evildoers, such as Sisera, King Jabin's general."

Then the priest paused and asked, "Which role do some of you prefer?"

"I prefer Deborah," said Joyce, with ease and confidence. "I want to lead our generals into battle." She was a pretty brunette, and like the other two of the coterie, she stood an inch or so taller than Priscilla's five feet five inches.

"I think I'd be better as a soldier," said Anna, the young blonde. "I don't think I'm strong enough to lead an army. But I could drive a peg or a stake into someone's temple. Or I might find it simpler to slip a pill or a vial of poison into a drink. Yes, I can do that. I'm sure I can do that."

"What about you, Camilla?" the priest asked. "Which role will you play?"

"Hmm, I need to give such an important decision more thought," she answered. "Then again, this is something that I should discuss with Father. I'm sure he'll know what's best for me." Camilla had red hair and freckles, and she stood the tallest of the three.

Astonished at what she had just overheard, Priscilla picked up her rag and stepped away from the classroom door. As she thought about what she had overheard, she dabbed her forehead with that dirty rag. She had just uncovered the reality of her new situation: the cathedral boarding school of the diocese was not an orphanage in the traditional sense of the word, nor was it a boarding school for privileged, racially mixed young girls. Instead, Priscilla now knew, it was a training camp, a charm school of sorts, for budding terrorists.

Priscilla knew about female soldiers—for she had often thought about the U.S. Congress's debates over the role of women in the military—but she knew hardly anything about terrorists, at least nothing about terrorists that were intentionally trained as such. Then again, she had never heard anything remotely like what she had just overheard. She had never even imagined there would be young women trained for such roles. But there she was—in the midst of such a place.

She walked a few steps away, turned a corner and leaned against a wall out of sight from anyone walking down the main corridor. She considered how little she knew about terrorism. The world she once knew had long since changed. The so-called Cold War that once existed between the Americans and the Russians had already taken a back seat to another level and type of adversity. International terrorists abounded the world over, many of whom did not associate with a particular government or political system but instead had agendas of their own for which they were willing to die. The groups seemingly sprang up from out of nowhere, aided mainly by advanced technology, which the South Africans, especially, managed well.

Priscilla wondered whether Tommy and his CF cohorts had placed her in the cathedral to ascertain such information. She was not so sure they would risk her life like that. But, for sure, she now realized that Father Mbuwayesango was not merely a priest but also a member of some clandestine organization.

But what type of organization is it? she wondered. *Who are the 'evildoers' that girl was talking about? And how the hell did they take over an Anglican cathedral in the middle of the capital of Zimbabwe? And most of all, who can I tell what I've learned, if anybody?*

But she was aware that she had left her cleaning post for too long. So as she thought about it, she wadded the dirty rag in her fist and went back to pretending to wipe down the walls in the hallway.

Priscilla might not have been so sanguine if she had known that one of these fierce girls who called herself one of the Judges had, in fact, begun to track her every movement.

Out of sheer curiosity, one member of the coterie of the privileged, Camilla, acquired a deep fascination with the new housekeeper. "Megan's quite different from Frances, our old maid. This one must really have been abandoned by her family. I feel so sorry for her," she said. In fact, she felt more uneasy than compassion with the new servant girl. But Camilla often did not trust most other people with her perceptions, not even the two other girls who were supposed to be her comrades. Even though the two other girls had the same social status as she did, Camilla detested them. Yet she was intrigued with "the commoner," Megan, perhaps the way a child is with a new prized possession, such as a pony; only Megan was nothing of the sort.

"Oh, Camilla," Joyce chirped, "you're the spitting image of your father, always looking for a new toy to fancy. Surely you're not contemplating communicating with the likes of her?" Joyce giggled, making sure to cover her mouth. Ladies do not show all their teeth, and never do they laugh out loud. Such were the lessons of the social elite, and the coterie of the privileged epitomized such lessons to the nth degree.

"Don't be silly, Joyce. I was only wondering who she is. Where did she come from? Does she know her father?" Camilla frowned. "Besides, haven't you noticed? Megan doesn't act as commonly as Frances. She walks a certain way. Good posture, not stooped over like Frances was. And when she and the headmaster talk, they actually talk. But with Frances, Father Jacob mostly told her or showed her what he wanted her to do. I'll bet Megan's educated, because she's certainly out of place here."

"Listen to me, Camilla, we do not have time to study the ways of the hired help," Joyce said. "Come with us. We're going to watch the news. Are you coming, Camilla?"

Then the coterie marched in lockstep to the lobby to watch the news.

Such was Priscilla's life as the CF caravan made its way to Lusaka.

15

Visitors
&
Three Engraved Wooden Statues

Apart from Priscilla's activities inside the cathedral compound, Onslow and the other sentinels also kept their eyes on the routine activities of the headmaster and other staff, such as the matrons, the kitchen crew, the librarian, and the groundskeepers. When they could, they listened in on the various conversations to monitor whether anyone had noticed anything about Priscilla's presence. In addition, Onslow and his team observed the staffers' work habits, their comings and goings from the boarding school, and especially their work schedules so that, if they needed to, they could access the facility as quickly as possible.

But they were not alone in their intelligence gathering and surveillance.

Disguised as an Anglican priest, PG Commander Longworth paid a few visits to the cathedral compound. What had prompted those visits was that he had gotten wind from one of his informants, Sleazy Duncan, that there was "a new young gal" in the cathedral compound.

Sleazy had described the newcomer as being older than the other girls. He said that she looked like she had mixed blood and added that she read books.

But what caught the PG commander's attention was the informant saying that someone in the compound had confided that this young woman "seemed to be American."

After that unexpected, though welcome news, the PG commander telephoned the headmaster, Father Mbuwayesango, and asked for a tour of the facility under the pretense of having a child for placement. In preparation for his appointment, he discarded his camouflage uniform and dressed in professional attire. He wore fashionable eyewear and kept his sandy-brown ponytail, but knotted it. Such a simple disguise, he believed, would at least complicate identifying him from a distance.

After Father Mbuwayesango and his guest got acquainted over tea in his office, the headmaster led the way for a tour of the facility. Pointing to three shut doors on his left, he said, nonchalantly, "These are just private quarters for the staff and myself." He was hoping to convey the message that whatever was behind those doors was of no significance.

The headmaster smiled at his visitor and gestured up the main corridor. "Shall we examine the classrooms and the library?"

As the two men turned and walked a short distance, Priscilla happened down the hallway towards them. She was carrying her duster and a pail filled with cleaning solution.

Stopping dead in his tracks, his mouth opened widely, and the PG commander asked, "Is *she* the housekeeper?"

"Yes." The headmaster barely paused, as if he hadn't noticed either Priscilla or his guest's apparent interest in her. "Now," he insisted, "the classrooms and library are straight ahead."

The headmaster took a step in that direction, but his guest did not follow. Instead, he stayed rooted to the spot and stared as Priscilla approached.

"Ahem, shall we," the headmaster politely prodded, "continue with our examination of the classrooms, my friend?"

"Oh, yes. Sorry, Father." A ghost of a smile hovered on PG Commander Longworth's thin lips. He had just seen for himself what Sleazy had reported. He noticed that Priscilla was apparently older than the other girls and that she had a certain comportment. Even Camilla had noticed that about Megan, the housekeeper. Megan walked and behaved as if she had pride in herself, which, in this racially charged and class-conscious country, was unusual for someone like Priscilla, who was anything but a "commoner."

Longworth pursed his lips. This housekeeper was the second young woman in the school who had caught his attention. He happened to be at the boarding school on a parental visitation day. In the reception area of the main office, he had noticed a vaguely familiar-looking girl sitting in the waiting area. Then, as Father Mbuwayesango and his guest walked through the area, once again, he stopped in his tracks, his mouth gaping in wonder.

"My, my, Father," he asked, "what have we here?"

"Oh, that's Miss Camilla," the headmaster said. "She's waiting on a visit from her father. Will you be expecting to visit your daughter? Or will your transaction be exclusively boarding school privileges?"

"Pardon me, Father," PG Commander Longworth said, "but I almost forgot this particular diocese is the one that operates a boarding school. I've not yet decided the extent of relations I'll maintain with my child. But since this is an open situation, may I ask the young girl's father's name?" *Who,* he wondered, *did that girl look like? Was she the daughter of someone he knew?*

"Like you, he's South African," the headmaster said. "However, we're not at liberty to divulge too much more information. Come, let us examine the rest of the facility."

By that point in their tour, the headmaster had begun to feel as if he would lose the contents of his stomach. His guest's sudden interest in Camilla was a mere distraction. The man had seen Priscilla's face. So, the headmaster mainly thought that, *now that Priscilla's cover had been compromised,* he had to get word to his CF contacts.

Just as Father Mbuwayesango and PG Commander Longworth entered the dining room of the cathedral boarding school, Moses Cameron walked into the reception area of the main office. But neither the PG commander nor Moses Cameron was aware of the other's presence.

In an instant, Camilla leapt from her seat and into her father's arms.

"Hold on there, young lady," Moses said. "Father's here now. Suppose you missed me, eh?" He guided his daughter outside for a stroll on the grounds and then took her by car to shop for new clothes. Camilla was aglow. Attention from her adored father meant the world to her. To anyone else looking at this scene from a distance, Moses behaved as if he had other than pure and "fatherly" motives for visiting his daughter—perhaps a secret rendezvous with another woman, a prostitute, perhaps. Yet the man who had walked into the

146

lobby of the main office was clean-shaven and well-dressed, the complete opposite of Moses Cameron, the SANM executive.

Later that day, just as her father was about to depart, Camilla told him about the new cleaning lady at the cathedral.

"You're not chumming up to the help, are you, my child?"

"Oh, no, Father," Camilla said. "I'm just curious about her. She's not like our other housekeeper. Megan seems educated. She reads books in the library, and sometimes she sneaks into the chapel, too."

"Really!" Moses said, his breath whistling through his teeth. His daughter had finally captured his serious attention. *Could this,* he wondered, *be where the American woman had been stashed?* "Perhaps you should figure out a way to get her trust." He went on saying, "When you can get away, take her a couple of books and ask her simple questions: what she likes to read and whether she travels. But keep the questions simple."

"Alright, Father, as long as you approve, that is what I will do." Then, "Oh, I almost forgot, Father. It's about the Judges. Which do you think I'd be best at, Deborah or Jael?"

"Why, Camilla, my child, it's Deborah, of course. We Camerons lead. And remember, Jael was not of our kind. Jael was a foreigner. She was not among the chosen people."

Onslow and his team were already searching through their picture files of the SANM Executive Committee and its Patrol Guard when Moses was departing from the cathedral compound. But finding a match was compounded by the fact that, aside from the red hair, the distinguished gentleman they had just seen at the boarding school did not look much like the disreputable-looking Moses Cameron in their file photos. But Onslow was able to make the tentative identification that Moses indeed had been sighted. Just to be certain, he obtained and transmitted the suspect's fingerprints from a doorknob in the cathedral boarding school to his supervisor.

Yet it was not long before Onslow apparently had something direr to worry about. Late in the afternoon, as soon as the headmaster got his chance, he notified his CF contacts about his visitor's interest in Priscilla, adding that he was certain the visitor had gotten a good look at the American woman's face.

Immediately thereafter, Onslow had been contacted by his supervisor, CF Agent Jordan, and ordered to: "Ratchet up your surveillance, Lieutenant." He and his supervisor conferred some more, and a new plan was hatched. Onslow was to enter the cathedral and make contact with Priscilla.

He struck before dawn when the moonless night was still in darkness.

Onslow used a screwdriver and an awl to pick the lock of the door that led into the garden. He raced up the main corridor, turned left and ran toward the private quarters of the headmaster. Soundlessly he opened the unlocked door.

Yet, since Father Mbuwayesango had been too anxious to sleep, no sooner was Onslow inside his room than the priest was on his feet. Quickly they conferred and then went together across the corridor to Priscilla's room.

Onslow urgently whispered as the two of them stood over her. "Wake her up, now!"

The headmaster bent over the sleeping Priscilla. He poked at her and even shook her shoulder, but she did not stir. So he knew that, once again, she had gone to sleep late, having read books through most of the night.

When she eventually awoke, she was stunned to see Onslow in her room. "You, here?"

Onslow lost no time in drilling her about Alistair Longworth. She had, in fact, seen the man in question, PG Commander Longworth, "twice." More disturbingly, he had seen her, too.

"The first time was during his tour with Father Mbuwayesango," she said. "Our paths crossed down the hallway. He said something about a child he wanted to bring here. The second time, well, that was during devotions in the chapel; I bumped into him accidentally on my way out."

Onslow frowned at the headmaster, who had been instructed that "Priscilla must be kept separated from the other girls." The priest shrugged.

Then Priscilla elaborated. "When I bumped into him, in the chapel this time, he actually spoke to me. The yucky trash acted as if he liked what he saw in me."

"I want you to think carefully, young lady," Onslow said. "Tell me every single detail of his appearance and demeanor."

After Priscilla described the man's face, Onslow said, "Ah, shit!" He turned his back on the other two, pulled out his cell phone, and, in a moment, had CF Agent Jordan on the line. "The cover is blown," Onslow said. Tersely he relayed what had happened. "We need to get her outta' here, *now*!"

"Damn it, man! How'd you let that happen?" Agent Jordan was shouting into the phone. "You told me she was secure there."

But, Onslow thought, *you and the commander picked this place.*

Then, he reported: "I can say with damn near certainty that at least one PG and one Executive Committee member were here today, separate visits though; but both men were here." Onslow paused and then said, "You ought to have received our transmission of those prints by now."

"Get her out of there!" Agent Jordan shouted. "Keep her safe, or it's your head." He disconnected the call and then thought hard. *How the hell do I break this news to our team?* Angel had doubted the wisdom of placing Priscilla in the cathedral in the first place. But what he dreaded even more than that was having to relay the news to Tommy and Carlton.

Onslow chewed his bottom lip until it bled. His instinct was that he had very little time to avert an incident with the PG, so he made a unilateral decision to move Priscilla. Previously, just in case he had to spirit her away, he had cautiously questioned the headmaster about possible "nests" at the boarding school or church. So he knew exactly where he would take her.

While Onslow had been talking to his boss, the headmaster had made a quick trip to the kitchen and returned with a bag of food and bottles of water. Already Priscilla had finished dressing and was munching on a chunk of cheese and a piece of loaf bread.

"Come with me, *now*!" Onslow said to Priscilla, who had already dressed for what she did not know.

Onslow grabbed the sack of provisions from the headmaster's trembling hands, took Priscilla by the arm and hurried her outside into the darkness. The next thing Priscilla knew, they were tiptoeing along a two-story granite wall with arched stained-glass windows that formed the north side of the cathedral. Near the end of that wall, Onslow suddenly stopped and dropped to his knees. He shoved open a panel below one of the stained-glass windows and gestured for Priscilla to crawl inside. After they both made it through, he pushed the panel back into place and latched it. Then he led Priscilla on a brisk walk along a dim corridor, taking care to stay close to the colorfully decorated walls of the sanctuary, until they reached the back of the chancel.

Then they came upon the first of three engraved wooden statues—this one of St. John the Divine, its two eyes, one glowing and the other dim, above the austere-looking face. Remembering what he thought the headmaster had once told him, Onslow pressed a lever to the right of the statue, waited a couple of seconds, and then said, "It's not opening, Miss Prissy!"

Before she could say anything, he peered down at the statue's base and read aloud the following words, engraved into old wood: "It takes only one of these to see you, but if you press the right one, the left one will pierce yours."

Looking at the saint's two eyes, Onslow said, "Well, here goes nothing," and pressed the "right" eye, the eye on his right. Suddenly a heavy door behind the statue opened, and the two of them entered through it.

Down deeper into the darkness they went until they reached a second engraved wooden statue—this one of St. Francis of Assisi, with engraved cherubim, birds, and woodland creatures around him. This time, Onslow had a more precise recollection of what the headmaster had told him. Rather than pressing down on the lever to his right, he first peered down at the base of the statue and read aloud the following words: "This helps me to eat. For my last meal, press down." Onslow kept still a moment, as if he were thinking, and then he spoke over his shoulder to Priscilla, "If I put my hand down one of 'em's throat, I'm bit to death! Got to watch these sweet little cherubs! Like snakes, every one of 'em!" So he pressed the cherub's tummy, and the heavy door behind the saint opened, and Oswald and Priscilla went through it.

As they crept along into more darkness, Onslow appeared to be having second thoughts. "I'm sorry, young lady, for hustling you off at this ungodly hour and for all this craziness with these doors. But my primary responsibility is your safety. That man didn't run into you by accident. He's one of the bad guys." Onslow sighed. "And thanks to the priest, we do have a little for you to eat and drink. But I'm going to have to figure out a way to get you more food."

As Onslow talked, Priscilla noticed the courtesy and considerateness in his language— "I'm sorry," "your safety," and "get you more food." She concluded that he was not quite as gauche as he had pretended earlier. *So why the façade?* And, too, she did not like the sound of "as this goes on." Surely he was not intending to go off and leave her here in the dark of this old church? Inwardly Priscilla sighed. She realized that sometimes she understood the gravity of her predicament, and sometimes she did not. But under the apparent circumstances, she still had difficulty believing. *One day, I'm watching my groom get gunned down at the altar, and the next day, I'm on the run in Zimbabwe. No one would ever believe this madness!* Still, she warned herself that for her own good, she had to be more cooperative. So from this point forward, she would try to do as Onslow instructed, without objection.

Onslow pondered his next move as he crept along in the darkness. He knew he had found the best new hideout for his ward. But beyond that, there were too many unknowns.

They soon came to a third engraved wooden statue—this one of St. Mary. Onslow read aloud the riddle written on the wooden ledge near the base of the statue: "Unable to see or hear, a child might know his mother by this."

Once again, Onslow kept still a moment, as if he were thinking, and then he said to Priscilla, "If I don't choose right, I'll be sliced into three pieces, maybe four. Well, here goes."

He reached out and clasped one of St. Mary's hands, and the massive door opened up all the way, and he and Priscilla walked through it.

Onslow and Priscilla carefully descended yet another flight of stairs. At last, they reached their destination, the lowest level of the cathedral. They were now in the dungeon, which also served as a crypt. When Onslow first brought her to the cathedral, it was in the dark of night. Since then, except for going to chapel, she had not ventured out the front door of the boarding school. So when Onslow turned on a lantern, Priscilla felt very tense amidst the close, stale air and the putrid odor of decomposed bodies. She felt a sudden nausea.

"Onslow," Priscilla managed to ask, "did anybody tell you about my phobias? I got this thing, you know, about darkness and close quarters and all. And you also need to know, I'm no good in basements. Or in high places, either, for that matter."

When Onslow did not answer, Priscilla realized she was mostly talking to console herself. She was afraid, even though she knew that Onslow was doing what he thought was best for her. Since he said he needed to bring her more food and other provisions, she'd already figured out that she was about to be left alone. She dreaded being alone in such a place. For the first time, she valued the company of Onslow, her protector.

She realized her eyes must be getting used to the darkness, for now she was able to make out shapes, and then objects. The first thing she noticed was the raised stone and marble tombs of the remains of holy people—*Probably bishops,* she thought—*from so many years ago.* A chiseled inscription marked each tomb.

Onslow told her—as he continued to lead her about the creepy crypt—that the headmaster had told him that the remains of yet other individuals who once played prominently in the life of the Anglican Church were buried underneath the walkway at the front entrance to the cathedral.

Priscilla felt as if she were in a mausoleum, and so she stood still and allowed only her eyes to roam. *Welcome to your new home, kiddo*, she thought. It was eerie and scary and reeked of death and decay. Never before in Priscilla's life had she faced such a seemingly unbearable circumstance. She did not like her new home.

16

Gone Missing, Propaganda
&
"A Scotch on the Rocks, Father"

As the day progressed, it gradually became apparent to the ever-more-anxious headmaster-priest-turned-double agent that Priscilla—a.k.a. Megan, "had gone missing." This, he told himself, would be his story. Still, he found little consolation in the knowledge that Onslow must have relocated her.

How the hell can I explain to the CF, who brought her here, that it was my fault the girl was compromised in the first place?

Father Mbuwayesango broke into a sweat as he pondered his precarious predicament.

The double agent then thought, *And what about the PG? Any second, their agents could come busting in, and it would not be long before they begin torturing me for information about the American woman's whereabouts.*

The headmaster shuddered. *Which of them was worse, the CF or the PG?* So far as punishing him or grilling him, he had no illusions about agents from either force. As Father Mbuwayesango continued pondering his predicament, he fell to his knees and made his peace with God.

But when he got to his feet, his serenity evaporated, as again his anxiety got the better of him. He decided his most imminent threat was Onslow. What if he came back to finish him off?

But the priest did not know what Onslow knew—that when Onslow decided to relocate Priscilla elsewhere, he had simultaneously severed ties with him, the headmaster, the priest, Father Mbuwayesango, or whoever he was.

There are times when a secret is only good if it is kept to oneself, and so it was with Onslow. He contacted CF Agent Jordan to report that he had "safely relocated our stash." Yet, fearing the phone line might somehow be compromised, he did not risk mentioning her name or sharing where he had stashed her. "Can't be too careful with these damn cell phones, Boss," he said. Onslow thought it was better to catch hell later for his apparent insubordination than to risk the life of his ward.

Agent Jordan was angry with Onslow, even though he was satisfied that Onslow was averting Priscilla's abduction by the PG. But he was angry because he was not accustomed to being disrespected by a subordinate.

"All the signs are pointing," Agent Jordan warned, "to an ensuing battle with PG Commander Longworth and the PG forces. It would not be long," he added, "before the enemies would be massing in Harare in pursuit of the American, PJ Austin."

Meanwhile, it was not long before PG Commander Longworth had gotten in touch with his own supervisor. He had shared with Hans the great news about his discovery of the American girl at the Anglican Cathedral in Harare.

When Hans, in turn, reported the news to the Executive Committee, they expressed much cheer.

"Now we're getting somewhere!" they all shouted in unison.

Above all the others, Moses Cameron, who was "attending" the meeting remotely from his room at the Salisbury Club, by telephone, managed to drown out the others as he yelled, "And I have a direct contact, right smack in the middle of the cathedral boarding school!"

There was an excited babble and demands to know the name of Moses' contact. "Who?"

"Yeah, who?" someone else queried.

"My daughter, Camilla," Moses said. "She's befriending the American as we speak. Oh, yeah, boys, we've got her now. With Hans's man on the case and my own unexpected visit to see my daughter again, we'll snatch the little American bitch. You'll see! I'm even considering coming outta' retirement for this one. Somethin' tells me this is the big one. Yeah, baby!"

"Well, I'll be damned," an outraged Simeon snapped. "Will you get a load o' this she-it!"

As for Heinreik, he just sat there and waited for the other shoe to drop in his direction.

Around the same time, CF Agents Jordan, Delgato, and Charlie were setting up their station of the ostensible international military unit amid the grandeur of mineral-rich Botswana. Situated on the country's northeastern border, Gaborone, the capital city, lies northwest of Johannesburg, by over 160 miles. An ironic difference between Botswana and South Africa was that the former was poor but democratic and stable, while the latter, though rich, was on the brink of a political revolution. Considered one of the longest-lasting and most successful of the African democracies, Botswana was also the most stable of African nations. Tourists loved it, too, because of the teeming wildlife in its parks and preserves, especially with its enormous elephants.

The CF had spent nearly three weeks in Botswana training its troops in the latest technological warfare. Now the time had come for the troops to receive their final instructions. Inside a large, dimly lit auditorium, a video played on the screen. The 300 recruits clustered close to watch it.

The video showed a raunchy-looking man, wearing a wrinkled white shirt and dark trousers stained with tobacco spit. He was sporting a head of ragged, dark red hair, and an equally ragged beard and mustache. In one scene, he spat what looked like a wad of chewing tobacco into a rusty tin can.

Charlie's voice-over intoned: "This man, Moses Cameron by name, is a descendant of one of the wealthiest and most powerful families in South Africa. He also has a daughter at the boarding school in Harare. He is now a member of the SANM Executive Committee and is no longer a PG agent. Reflecting that change in stature and role, he has been forbidden to rejoin the ranks of the PG agents on active duty. Still, this guy has a history of living outside all the rules. Just in case, you all need to see him up close, as he is very skilled in disguising himself."

Then the recruits watched videos they believed were of twenty-five additional members of the Patrol Guard. At the end, the voice-over, again the manservant, said: "Pay particular attention to those images. Hard to believe, but those are all the same man."

After the videos had played, Charlie proclaimed: "This is a 'kill or disable' order on all PG and SANM sympathizers."

Next, he showed the recruits video footage of how the PG tortured Black South African men to death using the infamous "necklace." The Guardsmen would begin by forcefully gathering a group of Black men. Then, they would coerce, with threats of severe punishment, a few of the men to stack a dozen or so rubber tires over their friends. Then each one in the group would be forced to pour several gallons of kerosene over his friend or neighbor, and then to light the fuel with a match and thus begin the friend's long and torturous death. When only one in the group was left standing, the Guardsmen would first force him to thrust the last of his friends or neighbors into a stack of rubber tires and again set to light the kerosene with a match; then, the Guardsmen would thrust the lone Black man inside his own stack of tires and hand him a match to begin his own grisly death.

At the end of the video came close-ups of the charred remains of those men. And the voice-over intoned: "A hideous way to kill another human being, just because of his skin color."

What came next in the video was footage of images of the missing American woman, PJ Austin. The recruits saw Priscilla in her more mature and sophisticated role as PR executive, moving about the floor of the Ohio Senate, directing her camera crew during Senator Callahan's speech on the SAD bill. Then they saw a close-up of a man in the background—PG Claus Fokker.

Charlie's voice-over said: "The PG are planted everywhere, in the halls of justice, in our legislative bodies, in our financial institutions. They are everywhere!"

Finally, the recruits watched footage that had been shot as part of the wedding package, that horrible day near the end of June at the Columbus church. They watched, amazed, as Priscilla and her nephew walked up the steps of First Church. She wore her lavish wedding gown, and Germane wore his tuxedo and pretended to be manlier than he actually was. The recruits saw Senator Callahan as he escorted Liza down the aisle to her seat. Then they heard gunshots and saw the bridegroom fall dead at the altar rail. Vivid close-ups illuminated Jonathan's brain matter splattered on the floor and on the bishop's discolored white robe.

At the event's conclusion, Charlie raised his voice and said, "And don't forget, my fellow CF soldiers of fortune! There's a bonus for rescuing the American woman unscathed."

He beamed at the troops, satisfied that once again he and his team had been successful in training and motivating their recruits with such vivid video-propaganda. He wanted to believe that the CF at Gaborone had set its forces up for success.

What he did not know did not hurt him, at least not yet.

In fact, the CF was at a slight disadvantage because the PG forces were already in place in Harare. Still, however, the CF had the advantage of manpower. The CF commanded the equivalent of a battalion, whereas the PG had a mere force of a dozen or so men in all of Harare.

Meanwhile, the PG was conducting its own version of a motivational program for its recruits. They issued orders to "kill the American girl, PJ Austin, and to kill or disable the headmaster." The Executive Committee was greatly upset that the double agent, the priest-headmaster, had deliberately withheld information pertaining to the whereabouts of the American girl. Every intelligence-gathering agency in the world was seeking her. Why the priest had not shared his information about her whereabouts with the PG would go with him to his grave.

Back in Harare, on a beautiful, sunny day in late July, three roughshod men called on the headmaster-priest-turned-double agent. PG Commander Alistair Longworth had cut off his ponytail, discarded his fashionable eyewear and now donned his camouflage uniform. Yet the priest still recognized him.

As soon as the commander entered the priest's quarters, along with his two companions, he pushed the priest violently into an upholstered chair and shoved it with him in it up to the small table that centered the room. "A Scotch on the rocks, Father? Something to take the edge off?" Without waiting for an answer, he removed a small flask and two shot glasses from his back pants pockets, poured two drinks, one for himself, and handed the other to the priest. After the priest had gulped down his drink, the PG commander then said, "Remove your shoes, Father."

Father Mbuwayesango looked into the bottom of his empty shot glass and envisioned his impending demise—a bloody one, to be sure, and very, very slow. But he still obeyed as he pulled off one black shoe, along with the sock, and then the other.

PG Commander Longworth said, "First, I want you to know that I'll go easy on you *if* you tell me where the American is."

"Believe me, master, I do not know." The priest trembled. Yet with over seventy years on this earth—close to forty of which were spent as a SANM agent—he knew he had already lived well beyond the life expectancy of an intelligence agent.

PG Commander Longworth beckoned to one of his accomplices, who, in turn, bent over the priest and said, harshly and abruptly, "Right hand on the table, Father. You know the drill."

The PG accomplice balled his fist and slammed it down onto the man's trembling hand. "Move your other fingers out of the way." Then he grabbed hold of his pulsating thumb, pulled out a blade and, in a single stroke, whacked it off.

The priest shrieked. His entire body shook visibly. Blood gushed.

"Act like a man!" the PG commander snapped and then said, "Now, let us try this another way."

Since the priest was a very short man, his feet barely touched the floor from his chair. The PG accomplice pulled out a pair of ragged, but sharp, pruning scissors, leaned down to the headmaster's right foot and, without saying a single word, chopped off its big toe.

The priest wanted to wail. Instead, he gnashed his teeth and held his silence. Tears coursed down his cheeks. Despite what was happening to him, he did not want to draw attention from the students or anyone else.

"My dear Father Mbuwayesango," the PG commander went on saying, "surely you can tell me something to spare your remaining dexterity."

"I swear to you, if I knew where the girl was, I'd surely tell you. Do you think I enjoy being mutilated?" he said, now more forcefully.

The PG accomplice looked up at his commander, who nodded again, and he scissored off the man's other big toe. The big toe dangled before it fell to the floor. Quickly, the accomplice stood back up and reached for the priest's other thumb and cut it off, too.

Emotionless, PG Commander Longworth said, "Now, sweet Jesus might rescue you from other possible agony, if only you'd point me in the right direction. Or, better still, perhaps you remember who might've aided in the removal of the American girl. Anything you say to my favor will be to your advantage, dear Father."

Blood gushed from the priest's hands and feet, spilling across the table and onto the floor near him. His eyes swelled. His body writhed in agony.

"Just kill me, master," he screamed. "I can't remember anything more."

But just as PG Commander Longworth reached for his own murder weapon, the priest, seeming to relish his role as a double agent, said, "Perhaps there is something, small as it is. But at least it's something."

"Pray tell, dear Father, pray tell."

"The man was called Onslow." His voice at first was a gasp, but then swelled along with his hope that this might not be the end for him after all. The priest sang like a tweedy bird. Mostly, though, he prayed for a quick death. "I'm almost certain that he, too, is American. He called on me early the other morning and asked to speak with Megan, the American housekeeper. The man drilled her about having seen you and scoffed at me for having allowed her to interact with the other girls. Then, later that morning, Megan was gone. But I swear to you, I don't know where he took her."

"Ah, ha! Now we're getting somewhere," the PG commander said.

Then he and his two accomplices walked out of the room without so much as a backward glance at the priest. Longworth was content with having disabled his victim. Although he still was not satisfied that the priest had told him all that he knew, he thought, *Let 'im stew awhile.*

Swift but methodic, the three PG agents searched the boarding school building and the grounds of the cathedral compound for any signs of the American girl. Then, once in the garden, they stopped at the impressive sight of the cathedral's towering granite ramparts, arched stained-glass windows and the soaring steeple.

"Ah, yes," the PG commander said. "I believe our little kitten is nestled somewhere inside the Lord's house."

Disturbed that so far this morning she had not seen Megan, Camilla marched down the hallway to the private quarters and knocked on Priscilla's door. When there was no answer, she opened the door and saw for herself that no one was there.

Instinctively then, she turned around and walked across the corridor to the headmaster's suite. She knocked on his door. When she heard a man groaning, she went inside the room. As soon as she saw the heap of groaning flesh and the blood on the small table and on the floor surrounding it, the heap that had once been Father Mbuwayesango, she screamed. Then a few other girls rushed down the corridor after her and looked into the headmaster's room. They all screamed, too, aghast at the bloody spectacle. In their *Book of Judges*, they had read about horrific scenes, but only now had they seen such. So, before they put their lessons from their manual into practice, they behaved like the young girls they were: they panicked and scurried about. Eventually though, one of them said, "I'm calling for an ambulance."

Camilla used the telephone in an office down the hallway next. She called her father. Frantically, she described what she had seen in the headmaster's suite. "And father," she added, "Megan's nowhere to be found."

Moses guessed precisely what had happened. So, come what may, he would definitely come out of retirement and rejoin the PG.

Then Moses told his daughter, "My child, I will be with you before nightfall. Go to your room and wait for me there."

In a shadowy corner on the far side of the cathedral, Onslow had his head together with the very informant who earlier had informed PG Commander Longworth about the American girl masquerading as a housekeeper at the boarding school. Because Onslow was paying Sleazy more money than PG Commander Longworth did, Sleazy had become an informant for the CF.

He told Onslow, "My friend on the kitchen staff says the man with the ponytail come back with two other men. Ah, yeah, ponytail gone and no eyeglasses. After they left, Father M didn't have no thumbs and no big toes." Since Onslow knew Sleazy provided information based on who paid him the most, he paid him handsomely.

But after he heard Sleazy's report, Onslow whipped a .38 out of a hidden holster, aimed it at Sleazy's forehead and pulled the trigger. *Can't be too careful with the likes of him.*

Only a few moments later, after he watched his men secret the informant's body, Onslow observed PG Commander Longworth and his two accomplices standing in the courtyard in front of the cathedral. He was well aware of CF Agent Jordan's strict instructions not to engage the PG until he got the word to take action. But now, since Onslow saw the severity of their situation, he changed the instructions to read in his words, "Once they attempt to enter the cathedral, we attack. 'We do what we must.'" Onslow and his companions may not have been special ops; still, they were seasoned fighters and so would do what they "must."

PG Commander Longworth and his comrades stood on the sidewalk outside the cathedral in plain view, unaware they were a hair trigger away from death. But the PG commander suspected he and his men were under surveillance, so he signaled for them to disperse while he figured out their next move. As things stood, he was still not entirely sure of his intuition that the American girl was, in fact, inside the edifice. And even if she were, exactly where was she?

17

The Privilege of Acceptance

Still alone, Priscilla waited in the darkness in the Anglican Cathedral crypt.

She had not eaten cooked, nutritious food for quite some time. She had lost track of nights and days, so she was not certain of the passing time. Nor did she know how long the battery-operated flashlight would last, so she kept it mostly turned off, and even though Onslow had come back twice and provided her with provisions, he had been clear that her use of the flashlight was conditional.

"Use the battery-operated flashlight *only* when necessary," he had told her. "And 'necessary' does not include your fear of the darkness, either."

As for the other provisions he had left for her, she understood the use of the blanket and the hourglass, as well as the chocolate bars, the nuts, and the bottled water. But Priscilla was not amused, wondering about the potential use of the other items: a hammer and a chisel, an oxygen tank and mask.

What on earth will I use this stuff for? I'm certainly not gonna open those darn tombs. Maybe I'm supposed to dig my way outta' here through a tunnel or something. She grinned. Priscilla was still somewhat oblivious to her precarious situation. Or was it that she was in denial? But she was more afraid of the dark and being boxed inside that dreary crypt than she was of any predator. Perhaps more importantly, she had yet to connect the dots between this Longworth fellow and the man who had shot and killed Jonathan, but not for too much longer.

Since Onslow knew she might have to hide in the crypt for an unknown period of time, he had suggested she occupy her mind by using the chalk that he had provided her with to tally the time and days. She used the hourglass to record the time of day as well as the days of the week; then she chalked tally marks on the wall accordingly. But sometimes she fell asleep and lost track of the time. Also, since there were no windows and her watch had gone missing, it soon dawned on her that she had no idea whether it was day or night. Overwrought, mostly because she lacked fresh air, she did not think of using the oxygen mask.

As once again she sifted through the various provisions, her thoughts drifted back to her wedding at First Church and to how everyone had said that would be the happiest day of her life. Instead, terrorism—there in her church! had turned that day into a horror show.

She thought about how sheltered she had been all her life. She remembered her loving father, Nelson, and how he had taught her to be strong and independent, while shielding her and her siblings from much of what she would eventually experience on her own, such as how mean-spirited some people could be. She thought about how, until Jonathan's death, the realities of terrorism had cast no shadows on her life.

As she settled down on the cold, dirty, debris-laden floor of the dark and dreary crypt, Priscilla remembered better times, that early last summer she had gone on what her family and friends called "a whirlwind vacation" to the Bahamas and Western Europe. She remembered that she and many other tourists had ignored the warnings from the U.S. Department of State and similar agencies around the world that advised citizens who traveled abroad "to do so with caution."

Stewing in the cathedral crypt, she recalled waiting on a Bahamian tarmac for three hours before takeoff to England. At the time, she had been vexed at the delay, not knowing or caring about the reason for it. Only later had she become aware that heightened security had been caused by Islamic militants hijacking a TWA jet en route from Athens to Rome. It was only after she had returned home safely from her Bahamian and European jaunt that she fully realized how plagued that year had been with international terrorism, beginning with a neo-fascist Italian group bombing a train as it traveled from Naples to Milan and later including kidnappings of academics and journalists in Beirut.

Priscilla sighed for her own lost innocence.

Stuck in this horrible crypt, she tried to take heart from the memory of her carefree European trip. After all, she told herself, she was only following Onslow's suggestion to keep up her spirits.

That year of her glorious Bahamian and European jaunt, Priscilla had been working so hard in her public relations business that she decided to treat herself to a much-needed vacation.

Her lips curled into a smile as she remembered the ups and downs of England, which were so different from home. Even the rooms in her sister Harriet's home were small by American standards; the miniature kitchen appliances seemed designed for doll houses. She and Harriet had made a day trip or two to London, where they had clamored atop a red double-decker bus and taken in the sights: Number Ten Downing Street, Buckingham Palace, old cathedrals, Big Ben, and palace guardsmen in tall, black, fluffy, plume-filled headgear. They had made a separate trip to tour Blenheim Palace outside London, and to a custom tailor's shop in the town of Leeds, where Priscilla had ordered a black wool cape with a gold jacquard silk lining that reminded her of something "Sherlock Holmes" might have worn. She had decided, however, that this might be perfect for back home. In Columbus, she mostly rode the bus and walked to her clients' offices. Her topcoat had to be stylish yet keep her warm and allow for ease of movement. The tailor said that he would make her a cape with "a classic understatement" and that he would finish it with a label that read, "Made exclusively for PJ Austin" and then "pop it in the mail so you will get it at home."

But not all of Priscilla's British experiences were, as the heroine of "My Fair Lady" once sang, "loverly." She had been especially shocked at experiencing racism in restaurants, pubs and shops. Priscilla's family tree, like that of many Blacks in America, included a racial mixing of Native Americans and whites. As a result, she and her sisters varied in complexion. Her sister Harriet wore a Nubian complexion, and Priscilla was pale, even though she was a tad darker than usual that summer because of her dedicated sunbathing in a West Indian sojourn with Julia just before she went to England.

But before they went to London for one of their day trips, Harriet had warned her sister of her previous experiences being denied service in restaurants and shops. "You'll be OK, Priscilla, because you're light-complexioned. But the British don't accept me, not at all. My natural color is black, and I mean black. There's no mistaking me as black. Sometimes when I go off the Air Force base at Croton, I have to present my military papers to get service. Otherwise, the shopkeepers ignore me outright."

Yet, for whatever reason, Priscilla had dismissed her sister's warnings. "But this is the mid-1980s. Surely the British aren't still racist? To boot, isn't part of your job here to protect the British from possible invasion, anyway?"

To Priscilla's distress, she discovered how right her sister was when they tried to have lunch in what looked like a quaint and atmospheric British pub. She led Harriet inside, but was stopped by the maître d' when they entered the restaurant part of the establishment.

"You may enter," he said to Priscilla. But then he pointed to Harriet and said, "But not her."

Harriet's eyes filled with tears. "I told you this would happen, Priscilla. I told you."

Priscilla yelled back at the maître d', "She's with me. If she can't come in, neither will I. Besides, she's my sister. She's my sister," she repeated. Never before in her life had Priscilla witnessed such blatant discrimination. Besides, how on Earth could she go in and sit down and eat and leave her sister outside?

Many of the other guests had already turned around in their seats to see about the commotion. Perhaps out of shock or fear that the Americans were intent on making a scene, the head waiter immediately relented and seated the sisters. But Harriet, as she wiped tears from her eyes, was not sure she wanted to stay. "You know, Priscilla, we don't have to eat here. We can go somewhere else."

But before Priscilla could respond, a young male waiter arrived at their booth. "Ladies, I apologize for any misunderstanding." Politely he asked to take their order.

Priscilla was as upset as Harriet, but she wanted her sister to experience one small victory in the war on race. Sure, they could have left that particular pub, but then no one there would have witnessed their being denied entry simply because of the color of their skin. Nor would those same people have witnessed how one Black American woman refused to accept mistreatment.

Life can be so interesting, Priscilla thought. *Here I am in England experiencing overt racism, of all things. Is this 1985 or what? How much longer, dear Lord, how much longer must we endure such foolishness?*

Suddenly she also understood something Senator Callahan had once said when she had expressed admiration for what she had said was "all things British." In the early 1970s, the senator had visited England as a member of a delegation of state lawmakers. Like Harriet, he had been denied entry to certain establishments and, as a result, had said he would never visit that country again.

She recalled, too, the particulars of how she had ignored specific warnings from Harriet.

"Listen to me," Harriet had said. "Life for me here is traumatic. On the Air Force base, all is well. But once I go out into the countryside around mostly white people, they openly discriminate against me. And that's just the way it is here!" Harriet, who had never been a weeper, had seemed about to cry. But she had wiped the tears from her eyes. "Well, it isn't different here. It's just as bad as and sometimes worse than back home in the States."

"Oh, Harriet," Priscilla had answered. "I didn't know it was like that. I'd just assumed since this was England, things were different. My goodness!"

Harriet had said more. "Don't you remember how it was at home when we were kids? We used to send you and Helen into certain restaurants to get us something to eat, because those ole white folks would cater to you two but not any of us in the family with darker skin. We were too black to be seen in their establishments."

At once Priscilla had been reminded, too, of how their father Nelson had felt when his Rotary associate, James Peterson, refused to enter their home.

Sitting at this disputed table in this London establishment, Priscilla realized it was one thing to experience the subtleties or intimidation because of one's race; it was something else to be denied outright. No matter how Priscilla hated to admit it, she understood that Harriet was right. *More often than not, society finds a way to accommodate people like me, but not like Harriet. How disgusting*, she thought. *How awfully disgusting.*

She patted her sister's hand. "We're staying," she said. But she remained puzzled about why she apparently was acceptable to that head waiter. "What the hell do they think I am?" she said to Harriet. "I don't even look white. Anyone can see that much."

"Oh, Priscilla, you're 'allowed' because of your looks. You're accepted, tolerated. These people are intrigued by you, but not someone who looks like me. I'm too black."

Priscilla sighed to herself, pained that her paler complexion had evidently made her less sensitive to some forms of racism than most other Black people. Even Senator Callahan had intimated as much to her one time when he said, "Don't let them make you think you're 'different' from the rest of us."

Ah, yes, Priscilla remembered all right. Sometimes she was slow getting the point, but that is how most people who are "allowed" to do something are; ergo, the expression, "the privilege of acceptance."

It was a hard lesson, and one she had never expected to learn on a vacation in England.

Paris was better, much better. Exquisite food and shopping, cafés where no one denied them seating, and monuments and palaces that took her breath away. Priscilla had arrived prepared to make her way with her high school and college French, along with a new credit card.

But although she did not encounter racism, the French did surprise her by being snobbish about dressing just right and not looking like what one hotel concierge said was "hippie riffraff."

The French, however, were sticklers about some rules, such as not turning up at the desk of a swanky hotel without a reservation.

She and Harriet had taken the boat-train to Paris and arrived looking, even Priscilla had to admit, a tad "disheveled." Harriet wore a black sweater and a matching skirt, which was considered an "acceptable" way of dressing. But she also wore her bizarre Doctor Seuss–striped leggings. Priscilla looked ready for combat in a brown leather jacket, jeans, and lace-up leather boots.

The two Americans stood at the desk of the Ritz-Carlton and asked for a room.

The supercilious clerk looked down his nose at them. But before long, the manager at another upscale hotel referred them to a nearby boardinghouse—or was it a hostel? —where the desk clerk welcomed them and, after looking them over, gave them tips about how to navigate the City of Light.

"If," the desk clerk said, "you plan to 'rough it,' as you Americans say, do not venture into the fine dining establishments, haute couture shops or the more reputable hotels. Otherwise, all other establishments will welcome you as you are."

Oops! Priscilla thought as she examined how she and Harriet were dressed. *We actually do resemble hippies and, yes, riffraff.*

Yet what followed were days of fun and enlightenment. They were mesmerized by the sight of and the ride up the Eiffel Tower. Priscilla wanted to take a boat ride on the Seine, but Harriet was not interested. Instead, they walked and walked and soaked in all the interesting architecture and statues. Since admission to the museums required tickets to be purchased in advance, which the sisters had not done, they continued to walk. Besides, even if they had tickets, they would have had to wait in extremely long queues for the opportunity to enter. As much as Priscilla wanted to tour a museum, she opted to nix the idea.

Eventually though, she turned to Harriet and said, "You know something, you really can't do Paris in a couple of days, can you?"

Shortly, they came upon an exquisite boutique with gorgeous clothes, handbags and shoes on display in the window.

"Oh, Harriet," Priscilla breathed. "I've got to go in there. Please! Let's go inside."

But Harriet was doubtful. "Now Priscilla, don't forget what the man at the boardinghouse told us. We must dress a certain way to go to some of these places. And we're not exactly dressed for fine dining or the haute couture shops."

"Let's at least check it out and see how they react to us."

As they walked into the small shop, the sales attendants turned around and smiled at them. "Bonjour, Mademoiselles."

Priscilla gave them her best smile. "Bon jour!"

"Americans, oui?"

"Oui, we're Americans," Priscilla said happily. She was thrilled that both she and Harriet were being welcomed so graciously. The sales attendants then walked over and asked, in fairly fluent English, how long they would be staying in Paris and what they were interested in purchasing. The attendants maintained friendly chat as they took the young women's measurements and then helped them to locate the type of garments they wanted.

"Everything!" Priscilla breathed.

As they moved about the small shop, Priscilla noticed immediately that the other customers, both male and female, disrobed and tried on garments right in the middle of the floor. Meanwhile, other shoppers, including men, moved about without apparently noticing the naked customers trying on clothes.

Priscilla's eyes widened, but she nodded. *Oh, so that's how they do it here.* Harriet chose instead to change her clothes in one of the small cubicles behind the curtains. But Priscilla undressed and tried on clothes right where she stood. She liked how uninhibited the French were about their bodies.

Priscilla laughed to herself at the memory of their return trip across the English Channel, a far different experience from their trip over. The huge ship tossed and turned, and rocked and bumped up against the stormy waves, made worse by torrential rain and wind. The ship rode against the current. With no relief in sight, Priscilla suggested that she and Harriet take up places near the bar, where a few other sick souls nestled together.

"Gin and tonic," she said, as if the phrase were understood. "And keep it coming until I pass out."

How the young women made it from the ferry back to Harriet and Judson's home is still a mystery, because Harriet was far from peak performance, and Priscilla—having not the foggiest idea where she was—was at the mercy of strangers for directions for their rail connection.

Back at Harriet's house, finally, Priscilla placed a transatlantic call to her mother. She had never gotten around to telling Liza about her plans for her European vacation. But she had written to Ellen about her trip, so she was not surprised that the news had leaked to her mom.

After listening to the highlights of the trip, Liza wasted no time criticizing Priscilla for taking such a risky vacation when there was so much terrorism going on. It was news to Priscilla that during her trip, the Frankfurt Rheine-Main Airport had been bombed. But even as absorbed as she had been with her trip, Priscilla had heard about the terrible crash of an Air India flight from Toronto over the North Atlantic, in which 329 passengers and crew members had been killed. She had not heard, however, that the Middle Eastern Black September terrorists claimed responsibility for an attack on the Madrid Airport.

"Girl, you take too many risks," Liza scolded her daughter. "And listen to me, Missy. One of these days, you'll be sorry. One of these days, I'm afraid you're going to learn more than you want to about terrorism."

Priscilla blinked hard. As she came back to reality, here in this dark and dreary crypt under the Anglican Cathedral in Harare, it occurred to her that her mother's warning could be considered as prophetic.

She stood back up and carefully paced the cold, debris-laden floor as she felt for familiar edges of the tombs and for familiar cracks and crevices in the walls, much like a visually impaired person would. Only now had she psyched herself into a more pleasant state of mind. Plus, she was no longer as afraid as she was earlier. But her memories about her "whirlwind vacation" had been the end of her most pleasant memories. *Now what?* she thought.

If she had only known that the ever-vigilant CF Lieutenant Onslow had stood watch over her from the bell tower of the cathedral in which she was stashed, she would not have felt so alone. But she did not know that.

18

Teeming at Hueston Woods Resort,
The Evildoer, and One of Our Own Kind

Onslow leaned carefully up against the rail inside the bell tower. He was content that he had secured the best possible hideout for Priscilla. But as he peered out onto the cathedral grounds, he worried about what the PG might do next. He figured that PG Commander Longworth had at least a dozen well-armed men at his disposal. He phoned his CF supervisor and requested backup forces:

"*Immediately,* like yesterday."

Onslow envisioned a likely encounter with the PG, not to mention their likelihood of discovering Priscilla's new hideout. Yet he was completely unaware of what the PG commander and his men had just done to the priest.

But CF Agent Jordan was in Gaborone, which was hundreds of miles away in Botswana.

"My God," Agent Jordan ranted, "it'll be tomorrow morning before we can get our guys up there. And that's *if* they can get a flight outta' here. Lusaka's closer. What'd Commander Wozniah say?"

"Haven't contacted those guys yet," Onslow responded calmly but firmly. "Anyway, was told before to go through proper channels, you fellas first, somethin' 'bout protocol and all."

"Alright, already." Perturbed, Agent Jordan snapped. "I'll call in your request for immediate backup. Meanwhile, Onslow, I'm still sending in reinforcements from my end. I'll be damned if I'm not covering my ass, and I mean that in every sense of the word."

Shortly, a conference call occurred among CF Commander Wozniah and Agent Bernhardt of the Lusaka-based unit and Agents Jordan, Delgato, and the manservant at Gaborone. After receiving a short but concise update on the situation at the Anglican Cathedral, the CF commander said, "Alright, folks, looks like anything that could go wrong has, and so we do what we must."

"We do what we must!" The voices reverberated back and forth over the secure phone lines.

Agent Jordan led his reinforcements to Harare, while the manservant stayed behind and continued to command the Gaborone unit. As for Agent Delgato, it was increasingly apparent that he needed to cultivate a relationship between the Executive Committee and the mine owners. Because he needed to solidify that relationship before the committee's impending demise, he made plans to fly to Johannesburg.

Halfway around the world in Ohio, PG Commander Leonard Genn and his dozen well-armed men finally experienced some success. He'd captured Julia at her home in Columbus and killed the two FBI agents who had been assigned to protect her. But despite his efforts to persuade Julia to cooperate, he did not get any information from her on the whereabouts of Senator Callahan.

And yet, after another final round of intense interrogation of her, Julia inadvertently revealed something that could be useful to him. Priscilla had reserved a place called Hueston Woods Lodge Resort and Conference Center in southwestern Ohio for her honeymoon.

Still somewhat frustrated, the PG commander reported to his Executive Committee supervisor: "They really must have the frigging senator at Fort Knox or something of the sort. So I'm going after the other targets."

Otherwise, Julia was not talking. Even PG Commander Genn had figured out that she detested him more than she feared him. But because he also knew Julia was an invaluable resource on all things PJ Austin, he kept her alive.

Therefore, he told her, "I'm taking you with me."

Off to Hueston Woods Lodge Resort and Conference Center, they drove.

By this point, CIA Agent Froley had teamed up with FBI Agent Rothschild. Why, even Columbus Police Detective Stoudemeir had been astute enough to know that what those guys were up against was well above his pay grade. Once Agents Froley and Rothschild realized they had lost Julia to the PG, they sped down the highway to Hueston Woods Lodge. "I always knew something like this could happen," Agent Rothschild said, "but I can only pray no harm comes to Julia." As it so happened, the two federal intelligence agents did not know about PG Commander Genn and that he had Julia with him and that they were also on their way to the Hueston Woods resort.

But PG Commander Genn and Julia were already there. The PG commander had stashed her in a motel, which, to his advantage, was situated off the beaten path. Then he'd headed over to the resort, where—after learning of Liza and Germane's safehouse—he immediately ordered his force of a dozen well-armed men to surveil and surround the place.

As he and his men conducted surveillance, the PG commander spotted young Germane playing alone outside one of the bungalows. But, for whatever reason, he decided to wait until dark before he would kill the young man. Meanwhile, he instructed his men to kill the security detail guarding the site and then to surround it until they received his signal to attack.

Then, just as the two federal intelligence agents arrived, they couldn't help but notice the absence of any visible protective detail for Liza and Germane.

"Surely both those guys aren't in the men's room or eating," Agent Rothschild said.

"Damn it, man, they're dead. Let's get inside. They must have us under surveillance, you know." Agent Froley left the obvious unspoken: Liza and Germane were absolutely vulnerable, but they probably did not even know it.

Inside their bungalow, Liza and Germane had already settled in for the night. They had relaxed their state of readiness and pretty much forgotten about the severity of their situation. But when the two federal intelligence agents knocked on their door, their senses of awareness heightened again.

"Oh, Grandma!" The boy's eyes widened with sudden fear. "I almost forgot. Who do you think—"

"Who's there?" Liza asked in a soft voice.

"Open the door, Liza. It's us. Marvin Rothschild and Jim Froley."

Swiftly Liza unlatched the door and let them in.

Then, after introducing CIA Agent Froley, Agent Rothschild talked fast, very fast. It was then that Liza grasped the gravity of her precarious situation, for she knew that C-I-A meant criminal activity of the highest order. However, Germane was laughing. He could not help noticing how much the CIA agent resembled "Lieutenant Colombo." Realizing what her grandson was thinking, Liza quickly covered his mouth and said, "Behave yourself, young man."

Germane shuffled his feet and said, "Sorry about that, Grandma."

But then, Agent Rothschild's next statements further frightened them.

"We're sorry, but we're going to have to relocate you *immediately*. Some things have been happening, and we don't think you're safe here anymore."

From a high knoll a few hundred feet from Liza and Germane's suite, PG Commander Genn had watched through his telescopic lenses as the two federal agents pulled up, knocked on Liza's bungalow door, and quickly disappeared inside. It was then that he decided to make his presence known. *Time!* Raising his repeating rifle, he aimed it carefully and, pulling the trigger, shot through the window of Liza's bedroom. Then he signaled to his team to shoot likewise. The *pop, pop, pop* sounds rattled the walls of the bungalow.

The guests in the adjoining bungalows heard the gunfire and scrambled for cover.

Throughout the gunfire, Agent Froley yelled, "Everybody, down on the floor. Take cover." Then, he pushed Liza and Germane to the floor and crouched down in front of them.

As Agent Rothschild began to shove furniture up against the doors and the windows, unexpectedly, Germane crawled over to him and said, "Don't get me wrong, man, I'm scared. But this is kinda' fun, don't you think so?"

"Oh, Germane!" Liza fretted over the speed at which the youngster had escaped the safety of her arms. Agent Froley was likewise fretting, for the boy had moved so quickly.

As Germane helped to push and shove the furniture, Agent Rothschild slapped the youngster's shoulder and said, "Welcome to the real deal, mate. Good to know I've got another pair of hands."

After Germane performed his manly role, he cuddled back up to his grandmother, behind Agent Froley on the floor.

Liza prayed openly:

"Dear God, please stay with us and protect us all from hurt and harm. And grant Thy great wisdom on these men who've come to help us. Be with us all in Thy son Jesus' name, we pray."

"But Grandma," Germane said in an admonishing tone, "didn't you forget to say, 'Forgive us for our sins and wrongdoing?'"

Liza nodded at the correction. He was her grandson, all right. "I said all that and more, in silence."

Then, alternately, Agent Rothschild—although he was Jewish—and Agent Froley and young Germane said, "Amen," "Amen," and "Amen."

The federal agents knew that whoever was outside shooting at them was not alone. But they did not know that the first battle between the CF and the PG had just gotten underway and that it was happening in the quaint community of College Corner, Ohio, in the American Midwest, not in southern Africa.

PG Commander Genn and his men surrounded the bungalow in which their victims were holed up.

Inside the bungalow, Agent Froley took out his cell phone and placed a call for backup from "all forces."

"Yeah, Frank, I need you to trigger some backup here in Hueston Woods."

Agent Rothschild turned to face him. "What exactly does that mean?"

"First," Agent Froley said, "the highway patrol will whisk through here and conduct a routine check of the premises. Shortly behind them, FBI and local SWAT teams will move onto the periphery of the grounds as if they're putting out a wildfire. And then helicopters will swarm about like nagging bees. That's what 'that' means."

Awestruck. "Wow!" Germane uttered.

"And the catch?" Agent Rothschild asked.

"We've got to keep the bad guys at bay. Their presence on the inside will only complicate things. That's 'the catch.' Now stop asking me questions I don't have answers to." Then, over his shoulder, he gave a rare wink of acknowledgment to Germane.

Agent Froley had tried to shed some relief and comfort on the situation by contriving that scenario, something straight out of Hollywood. But he really did call the CIA headquarters, and someone from the Langley office really did contact the FBI. And since the FBI had already sustained four losses, its agents would come to the Hueston Woods resort with a vengeance. Yet Agent Froley was keenly aware that the PG possessed capabilities comparable to those of a small army. He knew that the PG, including the heretofore unnamed PG Commander Leonard Genn and his cohorts, were equipped with enough artillery and advanced technological devices, the likes of which even the CIA would be surprised to discover. The days of *The Rifleman, Rat Patrol, The Godfather,* and make-believe action heroes had become passé. The age of the PG had arrived: biological and chemical warfare, nuclear weaponry, thermo-laser beams, drones, and smart missiles.

While the PG were attacking the Hueston Woods Lodge in Ohio, back in Harare, shortly before the ambulance arrived at the Anglican Cathedral there, Father Mbuwayesango convinced one of the young girls to persuade Camilla to return.

"Tell Camilla," he instructed the girl he had chosen as a messenger, "this is her opportunity to show leadership."

At first, when the young messenger arrived at Camilla's room, she had difficulty persuading her. Still, before long, Camilla eventually came out of her room, which she knew had been against the advice of her father.

Like the general she had trained to be, she stood boldly over the priest's pulsating, badly mutilated, bloody body. The blood—it seemed to Camilla to be everywhere. She calmed herself. She had been trained in how to respond to an emergency like this.

Bleeding and panting, the priest peered into her eyes and said, "This is real, Camilla. This is not a test. Megan is the evildoer, and it is your duty to destroy her."

At that moment, the medics arrived outside the boarding school building. But the other girls, having assumed their roles as obedient soldiers, diverted their attention. Instead of leading them to the priest's suite, they sent the medics to the girls' sleeping quarters at the opposite end of the compound.

The priest, meanwhile, continued trying to enlist Camilla's help: "Now you may call upon any one of the other girls you deem fit to fulfill this task, but you must choose wisely and quickly."

All the while, Camilla stood at attention and listened to her orders.

Next, the priest described the secret passages leading to the dungeon in the cathedral. Then he added, "I believe Megan is hiding out in the crypt."

Jacob Mbuwayesango had been playing a double game. But with these words, he made his final choice. He chose to fulfill his role as lord and master of the Judges.

He pointed to the chiffonier: "There on the top is a small box."

Camilla pushed a chair up against the chest, stood up on it and felt for the box. She stepped back down and opened it. There were four vials in it.

"Open one and pour it in my mouth."

Camilla briefly stared into his eyes. Then she did what her lord and master had instructed.

Jacob Mbuwayesango swallowed the toxic substance, slumped over in the chair at the small table—where he had just been mutilated—and died, very quickly.

Camilla replaced the empty vial back in the box and took the box with her back to her room, where she resumed waiting patiently for her father to come.

The medics finally reached the headmaster's room and found his bloody, mutilated remains slumped over in a chair at the small table, dead. They called the Harare Police. When the police arrived, even they could not fathom the horrific mutilation and death of the priest.

"But why'd those girls act like they didn't know which room the priest was in?" one of the Harare policemen said to his colleagues. "Obviously, they diverted the attention of the medics for a reason."

Since the headmaster apparently had been killed under suspicious circumstances and the only other boarding school staff were the instructors, the librarian, the kitchen crew, and several matrons, the Harare Police called headquarters and requested protective details for the schoolchildren. They also ordered that the priest's remains be transported to the coroner, "pending further investigation."

Outside the boarding school building, just as they were about to disperse from the sidewalk leading to the Anglican Cathedral, three roughshod men— PG Commander Alistair Longworth and two accomplices—watched in utter amazement at the sight of the arrival of the medical examiner, followed by the Harare Police. Then, moments later, they watched as the medical examiner and the Harare Police removed the priest's remains. But they did wonder who had killed the man—it had all happened so quickly.

PG Commander Longworth did not know about the services of the Anglican Cathedral as a charm school. He had been led to believe, "This is a boarding school for the mixed-blood children of some prominent whites." But Moses Cameron knew about the real role of the school; he was the grandson of a charter member of the Executive Committee, and his father had been privy to the establishment of the secret society of the Judges. Not only that, but Moses was a leader; he gave orders. Alistair was a soldier; he took orders. Also, PG Commander Longworth did not know Moses Cameron. Nor did he know of Moses's involvement in the pursuit of the American, PJ Austin, so PG Commander Longworth could only speculate that the CF was somehow involved. If he speculated correctly, and he believed that he did, PG Commander Longworth and his men stood in plain sight of the enemy. Still, he called his supervisor and reported the events of the day.

Hans was terse: "Retreat and regroup. Do as I say, man."

"But, Boss," PG Commander Longworth argued, "we're fairly certain the American is inside the cathedral."

"And she might very well be. But has it occurred to you that the CF is using her to fish us out? Retreat, I tell you." Hans hung up his telephone.

Not long afterwards, Hans and his colleagues were summoned to an emergency meeting of the SANM Executive Committee.

The atmosphere was tense.

Simeon fumed that Moses Cameron had left the Executive Committee to return to his role on the PG—an inexcusable act. No one was permitted to step down from the Executive Committee to return to field operations. And since Moses was the only case of a PG to have been so elevated, that scenario did not have a promising end. "We SANM Executive Committee members," Simeon explained, "possess too much vital information." If one of them were to be captured, or if heaven forbid, one of them defected or became an informant for the other side, at risk was the security of villainous secrets, including the financial affairs of one of the largest, notoriously operating conglomerates the world over.

At once, the other members were as furious with Moses as was Simeon.

"My God, we've never issued a kill order on one of our own kind," said Hans.

"What could possibly be so important that a man would give his life for something like that?" Joseph openly queried. For they'd all heard Moses boast about returning to the field, but no one had taken him seriously.

"This is an awful turn of events, just awful," Simeon said. "Let's wait for confirmation that he's actually made his move. Then Heinreik, you can—"

"Simeon," Heinreik interrupted him, noting, "I've already checked all that, and yes, there's plenty of movement in Moses's finances, plenty indeed."

After that unwelcome report, Simeon buried his head in his hands and sat at the head of the conference table for a moment longer in utter disbelief. Plainly, he knew what had to come next, but he did not want to confront the matter. *Why during my reign? Why me?*

"But Simeon, how will you handle the eventual hit?" Joseph asked. Then he reconsidered. "Come to think of it, I really don't want to know."

"Sorry," Dawker Simpson interjected himself with all the vigor of a marksman waiting for the signal to shoot his target. "But the rules are clear. Whenever there's reason to believe an Executive Committee member has violated the code of conduct, steps must be put into place to correct the situation. So the question before us, Mr. Chairman," he emphasized, looking directly at Simeon, "is which one of us will order the hit?"

Simeon glared at Dawker and spoke with much consternation in his voice. "And since you've given such logical forethought to the matter, Dawker, what answer have you come up with? Pray, tell us all, here and now?"

Dawker was the only committee member who did not automatically bend and bow with each and every word spoken by Simeon. So he continued his matter-of-fact explanation: "Well, Mr. Chairman, the rules also state, 'If an order is already in effect that directly relates to the issue in question, then the respective super—'"

This time, it was Hans who interrupted him, "Oh, shut up, Dawker," with even more contempt for him than Simeon. "I don't want to be the one issuing the order to take out one of our own kind."

After decades of association, some of the thirteen men had grown close, like family members.

Relentlessly, Dawker concluded with a certain degree of eloquence. "And since Moses has already imposed himself in an ongoing operation, that is, one in which Hans has already been charged, then it falls to Hans to designate the Guardsman to execute the order."

One by one, each Executive Committee member turned his shot glass upside down. That was a heartrending decision to make. But, after all, it was business.

Simeon was the last to turn his shot glass upside down. His eyes met Han's. "Done," he said. "So… Have we completed the order of business?"

"Done," someone else said, and the business of the emergency meeting of the SANM Executive Committee concluded.

They nodded as one and hurriedly stood to leave.

But Simeon lingered at the conference table a moment longer, deep in thought, he was. *This bad business all started with that Ohio senator as the sole target. But now it has mushroomed to unacceptable proportions: PJ Austin, her friend, her nephew and now, one of our own kind. Who would've thought?*

Simeon stayed where he was because another meeting followed the emergency meeting, the so-called meeting after the meeting.

19

Raid at Hueston Woods Lodge, Enter the Decoys, and Then Some

News agencies around the world issued sensational breaking news. The most poignant came from the *BBC* in Harare. A reporter stood in front of the Anglican Cathedral as the cameraman panned its entirety. He said:

> Today, sources here in the capital city of Harare say the local police have confirmed a strange incident involving the horrible mutilation and death of a priest affiliated with the Anglican Diocese of Harare. His thumbs and big toes were severed. A preliminary test performed by the medical examiner reveals that the priest, Father Jacob Mbuwayesango, ingested poison, although it is not yet known how it was done—or by whom.
>
> In an even stranger report, sources for the *BBC* say that nearly fifty female school-aged children, ranging from puberty to their late teens, may have

knowledge about the nature of the crime. But the young women are not talking.

Odder still is that nearly all the young women are what the Zimbabwean authorities deem to be 'unwanted.' That means, we are told, the girls are the children of mostly Southern Rhodesians and Afrikaner fathers and Zimbabwean and South African mothers, and some may even have been fathered by white men from other African nations.

The *BBC* has also learned from a member of the staff here at the cathedral, who wishes to remain anonymous, that the American, Priscilla J. 'PJ' Austin, abducted from Ohio recently on what was to have been her wedding day, 'worked here briefly as a housekeeper.' The staffer said, 'At least she did up to the day before the priest was killed.' Until this alleged sighting, the whereabouts of PJ Austin had all but eluded the authorities. But it now appears as if they have a new lead here in Harare, Zimbabwe.

Similar news stories were reported in Lusaka, Gaborone, Johannesburg, and major media outlets in Western Europe and North America.

But in Columbus, Ohio, what was bigger news was violence and killing closer to home, where the *CBS affiliate, WBTV*, broadcast the following news:

Sources close to *CBS News* report the FBI is on full alert after four of its field operatives were shot and killed. Two of the agents had been performing protective detail for the friend of the missing PR executive, PJ Austin, in the as-yet-unsolved case of the missing bride. The friend's name is being withheld, pending further confirmation. But sources confirm that the friend was Ms. Austin's maid of honor during her ill-fated wedding in which the groom, the Reverend Jonathan Morgan, was shot and killed in the assassin's foiled attempt to kill Ohio state Senator Daniel P. Callahan, who himself is still clinging to life. The whereabouts of Senator Callahan and the friend are still unknown, but it is believed that they may be in protective custody. Sources do, however, believe that the men who killed the two FBI agents in Columbus also abducted Ms. Austin's friend.

Two other FBI agents who provided a protective detail for Ms. Austin's nephew and mother were shot and killed at the exclusive Hueston Woods Lodge Resort and Conference Center in the quaint community of College Corner in southwestern Ohio, the heart of America's breadbasket.

CBS News has also been informed that the FBI and the CIA have scheduled a joint press conference for tomorrow morning. It is believed that they will address the possible involvement by the South African Nationalists Movement's Patrol Guard— also known as the SANM PG—in these seemingly related killings and abductions. The Patrol Guard is believed to be directly connected to the diamond, gold and platinum conglomerate of the SANM itself.

Meanwhile, there are unconfirmed reports of Ms. Austin being held by persons unknown in the vicinity of an Anglican cathedral in Harare, Zimbabwe, where she has reportedly been posing as a housekeeper.

We will have more on this breaking news story in a moment. Stay tuned to *WBTV-News*.

Meanwhile, in Harare, international news correspondents scrambled to stake out their space on the grounds of the Anglican Cathedral, as well as their space on the grounds of the opulent headquarters of the SANM Executive Committee in Johannesburg.

At the time of the breaking news, the quaint community of College Corner, Ohio, was turning into a war zone.

Germane, Liza and the two federal intelligence agents were pinned down in their once luxurious Hueston Woods Lodge Resort bungalow.

Reporters in search of that day's top story drove onto the grounds of the resort and met with rapid gunfire.

PG Commander Leonard Genn and his squadron had misjudged the situation. They believed that the media representatives were CF mercenaries disguised as reporters.

Several broadcast units had already set up their satellites and begun filming the periphery of the area, so they kept their cameras rolling even after it was apparent they had driven into gunfire.

From inside their bungalow, Liza, Germane, CIA Agent Froley, and FBI Agent Rothschild had no idea of the turn of events.

"What happened? Why'd they stop shooting at us?" Agent Froley asked.

But it was Agent Rothschild who figured it out. "Didn't the gunfire seem to change course? If I'm right, those guys have targets other than us." At that, Agent Rothschild dared to peek out of a crack in the pile of furniture covering one of the windows.

"My God, man, there are what look like news vans and trucks all over the place. Oh, no! Some of them are down! Shot!"

This time both men pulled out their cell phones and called their respective offices. Each man's message echoed the other.

"Why the hell," Agent Rothschild was saying in despair, "did you guys come in disguised as news reporters?"

"Yes, Frank, it's me again," Agent Froley said in similar despair. Then he shouted. "Why the hell did you guys come in disguised as news reporters? Some of them have been killed already."

Just as Frank cleared up the discrepancy in Agent Froley's take on the situation, that is, told him those were real news reporters taking actual gunfire, the Earth shook from beneath their bungalow.

"Damn it, Frank, someone just detonated a frigging bomb under us!" Agent Froley screamed. "Or was that an earthquake? Damn it, man, what the shit's happening?"

His cell phone went dead.

Then, "No! Oh, no! Not now!" Agent Rothschild hollered. "What the hell do ya mean, 'no service?'"

Suddenly, both federal agents looked at Liza and Germane. They shook their heads. "Sorry," Agent Rothschild said, "but we haven't the foggiest idea what that tremor was, and we don't know what's going on the outside, either."

"Outside," PG Commander Genn was struggling against the ever-changing odds to summon his team into retreat mode. He suddenly realized that those men and women who had poured out of those news trucks, looking and acting like real news reporters and photographers, really were "real" news reporters and photographers. But he and his men had already shot and killed at least three of them.

Emboldened by the murder of their colleagues, several other cameramen had jumped out of their vehicles and begun taping images of the Patrol Guardsmen as they scattered hurriedly back into the surrounding woods.

Unfortunately for the PG, however, people the world over had seen them: Commander Genn and his men had been captured on tape—live and in action.

An instant later, Ohio Highway Patrol cruisers advanced across the manicured slopes of the resort. Their sirens wailed. FBI SWATs followed. Like clockwork, they invaded the grounds and opened fire on the PG as they continued fleeing into the wooded grounds opposite the beautiful lake of the resort. Helicopters swarmed overhead and made loud, nagging sounds like swarming bees. Their spotlights ruined the cover of the fleeing PG. Agent Froley's account did, in fact, unfold Hollywood-style.

Liza, Germane, Agent Froley, and Agent Rothschild suddenly experienced a second explosion; a bomb had indeed detonated in the suite next to Liza's— the one in which Germane was believed to have been asleep. The youngster's room had just blown fifteen feet into the ground and an equal distance in the air, which they all saw for themselves because a portion of the wall that once connected to Liza's suite had just blown away with it.

Liza screamed. Germane did, too. Agent Froley turned beet-red but strengthened his hold on his two wards. "What the bloody—"

"Those bastards," Agent Rothschild cut him off as suddenly he realized what had just happened to Germane's room. "They meant to kill that little kid. And they almost succeeded."

So intent were the PG to exterminate Liza and her grandson that they had planted two bombs, one under each of their cabins. But the one under Germane's cabin had been the more effective.

As the battle raged, PG Commander Genn and his comrades fought hard against what had become overwhelming odds. They threw grenades, destroying some of the cruisers and killing three of the Ohio Highway Patrolmen. They also injured several of the FBI SWAT members as they chased them into the woods. Then, a PG raised his missile launcher and shot down an FBI helicopter. But the aircraft crashed into the woods, onto one of his fellow Guardsmen, creating a horrific scene. The weight of the helicopter crushed much of the man, and flames engulfed him; yet his wild screams indicated that he was still alive. Suppressed by what sounded like swarming bees overhead, the man's pleas for death went unheeded. Soon, the PG commander and his men were weaving deeper into the refuge of the dense forest. Still, thermo-laser beams enabled the federal troops to locate them, and when they did, they shot and disabled them, like fenced-in silly rabbits scurrying about.

After that, the rescuers began plowing through the debris of what remained of Liza and Germane's bungalow and mounted a gangplank for the survivors to make their way outside.

As darkness overlaid the scene, television cameras provided lights for the rescuers and the hostages to see.

Germane—half-jubilant and half-frightened—paced back and forth in the rubble of what remained of their suite.

"Oh, Grandma," he screamed, wiping the running mucous from his nose, "if they're doing this to us, what're they doing to Aunt Priscilla?"

It was Agent Rothschild who comforted the little boy. "Son, we have every reason to believe your Aunt Priscilla is fine and she'll be with you and your grandmother soon. But until then, she needs you to be strong and have faith. Grandma Liza has faith; she believes, and so, too, must you."

With each word the agent spoke, Germane swallowed his tears and seemed even visibly to grow stronger. The FBI agent had spoken in terms the youngster had understood. As he continued to hold the boy, Agent Rothschild felt tears forming in his own eyes. But he managed to hold them off; the boy had gotten under his skin. He truly wanted Germane to live to become the man that he knew he could be.

Just then, several members of the FBI SWAT gave the "all clear" signal, bungalow by bungalow. They also continued checking the perimeter for any casualties and wounded.

Almost simultaneously, a thunderous, bellowing sound came from above. "All clear from up here. 'Charlie that' for casualties and wounded."

Agents Froley and Rothschild looked silently at each other, disturbed at what the man had not said. *What about Julia?* But they waited anyway until the rescue team produced its final report. Nine PG were dead. Three survivors were captured, including PG Commander Leonard Genn. (Genn had led the SANM's American Mission, whereas Longworth commanded the African Mission, something that would come to light later.)

Then the two federal agents watched as PG Commander Genn, whose nostrils flared and his milky white skin juxtaposed against his flaming red hair, was shackled and frog-marched into the back of a squad vehicle.

"Too bad you didn't pop your little pill, my man," an FBI agent who shackled him said. It is more than a myth that secret agents, special operatives, and mercenaries carry cyanide capsules. Under the apparent circumstances, even PG Commander Genn understood the implications of the federal agent's remark. He had much to answer for, and he suspected life imprisonment or death would be the consequence of his life and his actions.

As it turned out, CIA Agent Froley and FBI Agent Rothschild were not the only ones watching as Genn and his comrades were captured and driven off to meet their fate. Every face, every gesture, and indeed even word was recorded and broadcast live by the news media.

"Brilliant," one reporter boasted to another.

"Every television in the country... maybe even the world, is riveted to this by now," offered a cameraman.

Guests from neighboring bungalows were also part of the crowd.

"Who can even imagine something like this happening here in America, at a luxury vacation resort," said one guest, shaking his head in disbelief.

"We could have been killed," said another guest.

But then each of the people who had just spoken fell silent when an elderly man, also a guest at the resort, said what they all had been thinking but dared not say: "This is utter madness; besides, what could that young woman (meaning Priscilla) possibly have done to wreak such vengeance?"

As the raid at the superb Hueston Woods Resort in the quaint community of College Corner, Ohio, in the American Midwest happened, Americans were astounded as the horrific events unfolded on their television screens in their living rooms and kitchens in real time.

Not far away, in the Midway Motel, Julia was watching the raid at the Hueston Woods Lodge Resort as it unfolded on the television set in her room.

Tears streamed down her cheeks as she watched in bewilderment the devastation at the lodge. She did not know who had been holed up in protective custody there: Liza and Germane, or even Priscilla. She shuddered at the devastation surrounding the abduction of her friend. And the news coverage did not make clear that the man who had mistreated her and who had brought her to this motel to die had himself been captured and taken into custody.

She did, however, have the presence of mind to be glad that PG Commander Genn had, at least, left the television on with the volume turned up as high as it would go when he left her. She supposed all he had cared about was muffling any of her moans, but without it, she would not have known what was happening.

Since the PG commander had covered her mouth to prevent her from calling out for help, all Julia could do was sit in bondage on the edge of her bed and weep. Or so she thought.

It would take her more than a moment to realize that her circumstances had changed for the better and that she could let someone know that she was alive at a motel not far from the resort. But the PG commander had threatened her so much that she feared doing much more than breathing and watching television. *In a minute*, she kept saying to herself, *in a minute*, to convince herself that she really could liberate herself without his permission.

Then, there before her very eyes on television was a live image of PG Commander Leonard Genn. He appeared to have sustained a gunshot wound to his shoulder. Even though he was grungy and had smudges on his face, she had no problem recognizing his milky white face and flaming red hair.

Julia tried to shout out through the cloth over her mouth. "That's him, all right. But the bastard's still alive."

She felt some relief seeing him surrounded by what appeared to be an army. She also realized, as if for the first time, *This is a big deal, serious stuff.*

Just as Priscilla was learning in Harare, Julia was also recognizing that terrorism was not confined to "those other countries." In fact, terrorism had come to roost in America, and the two friends were now caught up in its web.

The television news was now showing CIA Agent Froley and FBI Agent Rothschild walking out of the section of the lodge—where Germane's suite had been blown to bits and pieces, and where the connecting wall to Liza's suite had been blown to bits and pieces, as well—onto the gangplank in front of the cameras.

First, Julia heard Agent Froley making a short statement about what had just happened inside what remained of their bungalow. She flinched.

Then, she heard Agent Rothschild ask the news reporters to allow them a point of privilege, saying, "We'd like to bring out the brave young nephew and the mother of PJ Austin *incognito* because of the ongoing search for Ms. Austin and her friend." At that, she learned that Priscilla was not with them.

But then, the next thing she knew, she was mumbling behind the cloth covering her mouth. "Me!" Inside her gagged mouth, Julia was screaming. "But I'm 'her friend,' and I'm over here, right down the road from you! And, by golly, I'm alive!" Julia was trying so hard to be heard from behind the cloth that covered her mouth. "I'm alive!"

Back at the lodge, Agent Rothschild continued his special request of the reporters: "Please allow their safe and unimpeded passage. Afterwards, my colleague and I will try to answer your questions from our perspective, which, as you can see, is slightly different from yours."

The crowd of reporters backed up, and even though Liza and Germane's faces were covered, the crowd cheered and applauded as the two federal agents escorted them slowly down the gangplank. Equally impressive, although he could not see the faces of the reporters, Germane was so ingratiated that he stretched out his little arm from underneath the blanket that concealed him and waved. Then he and Liza were led to a police vehicle and driven away.

From the motel nearby, Julia welled up and continued weeping at the sight of Liza and Germane walking across the gangplank. She welled up, especially at the sight of Germane's little hand waving to the crowd. *They're alive! They're alive!*

The next thing Julia knew, she was rolling off the bed, and then, inch by inch, she began crawling feverishly over to the door. Tirelessly, she began kicking it. She had regained her will to live. She wanted to be rescued, so she kicked and kicked the door until someone eventually heard her. Soon, the manager came and unlocked the door, but Julia kept kicking. She needed to know she was really alive and safe, not dreaming, and that it was actually someone other than PG Commander Leonard Genn who was touching her.

After the motel manager's frantic call to the local police, sirens swirled in the vicinity of the motel. Already on high alert, the authorities were shocked to learn about another hostage in the area. So they quickly reported the incident, which was picked up by the local media.

When news of the incident at the Midway Motel reached the reporters at the Hueston Woods Lodge Resort, they, too, were astonished. One of them yelled out, "Excuse me, Agents Froley and Rothschild. You're not going to believe this, but another of the abductees, Ms. Austin's friend, whose name has been withheld for obvious reasons, has been rescued by local police over at the Midway Motel. Any comments?"

"Only that you might want to head over there yourselves and pick up that story firsthand," Agent Rothschild said. "My colleague and I need to report back to headquarters. And if we haven't already said so, God bless you one and all for your presence, without which there most probably would have been more casualties. And yes, God bless the families of all those fallen news reporters and cameramen who took bullets simply because they were doing their jobs." Agent Rothschild choked up with his last words. "Bless you all."

"Good PR, Marvin," Agent Froley said. "You're pretty darn good under pressure."

"No," Agent Rothschild answered. "Just too damn scared not to be thankful. That's all. Wanna run over with the others to check on Miss Julia?"

Nescient about what had just happened in Ohio to those she held most dear, a disheartened Priscilla lifted her voice in song inside the crypt at the Anglican Cathedral in Harare. Quietly, she refused to utter any words until she'd gained more courage. But there inside that dreary dungeon of the Anglican Cathedral in the heart of southern Africa, the daughter of a Methodist minister from America remembered who and whose she was.

She sang with all the force of her faith:

> O come, O come Emmanuel,
> and ransom captive Israel,
> that mourns in lonely exile here
> until the Son of God appear.
>
> Rejoice! Rejoice!
> Emmanuel shall come to thee, O Israel.

That it was nearly August 1986, not December, did not seem relevant to Priscilla. She sang the words that fitted her particular situation. She felt exiled from her home, her family, and her friends, and she felt as if the only way out was with the help of God. She wanted and needed to demonstrate her faith and her belief that she would be rescued, so she sang her hymn as her prayer to God.

Because CF Agent Jordan had told Onslow and his men about what had happened in Ohio, they knew that PG Commander Longworth and his men would retaliate with vengeance. They anticipated that the PG commander and his men would try to enter the cathedral sometime the next day, perhaps disguised as priests or maybe even as news correspondents.

Therefore, that night, Onslow and his entourage—five additional men and one of the PJ doubles—took up their stations in and around the cathedral.

The other CF forces—dispersed throughout the southern part of Africa—had also been apprised of the happenings in Ohio and made sure that their contingents were kept abreast of the good news as well.

As the Lusaka-based CF unit neared Zimbabwe, he sat proudly in the passenger's seat, as an army general poised for battle. CF Agent Carlton Elliott Bernhardt was no longer in the same military jeep with his friend and associate Tommy Wozniah but instead had teamed up with one of the three PJ Austin doubles. His driver, one of the PJ decoys, handled her vehicle as masterfully as any man. She shifted its many gears and dodged animal carcasses, tree branches, potholes, and other debris as she drove across the rugged terrain. When the jeep became stuck in mud, she jumped out and wedged whatever was at hand underneath the tires, enabling the vehicle to get traction and continue on its way. And she was an expert sharpshooter, too.

Each of the three PJ Austin look–alikes (decoys or doubles) was embedded within each of the three respective CF units. "We do what we must" was code for the teams to "bring out the PJ Austin doubles." As soon as that code had been sounded, each unit's leader had indeed brought one to the fore.

CF Agent Bernhardt watched his driver rev the engine and speed ahead. Like every special operative, these doubles—specially trained for this mission—knowingly put their lives in harm's way. They held several passports, credit cards, and, of course, a Swiss bank account, and they spoke several languages fluently. They performed their jobs with much care and pride, and should this one survive whatever was to happen here in southern Africa, doubtless she would return to the calm and serenity of her other life. Such work was not for the faint of heart. On the other hand, however, unlike the *James Bond* character, the CF special ops tended to live relatively subdued lifestyles.

"You know, Girlfriend," Carlton said to his driver, "Missy can be a bit of a snob, but mostly she's unassuming. She can enter a crowded room and ignore everybody there, save for the person she seeks. And if someone flatters her, she gives dead aim through her eye contact that the person's really serving up a pile o' shit, or as she often says, 'is blowing smoke up her skirt.'"

"I sound like an interesting woman."

"She—or do I mean you—is, indeed." Carlton grinned, but his mind continued to drift. He needed to share with this particular double as much about the real Priscilla as possible because she, more than the other doubles, needed to become Priscilla. They were en route to Johannesburg, where this particular double would be expected to play out her role to perfection. However, she might get her first chance to play Priscilla in Harare, where the other two look–alikes were either on their way there or had already arrived.

But as the Lusaka-based CF unit neared Harare, they were suddenly ambushed by the PG. Unlike Simeon and the other men on the Executive Committee, the priest had known enough about the so-called international military deployment to recognize it was more than sheer coincidence that its impending arrival had coincided with the arrival of the American PJ Austin and the many other unexpected guests at the cathedral boarding school. Father Mbuwayesango had not been a double agent for naught.

The PG, on the other hand, had not taken the warnings of the priest as seriously as they should have. They miscalculated the immense magnitude of the CF. It was the PG's own fault that they had sent a meager force of only thirty men for this particular raid.

Nonetheless, unexpectedly, CF Commander Wozniah, who rode at the very front of the caravan, and Agent Bernhardt and the PJ double, who rode a couple of jeeps behind the commander, were taken completely by surprise by the skirmish. The thirty PG snuck up on their caravan. With tremendous force, the PG destroyed two of their tanks and three supply trucks. But the CF quickly put down their attackers, after which, instead of killing them, the CF commander kept them alive "… for interrogation later. Never can tell. Everybody knows something," he said to his men as they escorted their quarry away.

Then the Lusaka-based CF unit continued on its trek to Harare with even more vigor for the possibility of another attack along the way.

At the same time as the CF's northern forces traveled down into Harare, their companion forces traveled up toward Harare from the south. The Gaborone-based CF unit, led by CF Agent Jordan, entered the vicinity of the capital first, and without incident.

The sensational news about the mutilation and death of the Anglican priest, together with the bulletins about the raid at the Ohio resort, permeated the airwaves. Local inhabitants lined the city streets in droves and cheered what they believed was an international military unit that had come to provide them with added security.

By the time PG Commander Longworth and his men got word that the so-called "international military unit" had arrived, they had already decided to enter the cathedral—against the orders of his supervisor, Hans Evekink. Aware that their enemies had the superior force of numbers, they had also prepared for the increased probability of their impending deaths.

But unbeknownst to PG Commander Longworth, Moses Cameron also had summoned some troops of his own. Although he had long since retired from the force, he still maintained reliable connections. Moses had put his own plan into action and called up several mercenaries who had been on alert for just such a command. The Cameron forces planned to arrive at the diocese in Harare in advance of the Gaborone-based CF reinforcements.

But as the CF reinforcements neared Harare, they still had not taken into account the actual whereabouts of the real PJ Austin. They merely assumed that Onslow and his substitute entourage had tucked her away securely. Nor did the CF appreciate the ambitious Moses Cameron.

And none of them—except possibly Moses Cameron—were taking into account any possible action by the young women at the cathedral boarding school. Both the CF and the PG still believed that the young women were merely teenage girls in a boarding school.

But both sides had taken into account the battery of international news correspondents on the grounds of the cathedral and had therefore planted some of their comrades among their ranks.

Yet each of these factions would be forced to hold off awhile in order that the priest could be eulogized. Nevertheless, the stage was now set for what would soon resemble a war zone.

20

Deemed Acts of International Terrorism, Making Haste, and Closing In

Around nine o'clock in the morning after the raid at Hueston Woods Lodge Resort, Liza, Julia, and Germane sat together in front of a television set at a second safehouse where the federal authorities had relocated them all together, this time. They were restlessly awaiting news that the CIA and the FBI directors might share about Priscilla's whereabouts, as well as about the circumstances surrounding the incident at the resort. They watched it on television as the two intelligence directors appeared together in a joint press conference at the CIA headquarters at Langley, and as the CIA Media Relations director set the stage and format for the press conference, which took place in front of the building. From the vantage point of Liza, Julia, and Germane, it appeared to be a hot, humid, and overcast day at Langley, and it was.

Just as the CIA director—a middle-aged handsome, fairly tall man with a big white handkerchief wiping sweat from his face—walked over to the podium to address the media officials and everyone else who was watching that broadcast—Liza, Julia, and Germane, in great anticipation, wiggled to the edge of their seats in the living room of their new safehouse. The CIA director seemed to stare at the podium, bristling with microphones in front of him. But he was not alone. The FBI director and a throng of senior staffers from both agencies accompanied him. Liza, Julia, and Germane watched as the two intelligence agency directors and most of the news correspondents all wiped sweat from their faces continuously.

Then, with even greater anticipation, Liza, Julia, and Germane watched as the CIA director cleared his throat and began talking:

> The sequence of events leading to the episode in Ohio last night appears to have begun this past spring, when the Ohio General Assembly passed a divestiture bill pertaining to South Africa. The chief spokesman for Senate Bill 71, which became known as the South African Divestiture Bill, was Ohio state Senator Daniel P. Callahan.

Liza, Julia, and Germane all reacted the same way, saying in unison, "Oh? We didn't know that." Of the threesome, only Julia fully understood the significance of the SAD Bill. Then, in the lower left-hand corner of their television, they watched video footage showing the senator debating the bill on the floor of the Ohio Senate.

The CIA director continued:

> However, this past March, Senator Callahan and a committee of anti-apartheid supporters also hosted an event featuring the life of South African activist Nelson Mandela. Then, in June, the Ohio General Assembly enacted the South African Divestiture Bill, also called the SAD Bill. As it so happened, PR executive Priscilla J. 'PJ' Austin, the former legislative aide to Senator Callahan, was instrumental in both those activities.

At that, Liza, Julia, and Germane then watched the footage of Priscilla directing the videotaping of the Ohio Senate debating the bill. Except for special events and receptions, such as the Ohio premiere of the documentary

Mandela, this televised news story marked the first time that Liza and Germane had ever seen Priscilla performing her work as a PR person.

"Wow!" Germane exclaimed. "Look at Aunt Priscilla, Grandma."

But their mood became somber when the CIA director began talking about the wedding, and a photo of Priscilla in her wedding gown popped up in the lower section of their television screen. As if on cue, the three of them all turned their heads away from the screen, and when the director started talking about the fatal shooting of Jonathan and about the wound that the senator sustained, Liza said, "We don't need to see any of that anymore."

But when the CIA director began talking about the perpetrators of the crime, Liza said, "Turn up the volume, Germane. Let's listen to this part."

> At the outset, intelligence officials suspected involvement by the South African Nationalists Movement, the SANM, which is comprised of individuals sympathetic to the cause of the white-ruled South African regime. The SANM itself is a global conglomerate that controls the extraction, manufacture, and distribution of diamonds, gold and platinum, and possesses incredible financial investments and other such holdings.

"Wow!" Germane breathed.

As it turned out, Priscilla's family and friends, along with many other people the world over, were learning about the South African-based conglomerate for the first time.

But then the CIA director informed the audience of the enforcement arm of the organization, the Patrol Guard, which had been news to virtually everyone following the news. Notably, however, when he informed them about the mutilation of PG Commander Claus Fokker and that his remains had been discovered in the basement of the missing bride's West Third Street home-office in Columbus, that came as a shock to nearly everyone, particularly Liza, Julia, and Germane.

Germane even belted out what Liza and Julia must have been thinking, "My God, that man was killed in Aunt Priscilla's basement!"

By this point, the threesome had moved away from their individual seats and cuddled together on the couch. Speechless, tears rolled down their cheeks out of their unspoken fears about Priscilla's fate, which only increased when the CIA director talked about "the mysterious mutilation and death of the Anglican priest at the cathedral of the Diocese of Harare, Zimbabwe" and about "an alleged sighting of Ms. Austin at the cathedral boarding school."

Liza screamed. "You have got to be kidding me! That girl is in *Africa!* Is she?" She covered her mouth. Julia and Germane wrapped their arms around her as she trembled.

Julia cried out: "No, Lord, no! How on Earth did she get mixed up in all *that?*"

But it was when the CIA director expounded on the events surrounding the raid at Hueston Woods Lodge Resort that the three of them really cringed. Suddenly—outside of the events which they had just survived a few hours ago—they saw themselves, for the first time, linked to this international web of violence.

Germane broke out in laughter. Then he wept as he saw himself there, on the television screen, covered in that blanket, waving to the news reporters and cameramen. Julia and Liza just sobbed.

In Johannesburg, Simeon Johannes and the Executive Committee were also riveted by that same joint press conference on a big screen at Simeon's palatial estate. The men were primarily interested in the parts that dealt with their organization, especially the failed siege at the Hueston Woods Lodge Resort.

"Incredible. I don't believe that bullshit," Simeon said, shouting above the others' outrage. "Nah, that can't be true. Those were some of our best men."

The CIA director rolled on:

> Federal and state authorities arrived and put down the incident. Although the Ohio Highway Patrol ended the Patrol Guard's attack, three Ohio Highway Patrolmen lost their lives, and several FBI SWAT members sustained injuries.

> By the end of the tragic affair, nine Patrol Guardsmen were killed, and PG Commander Leonard Genn and two of his men were taken into custody.

Simeon and his colleagues, along with other viewers worldwide, could see footage of the shackled PG commander and his two men in the lower right-hand corner of their television screens, being frog-marched to a waiting vehicle. "Nah! Why didn't they pop their bloody pills?" Simeon fumed.

Meanwhile, the CIA director continued speaking:

> Immediately following the raid at Hueston Woods Lodge Resort, local authorities successfully rescued Ms. Austin's friend from the Midway Motel nearby.
>
> These tragic events have been deemed acts of international terrorism, and all affected parties are dealing with situations as they arise.
>
> Meanwhile, the president is in discussions with the British prime minister, the president of Zimbabwe, and several other heads of state, as is the Secretary of State and her counterparts, and, of course, the respective intelligence agency officials.
>
> There will be no comment about the whereabouts of Senator Callahan nor about the relocation of Ms. Austin's friend, her nephew, or her mother. But we are happy to report that Senator Callahan's condition has stabilized.

Given the seven-hour difference between the time zones of Ohio and southern Africa, viewers and listeners in the eastern and southern African nations saw and heard the joint press conference at three o'clock in the afternoon. Meanwhile, telephones, cell phones, fax machines, and shortwave radios beeped and buzzed across the southern African countryside.

As the two CF units—one led by CF Commander Wozniah and Agent Bernhardt, and the other by Agent Jordan—continued their trek to Harare, they were all elated at the news: they no longer needed to concern themselves with events back home. The American intelligence agencies and state and local law enforcement had successfully rescued Priscilla's friend and family members, and the senator was safely tucked away in a place that surely must be as safe as Fort Knox. The news about the capture of PG Commander Leonard Genn gave additional confidence and encouragement, for a special operation's commander is rarely captured—alive, that is.

SANM Executive Committee members continued lingering around the big screen at Simeon Johannes' palatial estate in Johannesburg.

"At least they're not calling us 'a cartel' anymore," Simeon said.

"Oh no! Calling us 'international terrorists' is no improvement," Joseph Sabato said. "My God, man. That means they can shoot to kill us on sight!"

"Hold it, Joseph," Hans suggested, "Not necessarily. We're the executive committee of the diamond, gold and platinum conglomerate, the SANM. Otherwise, they don't have a thing connecting us directly to the Guardsmen, only suspicions; that's all."

"But an even bigger deal," Simeon fretted, "is that we could be damn near broke by the time this fiasco concludes. According to Heinreik's last report, every one of our distribution centers has all but ceased operations because the damn authorities are all over them. Our wells are going dry!"

"But Simeon, we do still have—" Heinreik attempted to speak.

Simeon smoothly cut in, "I wouldn't hold out on you guys. But as the CEO, I had to make provisions for a rainy-day fund. Something to jumpstart a new life once a catastrophe such as this occurs. And now that one has, that's why I called this little get-together. Heinreik here will update us on our primary option. Go ahead, Heinreik, bring the fellas up to date."

When Heinreik began, "Well, first of all, we need to suddenly and quietly leave South Africa," everyone was outraged, well, except for Simeon.

"Oh-h, no, you don't. Like hell am I leaving," Dawker said, pouting like a child. "We've got too much invested here: our families, friends, our lifestyles."

"But Dawker," Simeon interrupted, "we've always known of such a possibility. Now give Heinreik a chance to finish his report."

200

"After we're settled in our new communities," Heinreik went on, "we may reconnect with our former businesses, but under assumed identities. And we still possess our accounts in Switzerland and the Cayman Islands. Plus, none of the countries we're relocating to have extradition agreements with South Africa, America, or their Western European allies. Besides, if you keep your identity, you'll surely incur unnecessary scrutiny. So, I strongly recommend that you adopt the identities portrayed in the passports we've prepared for you. Sever all ties with the SANM Executive Committee, and begin new business ventures, such as that sugarcane business you've always talked about starting, Dawker, or that cigar business you wanted to invest in, Joseph. But whatever you do, let go of your connections to South Africa."

Each word spoken by Heinreik met with grumbles and frets.

"Humph!" Dawker fussed.

"Well, I'll be damned," said Joseph.

None of the men had ever envisioned the day would actually come when each of them would have to make such an important decision. But here they were—in the midst of perhaps the most important decision they would ever make. The decision to leave also included the decision to leave their families.

"But losing all that money!" Dawker wailed.

"Yes, Dawker," Heinreik said, "and how many times have I advised you to move some of yours away from here? But no-o, you wanted to keep your precious money at your immediate disposal; only now you can't touch any of it. But you do have holdings in a Swiss account. Plus, there's a substantial sum in the local banks where each of you will relocate."

As Heinreik tried to appease his lifelong colleagues and friends, Simeon nodded in finality.

Then Simeon added, "Now, I realize part of your frustration is having to leave your families, but it's only for a short while. Besides, you wouldn't want to put them in harm's way, now, would you? My assistant here has your new passports, credit cards and some currency. Also, to expedite matters, private jets, even as we speak, are already available at the airport."

His face was grim. "And what of Moses Cameron?" Dawker asked, as only he could have at such a critical moment.

But Simeon did not respond. This time, it was Heinreik who said, "Well, Dawker, remember, one of Hans's men has already been given that particularly regrettable assignment." Interestingly, Heinreik, the money man, so to speak, never imagined himself in that role, that is, as the supervisor of PGs. However, by definition, membership on the Executive Committee required that.

Meanwhile, Hans said what had to be said: "And as this is most probably the last time we'll be together, I should tell you that one of my best PG agents is already in place in Harare and will do the dirty deed." He hesitated, then decided he did not need to share the agent's name. When he had told Longworth to snuff out Moses Cameron, he had faxed a photo but had not mentioned that Moses was both a former PG agent and a former SANM Executive Committee member.

After that, Simeon watched in silence as these men who had been his lifelong colleagues and friends scurried away, leaving him to defend his little kingdom 'til its impending demise.

As the Executive Committee dispersed, PG agents and sympathizers across the continent were brooding over the shocking news that one of their agents—one of their own kind—had been captured by the Americans. Throughout their existence, the SANM Executive Committee (and the PG, too, for that matter) was accustomed to conducting its business affairs somewhat unimpeded and never imagined it would lock horns with the Americans. So, as the events unfurled, Afrikaner sympathizers the world over loathed images of the CIA headquarters at Langley, where PG Commander Leonard Genn and two of his comrades would surely undergo harsh interrogation before being handed over to the U.S. court system.

"Ah hell," Dawker had blurted out about the captured men at one point to the few still lingering, "will they even survive before they get to Langley?"

Also, it was fairly evident that, except for the CIA report, not a single news correspondent had ever even broached the heinous murder of Claus Fokker, which was also disregarded by the Executive Committee and his fellow PG comrades. It seemed almost sacrilege for anyone even to mention Fokker's name. As it turned out, as some of the committee members made haste their getaway, they'd all been deeply humiliated behind Claus Fokker's botched assassination attempt that had started the debacle in the first place.

It seemed the only one unmoved by the news was the resourceful PG Commander Longworth. All that mattered to him was his two targets: PJ Austin and the man whose name he now knew was Moses Cameron. He had done enough basic research on the face in the faxed photograph. It had not taken him long to discover that his target was a former Guardsman and, so far as Longworth knew, a current member of the Executive Committee. *Some falling-out must have occurred in Joburg*, he surmised. *Surely there would be a hefty bonus for taking out a man like this.*

Still in transition from the Ian Smith era, Zimbabwean news media had yet to develop a sophisticated communications system. In fact, it operated much like that in closed societies, reporting Prime Minister Robert Mugabe's propaganda with little if any differing points of view. Added to that, there was only one television channel or network, and it was government-controlled. So anyone who desired unbiased news often gleaned it from the *BBC*.

Interestingly, however, international news media were allowed access and entry into the country, hence their presence on the grounds of the Anglican cathedral. And given the relaxed security, it was easy for the PG commander and some of his men to disguise themselves as members of the press corps. Even so, the authentic reporters did not even bother to question any of the new faces, because they were too busy scrambling to be the first to break any news. Consequently, PG Commander Longworth experienced no problems as he mingled amongst the international news correspondents. Why, he even went inside the cathedral compound to conduct interviews with some of the kitchen staff and the matrons.

On one such occasion, inside the school, he broke away from the other reporters. Even the Harare Police, who guarded the girls, were somewhat relaxed in their role. Therefore, the PG commander was able to, with relative ease, wander about the grounds, where he happened upon the coterie of the privileged in the garden. So quite by accident, as he stood by the garden entrance, unseen by the coterie, he overheard a conversation during which Camilla gloated over her father's plan to enter the cathedral "shortly after dark." Camilla was not supposed to tell anyone about her father's plans to enter the church. Yet, there she stood, blabbering: "Father is fairly certain the missing housekeeper, Megan—who he believes is the missing American woman—is somewhere inside the cathedral."

Ah, ha! PG Commander Longworth smiled. *So she* is *in the cathedral.*

"No!" Her friend Joyce was shocked. "Camilla Cameron, are you sure you're not making this up?"

"But yes, Joyce, Anna!" Camilla said.

Nearby, the PG commander continued listening to what the girls thought was a private conversation. Then he ambled up to them and introduced himself as "Christian Henry, reporter for the local news."

As the PG commander pretended to conduct his interview, he asked, "Now, for our readers' understanding, what exactly is the name of your father? Where are they? And what are their occupations?"

Camilla proudly responded; however, the two other girls hesitated to tell the stranger anything.

"And my father's name is Moses Cameron," she said. "He's in the city right now visiting some friends, but he'll return before nightfall. After he finishes his business here, he's taking me out of this despicable place."

Surprised by what he had just heard, "Oh-h, so you're going back home with your father?" the PG commander asked. Unknowingly, Moses Cameron's own daughter had just confirmed his identity to his assassin.

"No, Sir. We're going away to Europe," Camilla said, with an uppity air. "Father says it's a secret, though. But I'm very excited to start a new life with him—in Europe, of all places."

"And the two of you?" the PG commander turned and asked of Joyce and Anna.

"Well, Sir, we're not sure. We're simply not sure," Joyce said, referring to herself and Anna. She was uncomfortable with the man, who seemed too keenly interested in them, and she was even more uncomfortable now that Camilla had talked so much. After all, the man was a complete stranger, and Camilla should have known better than to talk so openly with him. But Camilla had all the enthusiasm of the immature, sheltered teenager that she was.

The PG commander returned to his comrades and shared his interesting news.

But all the while, the CF had him under their surveillance because some of them were also disguised as members of the international press corps—and as members of the boarding school's kitchen staff, too. They had baited a trap, and now they watched patiently for the actions of their prey to unfold.

Until now, however, none of the CF, not even Onslow, Charlie (the manservant), Commander Wozniah, Agent Bernhardt, nor Agent Jordan had any idea that Moses Cameron had a daughter at the Anglican boarding school, so that was useful information to know.

Now the CF needed to find out more about any possible involvement by the young women in the death of the priest.

21

Eulogizing the Headmaster-Priest-Double Agent

In the shaded garden of the cathedral compound, most of the international news correspondents listened as the spokesman-priest of the Anglican Church of the Central Province of Zimbabwe set the parameters for the funeral of the murdered headmaster.

"The funeral for the late Reverend Father Jacob Mbuwayesango will take place tomorrow at 9:00 a.m." He paused, noting to himself that the media ranks had swelled from the garden to the sidewalk leading to the cathedral.

As a precautionary measure, Anglican Church officials had met with the local authorities. They decided to minimize the public funeral rites because a priest had been brutally murdered, and the authorities were investigating the circumstances surrounding his death.

Then the spokesman-priest explained the protocols, such as "prohibitions on the use of electronic devices and cameras inside the sanctuary. You may film the processional, but that is all," he added matter-of-factly. "Once inside the sanctuary, you may sit and observe, but you may not move about or interview anyone. We must respect the sanctity of the service."

Just as the news correspondents were filing their reports on the funeral procedures, a police brigade on motorcycles roared into view in front of the cathedral along Baker Street. They led an entourage of Anglican dignitaries riding in a variety of makes and models of mostly old cars, black limousines, and church buses. Women, wearing black and gray habits, climbed out of the buses; they had come to prepare the cathedral sanctuary for the funeral. The women were followed by several priests and finally the archbishop of the diocese, wearing a tall and colorful miter and carrying a crozier.

The news correspondents also filmed the appearance of what they had been told was the international military unit, whose presence served as a reminder of the gravity of the situation. Men fully dressed in camouflage uniforms and carrying heavy weaponry spread out around the grounds. Some of the soldiers paired alongside the Harare Police, while others created a pathway for the Anglican dignitaries to walk through safely. Yet others entered the boarding school building, fanned out surrounding the oblong-shaped structure, and stood guard throughout the downtown neighborhood.

Perhaps it was the excitement among the CF that things back in the States were under control, or, as was also the case among the PG, that they had readied to retaliate over their recent losses in that quaint Ohio community. Still, news about the funeral for the priest had come as a surprise to them all. As for the boarding school students, they had never before witnessed a funeral, so they had not given any thought to the final arrangements for the priest, either. As it turned out, the funeral for the priest created a little chink in all their plans.

That evening, the lights from the cameras of the international news corps lit the grounds of the cathedral compound as never before, when, at about nine o'clock, the spokesman-priest once again appeared behind the makeshift podium. This time, he handed out copies of a press statement, and then he read it aloud as it was broadcast live:

> The Reverend Father Jacob Mbuwayesango served as
> headmaster at the Harare Boarding School for Girls for
> nearly forty years. He devoted his life to teaching and
> caring for hundreds of young girls, imparting the Word
> of God, as well as etiquette and other social graces that
> would enable the young women to become successful

members of society. The Reverend Father was first and foremost a loyal and faithful servant of God.

Our thoughts and prayers are with his family and loved ones as they grieve over the horrible circumstances behind his death.

The archbishop will conduct the eulogy.

There will be no further statements from this podium or from the Church regarding the death of our dearly departed Brother Jacob.

As the spokesman-priest walked away, several reporters shouted questions at him.

"Is the death of the priest," one reporter asked, "connected in any way to the missing American?"

Another reporter asked, "Was the priest an unfortunate victim of circumstance?"

But the spokesman-priest continued his stride without responding to any of the reporters.

During the news conference, Onslow and his men stayed put in the nooks and crevices of the cathedral and the bell tower. Since the bell tower was ventilated with openings in its exterior, it was a perfect lookout station. Onslow's men were also hiding near each of the secret passageways that led to Priscilla's hideout in the dungeon.

As for Moses Cameron, he stood amid the reporters and watched as the spokesman-priest completed his press statement. He was oblivious to the fact that PG Commander Longworth had already spotted him. But Longworth decided that it was neither the right time nor place to eliminate his target, so he decided to wait before making his move.

The unsuspecting Moses Cameron went back inside the cathedral boarding school and updated his daughter on what he had just learned. "Things being what they are, we must adjust our plans, my child."

Camilla wrinkled her forehead. "But no, Father! What could possibly have happened?"

"The funeral. We forgot about the funeral for the headmaster; it's in the morning. Besides, the place is swarming with police and soldiers. So we have little choice but to wait."

Moses kissed his daughter goodbye and left. He headed out the rear of the boarding school building through the darkness of the garden. But Onslow spotted him from his lookout in the bell tower and then contacted CF Agent Jordan about the mysterious man's reappearance. Agent Jordan, in turn, reported the sighting to CF Commander Wozniah. As for PG Commander Longworth, he lost the trail of one of his primary targets.

Throughout the unexpected drama of that day, only Onslow gave any thought to the horrible situation that Priscilla endured.

Inside that dreary dungeon, she said to herself, "I feel like I've been here forever."

Apart from song and prayer, she had only memories and wild thoughts to occupy her mind. Desperate to pass the time without sinking into self-pity or depression, she resorted to her habit of doodling. She drew fanciful images on the walls with the chalk that Onslow had given her; it had some other useful purpose, after all. She had seen enough rodents (which she detested) and cobwebs (which frightened her even more) to create her own *Indiana Jones* movie. With the chalk, she drew enlarged faces of some of the bugs and rodents she saw. For example, she drew an enlarged image of a rat that had scurried over the dungeon floor an hour ago, terrifying her. To ease her terror, she gave the rat long whiskers and an upside-down half-moon mouth to reassure herself that the rat was disappointed because it could not have her. She also drew enlarged smiling faces—faces of her family members and friends— "to bring some cheer into this dreary place," she said to herself.

Suddenly Priscilla was disturbed by a massive pounding sound, the loud ringing of bells. She heard what she thought might have been one of the priests pulling the ropes attached to the bells. The noise penetrated the very mortar of the floor above her head. Then, the pounding and ringing stopped, but those of an organ grinding quickly replaced those sounds.

Priscilla had no way of knowing it, but the funeral for the late Father Jacob Mbuwayesango was underway.

The procession was already formed at the rear entrance to the cathedral. Leading it, the cross bearer carried a big, heavy crucifix. He was followed by two acolytes, whose candles would be lit upon entering the cathedral. The bishop for the Central Province of Zimbabwe was next in line, and he was followed closely by the archbishop of Zimbabwe; both wore colorful miters and carried decorative croziers. Yet all the clerics, including the high-ranking ones, displayed the black side of their stoles. Next came the pallbearers; they carried the casket containing the remains of the late Jacob Mbuwayesango, priest, headmaster, and (double) intelligence agent for the PG and the CF. But his role as an intelligence agent for both the SANM Executive Committee and the Collective Force was about to be buried along with his remains.

As the bishop began reading the *Twenty-Third Psalm*, the pallbearers entered the sanctuary, followed by the priest's family and close friends. When the pallbearers reached the altar, they set the casket down on a stand that had been erected in front of the altar.

The family and friends expressed tremendous anguish. Some wept and even screamed. Others were silent, carrying too much pain to speak. Each of the mourners carried a terrible question: *Why did Father Jacob die so horribly?*

But soon the procession of the young women from the boarding school brought a different mood to the grieving family and other attendees. The coterie of the privileged led the way: Camilla first, walking alone; Joyce and Anna next. In a display of grief, each girl carried a handkerchief and periodically patted her eyes and nose, as if they were grieving. Following them, the other girls walked in lockstep, two-by-two.

In a dramatic mood change, the organist stopped playing the somber Bach funeral dirge and began playing the well-known cheerful Beethoven arrangement with lyrics by Henry van Dyke, "Joyful, Joyful, We Adore Thee." One measure into the organist's melody, the trio of the girls with the melodious voices that Priscilla so adored began singing:

> Joyful, joyful, we adore Thee,
> God of glory, Lord of love;
> Hearts unfold like flow'rs before Thee,
> Opening to the sun above.
>
> Melt the clouds of sin and sadness;
> Drive the dark of doubt away;
> Giver of immortal gladness,
> Fill us with the light of day!

The trio sang the same calm and uplifting verses as if they understood they were bringing joy to the family of the deceased priest. They repeated the verses until all the guests were seated inside the sanctuary.

As the cathedral filled with an anticipatory hush, a few late arrivals crept down the aisle: a few parishioners, some of the international news media, local businesspeople, and a few strangers—most notably, what onlookers believed to have been the missing American, PJ Austin. The pale, "red-bone" young woman—wearing a beige, sleeveless, tea-length, pleated linen dress—was accompanied by a tall, handsome, olive-complexioned man—wearing a matching beige linen suit with shirt and tie, and donning a ponytail of long, wavy, black hair and an impressive moustache. Only a few of the well-disguised guests knew that he was none other than CF Agent Carlton Elliott Bernhardt. The couple trailed behind a few other guests. Then they walked all the way up the center aisle, touched the coffin, and pretended to pray. After showing their respects, they found seats near the front section of the sanctuary.

Those in attendance watched, in amazement, as someone who indeed resembled Priscilla carried herself as if not a care in the world. But was that "someone" really Priscilla? If so, why did she appear so calm, as if she were unaware of the international search and rescue operation underway for her?

As for the keen PG Commander Longworth and Moses Cameron, who sat separately—unbeknownst to each other's presence—they watched in utter bewilderment at what they both saw: someone who looked a lot like PJ Austin. But, unlike PG Fokker, who had violated the longstanding Guardsman's rule forbidding the taking out of a target during an act of worship, Moses Cameron and Alistair Longworth still observed the sanctity of an act of worship. And so it was that, once again, a primary target was well within each man's grasp, but the circumstances (so both men thought) were preventing them from carrying out what would have been in perfect order in their line of business.

22

The Funeral, the Sighting, and Heinreik's Turn at Bat

During the funeral, CF Agent Bernhardt hid his anxiety and played the role he had been assigned with the PJ look–alike who sat next to him. He cast fond glances at her and even sometimes held her hand. He wished that, in fact, she had been Priscilla. He carried a heavy burden: *Missy, where are you?* If he had only known that Priscilla was right there in the dungeon beneath the very seat in which he sat, he would have risked his life saving her. But he did not know that she was there, so he sat and pretended the look–alike was his "special someone."

As he thought about the one and only time that he and Priscilla made love, he caressed the shoulders and hands of her look–alike; and she performed her role, accordingly, moaning with pleasure beneath his massaging hands.

PG Commander Longworth sat several rows close to the rear of the sanctuary, quite some distance from the CF agent and the PJ look–alike. He now knew that Moses Cameron, who sat in the opposite section, four rows in front of him, was there, too. But Moses did not know that a PG was so close to him, and if he had known, he would not have believed the man had been there

212

to eliminate him. Even so, both men shared one common motive—the elimination of PJ Austin—and suddenly, they both saw her double sitting in front of them, in plain sight.

As the two men sat stunned at the sight of whom they thought was their target, the congregation stood and chanted some verses from the *Book of Common Prayer*. But when the congregation, which included PG Commander Longworth and Moses Cameron, sat back down, the PJ look–alike had disappeared. Then—as if it were orchestrated, or as if someone had demanded the two men stand back up—both Moses and the PG commander stood back up. When some of the people in the pews nearest to each of them turned around and stared at them, both men then realized that they had just now put themselves out front, which would make attacking them much easier for the CF agents, who also were masquerading as parishioners and media officials. So if there had been any doubt regarding the identity of the two men, the CF agents had just gotten all the validation they had needed.

Then, just as PG Commander Longworth sat back down, the CF agent— who had been sitting behind him all this time—clutched the back of his neck. Onlookers assumed that the CF agent was merely comforting the man. But as the CF agent clutched the PG commander's neck, with a small syringe, he injected a paralyzing serum. Then he whispered what the onlookers could not hear: "Sorry, ole boy, but you ought to be more careful next time." Then: "Oops! There won't be a next time, now, will there?"

Just then, the onlookers saw the PJ decoy (They did not know that she had pretended to go to the powder room) returning to her seat, where she and CF Agent Bernhardt remained until the benediction.

When the ceremony ended, the guests began walking out behind the recessional.

The CF agent who'd injected the paralyzing serum into PG Commander Longworth's neck told the onlookers nearest him: "Go ahead, please. We'll stay with him for a while. He's still a little shaken up by the ceremony. We'll see him home."

Unknown to the onlookers, PG Commander Longworth was keenly aware of his predicament. He could neither move nor speak, but his eyes were open and his mind clear enough to anticipate his eventual fate. For he knew that the CF agents would surely torture him, in much the same way as he and his fellow Guardsmen had tortured so many of their prey.

Immediately after the funeral, the CF agent, who'd injected PG Commander Longworth with the paralyzing serum, and some soldiers took their catch of the day to a meadow on the outskirts of Harare, where, after interrogating him, they disposed of him much in the same way that he and so many of his comrades had made sport of so many Black men.

A short time later, passersby walking through the meadow smelled the stench from what appeared to have been a stack of burnt rubber tires. Most Zimbabweans knew precisely what the burnt tires symbolized, so they did not venture too close to the stack. Yet someone eventually called the Harare Police, who, upon close examination, determined the charred remains were those of a man. But they were never able to identify his remains fully.

Being a more seasoned agent than PG Commander Longworth—and PG Commander Longworth had indeed been an outstanding agent, until his fatal slip-up—Moses Cameron had disappeared from the scene, although not from the ongoing range of the CF surveillance. Yet he did not go far, because he still planned to return to the cathedral boarding school that evening.

On their noon report (Zimbabwean time), the *BBC* broadcast a gripping story to television viewers worldwide:

> Several reporters, including me, saw the mysterious PJ Austin in attendance at the funeral of the Reverend Jacob Mbuwayesango this morning. Although we have yet to confirm the name of Ms. Austin's escort, he is believed to be associated with a Washington, D.C.-based lobbying firm.
>
> Unfortunately, strict protocol forbade the use of electronic devices during the funeral, so we were unable to capture any footage of the couple. By the time the service ended, they had moved too quickly out of our reach.
>
> Stay tuned to *BBC World News*, where we provide up-to-the-minute coverage on this ongoing mystery in Harare.

The Funeral, the Sighting, and Heinreik's Turn at Bat

As the *BBC* delivered its latest report, CF Agent Bernhardt and the PJ decoy met up across the way in Cecil Square with CF Commander Wozniah and several other members of the CF unit.

During the rendezvous, two other CF agents reported: "We disabled PG Commander Longworth and took him to a beautiful meadow for him to commune with nature. We also disposed of three other bags of garbage in dumpsters nearby."

The CF Commander nodded. "Well done, fellas. Seems as if we've finished our business here.

It would, however, be much later before Harare law enforcement officials would learn about the three other Guardsmen who had been killed, because it was anybody's guess when the meager sanitation force would collect the trash again. Still a relatively new nation, Zimbabwe had yet to develop the type of public services, such as waste removal and infrastructure, that most Western societies take for granted.

Then the CF commander turned to Carlton and the decoy and said, "Shall we assemble at our favorite watering hole for some tea? And, by the way," he noted, "You and PJ were marvelous, absolutely marvelous."

Sometime earlier, during the funeral, CF Agent Jordan had joined Onslow in the bell tower, where they enjoyed a bird's-eye view of many of the morning's activities.

That was when Onslow briefed his supervisor about Priscilla's experience at the boarding school, about Moses Cameron and his relationship with one of the students, and about the peculiar circumstances surrounding the students at the boarding school. But intentionally, he did not mention perhaps the most crucial fact. His CF training cut deep. He'd had drilled into him that the fewer who knew about an ultra-secret, the greater the probability of keeping that information a secret. Therefore, he did not tell Agent Jordan, his supervisor, Priscilla's hiding place.

But when Onslow handed Agent Jordan a copy of *The Book of Judges*, the subject and tone of their conversation took a different turn.

"Onslow," Agent Jordan spoke with a raw edge. "Do you have *any* idea what this is?"

Onslow nodded. His voice was matter-of-fact, but what he said was sensational. "My men also discovered a secret compartment behind one of the bookshelves in the library. There were enough weapons to start a small war. Some of 'em kind of small, but still they can kill ya."

Slamming his fist against the manual, Jordy said, "My God, man! This is a sophisticated training manual for young female assassins." During his time in southern Africa, his hair had grown longer. When he slammed his fist down, it fell forward, covering his stubble. He pulled it back and said, "This is no boarding school; it's a damn charm school. You know, the type that the Soviets used to create their brand of Americans. Only these little wenches don't want to be Americans. They prefer to go for the kill, especially on the likes of Senator Callahan and Miss Prissy." The pitch and pace of his voice escalated with each word. "This is the missing piece to the mystery. Wait 'til Tommy and the others get a load of this!"

Jordy realized that Onslow had stumbled onto some of the most significant data about another of the clandestine operations of the SANM, a special operations unit called "The Judges." It was comprised of teenage females—categorized as judges, generals, and soldiers—and they were trained at the Anglican Cathedral's boarding school in the Diocese of Harare. The instructor had been the headmaster, the late Father Jacob Mbuwayesango.

The CF agent's concern for Priscilla's safety suddenly heightened. She was not only targeted by the PG but possibly by the Judges as well.

Simultaneously, the two comrades in arms spoke: "And Camilla's the judge, isn't she?"

Around the same time that Jordy and Onslow met, after trying to reach PG Commander Longworth via his cellular phone for a third consecutive time, Hans Evekink suddenly realized that his star assassin had been eliminated. For surely he would have contacted him by now.

Grimly, he clenched his teeth. Intuitively, he knew he was right. Longworth was dead. Hans then reasoned that the kill order on Priscilla seemed to have inadvertently fallen into the hands of Moses Cameron, of all people, and his daughter Camilla.

But Hans did not know that, soon, another member of the SANM's Executive Committee would unleash yet another assassin to eliminate Moses Cameron and PJ Austin—a PG who was more formidable than Longworth, or

Moses Cameron, for that matter. According to the SANM rule book, each supervisor got three chances to effectuate a kill order. Hans Evekink had exhausted his three chances with Claus Fokker, Leonard Genn, and now, Alistair Longworth. After a supervisor exhausted his three chances, his supervisory authority was automatically terminated. After that, the Executive Committee either pulled lots or CEO Simeon Johannes selected another committee member to complete the task; either way, Heinreik Lipponeg was next in line. And when there were no more members on the Executive Committee, the PG would choose a new commander from among themselves.

And so it was that the remaining Guardsmen in Harare regrouped at a pub near the Anglican Cathedral compound. They were aware, having caught a whiff of those burning tires and not having been able to find Longworth since the funeral, that they had lost their commanding officer.

Jerome Funderburke, the next in line, took charge and called Hans, who was not surprised to hear the news of Longworth's demise. So Hans told PG Funderburke that his own supervisory authority had automatically ended at the death of Longworth.

Meantime, Funderburke and his men, down the line, waited to hear from their new supervisor, Heinreik Lipponeg, who was himself only just now learning about his new commission.

Unknowingly, however, PG Funderburke and his comrades in Harare were jumping the gun, albeit only for a moment.

In short order, Hans informed Simeon about the situation with his PG commander.

Simeon convened another Executive Committee meeting, at the start of which, without a written agenda or even small talk, "Heinreik," Simeon said, peering directly into his eyes, "it's your turn at bat, my friend. This one's yours."

Once Heinreik realized that Simeon really was talking to him and that Simeon had just informed him of his role as the new supervisor of the PG, he squirmed in his seat. He sweated profusely, too. "No! No! No! I cannot. I will not do it." Heinreik felt like vomiting, but nothing came up his throat. He wanted to leave the room, but he could not move.

Besides, he had watched with growing horror the *BBC World News* noon broadcast about the man seen escorting the missing American at the funeral of the priest. Like his nephew, Heinreik (Bernhardt) Lipponeg, the man was described as tall and handsome, and he wore a head of thick, long, wavy, black hair in a ponytail, and he was olive-complexioned, too.

To Heinreik, it seemed like a lifetime ago when he had asked his father for his inheritance and departed for South Africa. And for sure, he could not erase the image of the man who had been standing in the Ohio Senate gallery during the debate on the SAD Bill.

So Heinreik prayed as he had never done: "My God, please remove this horrible charge from me. I dare not do it. I will not do it." Although Heinreik had not been commissioned to execute a kill order himself on the CF agents—and by implication, on this young man he strongly suspected was his great nephew—he still did not regard himself as a murderer, and he had no intention of descending that low at this stage in his life. With each thought, Heinreik's naturally radiant complexion yellowed.

When Simeon noticed the reluctance on Heinreik's face, he let loose vigorous laughter. "Oh, I get it! You've never killed anybody! Mr. Numbers Cruncher has never ordered a kill!"

Simeon laughed and laughed and laughed. He pointed his index finger in Heinreik's face. "But you'll do it now or face your own demise." Then he got up and, still laughing, walked away while Heinreik sat at the impressive conference table at the SANM headquarters and stewed.

Following the Executive Committee meeting, later that afternoon, Hans Evekink prepared to leave the office early.

"I'm a tad ill," he told his secretary. "I'm just feeling a little queasy."

When he arrived home earlier than usual, he told his wife that he had forgotten some important papers, and then he locked himself in his study. There, he recounted his three failed attempts at the most crucial assignment he had ever been given by the Executive Committee, as a leading member of one of the most highly revered conglomerates in the world. As far as Hans knew, two of his PG had been killed, and the other one, captured.

"Such failure," he whispered to himself.

He thought about how the SANM Executive Committee had begun to crumble before his very eyes, and about how he and his colleagues had been urged to go into exile. But he refused to think about his wife and children, or else he might not have the courage to do what he felt he needed to do.

Hans reached into his desk drawer and took out a revolver; he pointed it at his right temple and pulled the trigger.

At the sound of the gunshot, his wife ran to the door of her husband's study and banged on it. She burst into tears when there was no response. She did not have to go inside the room to find out what had happened. She called the Johannesburg Police.

After the police arrived at the lavish estate, they confirmed what the wife had already suspected.

"Hans Evekink is dead, apparently by his own hand," one policeman said when he called in the incident.

Hans Evekink's suicide documented for the first time the link between the SANM Executive Committee and the PG since the horrific tragedy at the Anglican Cathedral in Harare had begun. Evidence of that connection had already been obtained from U.S. intelligence officials while interrogating PG Commander Genn and others since the Ohio resort rampage. In fact, the PG commander had already confessed that Hans Evekink was his supervisor. Then, after more unpleasant physical inducements, he'd informed the American intelligence officials of many other "villainous details" about the organization's operations as well.

Before long, in Johannesburg, the reception area of the posh SANM executive offices was filled with international news media. The two-story suite of offices restricted visitors to the reception area on the first floor. Because only committee members and a few select staff had key cards to the penthouse office suites, they were fairly well-shielded from the media and other visitors, including some disgruntled investors.

As it turned out, Hans' suicide and the presence of the international media alleviated much of Heinreik's trepidation. Simeon, not Heinreik, suddenly became the subject of international intrigue, for Simeon Johannes was, after all, CEO of the SANM, the global diamond, gold, and platinum conglomerate. Heinreik's time would come, but not this day.

Back in Harare, what the media were describing as "the international military unit here to keep peace"—and what in reality was, in fact, the CF—

maintained the pretense on the grounds of the Anglican Cathedral. They let it be known that they were staying in place to help law enforcement protect the young women at the boarding school.

But when Agent Jordan shared with CF Commander Wozniah and Agent Bernhardt the information Onslow had reported about "the charm school," they all agreed they faced a far more complicated set of circumstances than they had previously believed—namely, how to deal with almost fifty teenage female assassins, maybe more. They also now realized the magnitude of the mysterious circumstances surrounding Priscilla: she faced danger on two fronts, the PG and the Judges.

While the CF agents met, so, too, did the PG—including a man named Damien. The remnant of PG in Harare, led by PG Funderburke, had finally received their official orders from the reluctant Heinreik Lipponeg, and they continued to function just as they had under Hans Evekink. So they returned to the cathedral grounds and met with the teenage assassins. By now, even the teenage students knew that PJ Austin, who'd gone by the name "Megan," was in the cathedral dungeon.

While both the CF and the PG held their respective confabs, the Judges held one of their own, during which the young girls made plans to fortify and defend their quarters. After their confab, the forty-seven teenage girls teamed up into twenty-three pairs, or groups. The judge, Camilla, who had been elected as their commander, dispatched the groups to cover the windows and doors of the building. The smaller girls brought the weapons and ammunition to the bigger girls and prepared to reload the weapons as they were needed. Like the little hobbits they were, the forty-seven teenage girls moved about the boarding school building quickly and with great zeal. Indeed, the priest had trained them well, leading periodic drills, during which the young women behaved much like schoolchildren practicing fire drills, but not this time. This time, they behaved like the little soldiers they'd been trained to be.

After Camilla had performed her role as commander, she handed the command over to Joyce and Anna.

Then, unbeknownst to Joyce and Anna and the other girls, Camilla carried her rifle and an unlit lantern as she slipped out of the boarding school quarters into the cathedral, where she hoped to join her father in hunting down Priscilla.

23

Raid at the Anglican Cathedral
and
Moses Cameron's Mistake

In the early evening after the headmaster's funeral, a man dressed in a fashionable suit and necktie walked briskly onto the grounds of the Anglican Cathedral. He even nodded at some of the soldiers and news correspondents as he passed them. When one of the reporters asked his name and his business at the cathedral, the man spoke openly and willingly, "I am Moses Cameron, and I have come here to visit with m—"

Before he could finish his sentence, gunshots rang out rapidly. Then he saw the soldiers around him crumple to the ground, one by one. Suddenly, the reporter who had been asking him about his "business at the cathedral" wore an expression of fear and anguish on his face. Others screamed and scurried about frantically.

Moses then watched as some of the cameramen dropped to their knees to film what was happening.

"Stupid idiots," he said.

His initial instinct was to get to the bell tower, but as he attempted to move in that direction, he saw several reporters running toward him. The loud, rapid rattling of gunfire confused him and everyone else. As some of the reporters bumped into him, he shoved them aside, toppling some of them onto the lawn.

Then he heard what sounded like missiles flashing through the air. Instinctively, he held up his hands for protection from the gunfire. But when he realized that he could not remain out in the open, Moses dived for cover.

Before long, Moses, along with everyone else on the cathedral grounds, could make out automatic rifles mounted in the windows of the boarding school building and could see that the gunfire was coming from there.

From the bell tower, Onslow watched in utter astonishment as the soldiers and a few news correspondents dropped to the ground, including a few of his own men who were masquerading as news correspondents. It was dusk. So it was hard to distinguish between the camouflage uniforms worn by the CF and those worn by the PG soldiers. He thought about Priscilla, so he radioed to some of his men assigned to the secret passages leading into the dungeon.

Yelling into his radio, Onslow said, "Hey, man! I need you guys outside now—like yesterday." What seemed to Onslow like an instant later, a battalion of troops arrived, running headlong from the street onto the cathedral grounds, only to be met with the cracks and flashes and sputtering of what sounded like hundreds of AK-47s being fired simultaneously. He saw soldiers grabbing their heads and slumping to the ground. Onslow quickly realized that the shooters were the teenagers inside the boarding school building. He also realized that they were darn good sharpshooters, too.

Just as Onslow had figured out who the shooters were, so, too, did Moses Cameron, the soldiers, and some of the international news correspondents, who had spotted the young girls who were firing. Still, no one really wanted to believe that the Anglican Cathedral was under siege by teenage girls with guns.

In spite of the commotion and gunfire, Moses Cameron managed to crouch low enough and to dodge this way and that until he made his way inside the cathedral church. Onslow saw him, but he assumed that at least one of his men had remained at his post at the strategic passages to the crypt. What he did not know was that Jordy was the only CF agent still present inside the church.

Television cameras were capturing much of the action. All over the world, people were glued to the live coverage at the Anglican Cathedral in Harare. There, in real time, was a war zone smack in the capital city of Harare, across from Cecil Square and the Salisbury Club, and within a mere three blocks of the Parliament Building. Despite the televised images, viewers could not discern the good guys from the bad ones, and they found the images of those teenage white girls holding and firing high-powered rifles unbelievable.

As the gunfire crackled and sputtered and flashed from the windows and doors of the Anglican Cathedral compound, viewers soon saw many of the soldiers raising their weapons and firing back. After several minutes of a prolonged gun volley between the teenagers and the soldiers, the gunfire from inside the boarding school building abruptly stopped. The soldiers, believing that they might have killed enough of them to stop the battle, rose from their crouched positions with nearly audible sighs of relief. But they quickly ducked when a volley of launched grenades spouted dirt and flames in front of them.

Then, a young commanding officer among the soldiers yelled, "Gas the damn place!"

The TV viewers then saw a few of the soldiers loading teargas canisters and firing them toward broken glass windows in the boarding school building. Within minutes, there was silence. And this time, that silence held.

By the time the soldiers entered the school building, they discovered the small, fragile bodies of teenage girls lying dead on the floor at the front and rear entrances. The manual for *The Book of Judges* had instructed its followers, "If at all possible, never be taken prisoner." As the end approached, some of the surviving young women had turned on the others and shot them before killing themselves.

"From the looks of it, they killed one another in sync," a soldier said to his captain as he radioed to headquarters. "We've got what looks like forty-six teenage white females down, most all shot by single bullets in the head. My God, what is this place?"

After a short while, several international news correspondents bravely entered the school building, their cameras poised to capture whatever they would find. Almost immediately, some of them grabbed their own foreheads, spun around with sudden dizziness, and fell on the floor. The sight of all those young girls with bloody and lacerated bullet wounds to their foreheads was unbearable. One cameraman even spilled his stomach. No one, not even the television viewers, believed the massacre that had just occurred.

Back inside the Anglican Cathedral, Moses Cameron had already met up with his daughter. He and Camilla were making haste toward the crypt. At the back wall of the chancel, they came upon the first of the three engraved wooden statues—this one of St. John the Divine, its two eyes, one aglow and the other dim, above the austere-looking face.

Moses peered down at the base of the statue. He read aloud the words engraved into the old wood, the first of the three riddles that Onslow had encountered when he had taken Priscilla into the dungeon for her own safety: "It takes only one of these to see you, but if you press the right one, the left one will pierce yours."

Studying the saint's eyes, Moses told his daughter to step aside. He was not sure which eye the riddle referred to. But he pressed the "right" eye, and the heavy door behind the statue opened. They entered through it.

Then, aided by the lantern, now lighted, that Camilla had brought with her, they walked together through the darkness. Camilla's adrenaline rushed. Even in the darkness, her face, like that of her father's, reddened with excitement. Emboldened by the presence of her father in carrying out her charge, Camilla stepped like a proud commanding officer down a flight of stone steps into more darkness.

They reached the second engraved wooden statue—this one of St. Francis of Assisi, with engraved cherubim around him.

Again, Moses peered down at the base of the statue and read aloud the following words of the riddle: "This helps me to eat. For my last meal, press down." He realized that if he put his hand down the throat of any of the cherubim, the cherub would prick him with a serpent's venom. So instinctively, and correctly, Moses pressed the cherub's tummy. The heavy door behind the statue opened, and father and daughter entered through it.

By the time they reached the third and final statue, Moses felt so close to his prey that he was nearly overcome with delirium. He handed the rifle that Camilla had brought him back to her and then told her, "Go back up to the top of the stairs and keep watch."

Camilla objected vehemently. With her excitement to conquer her prey dashed, her face reddened even more. But she did as her father had instructed. When she reached the top of the stairs, she suddenly felt a peculiar-smelling cloth wrap over her face, and then she fell unconscious.

Raid at the Anglican Cathedral and Moses Cameron's Mistake

Not knowing that the CF had just captured his daughter, Moses stood in front of the last engraved wooden statue, St. Mary, and read the riddle on the ledge near its base: "Unable to see or hear, a child might know his mother by this." Of all the riddles, this one caused him the most difficulty. Indeed, he had spent much of the previous night contemplating the answer. Moses already knew the three riddles would await him at the guardian statues. That was because he knew that, as far back as the 1890s, many of the Shona and the Ndebele, especially the educated and English-speaking ones, had so despised the early Anglican missionaries, that to protect themselves, the missionaries had installed the three wooden statues—together with the three traps and their corresponding riddles—in the main passageways leading to the crypts that housed the future tombs of the Anglican clergy. The riddles had been written, therefore, as an added precaution to any future desecration on the part of the unwelcoming locals.

Moses studied the statue of St. Mary. He knew that if he chose wrongly, three sharp, curvilinear blades would swiftly slice him into pieces—or, more precisely, four portions. He reached out and clasped one of St. Mary's hands, and the massive door opened up all the way.

With nary a thought about his daughter, Moses Cameron walked through the opening jauntily, as if he were expected.

The creaking of the door opening caught Priscilla unawares. She rose from the dreary darkness and the cold, damp, debris-laden floor in the corner, which had become her resting place. She stood silently beside one of the monumental tombs. At first, her heart pounded with glee because she thought that it was Onslow calling.

Squinting her eyes, she looked up and saw a tall, husky man in a dark suit standing at the top of the stone stairwell. He held a lantern in one hand. His face was twisted into a lascivious and leering grin. Priscilla grew nauseous. She readily discerned that this visitor did not bring her any relief. The man she observed seemed as if he would eat her up and spit out her remains for the sheer fun of it all. She sensed a most terrible fate.

Moses Cameron stood rooted at the top of the stone stairwell, gasping at this ghastly and unkempt creature. He held the lantern up higher. Priscilla's hair had grown out somewhat and was filled with dirt and cobwebs. Her skin was soiled from the dirt and debris in the dungeon. She stank of her own waste, despite the small, covered pail situated on the floor not far from the corner that she had claimed as her space. Candy wrappers, shells from nuts, and other debris were scattered about and made a mockery of the holy burial place.

Moses took a couple of steps down the stairwell. He held the lantern up even higher. Surely this was not the woman for whom he had been searching! *She can't be the attractive American whose picture has been all over the television news in her bridal gown.* He recalled, too, the stunning and stately woman he had seen at the priest's funeral.

Puzzled, his pace quickened as he descended the stone stairwell for a closer look. Then suddenly, he stopped. *This could easily be her if she's been here not hours but days, maybe even a week or longer. If that's the case, no wonder she's a mess. But if so, who was the blazing beauty I saw at the funeral?*

With renewed purpose, Moses Cameron strode down the few other steps toward his prey.

While Moses entered the dungeon where Priscilla was stowed away, upstairs in the central aisle of the cathedral, CF Agent Bernhardt stood—disguised in a baseball cap, sunglasses, and a sandy-brown ponytail—impersonating PG Commander Longworth—holding the collar of a PJ decoy. Just as he saw soldiers (some of them from the CF international military force, some of them from the PG) enter the church and head toward him, he shouted as loud as he could: "Will ya looka' here! I've got the American."

Then, as if on cue, the CF troops retreated with great speed, running out of the church, all the way to Baker Street. But the PG soldiers, unaware of the CF's scheme to retreat, kept their eyes fixed for too long on the PJ decoy. By the time they realized that they alone were in the church and that they should leave it as soon as possible, it was too late for an orderly retreat. Then, just as they ran out onto the grounds, they were, to the man, gunned down by the CF troops, who were waiting for them outside.

As Onslow listened to the gunfire and then the shouting about the fantastic "capture of the American," he decided it was time to leave the bell tower and check out the situation for himself. As he descended the narrow spiral stairwell, he perspired profusely. His thoughts ran rampant: *No, Miss Prissy couldn't be in danger! No one else knows how to enter the dungeon!* But in his rush to check on her, he did not notice the television news cameraman following him at a distance with his camera rolling.

Onslow reached the first engraved wooden statue and pressed the "right" eye, and the great door opened up for him.

Then he ran swiftly down the stone steps until he came upon the second statue, where he pressed the belly of the little cherub and entered through the opening. As it so happened, he had no idea that someone else was there and that someone heard him panting and saw his eyeglasses glaring in the darkness.

Then, just as he was proceeding hurriedly down the next stone stairwell, he also sensed the presence of someone else. When he stopped abruptly, his spectacles slid down his nose. From behind him, someone whispered, "Onslow, is that you?"

The voice sounded familiar to him, so while pushing his eyeglasses back up his nose, the already agitated Onslow spoke in a dampened whisper, "Damn it, Jordy." Jordy may very well have been Lieutenant Onslow's supervisor. Still, the two men had long since been friends, and their difference in rank rarely affected their personal or professional relationship. So, at this critical point in his assignment to protect Miss Prissy, Onslow hardly observed proper protocol, hence his damning tone with Jordy.

"Where're you off to in such a hurry?" Jordy whispered back to him.

"The damn crypt, you fool. Someone's got our game."

"Not yet, they haven't. And even if they have, we've got one of theirs, too." Jordy shoved Camilla out for Onslow to see her.

"But then, who," Onslow asked, "is the woman the soldiers have outside?"

"She's one of ours, Onslow. You'll see."

Then Jordy and Camilla (and, unknown to all of them, the cameraman) followed Onslow as he continued to run down the stone steps. When they arrived at the third statue, Onslow said, "Stand back." He pushed his horn-rimmed glasses up his nose, cautiously grabbed hold of St. Mary's hand, and slowly but surely, the great door opened.

Just as Onslow stepped over the threshold, he paused, and Jordy and Camilla almost bumped into him. He held up his lantern and surveilled the dungeon. Seeing no Priscilla there, he panicked and rushed down the stone stairwell into the dungeon to see for himself where she could be.

But first, he observed a man slumped against the opposite wall in a high-backed wooden chair. His shoulders drooped, and his eyes were dull, as if life had gone out of them. A large tin pail was upended over his head, black waste dripping down his cheeks. Yet the stench was so overwhelming to Jordy and

Camilla that they crept slowly down the stone steps, and the cameraman, not far behind them, remained at the top of the stairwell, his camera still rolling.

Soon, all the visitors were watching the man in the high-backed wooden chair, whose body pulsed sporadically and who cried out, "Just shoot me. Please kill me, so my people will not say about me, 'A woman castrated him.'"

At first, Onslow ignored the man. Then, *Where is she?* he thought as he stood beside the crying man in the chair, the man Camilla knew instinctively was her father.

Moses made his first mistake when he tried to engage Priscilla in conversation instead of killing her on sight. As such, he'd foolishly chosen to spar with his prey.

"And if you answer my questions properly," he had said, "then I will go easy on you."

Out of fear of the man, Priscilla had dutifully nodded.

Then Moses had asked her the first of his questions: "Will you sit on your little potty and then bring it to me?"

At first, Priscilla had pretended to oblige: she picked up the pail and started for the dark and smelly niche where her "bathroom" was. But then she turned around and blurted, "I thought I had to go, but I don't, and so—"

Quickly, she walked to Moses, who was seated in the high-backed wooden chair, holding his exposed penis in his hands. Then, spontaneously, she dumped the pail's contents onto his head and left the pail upended.

As she stared at him, soaked in her waste, she remembered the time, long ago, when that "thug" Dennis had thrust himself upon her. In memory, she heard his rough and belligerent voice: "Spread your damn legs, bitch!" She feared Moses was another Dennis and would do bad things to her, most probably sexual in nature. Out of fear, or out of self-preservation, she decided to disable the man as quickly as she could.

While Moses ranted profanities, Priscilla removed the hammer and chisel from the pockets of the apron she still wore from her days as a housekeeper. Aiming the chisel at the man's exposed penis, she raised the hammer and slammed it down hard. But when she realized she had missed his penis and saw the "darn tool" sliding toward his groin, she hammered the chisel down again. With each hammer, Moses hollered to the top of his lungs. But Priscilla continued to hammer with all her might. "Three times to make it holy," she'd declared.

So, it had been after Priscilla had disabled Moses Cameron that she had gone back to her corner on the cold, damp, debris-laden floor, covered herself back up in her blanket, and pretended that she had had a bad dream.

Unfortunately for Moses, neither Jordy nor Onslow nor the muzzled and handcuffed Camilla would carry out his plea to kill him. So the whole world, via the *BBC News* cameraman who was already videotaping, would soon see the mysterious injury he suffered at the hands of a woman—a Black American woman, at that.

Onslow removed the pail from Moses's head, but as he snatched up the chisel from his groin, Moses collapsed. Onslow then radioed his CF comrades for assistance.

All the while, Jordy and Camilla stood still on the stairwell, speechless, unable to believe what their eyes saw, and what their noses smelled. As for the relatively constrained Camilla, she could not react because her mouth was muzzled, and her hands were clasped in cuffs behind her back. Still, the young woman was distressed over her father's apparent misery, even though she herself was deeply humiliated by the scene.

After dealing with Moses, Onslow instinctively walked toward a hump on the floor in the opposite corner of the room. Cautiously, he pulled off the blanket that covered it, which he soon discovered was indeed Priscilla. *Ah!* He was glad he found her, but he quickly covered her back up. Even he had enough sense to know that she was too ashamed for anybody to see her like this, so dirty, so smelly, so unkempt.

As the visitors and Priscilla prepared to ascend the stairwell, Onslow covered Priscilla, and Jordy tried to shield Camilla. But the television viewers worldwide had already seen her muzzled face. Then again, perhaps Jordy had intentionally allowed that brief glimpse of her, thinking, *Bait is bait.*

Back on the main level of the cathedral, as they neared the entrance to the sanctuary, Onslow discreetly beckoned to Jordy. "No, not that way. Follow me." The blanket still covered Priscilla because Onslow did not want to subject her to the indignity of the television viewers.

So they exited the cathedral through the secret passageway leading back outside the edifice, thereby eluding the lone cameraman who had followed them and the swarms of international news correspondents waiting outside.

Shortly, Jordy called for additional men to aid Onslow's men in removing Moses Cameron from the crypt. Then he took charge of Camilla. Onslow took charge of Priscilla.

Then the four of them boarded a high-riding military-style, canvas-covered jeep, and off to the CF central command outpost they all rode.

24

Breaking News, An Unlikely Truce
&
Sights and Sounds and Foul Odors

Around eight o'clock in the evening, Harare time, the raid at the Anglican Cathedral dominated television airwaves around the globe. The *BBC World News* broadcast was perhaps the most riveting. Once again, a reporter stood in front of the Anglican Cathedral in Harare as a cameraman panned over it:

> Shortly after dark this evening, gunfire spread
> rapidly here at the Anglican Cathedral in Harare.
> It all began when a man—who identified himself
> as Moses Cameron—walked onto the premises.
> His very presence seemed to signal to someone
> inside the cathedral boarding school building to
> start shooting. As ludicrous as this might sound,
> forty-six teenage females, reportedly pupils at
> this boarding school, turned to violence. In
> groups of two, they positioned themselves at each
> of the windows and doors, and then they shot and

killed almost every soldier standing guard outside the building.

Next, they launched grenades and killed more soldiers *and* news correspondents. Military reinforcements arrived. The soldiers tossed teargas through the windows, and the gunfire soon stopped.

In total, thirty-eight soldiers were killed, and twenty-eight were wounded. Additionally, three news correspondents were killed, and four were wounded.

When the soldiers entered the building, they found forty-six female teenagers at the entrances and throughout the structure, all dead. Each of the forty-six young women had been shot in the head with a single bullet. Sources close to *BBC World News* say the authorities believe the young women had made a pact to kill each other rather than be taken captive.

Amid all the furor, there was another sighting of the American PR executive PJ Austin. Only this time, she was reportedly seen on the walkway in front of the cathedral in the company of a Patrol Guardsman. Why does the SANM PG want Ms. Austin? Does her abduction have anything to do with the attempted assassination of her former boss, Ohio state Senator Daniel P. Callahan? Is there a connection between Ms. Austin and the mass killings?

Even more puzzling, we followed some of the soldiers into the cathedral church—what they were seeking, we do not know. But when we heard a man shout, 'We've got the missing American,' indicating that the American, PJ Austin, had either been rescued or captured, other soldiers ran out of the church and were instantly gunned down.

Then, our cameraman—who remained inside the church—followed three mysterious people down three flights of stairs into the dungeon. At this point, we warn viewers about the graphic nature of these scenes. The man seated in the high-back chair is Moses Cameron—a SANM Executive Committee member. A pail of excrement covers his head, and someone has hammered a chisel into his groin.

Finally, we see a figure covered by a blanket.

A third figure is a young woman muzzled and handcuffed, but she is not Ms. Austin. Indeed, she is believed to be the only surviving student from the Anglican boarding school. Otherwise, as of this report, none of the other students has been identified.

What happened next is equally puzzling. Two men, the muzzled woman, and someone wrapped in a blanket left the cathedral; they eluded our cameraman on the first floor and seemingly disappeared into the darkness.

Stay tuned to *BBC World News* for up-to-the-minute coverage in this ongoing mystery in Harare.

Back in the American capital, senior government intelligence officials broke another news story, which followed the *BBC World News* exclusive. In a press release, the FBI director said:

Medical doctors treating Ohio state Senator Daniel P. Callahan inform us that the senator's condition has stabilized and even begun to improve. It had been believed that his brain injuries were too severe for him to recover fully, but now doctors are what they term 'cautiously optimistic' he may even have a chance to return to his work in the Ohio Senate.

His beloved wife, who has been with him since he was struck down at that aborted church wedding, asked us to thank everyone for their prayers.

Still in protective custody, this time the FBI stashed Liza, Germane, and Julia in yet another secure place. They were in Niagara Falls, New York, a place close to Priscilla's beloved hometown of Prendergast. The three of them sat on a long sofa, three in a row, watching the news bulletins. Over the course of the Austins' time in Prendergast, they used to drive visiting relatives and friends nearly ninety miles to see the magnificent waterfalls. But Priscilla did not know that her mother and nephew, and her friend Julia, were there. Although Liza reminisced with Julia about her family's life in New York, even she'd forgotten how much the waterfalls meant to her daughter.

Besides the new locale, another difference was that all three of them, perhaps because of their close call back at the Ohio resort, had finally come to terms with their new circumstances.

Liza and Germane had begun treating Julia like a member of their family, mostly because she was so close to Priscilla that having Julia there with them seemed the next best thing to having Priscilla herself.

They were all cheerful about the good news concerning the senator's road to recovery.

"Priscilla will be so happy to hear he has a chance, after all," Julia said. "They were always so close." Her voice had a raw edge to it.

Liza nodded. "Maybe too close sometimes. But we all—Nelson, too—always knew Priscilla had her own mind. We never knew just what she was capable of doing. But I've been praying she makes it through this mess, whatever it is. 'Cause this water is too deep for me."

"I think I know what you mean," Julia said.

But neither woman could make heads or tails of the incredible *BBC News* story about the raid at the Anglican Cathedral in Harare.

"If you want my two cents," Julia said. "None of those women we've seen on television is really Priscilla. They don't have her hair or her complexion, and certainly not her mannerisms. Looks to me like they're doubles. You know, decoys? Where'd they get those women? Do they think we're all fools or what?"

"Never can tell with the media or the government," Liza said. "Seems to me, too, they sure haven't shown us that child yet."

The two women laughed.

As the CIA officials at Langley, including Agent Froley, watched the news about the raid at the Anglican Cathedral in Harare, some of them frowned. Then, after studying the images for a while, one of the agents determined that they were none other than CF Agent Bartholomew Jordan and Lieutenant Jeremy Onslow. But the colleagues knew Agent Froley to be "camera shy."

They also knew that had they not been personally acquainted with the two men in the footage, they would not have been able to discern their real identities. Jordy's thick, long, black hair nearly reached his shoulders; he donned camouflage, a military-style helmet, and night goggles; and black stubble covered much of his face. As for the ever-elusive Onslow, he wore tattered, dingy civilian clothes, baggy, high-water pants held up by a rope; rolled up sleeves revealed his snake and tiger tattoos; and he sported a bushy head of sandy-brown hair pulled back in a ponytail, and black, horn-rimmed, smudged eyeglasses.

"Nah, Jim. You're making too much of this," said one of Agent Froley's colleagues.

Yet another CIA official said, "Why, hell, if we didn't know the bloody bastards, we couldn't identify them ourselves. For sure, no one can identify Onslow in his crazy disguise."

Still not convinced that their "boys" were not easily identifiable, Agent Froley continued his tirade: "And if they're stupid enough to get captured on tape, then that's their own bloody fault. Damn fools." Then again, he thought, at least they were smart enough to conceal the identity of the young woman.

And while the devastation in Harare subsided, back in Johannesburg, Heinreik and Simeon seemed to have reached a truce, tenuous as it was. In light of the devastating news coming out of the American Midwest and, more recently, Harare, not to mention the *BBC World News*, Simeon needed someone to stand with him as he addressed the international news correspondents. He was aware that he lacked PR savvy, so he smoothed things over with Heinreik in exchange for his assistance in presenting a hastily packaged PR campaign.

The unlikely truce depicted Simeon Johannes, CEO of the global conglomerate, flanked by Heinreik Lipponeg, the Financial Officer, whom most people had never seen, at least on television. Simeon read the following statement:

> We, the SANM Executive Committee, wish to express our deepest condolences to all the families suffering from the unfortunate events in Harare. Although we acknowledge neither credit nor blame, we are offering some relief:
>
> First: Restoration of the boarding school at the Anglican Cathedral in Harare, making it available to *all* orphans of Zimbabwe, including those of mixed race. We will restore the boarding school to its original purpose and operations. Our finance officer, Heinreik Lipponeg, will work hand-in-glove with officials of the Anglican Church to endow the school into perpetuity.
>
> Second: Establishment of comparable boarding schools and orphanages in Zimbabwe, as well as here in South Africa.
>
> Third: We have initiated procedures to improve working conditions for Black workers and to bring their pay scale more in line with wages paid to others in our diamond, gold and platinum industries.

Following that mind-boggling announcement, Simeon and Heinreik refused to answer any of the reporters' questions about possible links between the SANM and the PG.

But one reporter persisted, "Mr. Johannes," he asked, "what about the confession by PG Leonard Genn that he took his kill orders from your Executive Committee associate, Hans Evekink?"

Simeon ignored the man as if the question were meaningless, along with other questions about apartheid, mainly those dealing with fantastic proposals to establish boarding schools and nursing homes in Zimbabwe and South Africa and to provide financial support in perpetuity, something that clearly flew in the face of the apartheid-era regime.

But Heinreik did comment: "We're not so close-minded as to presume ours is the only way. For we too sense the changes in the wind."

As the two SANM executives hastily retreated from the microphones and left the room, thoughtful reporters pondered the significance of what they had just heard. Surely these comments would give Afrikaners pause as to the state of affairs in the country. Had Simeon signaled to the parliamentary members in the House of the Assembly that he was in favor of legislation to modify or to eliminate the apartheid system? Why else would he sanction racially inclusive policies for the orphanages and boarding schools? Or was his media statement a mere ploy to sidetrack interest in the bad news about the SANM's connection to the Patrol Guard, the terrorist organization responsible for all those killings?

Back in Harare, the blanketed Priscilla sat next to Onslow—unknowingly behind Jordy and Camilla—as the high-riding military-style jeep sped away from the Anglican Cathedral to the CF central command outpost, the vehicle transporting Moses Cameron, behind them.

As they motored down Baker Street past Cecil Square through the heart of the capital city, Priscilla noticed the sights and sounds of the nightlife as well as similar foul odors that she had smelled at the Prospect compound and then in the cathedral garden. Cautiously, she lifted her blanket enough to see what was attributed to such smells and sounds. Then, for the first time since her time in Africa, she saw Black people, that is, many more than the headmaster and the few staff at the Anglican Cathedral compound. She saw street vendors clustered along the streets showcasing, via candlelight, avocados, beans, cucumbers, and sun-dried kudu and ostrich. She saw people wearing dingy-colored, ragged clothing, both African and Western wear; some of the people were even barefooted. Some were packing up and shutting down. Old men and women were sitting on wooden stumps and broken chairs alongside their display stands and tables, some helping with the sales, some covering up their wares, while others were just sitting there. Barely clad small children lay asleep on the barren Earth, whereas others frolicked about. Throughout the multitude of vendors, Priscilla noticed much pride in the people's faces.

She stood up from her seat in the canvas-covered jeep at the sight of live chickens in wooden cages and skinny goats roped to racks of colorful fabrics and clothing. She marveled at the wood carvings of elephants, giraffes and turtles stacked up against themselves on the ground, right beside the live animals. She sat back down as some people ran up to the moving vehicles, pushing their produce and wares in the faces of the drivers. At that moment, she remembered the time when her family had no food, so her father took her and her sisters to the back of Jeff Richards Grocery Store in Connersville, North Carolina, where they picked bananas and cabbage out of the grocer's dumpster. As she thought about it, the food in that dumpster was far more appealing than anything her eyes fell upon this evening.

Another image etched in her mind was of the women walking along the street carrying large baskets on their heads filled with fruits like mangos and small melons, bottled water and assortments of trinkets. Some even carried babies or small children wrapped snuggly around their backs in drab-colored material like those covering their heads: faded-blue, dingy-white, gray, and black-colored turbans. *How on Earth*, Priscilla wondered, *do they do that?*

She saw some developmentally disabled people, hobbling along on makeshift crutches, and some other people who, to Priscilla, looked like lepers. These people, mostly men, did not use crutches of the type Priscilla knew, slightly curved and padded at the top for a comfortable fit under one's arm. No, these crutches were hand-made from tree branches with crude V-shaped tops, rendering anything but comfort.

But when she saw three men seemingly peddling about on makeshift, mobile carts like Sidney Poitier in the movie *Porgy and Bess*, she almost upchucked whatever was left in her stomach. Apart from the main character in the movie, she had never seen anyone on such an apparatus. No one was outfitted with a prosthesis or cane, wheelchair, or other such apparatus used by physically impaired people in America and other Western societies. These people were too poor to purchase such apparatuses; neither did the Zimbabwean government provide disability benefits for its citizens, something that America and many other Western societies provide for the general welfare of their people. And Priscilla knew that, back home in the States, there was a charity for whatever ails a person, including food banks and shelters, but not in Zimbabwe, where many people she saw begged for a livelihood; pale palms extended from their grungy Black bodies to passersby for whatever they would give to them. The darkness of the night only dramatized what she saw.

As Priscilla, Onslow, Jordy, Camilla, and the rest of the CF relief team, along with Moses Cameron in tow, drove through and away from downtown Harare, the more commercial establishments she saw: banks, oil and gas companies, tobacco, fast food, and telecommunications businesses.

She could not see the better parts of the city: the Salisbury Club, Meikles Hotel, signs leading to nearby golf courses, exquisite hotels and resorts, Coronation Park, the National Art Gallery, and the Chapungu Sculpture Park in nearby Msasa, which featured the Shona culture.

To Priscilla's discerning eyes, there did not appear to be any order to the design of the capital. But she did notice the Parliament Building—an imposing, self-contained, heavily-guarded structure with an uninviting entrance—and what she later learned was Cecil Park were within a comfortable walking distance of the Capitol.

She found the traffic frenzy somewhat frightening. It was as if there were no rules and regulations governing it, as if everyone fended for themselves. Drivers waved their hands, yelled out obscenities, honked their horns, and raced in and out of lanes, which, as it turned out, were not even marked. Nobody used signals of any kind, and if they did, the other drivers were blinded by soot and fumes oozing out of the tailpipes of rusty, weather-beaten, and a few new automobiles, motorcycles, vans, and trucks. Priscilla had no way of knowing it, but she was amid rush-hour traffic of people going home after a long, hard day's work in the city.

None of the drivers seemed to observe their vehicle's capacity. Two to three times the capacity filled the vehicles. Priscilla felt herself pulling back into the gulf of her seat as crowded vans of people leaning out the windows, sitting on the rooftops, and standing on the back and side fenders weaved close to her jeep. "Please don't fall off," she mumbled.

Major intersections were incredibly chaotic. Usually in heavily congested areas such as the Arc de Triomphe in Paris or Times Square in New York City, ah, heck, even Paradise Island in Nassau, Bahamas, a policeman directs the flow of traffic, or so Priscilla thought, but not here in Harare, the bustling capital of Zimbabwe.

Then, on the outskirts of the city, she saw small groups of people with large lesions and scabs on their bodies. Already, the deadly effects of AIDS were beginning to show; however, Priscilla did not recognize them as such. She thought the people had some illness, maybe even cancer. She never once thought about AIDS. At the time, in the summer of 1986, Priscilla was not too familiar with AIDS. She, like many people, attributed it to well-to-do white homosexual men. By the time she learned more about the disease, she had already lost some of her friends to it, and they were not well-to-do white homosexual men either.

One such acquaintance was a young municipal judge in Cincinnati, Ohio. When the man realized he had contracted the deadly virus, he drove his Mercedes to an alley, took a pistol from his glove compartment, and shot himself in the head. That was primarily because, at the time, being Black and gay was considered shameful. But the man had not been gay; instead, he'd dreaded the stigma awaiting him once it was revealed that he had somehow contracted the deadly virus.

It followed, therefore, that whenever Priscilla attended funerals of Black people who had died from AIDS, their obituaries almost always read, "… died from complications due to pneumonia," which was another way of saying AIDS, particularly in the predominantly Black churches and communities of which Priscilla was familiar.

As the years progressed, the death toll from AIDS in Zimbabwe and neighboring South Africa would escalate to epic proportions. Yet neither government would adopt viable policies to combat the disease. Even more disturbing, deaths from AIDS would escalate disproportionately among Black American women well into the twenty-first century.

25

Welcome to Your New Home!

After her long, revealing, and exhausting ride (which seemed to Priscilla like twenty miles), she could hear the sound of birds and small animals. She could smell the sap of exotic trees and plants, which were so unlike the bland, sometimes foul odors of the city or that safehouse in Prospect, or the putrid atmosphere inside that cathedral crypt. So she occasioned yet another peek from underneath her blanket and saw that they were approaching what looked like a fenced-in military compound. She saw several single-story cabins constructed of cinderblocks or cement, along with a few shanties with canvas covers flapping about. The makeshift structures appeared to shelter troops. The place reminded Priscilla of the television series *M*A*S*H*. She noticed one sturdy structure, much bigger than the rest; it looked like a warehouse. Mostly, she saw soldiers carrying big rifles, lots of them milling about the grounds.

As the high-riding military-style jeep slowed, Onslow nudged her and said, "Welcome to your new home!" He was careful not to call her by her name or to say, "the CF central command outpost."

When the passengers inside that high-riding military-style jeep arrived at the outpost with their catch of the day, namely Moses Cameron, they were met by rousing cheers.

Onslow continued taking care of the blanketed Priscilla, as did Jordy with the muzzled and handcuffed Camilla. At the same time, some men from the other vehicle transported Moses Cameron directly to the medical center, where curtains drawn on either side separated him from the other patients. But Priscilla was unaware that Moses Cameron had also been transported here. And neither she nor Camilla was cognizant of the other's presence.

Jordy escorted Camilla straight to CF Commander Wozniah. Because he and the commander needed to talk, they isolated Camilla until the commander was ready to interview her. That was especially true after Jordy told him about the mysterious charm school.

And although the commander was shocked to learn about the mysterious charm school, of the three "guests," he was most interested in Moses Cameron.

"Are you sure all the other girls have been eliminated?" he asked Jordy. "You don't suppose there are other such places? Nah, not in South Africa, do ya think?" Tommy spoke as if answering his own questions.

Jordy handed him the manual entitled *The Book of Judges* and noted, "And there's plenty more where that came from."

"Okay," the CF commander said, "Let's see what our interrogation produces."

"And what of Miss Prissy?" Jordy asked, pulling loose strands of his hair away from his stubble-covered face.

"I believe we're about to find out," the commander said. "But first, we have the matter of Moses Cameron. Can you believe that bloke had the audacity to come out of retirement and go back into the field? And to meet with such a humiliating end!" He shook his head. "Oh well, so where'd you put him?"

"We had a bit of a problem. You see—"

Arching an eyebrow, the commander said, "I did see, and I saw all of it, along with the rest of the world, on the televised news."

"Alright, then," Jordy said, "but we had to lose the cameraman before our guys could sneak back inside that place." Then he spoke with a bit of humor. "It took some doing, but he's over in the medic center. Suppose he's on ice?"

The CF commander ignored Jordy's question because he had something else on his mind: "Do you know who almost castrated the man?"

"I have my suspicions. But it pains me to relive what I saw. And if I think who did that to the man, I sure as hell don't ever want to be on her bad side.

While CF Agent Jordan briefed CF Commander Wozniah on the current state of affairs, Onslow hurried Priscilla—still under wraps—through the crowd of curious CF soldiers. They made their way to the back of the barracks, where he ordered a couple of men to stand watch. Then he pulled the blanket off Priscilla.

"Young lady," he began, "do you trust me?"

Priscilla wore a puzzled expression on her dirty, almost unrecognizable face. She stared at the scary tattoos of snakes and tigers crawling up Onslow's neck and arms. "Why, Onslow," she quipped, "I'm more afraid of your snakes and tigers than I am of you." She giggled and finally said with a heavy New York accent, "Get outa' here. What a stupid question."

"Then I need you to strip. Take off everything. You need to be scoured of possible germs and other stuff."

"Oh, no, you don't!"

While Priscilla balked, Onslow pulled off her clothing, and then he put her under a hot shower and, impersonally but thoroughly, lathered her up and began scrubbing her all over. After he was pretty sure that he had cleaned her body of any germs and other filth, he turned on the cold water; Priscilla hollered again.

Several curious men heard what sounded like a woman screaming. They rushed over to the barracks and asked the two soldiers standing guard, "What was that? We thought we heard a woman scream."

"And so you did, Bro," one of the guards said. "Onslow's just giving one of the little wenches a scrubbing."

The men laughed. "Wow!"

Then one of them whistled and then said, "She must be awfully dirty."

After Onslow had scrubbed her clean, he gave Priscilla a slightly oversized camouflage shirt, a pair of pants, and a pair of men's boots. She put on her new clothes. Then, Onslow took her on a tour of the CF central command center. Starting at the back of the facility that Priscilla had regarded as a massive warehouse of sorts, she saw a kitchen, a storage area and several shower stalls. She also saw a bedroom that had been prepared exclusively for her. It looked like a storage room with a bed and a nightstand. Grateful, "This'll do," she said.

Then, the two walked out into a corridor that led directly to the immense and vibrant central command center. "This is where everything happens," he proudly told her.

"Okay, Onslow, what exactly do you mean by everything?"

"Miss Prissy, the fellas in that room over there," he said, pointing to some distance away from them, "well, they will bring you up to speed." He could see the CF commander and Agent Jordan talking in the commander's office. Since he had some idea of the commander's need to update Priscilla on her situation and the impending trek ahead of them, he took his time bringing her before him. So, he continued showing her around the command center.

But Priscilla did not see the men who were talking in the commander's office. Since her time in Africa had begun, she had not seen Tommy Wozniah. In fact, since her time at the safehouse in Prospect, she had not even seen Jordy.

At the same time, in the medical facility, the physician was speaking with Moses Cameron.

"Now, my good friend," he said, "I have a syringe of analgesic here to lessen your pain. But my instructions were to administer it only if you—"

"Please, Doctor, please," Moses begged. "Have mercy."

"Oh, my good friend, I would if only I could! But you see, my good friend, if I do not do as they tell me, they'll kill me. And so, please just tell them what they want to know. Besides, even the ice on your wound will melt very shortly." Then the doctor leaned over Moses and held the syringe in his face for him to see it. "So-o … tell me, how does the SANM select its PG? And how many of them are there? And then I have some questions about the finances and, of course, about certain policies of the SANM Executive Committee."

"I don't know. I tell you, I don't know anything," Moses gasped. "I don't know," he said, again and again. Then he lost consciousness.

The doctor splashed cold water on Moses's face, woke him back up, and whispered in his ear. "My dear friend, Moses, I'll tell you a secret. I also hold here in my other hand the power to restore your manhood. What will you tell me, my friend, to have me do that?"

"Anything. I'll tell you whatever you want to know."

"Now we're getting somewhere. Yes, my good friend, now we're getting somewhere."

The doctor signaled to one of the soldiers to fetch the CF commander. But Jordy was about to tell him about Carlton and Priscilla's previous relationship. While Jordy followed the commander, he realized he would have to keep his secret a little longer.

At the sight of Moses, Tommy smiled and said, "Ah, I see our patient is back with us, and I hear he's ready to talk."

Moses spoke between his clenched teeth. "Damn it, man, I know what you people are trying to do. But I know my rights. What you're doing constitutes crimes against humanity!"

The commander shrugged. He also laughed. "Ha! Ha! Ha! Yes, yes, but you and I both know beyond a shadow of a doubt that no government on the face of this Earth even recognizes our existence. So, my good friend, start talking, because we're definitely your only hope."

Hope filled Moses' eyes. "Are you going to restore my manhood?"

"That's between you and the doc." Again, the commander shrugged. "Your manhood is of no concern to me." He leaned over Moses and whispered emphatically: "I only want to know about the operations of the PG and the SANM." Then he straightened up and said, "Now, start talking! And whatever you say had better be reliable. Or else…. Are we clear?"

"We're clear. All right then."

Moses confirmed much about the PG and the SANM that Tommy had already suspected. But he also revealed some new information about financial operations. Then he mentioned something even more unexpected: "And we've got women special ops all over Paris, Rome, London, lots of places. You name it, we've got 'em—"

Tommy interrupted him. "Hold on! Are you telling me, even as we speak, the SANM has female special ops scattered about Europe?" When Moses nodded, the commander pressed for more. "And where might we find records of those women?"

"The priest kept all that information under lock and key somewhere in that chiffonier of his. You know… that one big piece of furniture in his private quarters."

The commander nodded and turned to walk away. "Give the man some more damn morphine. I'll come back later."

But just as he turned to walk away, Moses tossed him another tidbit.

"Not so fast, Commander. It might also interest you, Yanks, to know the guys on the Executive Committee released the man called Damien. I overheard some of the fellas mention that during the raid. He's looking to take me out. And that little wench PJ, too. Can you believe that? The SANM gave a kill order on one of its own kind." Moses intended to say more, but he grew groggy, very groggy. "And yeah, before I forget. Damien reports to the moneyman, Heinreik Lipponeg."

Then Moses slipped into unconsciousness again.

Amazing, CF Commander Wozniah thought as he walked back to his office. *Just damned amazing how much a man talks when his manhood's on the line. I wonder, though, what else can the bastard tell us?*

As soon as he entered his office, he caught sight of Jordy, who had returned a little earlier. He looked troubled as he stared into space. "A penny for your thoughts, Jordy. I offer my friend a whole copper cent."

"Oh, Tommy, it's you."

"Yeah, man, expecting somebody else? What's on your mind? You seem far away from here."

"Tommy, my man, sit down. I have something you need to know. It's about Carlton and PJ." As if there would never be a better time than the present, Jordy talked nervously and fast; he put it all out front. But what he did not notice was the immediate reaction of his long-time friend and CF associate.

The indomitable CF Commander Tommy Wozniah looked as if he had been caught completely unawares. "Nah, man. Now stop right there. Surely you're not telling me that—"

This time, Jordy peered intensely into Tommy's eyes and spoke: "Afraid so, my man. Apparently, it didn't go on for long. But from what Carlton told me about it, it seemed…." He sighed. "Well, they broke it off shortly before the wedding announcement."

"Ah, hell! Talk about added complications. That scoundrel! Wait 'til I get my hands on him."

"Back off, will ya, Tommy. I don't think what they had was just a fling. When you see the two of them together, the sparks shoot big time. I think there's something between them still." Jordy hesitated; then he added, "And I'm afraid it might pose a bit of a problem as we try to wrap things up."

"I'll say. But I'm still gonna get back at him because he led me to believe, 'My work is my life,' as if he didn't even have a significant other. The sneaky bastard. I'll get him for this one. Damn, Jordy, how'd it happen?"

"Long story, that we can maybe save for later. But I just wanted you in the loop, things being what they are."

"Alright," Tommy said and paused. "Now, let us resume with Moses …." Since Jordy had left the commander's interrogation of Moses early, the commander filled him in on the parts that he had missed.

While Tommy was consumed with what he'd learned about the SANM and the PG, Jordy openly pondered Moses' relationship with his daughter, Camilla. "Didn't you think it odd the man didn't even ask about her, his own daughter?"

"Who knows? We'll give him the opportunity to demonstrate fatherly love, just not right now. For the moment, we get the daughter to pin her little ass on her father. And then we see how hard Moses tries to shake her loose."

"I see." Jordy frowned at the thought. "I do indeed."

"But right now, we need those records of the female assassins," the CF commander stressed, ending with, "Then we'll see where Miss Camilla's loyalty lies, with her earthly father or the Judges."

26

A Tense Reunion at the Immense & Vibrant CF Central Command Center

Dressed in her oversized camouflage uniform, with CF Lieutenant Onslow standing beside her, Priscilla stood enthralled with the immense and vibrant CF central command center. She looked up and saw ceiling fans that actually worked, spinning round and round. Then her eyes fell on a movie projector that showcased aerial maps and what appeared to be troop movement. She walked to the center of the vibrant space and was caught up between several soldiers seated at computer workstations tapping away on their keyboards, as two more soldiers paced back and forth talking loudly on clunky walkie-talkies—or, they might have been cellular phones—and another soldier yelling across the way at someone talking on a black rotary telephone when, suddenly, upon seeing her, they all lowered their voices and stared at her and stopped whatever it was they were doing. Then, just as quickly as the soldiers had stopped what they were doing, Onslow gestured to them to resume their work, and the vibrancy of the central command center continued. Mesmerized, Priscilla could not help noticing that none of these soldiers sported heavy weaponry, at least not the big automatic rifles that Onslow and Jordy carried. Yet they all sported big pistols in holsters under their arms or around their waists.

She walked over to a table that displayed an array of electronic devices. Observing her fascination with the equipment, Onslow told her that, "Some of these are encryption devices and scramblers and scanners, even fax machines."

"Hmm," she said. Then, "So 'this is where everything happens.'" At that, she suddenly realized that she was involved in something much bigger than the murder of her fiancé or her apparent abduction so far away from home. Then she thought, *Why the hell am I in the middle of a military complex in Africa, of all places? I wonder what their party line is this time.*

Priscilla had no way of knowing it, but she was in the belly of something much more sinister than any political farce she could ever have imagined back in the Ohio capital. As she pondered her precarious situation, she happened to look up and notice a soldier walking into an office across the way. He had some papers in his hand. There were two people inside the office, and they looked vaguely familiar to her. A tall, otherwise nondescript, clean-shaven man donning a knotted ponytail of brown hair, seated in a wooden, executive-style swivel chair behind a huge metal desk, reached out and took the papers from the soldier. *Why, I haven't seen Tommy in two or three years.* Yet she knew she had heard his voice more recently. *But where was that, and why is he here?*

The CF commander was leaning over his desk, talking to another man, who was also dressed in a camouflage uniform. Priscilla would recognize her former high schoolmate anywhere. Of similar stature to Tommy, Jordy was nearly six-feet-three. His hair nearly touched his shoulders; he sported a haircut longer than usual. Priscilla remembered his habit of pulling his hair behind his ears. But she had never seen his hair this long. Jordy wore his hair off his face, which was covered in what Priscilla regarded as black porcupine-like spines.

A stern, pensive expression covered her face. *Not again,* she thought. *Didn't I just see Jordy and Angel at that place where the ceiling fan worked when it wanted to?* But Angel was not here.

But seeing Tommy and Jordy here was too much. Unlike her situation in Prospect, when she had been sedated much of the time, this time she had the full range of her mental faculties. *And why're they dressed in camouflage ... and all these soldiers? My God, what is this place?*

When, like Bette Davis, she strutted closer to the familiar faces, Onslow did an about–face—as if that had been his cue—and he departed, as if he had never even been there.

At the very sight of her, the CF commander wore an expression of amazement. He stood up to greet her.

Jordy turned around in his chair to see what or who it was Tommy was acknowledging, and when he saw Priscilla, he also stood up to greet her.

Both men wore pleasant expressions on their faces.

For a brief moment, though, silence permeated their midst.

Tommy suddenly realized that he had not seen Priscilla since her abduction in her bridal gown on that ill-fated day of her wedding. So, absent her wedding gown and with her new short hairdo, which was still short in comparison to its natural length, she looked pretty much the same to him. Yet he had no idea of the ordeal she had endured in the crypt of that cathedral. But at the sight of her, he was reminded of something else. "My God, where's Carlton? He's got to see how similar his doubles are to the real deal."

But Priscilla shocked Tommy and Jordy when she held up her right hand, palm turned out, beckoning them to stop whatever it was they were about to say or do.

"Now, before anybody says anything, please tell me you didn't bring me into this rat hole to make me another job offer," she said in reference to the time they had visited her in Senator Callahan's office with the plum offer of a lifetime, which she refused. "I mean, this is sheer madness."

Tommy gave up his seat for her. "Here, PJ, take my seat." Then he grabbed hold of a metal chair from the other side of his desk, found a place to sit a safe distance away from her direct contact, and braced himself for the duration.

While Priscilla was making her declaration, executive decree, whatever, through her peripheral vision, she caught sight of yet another familiar face— the man with whom she had had the one-time affair, her "special someone" she had only confided to her sister Harriet. Her eyes flashed fire. "You, too!" she roared, as a million sensations—shock, joy, anger and something else that could have been hope or even something more substantial—flooded her. Rage won.

She tilted her head slightly and then quickly ordered, "Oh, no, you don't! Carlton Elliot Bernhardt, front and center with the others."

As Carlton did as he was told, he smiled at her but quickly grabbed hold of one of the other metal chairs and sat in a corner some distance away from her and Jordy and Tommy. For, at that very moment, Carlton, Tommy and Jordy all knew that it was Priscilla's turn to talk, and boy did she have questions that needed answers.

She sat in the commander's oversized chair as if it had been made exclusively for her. Then she spoke as if this would be her only chance to do so. "Why, hell, fellas, I've lost over one month of my life—maybe more, and under the most mysterious of circumstances. I need answers to my questions. Pronto. Quick, fast, and in a hurry, before you stash me away again in some other god–awful place." Priscilla could not have been clearer, demanding to know her situation. "I mean, come on, fellas." Then she snapped: "What on Earth could I have done to bring about the horrible death of my fiancé? And what about my mom, Germane and Julia? How are they and where are they? Do they even know where I am? And why are you guys dressed in camouflage uniforms? Why, I just spent an eternity in the company of 19th-century tombs of Anglican bishops in a rodent-infested crypt. So, please, whatever you say, do not drop that 'we're on safari' line on me. 'Cause you're certainly not high-powered Ohio lobbyists on a big game hunt or safari."

Priscilla thought her voice sounded like a tape recorder, and it did. She had raised almost the same questions to Jordy, Angel, and Charlie at the Prospect safehouse. Only now, here in Harare, she was with two more of "the boys," Tommy Wozniah and Carlton Elliott Bernhardt, in person.

Tommy spoke first. "Well, now, you see, Miss Prissy. ... It sure is good to see you. I mean, it's been a while," he said as he conjured up the line he would feed her. "You see, Carlton, Jordy, Angel, and I are, well, we're reserve officers in an international military unit that's been called into service on behalf of the African Union." But Angel was not present. He was with the manservant in Botswana. Or was it that he was already in Johannesburg? But he was not at the immense and vibrant CF central command outpost near Harare.

Wordlessly, she stared at them and thought, *All right, so I'll play along. Let's see how far he's going to run with that ball.*

Then the CF commander began telling the truth about everything else that had happened, beginning with the Ohio SAD Bill and its connection to the SANM and the PG.

But Priscilla interrupted him, "Yeah, yeah, I've heard something about all that. Cut to the chase."

"But PJ," Tommy spoke more emphatically, "it's the PG—the Patrol Guard—we're confronting. They're assassins. They're the ones who killed your fiancé and caused the senator's incapacitation. They're the ones we're fighting."

Priscilla frowned and asked for a drink.

"Gin and tonic, Missy!" Carlton stood and said confidently. "Give her a gin and tonic."

With not much of a moment's notice. "No," Priscilla said, "this much crap calls for bourbon. And leave the bottle on the desk."

"PJ," Tommy continued. "I'm not so sure you want to hear all the lurid details—"

"Oh, but I do, Tommy. Tell me all that has happened."

"Alright then." Then the men, by turns, leaned forward in their chairs and told her about the many events that had occurred since the date of her ill-fated wedding.

Jordy picked up a stack of newspapers and handed them to her. "I think you'll find these illuminating."

As she sifted through the newspapers, each of the men attempted to inject additional tidbits about the various events that had occurred.

Nearly an hour later, Priscilla let out with an exclamation and waved a newspaper at the men. "A frigging bomb was detonated under my nephew's bedroom at that resort in Ohio! That's how good the FBI's protective custody was, eh?"

It soon became apparent that the "everything" that Priscilla had asked for was too much. She grew exhausted from the horrible news, so she attempted to end the meeting. "Listen, fellas, forget about me. Just take care of my mom and nephew and my friend Julia. They're all that matter to me anyhow. Just forget about me."

"But Missy," Carlton pleaded, "you don't seem to understand. Those bad guys are after *you*."

"Ah, come on, Carlton, what would anybody want with a pawn like me?"

"Oh, Missy, no-o," he held her with his eyes. "You're in an awful mess only because of your association with the senator. I'm sorry to tell you this, but those guys are out to make a statement that nobody messes with their money, or, for that matter, with their political system, which is what the Ohio SAD Bill does. Added to all that, now they've got to avenge the deaths of all those PGs they've lost. With Senator Callahan out of reach in some secret medical facility, you're the next best target. Don't you see, Missy? We *have* to finish our mission in order to protect you."

Priscilla stared into Carlton's eyes. She felt his love for her once more. She flushed, confused. She looked away and then back at him. Her blush deepened. Oh, how she hated it all!

Tommy looked at Carlton, and then at Jordy, to whom he nodded. The CF commander finally witnessed some of what Jordy had told him earlier, and the sparks were indeed amazing to watch.

Jordy broke through the highly-charged atmosphere: "And another thing, your treatment of Moses Cameron—"

"Moses, who?" she asked.

Amusing images appeared on each of the men's faces, who tried and failed to hide very small smiles.

"Let's just say," Jordy went on saying, "he's the one you practiced surgery on with your little hammer and chisel. Thank God, you missed that—and missed an artery to boot!"

"Oh!" Carlton's handsome eyebrows arched nearly to his hairline. "So it was *you* who practically whacked off Moses Cameron's manhood? I had no idea. Woman, you never cease to amaze me!"

"Speak for yourself, my friend," Tommy said in an outrageous tone of voice. "Speak for yourself."

"My goodness, Tommy!" Carlton came back saying, "Where'd all that come from?"

Priscilla took another drink and settled back into the gulf of the CF commander's comfortable chair to watch the two men spar.

Then Tommy said, "So when exactly were you going to tell me about …?" He hesitated, and then he nodded in Priscilla's direction.

But Carlton responded in a deliberate matter-of-fact way, "Oh, Tommy, man, even you have secrets."

"Yeah, Carlton, man. But nothing that could jeopardize a mission. Under the circumstances, didn't you—?"

"Okay, fellas," Jordy came to the rescue of his colleagues. "Take a station break. And let's finish up with Priscilla. Then you two can go out back and have at it. Besides, we're running out of time. We've got to bring her up–to–date, particularly the part about Joburg."

Disillusioned, Priscilla almost dropped her drink. Then she reentered the conversation. "Oh, no, Jordy! There's more? I really don't know how much more of this I can take. I just want to go home and pretend none of this ever even happened."

The telephone rang, bringing much-needed relief to everyone.

Tommy ran over to his desk and picked up the phone on the first ring, listened and briefly nodded before hanging up. "Our man at the cathedral says things are trickier than expected… crawling with soldiers, police, and forensic folks. We can't get inside the headmaster's quarters just yet."

Then, after the three friends and CF associates told Priscilla about the teenage assassins at the Anglican Cathedral and about their connection to the PG and the Judges, her original suspicions were finally confirmed. Still, she found what they told her hard to believe. Had Priscilla grown delirious? Or was she just a little tipsy from all the bourbon she had drunk?

Carlton's dark eyes grew even darker with concern. "I think, guys, this is enough for now. We have work to do, and I think Missy here needs some time to process all this."

"Incredible, just incredible," she kept saying. Pensively, she walked back through the immense and vibrant central command center to the bedroom that had been prepared exclusively for her. She lay down, shut her heavy eyes, and felt herself drifting off, drifting back to that day of days. "Incredible…."

They first met in the summer of 1982 at the governor's mansion in Columbus during a political fundraiser for a Democratic gubernatorial candidate. During the crowded reception, a distinguished gentleman walked over to Priscilla and asked her what she was drinking. When she told him, "A gin and tonic with a twist of lime," he called a drinks waiter.

Always underestimating her own persona, Priscilla had no idea of her aura. Whereas at the time many other women wore the trendy padded-shoulder suits and beaded dresses, Priscilla wore the earth-tone rayon culottes she had purchased during her visit to her college friend Cathy's home in Cheyenne shortly after her father, Nelson, died. Nor did Priscilla sport a bouffant hairdo. Since she felt that her race and gender attracted unnecessary attention, she wore her hair like the British band members, *The Beatles*, and settled on a more classic outfit as part of her political life in Ohio and for the fundraiser.

Yet it had been that very understatement of hers that had attracted the mysterious admirer, who spotted her almost immediately. Priscilla did not notice someone had just offered her a drink—a common occurrence at such events—until she had nodded her acquiescence to that offer of a drink. She looked him in his eyes to acknowledge his kindness, but then she almost fainted. *My goodness*, she thought, *my very own Charles Boyer*.

"I'm Carlton Elliott Bernhardt. How do you do?"

As she was to discover not long afterwards, he already knew about her. At that time, Priscilla had become popular— "but in a good way," Carlton had taken care later to reassure her—as author of a letter that resulted in a Democratic state senator returning to the fold just in time to secure that party's control of the Ohio Senate. At the time, Carlton was the Congressional liaison for the governor's office. Because he spent much of his time in the nation's capital, Priscilla had seen little of him.

In those days, when Priscilla had worked as Senator Callahan's legislative aide, only one other politico—Bill Scott, financial aide to the Senate Republican Caucus—so captured her attention. Yet not even her fondness for Bill compared to the intense feelings that quickly developed between her and Carlton after their meeting at the gubernatorial reception.

Sometimes they shared coffee at Mary's Café at the Statehouse, and, after that, they told whoever asked that they were "just mutual acquaintances." But anyone in the company of the couple could easily see the natural attraction growing between them. Priscilla all but melted at the sound of his voice, especially when he would say, "Hello, Missy." Always he called her Missy or Prissy, never PJ or Priscilla. Back home in Prendergast, her family had called her Missy. When they teased her, they called her Miss Prissy, too.

As for Carlton, he could not quite restrain himself from planting a kiss on her cheek, regardless of where he saw her. To him, it seemed so perfectly natural to touch. From week to week, he wanted to touch her more.

Yet aside from his pecks on her cheek, over the course of their mutual acquaintance, it seemed they kept each other intentionally at bay.

But for the occasion of Priscilla's homecoming from her Bahamas and European excursion, Carlton could no longer play it safely.

So it was there, at Port Columbus International Airport, that the two mutual acquaintances breached the unspoken rule that had existed between them. Together they walked the long concourse to the escalators and descended to the baggage claim area. After he collected her two large suitcases, filled with collectibles from her trip, they headed to his car. Then they drove the short distance to his condominium, where, upon entering, he told her, "Sit down, anywhere. Relax, Missy. I'm sure you're thoroughly exhausted from your trip, especially that long return flight."

Still standing and taking it all in, Priscilla finally said, "Gee, so this is what a bachelor's pad really looks like." She had half-expected a lot of black and dark colors—masculine, maybe even plastic furnishings, here and there. Instead, she saw neutral and Earth-tones, and the furniture even matched. It would be a long time before she'd learn of his family's relatively high net worth. Nevertheless, she did not broach the subject of whether he had decorated his home himself or had hired an interior decorator. Nor did she realize that his simple, understated elegance had matched her very own style.

Carlton had already asked her if she wanted a drink, but Priscilla's mind lingered on the décor of his home. He asked her again. "Say, Missy, I said, 'Would you like a drink?' Maybe a light cocktail?"

"Perhaps a bit of white wine."

"White wine coming right up for my lady friend."

Then, one thing led to another—and it really did happen in an instant. Their bodies glided back and forth and created the most wonderful sensations. Priscilla could not remember how it all started. But she later remembered that she enjoyed the sweet taste of the salty sweat of his body so much that she kept licking more of it from her upper lip.

At one point, she peered over at the nightstand and noticed a saucer filled with lemons. "My goodness, Love, where'd these come from?"

"Don't you remember, Missy? You told me once, the first time I got you a drink, 'I like the taste of lemons or limes with my gin and tonic.'"

"Gin and tonic? When today did I ask for a gin and tonic?"

"Shortly after our first kiss, when you said, 'Now all I need is a stiff gin and tonic with a twist of lemon, or is that lime?' Missy, don't you remember?"

"And how'd we get from the sofa to your bed?"

"Ah, come on, Missy. We were making out. I asked you if you wanted to stop, and you looked dead in my eyes and said, 'I'd hate to go through life wondering what could've been.'"

"And then what?"

"And then we stood up, barely," he laughed, "and ran in here to the bed. And you've been hollering and screaming until a moment ago when you calmed down."

"Wow! Who would've thought?" she said as she reached out and kept eating those lemons, the rinds and all.

"Excuse me a minute, will ya," Carlton said. "I've got to make a pit stop to the little boy's room. Meanwhile, catch your breath, 'cause there's plenty more where that came from."

"Oh, Carlton, my darling Carlton, I just love the sound of your name. Bring me a damp towel when you come back."

"Okay, Miss Prissy."

While Carlton always called her "Missy" and "Miss Prissy," she called him "Darling" and "Love."

When Carlton came back to the bedroom, he was amused at the sight of her still eating those lemons.

"Why are you eating those lemons like candy?"

"I don't know 'why', but the taste seems to suit the taste of your body, which is good. My goodness, you taste good."

Spontaneously, he pulled her ankles and slid her down to the edge of the bed. He kissed her gently, whispering, "Well, now, Missy, it's time for me to taste more of you." He licked her cheeks and her neck and played with her voluptuous breasts. He looked up at her and laughed again. Priscilla dropped her lemon onto the bed, clamped his head between her hands, and planted a hard kiss on his lips. Then she streamed tears of joy as he licked the insides of her thighs.

Moved by Priscilla's display of emotion, with sheer grace, Carlton recited the words of King Solomon:

> Your rounded thighs are like jewels,
> the work of a master hand.
> Your navel is a rounded bowl
> that never lacks mixed wine.

But before she could react, he parted her vulva.

"Now, Missy, I want you to come for me. Come as if it's the last thing we'll do together."

Priscilla fell back and cried out: "Oh my . . ., what is . . .?" She could not continue to speak.

Carlton tossed her a small pillow; she muffled the sound of her voice, and he continued to feast in her vineyard. After a while, the lovers fell asleep, and they slept for hours.

When Priscilla awoke, reality set upon her. At once, she knew her time with her mystery man was transient, for there was absolutely no way she could take him home to her family—certainly not to her mom. Liza had always insisted her girls never bring home a white man. But Carlton was an Arab, Palestinian, more precisely. His family was from Lebanon, and he had a swarthy skin tone. But that would not count for Liza. Still, Priscilla thanked God for their time together. As she absorbed the moment, she fawned over her lover's magnificence.

Aroused by the gentle touch of her hand, Carlton embraced her petite body and held her close.

"Any regrets, my Love, any?"

"No, my Love. Not a single one."

The two lovers held each other tightly and silently appreciated what both knew might be their only time together—intimately, that is.

A little later, she reminded Carlton that she needed to call her friend, Julia. She had not contacted her since her arrival, and she knew that Julia would be concerned. Carlton handed her the telephone and asked her to call out the numbers for him to dial.

When Julia heard Priscilla's voice, she knew instinctively what had transpired, but not with whom. She guessed it must have been with someone she had met on her vacation. "Okay, now Missy, exactly when are you actually coming home?"

"Oh, Julia, I'm sorry, but I got a little detained," Priscilla had told her friend. "I should arrive first thing in the morning." Then she gave the telephone back to Carlton, and he hung it up.

"So, we're in agreement. You will spend the night, and I will take you home after breakfast."

"Why not?" she said, and they resumed making love as if it would be their last time, again.

The next day, Saturday, Carlton drove Priscilla to her home office, which was quite a distance from his condo and the airport. Still, he was hesitant to leave her. In fact, neither would say, "Good-bye." Instead, they kept saying, "See ya," "See ya, again soon," knowing full well they most probably would never be together again, at least not like this....

It was not long afterwards that Priscilla had met Jonathan, and shortly after that, she'd agreed to marry him.

Remembering all that had been bittersweet. Priscilla's eyes opened wide on the bed at the immense and vibrant CF central command center in Harare. She was not so sure how she would handle her unexpected reunion with Carlton. *Right now,* she thought, *my survival is paramount. I'll deal with my love life later. Tomorrow, maybe.*

27

Vital Intel, the Man Called Damien
&
Ambush at Chitungwiza

It was nearly midnight. While Priscilla had been catnapping, CF Commander Wozniah and his chief agents were about to collect some more vital information from inside the Anglican Cathedral compound.

A CF soldier, known as "Joe," walked briskly past the Harare Police guarding the cathedral boarding school with all the zeal of someone important, lying, "Gotta check on one of my men."

Twice he was stopped, and each time he told the same lie: "It's getting kinda' late. I need one of my men to check back in at headquarters."

Once inside the mostly unlit boarding school building, aided by his night goggles, Joe hurried down the main corridor to the private quarters of the deceased priest, where he saw little flags all over the room and the many blood stains that evidenced the priest's mutilation and the students' suicides.

He headed straight for the chiffonier and began rummaging through its drawers and compartments. Then he turned around and rummaged through an old wooden desk and a tall aluminum filing cabinet.

"Nothing, damn it!" Joe cursed.

It then crossed his mind that there might be a secret compartment in the chiffonier, especially since the CF commander had told him to look there first. Joe rapped his knuckles on the drawers and the doors of the furniture, feeling for anything unusual, but still, there was nothing.

Then, out of frustration, he banged on one of the ivory knobs of the chiffonier's top drawers.

"Voila!" he cried out.

A slab slid out from the wall right beside this tall chest of drawers. The slab covered a secret compartment, which contained a brown leather folder. Joe opened the top flap of the folder and leafed through several pages of names—all of them were feminine names. Then he slid the folder under his shirt and shoved it above his belt to secure it.

Just as he turned around to leave, the lights came on in the room. The guard approached Joe and asked him what he was doing.

Joe drew a switchblade from his right pocket, flicked it open and swiftly slashed the guard's throat. Then he shoved the guard's body under the deceased priest's bed, turned off the lights, and continued on his way.

After Joe met up with his comrades, they set out together in the darkness of the night for the CF central command outpost. But the CF comrades were followed, unknowingly, by the man called Damien.

Damien, with the patience of Job, had staked out the Anglican Cathedral compound after the raid at the cathedral, so he was well aware of the role of the CF having captured his targets—Moses Cameron and PJ Austin.

He was sure his persistence paid off when he began following the CF soldier out of the cathedral compound into the darkness of the city. He believed in hunches, and his hunch was that this soldier would lead him to the CF nest. All Damien had to do now was follow the guy.

Back at the CF central command outpost, Priscilla returned to the commander's office, where the three friends and CF associates continued briefing her on the circumstances confronting them.

"Missy," Carlton said, "I'm not sure how to tell you this, but we're headed to Joburg, as in Johannesburg, South Africa. And, well, let's just say, those folks aren't kind to Blacks. Tommy, Jordy, you tell her the rest."

"Here's the deal, Priscilla." Jordy chimed in and said, "We're infiltrating the SANM's turf. Angel has been setting up things for us there, so everything's pretty much in place. But to bring everything to a head, we're going—"

"Oh, I get it," Priscilla interrupted without apology. "You need my behind for bait, again."

Carlton reentered the conversation: "That's about the size of it, as you're prone to say, 'no pussyfooting around.' But don't worry. We have decoys. So we can use them at least some of the time." He stopped talking. Suddenly, he could not bear to explain the details of these dangers to the woman he still loved.

"Tell me, Agent Bernhardt," Tommy wanted to know, "Do we have a problem here? Are you going to be able to work with her, or not?"

"Don't worry, Tommy," Priscilla interjected. "You guys have risked your lives for my family and friend, and for me, too. So whatever awaits me in Joburg, so be it. Besides, it's time I did my part to help even the score, don't you think? So try not to scoff at Carlton. After all, he's only a man. Now, tell me what it is you want me to do."

As soon as she spoke those words, stunned, Carlton raised his handsome eyebrows. But then he shrugged. It was easy for her to take out her frustrations on him. But he guessed she also needed to show Tommy that any previous encounters between the two of them were not going to endanger the mission.

Once it was clear to Priscilla that their mission was nowhere near over, she was determined to be strong for the duration. She already knew the men had not exactly been forthcoming with her, but she still trusted them because of their shared history.

The three men seemed to feel both her zeal to live and her tremendous faith as well.

When Priscilla returned to her makeshift bedroom, she packed a small backpack and then knelt and prayed. *What else,* she thought, *can I do?*

With such limited knowledge about her situation, she decided it was time to have a little talk with the only Being who was absolutely true to her.

Her prayers were simple.

First, she asked God for forgiveness of all her sins and wrongdoing.

Then she thanked God for looking after her family and friend, including the senator. She also thanked God for Onslow.

Finally, she said, "Now if you would only give me the courage and strength of my convictions to do that which is necessary to help these rascals fulfill their mission, then I'd be truly grateful."

That prayer was about all Priscilla had to say. She had already learned the hard way the difference between prayer and promises. Just ask for the blessing and leave the promises to God.

Word soon came that Joe, the CF soldier, and his comrades had almost arrived from the cathedral. Joe had already called ahead to inform the commander that he had secured the folder about the female Judges. In fact, he and his men were less than a mile away.

The level of excitement among the troops at the outpost reached a fever pitch.

But in their haste to return, the CF soldiers had failed to cover their tracks. Nor had they taken added precautions, such as devising alternate routes in case they were followed. Perhaps this might have been different if the ever-cautious and meticulous Onslow had been with them instead of remaining at the CF outpost catching up on much-needed rest.

So it was that Joe and his men were unknowingly leading the man called Damien to the CF outpost.

Even before the CF soldiers reached the outpost, Damien was already seeking a hiding place in nearby thickets in the darkness, where he could wait for his chance to enter it—and to kill Moses Cameron and Priscilla.

Back inside the main office at the outpost, Jordy said, "You know, Tommy, I'm not liking something. It's as if things are too good to be true. Besides, we're rarely this relaxed."

"I'm with Jordy," Carlton said. "It's as if someone is waiting on the chance to ambush us or something. So once you get your hands on those darn papers from the boarding school, let's get the hell out of here."

"All right. All right, fellas. But" Tommy said in jest, "do you think a few more minutes will make much difference?"

"Ah! Here's Joe and his men now," Carlton said, pointing to the men who were just entering the main office and hurrying their way.

Without a word, Joe handed CF Commander Wozniah the brown leather folder he had ferreted from the dead headmaster's quarters.

The commander opened it immediately. To the dismay of Carlton and Jordy—who were anxious to evacuate the outpost and begin the long journey to Johannesburg—Tommy sat down and began reading aloud some of the names and locations on the list of the female assassins: "Camilla Cameron–Vienna; Alecia Favre–Zurich; Mariel Hansen–London; Francesca Spaulding–Paris; Jessica Swanson–Rome; Joyce—"

Then, unexpectedly, he was interrupted by a wailing sound. He looked up from his papers. "It seems to be coming from the medical center."

Tommy then ran out into the corridor, where Priscilla and Onslow were seated on their bags, waiting for the signal to depart. "Good, Onslow," the commander said, "Stay with Miss Prissy until we can see what's happening."

Then he signaled for Carlton and Jordy to join him.

Back at the operating room of the medical center, they stared at what they found. They could barely hold their eyes steady.

Moses Cameron's torso had been chopped up into three sections, yet he still appeared to breathe. Blood gushed out of his nose. His bloody arms and hands flapped about aimlessly. His bleeding lower limbs rattled on the table, like skeletal limbs searching for their body.

Damien had worked fast. Without uttering a single word, he had used a hacksaw and cut Moses Cameron's torso into three sections. The man knew his job. For him, a kill order was just that, an order to kill. It would take a few minutes before Moses Cameron would bleed to death, long enough to comprehend the fullness of his defection from the Executive Committee of the SANM. His slow death was the point of the grotesque dismemberment, a PG trademark of final agony which they imposed on their victims.

After he had eliminated one of his primary targets, Damien returned to his hiding place in thickets behind a nearby munitions truck. He contemplated his next move: *Now that I've eliminated one of my primary targets, shall I go inside the principal office of the CF central command center to find the American woman? Nah, too many people. Since I already know they're headed to Joburg, should I go ahead of them or wait and follow them? What the hell, no hurry. I'll just follow them.*

Then Damien pulled out his cell phone and placed a call to his supervisor, who happened to be working late at his Johannesburg office. "Disabled my first target," he said. "Chopped him up. He'll be dead shortly. By the way, I overheard someone say they're closing down this camp and headed our way."

Heinreik dropped the telephone, leaned over, and puked all over his desk. He vomited until there was nothing left in his stomach. Then he ran into the washroom, rinsed out his mouth, and splashed cold water on his face.

"Dear God, no," he cried out. "Please stop this madness." Heinreik then fell to the washroom floor and cried like a baby.

Back at the bloody scene before them at the medical center, the three CF senior agents stood for only a moment over what was left of Moses Cameron, and then all three nodded and turned. Without having to talk it over, they all responded in tandem to the same instinct.

"Let's get out of here, *now*!"

"So ordered," said CF Commander Wozniah.

But before they departed the outpost, the commander ordered a squad of his men to bury Moses Cameron's remains near the wooded area behind the medical center. The men dug a deep hole in the ground, put the remains in it, doused it with kerosene, and lit a match to it. After the flames faded, the soldiers covered what was left with dirt, climbed into their jeeps, and drove away.

Not far away, Damien, too, prepared to leave.

Before long, in the darkness of the night, as the CF caravan drove away from their outpost outside Harare, they entered the neighboring city of Chitungwiza. It was there that Jordy struck up a new conversation.

"Moses' daughter, Camilla. What's our strategy with her now?"

Absently, the CF commander responded. "I suppose I'll find a link that can help us with that somewhere in that list of female assassins." Then he raised what he considered a more pressing issue. "Damn-it all. I'm sensing Moses' killer is still with us. Radio ahead to Carlton. Maybe we need to create a little diversion. This might be a good time to unleash another of our PJ decoys."

"I was thinking the same thing," Jordy said. "Let's send word out through the ranks that we're dropping off the American and Camilla at Gweru, and that the courier will deliver them to our Bulawayo camp. Afterwards, the caravan will continue to its destination in Joburg. How's that?"

"Sounds like a plan to me," the CF commander said.

Almost immediately, cell phones and radios beeped and buzzed across the CF caravan, all announcing in code the plan to make the drop-off at Gweru for delivery to Bulawayo, and then to proceed to Johannesburg. As soon as the soldiers heard the message, they were pleased, because many of them thought that the two women civilians posed too many problems, anyway.

When Damien overheard the message from the man driving the munitions truck in which he was hiding, he, too, was pleased. He slumped back down in his hiding place.

Just might get my chance before Gweru, he thought, *and certainly before Joburg.*

On the other side of Chitungwiza, in the pitch blackness of the night, the caravan was creeping along a narrow road, with branches and tree limbs cluttered off to the side of it, when, suddenly, Commander Wozniah called out from his jeep, "Hey, I feel like we're entering a trap. Something—"

Before he could finish, a bullet whizzed by his ear, he saw fifty or more PG jump from under the branches and tree limbs, firing their rifles and pistols sporadically at the caravan.

As it turned out, Simeon had been so angered by the situation in Harare and all the news about the deaths of his PGs that he'd taken unilateral action. He called colleagues for reinforcements, and they'd willingly obliged. But they also reminded him of the need to reserve a sizeable battalion on their home turf, for even they knew about the CF's plan to bring the fight directly to them.

But Simeon did not see the situation the way that his colleagues did. In fact, he did not see anything their way. When news about the devastating PG losses reached his office, it was another bad day for Simeon Johannes.

During the ambush on the caravan, a Guardsman hid under some branches. As Priscilla's jeep neared, he sprang forth and aimed his rifle directly at her head. But one of the CF soldiers who rode in her jeep shot him, although not before the PG got off a round. A bullet grazed Priscilla's temple: she fell over. But no one noticed her wound until after the ambush ended.

Only one CF soldier was not accounted for after the ambush. His body lay across the piles of ammunition in the truck where Damien had shot him earlier. Since he had used a silencer, no one had heard the deadly shot.

"As I said before, we're too relaxed," Jordy shouted out. "Where're our advance men?"

"Perhaps we ought to perform a check now," Tommy said, in his not-so-subtle way of appeasing his men. "Sound off," he ordered.

266

But no one responded when the commander called out for John Becker, who was one of Onslow's men. So the commander sent another soldier to the munitions truck, where John Becker had last been dispatched. The man's body was found on the floor of the truck.

Suddenly, then, the last jeep in the convoy swerved out from beside it and sped away.

The driver of the munitions truck stared at that other jeep and noted, even in the darkness, that its driver was no one he knew. "The bastard who killed John is getting away. I'm after him!"

Indeed, it was Damien.

But the CF commander brought a halt to the matter. "We can't afford the time or manpower to give him chase. All right, men," he said. "Let's move on." The commander had made a calculated decision not to risk unnecessary loss of life to pursue the lone PG. Besides, he did not wish to get off track, especially not in the pitch blackness of the night.

Since they were still near Harare International Airport, the commander arranged for the transport of the remains of the three dead soldiers to Langley, and he also paused to have the wounded treated. Then he, Carlton, and Jordy lowered their voices and talked among themselves. If the CF kept losing men at this rate, they would need more reinforcements sooner than planned. During this battle alone, they lost three soldiers, and seven others suffered serious injuries. Since their venture first began in Nairobi, which seemed like a lifetime ago, the CF had been reduced considerably in size.

"Carlton, take over," Commander Wozniah said. "I'm going to have a little chat with Miss Camilla. I wish like hell we hadn't lost Moses Cameron."

At the sight of the CF commander entering the jeep where she was imprisoned, Camilla leapt to her feet. Then the commander unsnapped the muzzle that had kept her silent.

Camilla shouted out, "My father! Where is my father? Surely you didn't bring him on this journey. Where are you taking me? I heard gunshots. What's happening? Please tell me!" Oh, how she ranted.

"You want to know something, and I want to know something, so let's start there," the commander said. "First, let me say that, whatever happens, you will be treated as an adult. Had you been younger, say, eleven or twelve, things would be different. But you're nearly eighteen years of age. So start talking."

"Am I on some sort of trial?"

"No, Camilla. But let's continue with my questions. We already know you've been placed, shall we say, in the care of a certain *Swiss* guardian for your entry into European society." The commander emphasized "Swiss" for two reasons. First, he wagered the young woman had preferred not to be placed in the already fully covered environs of Britain. Second, he knew, from the late headmaster's papers, that Camilla had been assigned not to Switzerland, but to Austria—to Vienna, precisely. But to confirm his suspicions, he still asked for verification—and gave her the leeway to lie.

"Where is your assignment and under whose care?" he asked her. "Think very carefully before you answer. You do want me to answer more of *your* questions, don't you?"

"Yes, I see. I have been placed in Zurich, Switzerland. My father was going to take me there earlier, but then everything got turned upside down."

Camilla pretended to cry.

The commander ignored her fake tears. "Now, as promised, your father is in Harare. You were correct. But he's not in any condition to travel. So tell me, who is your contact in Zurich?"

"I really don't—"

"Young lady, you're not playing a game with your friends. I want you to tell me the name of your contact, or this conversation is over. And believe me, you don't want our relationship to end this way."

As the truck lumbered over some rugged terrain, Camilla stumbled and fell on the floor of the jeep. One of the guards picked her back up, but she had difficulty standing on her own because her hands were still cuffed behind her.

"I'm waiting, young lady. I'll have that answer now."

"I'll tell you when you let me see my father."

"That can be arranged, but we have a slight problem. You see, we're on our way to Joburg, and your father is in Harare. He'll be there for quite some time. But we can't arrange for your placement without the name of your contact. Comprenez-vous?"

"Oui, Monsieur."

"Quel est son nom, Camilla?" ("Give me the frigging woman's name" was what he really meant to say.)

"Madame Katrina Denieuvre."

Camilla was acutely aware that the CF wanted the list of the European contacts affiliated with the Judges, so she had already concocted a credible answer. She was desperate to learn the truth about her father, whom she now feared was dead.

"Etes-vous sûr?" the commander asked, nearly shouting. "We'd hate to make arrangements with the wrong contact for you."

He was acutely aware that the first answer given by any special op, teenager, or otherwise, was almost always a variation of the truth. Therefore, he accepted the name that she provided. He also knew that he held the ace that his young hostage so desired. So he was letting her play for it.

"Oui, Monsieur. Il a déjà été convenu."

"Très bien, Camilla. Now you asked about the gunshots. We were ambushed. They didn't say what they wanted, and we're not sure who they were. But that's all over now. You're safe. Okay?" The commander snapped the muzzle back across her face and left her.

On his way back to his command post, he checked on Priscilla. She had already hidden the wound on her forehead with a cap, and given the darkness of the night, he did not detect the scar.

Satisfied that both Camilla and Priscilla were fine, he returned to his jeep, where one of his men told him, "Boy, those South Africans are tricky. Found a tracking device under the truck carrying the female prisoner. We almost didn't see it 'cause it was so small. What do you want us to do with the darn thing?"

"Leave it for now," the commander said. "But when we reach Gweru, put it under the courier's truck, the one headed for Bulawayo. After all, that's where we said we were going today."

But then he added, "If Damien had been that darn close to the girl, why didn't he eliminate her? Surely he must have known she was in that truck."

With that surprise attack by the PG, Priscilla finally got a taste of the action the men protecting her were facing. Even though she was terror-stricken at so much adventure, she had already psyched herself to endure whatever else she would face.

"This is my first real safari, and so far, so good," she said, being careful not to look her driver in the eye when she said that.

But the driver simply thought she had an odd sense of humor. Then again, it was his job to drive Priscilla, not to engage her in conversation.

In another vehicle of the caravan, Carlton and Jordy were discussing Priscilla.

Jordy was saying, "I don't think she bought our story about our being in some special international military reserve unit."

"If she did," Carlton said, "she has the best darn poker face I've ever seen. But Jordy, that's not her MO. Missy's very transparent."

"I know, but I wonder what she really thinks."

Both men were right because, apart from having psyched herself for the journey ahead, Priscilla had already thought about why the men had lied to her. *There are NATO forces, special UN forces and a host of others for such matters. Do they take me for a complete fool?*

28

The American Investor, The Winds of Change
&
Connecting the Dots

The CF faced a long journey. If they flew to Johannesburg, the trip would take two hours at most. But they had a whole militia of 200 men, in addition to four women: the two PJ Austin look–alikes, Priscilla, and Camilla. They needed to transport their personnel, munitions, tanks, and other equipment, not to mention the food, cooking utensils, and other essentials such as medical supplies and a makeshift medical unit, overland. The 600-mile trek, with a three-day span, would be across unreliable roadways and a myriad of climates. They could face more attacks by the PG, mishaps with wild animals, and many other problems. But the timing of their arrival in Johannesburg was important to CF Agent Delgato, and what was important to him was essential to the entire CF.

CF Agent Angelo Delgato of Delgato Construction Contractors made an appointment for an important meeting in Johannesburg with the Executive Committee of the SANM. Delgato Construction Contractors was after investor rights in South Africa's lucrative gold industry, primarily in the mining sector. At the time, the most effective way to infiltrate the industry was to finance mining companies that were already there, which, in fact, was what Angel was in the process of doing. The final, though most difficult, part of the arrangement was to secure the approval of the SANM Executive Committee. And Angel wanted to make very sure that he had his own army to back him up.

A day and a half later, Simeon convened the Executive Committee to vote on admitting the new investor. "With so many of our lifelong investors having already pulled out," Simeon said to the seven remaining committee members, "I can't understand why an American firm wants in. And it's particularly puzzling given the actions by their Congress and the recently enacted state divestiture laws, especially the Ohio law."

Then he asked, "When do we meet our new investor?"

Heinreik said, "I told him Friday at nine would be a good time. That would give me a couple more days to prepare the necessary paperwork for a new investor, which, incidentally, I haven't processed in over thirty years. Ours has been, after all, a somewhat restricted enterprise."

Apart from Simeon, Heinreik was the only other member of the Executive Committee familiar with its finances. And although Heinreik had been with the organization since the late 1940s, he was neither Dutch nor British nor Portuguese—but rather Lebanese. On the other hand, Simeon and three other committee members were direct descendants of charter members, fifth-generation Afrikaners. The two other men were of British descent.

The SANM was organized on January 1, 1875. At the time, fewer than a dozen men had amassed immense wealth in mining and refining gold, and later in mining diamonds. A short time later, some of the original group sold their shares and set out for other adventures, whereas the others had remained and invested their fortunes in corporations and industries near and far. They'd bonded and eventually became the leading social and political figures in the mineral-rich territory. There, they'd formulated rules governing South Africa from the perspective of the nationalists, white supremacists mainly. Out of the nationalists' financial endeavors was formed the Executive Committee of the SANM. As their business and commercial interests flourished, they established supporting financial and political institutions. No one could recall for sure, but it was generally believed that the same men who'd created the SANM had also created the apartheid system and the tri-cameral parliament, in which the National Assembly possessed almost all rule-making authority for the South African government.

But throughout the 1960s and 1970s, some of the SANM's most valued investors had slowly but surely divested their holdings. The gradual divestiture started when former British Prime Minister Harold MacMillan addressed the South African Parliament on February 3, 1960:

> "The wind of change is blowing through this continent, and whether we like it or not, this growth of national consciousness is a political fact, and our national policies must take account of it."

Specifically, in northwestern Africa, Ghana and Nigeria had already gained independence. To the east, Kenya, along with several other African nations, became independent during MacMillan's visit or shortly thereafter. Zimbabwe was among the last to gain independence. But South Africa had proved the most resistant of all to social or political reform, resisting those reforms up to and shortly after Priscilla's appearance there.

As it turned out, however, Delgato Construction Contractors were the only ones who'd stepped in to fill one of the seats once held by previously loyal shareholders.

So it was mostly for his love of yet more money that Simeon had taken the bait. In fact, despite his seeming reluctance, he was quite eager to meet the American investor, Angelo Delgato.

"Well," Heinreik said, "I've heard it said that the best time to buy into something is when all the other birds take flight. Besides," he pointed out, "the marketplace will always need gold. I agree with that reasoning, Simeon. I do."

"And the effect of the Ohio SAD law?"

"There's nothing in that statute prohibiting Ohio firms from doing business with us. It merely 'encourages' them not to do so. Americans are as predisposed to capitalism as we are."

"I don't know, Heinreik. Something is unsettling about his timing."

"Again, Simeon, the Delgatos came here well within the thirty days of the bill's enactment. To me, that's indication enough they're serious contenders."

"Oh, all right then. But for the record, mine is a weak 'aye.'"

After Simeon approved Heinreik's proposal, the other five members all voted, "Aye," in near unison.

"The motion passes," Simeon said, "without objection."

While the Executive Committee met and approved admitting Delgato Construction Contractors into their ranks, the CF caravan came upon the magnificent splendor of the Inyanga and the Mtarazi Falls National Park. Mtarazi Falls is unusual in that it is a two-tiered waterfall, the top tier almost hidden. Because the soldiers could not resist the appealing scenery, the caravan slowed to a stop. Several soldiers slipped out of their vehicles and ran to the base of the waterfall, the fifth highest in the world. But because the soldiers were on high alert, the CF commander once again reminded his troops, "This is a military mission, fellas, not a frigging bucket list adventure." At that, the soldiers scrambled and returned to their jeeps.

At the same time, a defiant Priscilla stood up from her seat and shouted, "Now, this is what I'm talking about! Is this the good life or what?"

The men in her jeep stared at one another. Then one of them said, "S'pose she needs to get out a little more or something, eh?"

Even though Priscilla could barely breathe because the forest was dense and the humidity overwhelming, she loved the beauty and splendor of the scene. After she sat back down, she turned to the driver and said, "You'd love all this, too, if you'd been locked up in a frigging crypt as long as I was."

At that, the driver realized that Priscilla was not really crazy after all. He cracked a smile. She was truly happy to be alive and outside of that crypt.

A short time later, the caravan came upon an open plain filled with bushes and shrubs, where at once they encountered a variety of animals.

The men could barely refrain from laughing as Priscilla giggled and said, "My goodness. Look at their color." She was referring to the so-called "blue monkeys" that were swinging back and forth in the tall trees.

She saw some hyenas, too, which she mistook for foxes. She also saw lions, kudus, reedbucks, antelopes, and water buffalo. But when she spotted a leopard, she heard the sound of guns being cocked.

Whereas Priscilla behaved as if she were traveling through a zoo of sorts, the soldiers recognized the predators for what they were. Their orders, however, were, "Kill the beasts if they attack, but never for mere sport."

Throughout their drive through the national park, the CF commander anticipated another surprise attack by the PG, but none was immediately forthcoming.

They finally arrived at Gweru, a city with a population of nearly 150,000. Situated in the center of Zimbabwe, Gweru rested alongside a river that bore its name. Its claim to fame was the country's first bank and its first stock market exchange. Moreover, the arrival of the railroad at the turn of the 20th century connected the landlocked territory to its neighbors—Bulawayo, Botswana, to the west, and Maputo, Mozambique, to the east.

Once most of the caravan had entered the city, some of the soldiers went inside the shops and purchased supplies. In Gweru, miners sold their precious stones and minerals, including asbestos, chrome, gold, iron and platinum. But what the CF soldiers needed was to replenish their building materials, dairy products, textiles, and even footwear.

On the outskirts of the thriving city, Priscilla and the CF soldiers saw farms and enterprises of cattle, crop farming and gardening for export, which they did not know were only a small representation of the hundreds of profitable farms that faced devastation under the leadership of President Robert Mugabe.

CF Commander Wozniah met the courier while the soldiers quickly attached the tracking device inside a panel on the door of the driver's side of the vehicle, which resembled an American armored car.

A soldier escorted Camilla to the commander, who grabbed hold of the young woman's arm and told the courier, "Watch this one. She lies with ease."

The courier pushed Camilla over to one of his companions and ordered, "Lock her in the back with you."

"You lied to me," Camilla mumbled to Tommy from under her muzzle. "You said you were taking me to see my father. Liar!"

"And you lied to me. You gave me a mismatched name." Then he ordered the courier, "Get her out of my sight."

Next, he called for "Ms. Austin"—that is, one of her decoys. Shoving her to the courier, he said, "Let me caution you that although this one is feisty, she carries a huge bounty. So she must be delivered unscathed, or we'll all pay miserably."

"Ah!" the courier exclaimed. "So she's the American everybody's going on about!"

"Yes, the American," Tommy said, and the decoy pretended to spit at him.

Following those two exchanges, the courier handed one of the CF soldiers a heavy metal box. It was no secret that the box contained much currency for the ongoing operations of their mission. After the men exchanged a few more words, the courier departed for Bulawayo.

As it so happened, Damien had observed, from a distance, the transaction between the CF commander and the courier. He was pleased to see both Camilla and the woman he assumed was PJ Austin were en route to Bulawayo. He drove the jeep he had commandeered behind the courier's bugged armored car, which he was unaware had been discovered. But Damien also assumed more of the caravan would have gone with the courier to Bulawayo, so he was somewhat disappointed—and not only about the size of the caravan. But he did wonder why such a significant transaction was conducted in plain sight.

Meanwhile, CF Commander Wozniah conducted another transaction, but Damien had already left, so he missed it.

Tommy ordered a staffer to transmit a copy of the list of the female assassins to CIA headquarters at Langley, which he did. Upon receipt of the list, CIA Agent Froley immediately contacted MI5 and Interpol, triggering an international search for the women whose names appeared on the list.

Within hours, the names and faces of several prominent European women appeared on computer screens, flat screens, and fax machines at intelligence-gathering agencies worldwide. Within hours of those transmissions, the European women were detained by local and regional law enforcement officials, and stakeouts were put in place to arrest even more.

In less than twenty-four hours, curious international news correspondents, who were investigating the rumors about the arrests, had begun to connect the dots. The *BBC* was the first to break the story:

> It is widely believed that several prominent European women are active members of an international terrorist group linked to the South African Nationalists Movement, also known as the SANM. Reports indicate that these women are highly trained assassins who operate similarly to sleepers in terrorist organizations.

276

We will provide more details later in this broadcast as
we receive information from Interpol.

Several hours later, an updated version of that same story ran on nearly
every communications network worldwide. Meanwhile, international news
correspondents checked and confirmed their reports.

And back in Columbus, Ohio, in the American Midwest, a local television news
anchor reported:

> Sources close to *CBS News* have learned that the local
> missing PR executive, PJ Austin, may have been
> targeted by an international terrorist organization
> associated with the South African Nationalists
> Movement. The young women who turned their guns on
> themselves at the Anglican Cathedral in Harare,
> Zimbabwe, were part of a terrorist training group called
> 'the Judges'. The mutilated priest, Father Jacob
> Mbuwayesango, was their headmaster. Upon graduation
> from the so-called boarding school, the young women
> would be matched up with other women who, like
> themselves, were also alumnae. The older graduates
> would introduce the younger ones into European society
> and arrange for their marriages to socially or politically
> prominent figures. Once established, the women would
> wait for orders to assassinate someone with whom the
> SANM found disfavor.
>
> *CBS News* has now confirmed that Ms. Austin is
> indeed targeted by the SANM Patrol Guard, also known
> as the PG, because of her association with Ohio state
> Senator Daniel P. Callahan. After the PG's failed
> attempt to assassinate the senator, Ms. Austin became
> their primary target. However, there have been no
> further developments since her alleged sighting at the
> Anglican Cathedral in Harare.

In related news, the mutilated remains of South African Moses Cameron were discovered in an unmarked grave in the vicinity of an evacuated medical center of the international military unit near Harare. Cameron was a third-generation member of the SANM Executive Committee. He is survived by a daughter, Camilla, who is believed to be the only surviving member of the Judges' terrorist group. There have been no further reports on her whereabouts.

In other news, it has been reported that the international military unit is en route to Johannesburg, South Africa, where it is expected to provide 'added security' for some of the diamond, gold, and platinum mines there. Several unconfirmed reports also allege the military unit will assist in the dismantling of the Executive Committee of the SANM.

Stay tuned to *WBTV News* for further details on this riveting international mystery, which began in Columbus, Ohio, and has since spread across the Atlantic to southern Africa.

29

A State of Emergency
&
Reeling in Heinreik Lipponeg

Back in Zimbabwe, as the CF caravan neared the town of Musina, they prepared for the most challenging part of their journey, the Mushandike Sanctuary. This borderland to northern South Africa consisted of a myriad of interconnected, barely navigable rivers.

Along the way, Priscilla's guards were changed periodically to lessen any familiarity between them. Their mission was a military one, and they did not want it complicated by emotions.

During a break in the caravan's journey, as CF Commander Wozniah and his men reviewed their plans to tackle the passage over the dangerous rivers, the commander expressed his dismay with the leak about their mission.

"My God," he said, "why the hell did those guys leak our mission? How the hell can we launch a surprise attack if everybody's expecting us?"

"Let's try to work this to our advantage," Jordy said.

"There is no advantage," Tommy groused. "Do you suppose the goddamn South African Army is simply going to step aside and say, 'Welcome to South Africa, mates? Come on in.'"

"Maybe not, but if we get the Brits to tell them we really are a peacekeeping unit to protect their diamond, gold and platinum mining interests until this mess blows over, then—"

"Well, now, Jordy, I think you might be on to something. I believe we've got the best damn cover yet. I'll call Langley. Now, if only we could maneuver these damn rivers."

Carlton gave an update saying, "On that note, Onslow's ahead of us. Back in Gweru, he purchased some lumber to build rafts sturdy enough to load the tanks. The jeeps and trucks will fit on the regular ferries, so we're good there. But building the sturdier rafts will take the better part of the day."

Tommy then said, "We need to get word to Angel that we're not going to make it in time for his meeting. And you know . . . he's not gonna like that."

"Yeah, well," Jordy said, "Things being what they are, we don't have much choice. Besides, are we even sure the blokes will keep the appointment now that they've heard the news about our mission?"

"How 'bout giving Angel a call to see what's happening down there? I'm going to talk to Onslow. Take over command, Carlton."

As the CF caravan prepared to cross the barely navigable rivers, Damien made a remarkable discovery after forcing the courier's armored vehicle off the road and instructing the driver at gunpoint to open the back door. When Camilla and the PJ decoy stepped out, Damien called out, "Hello there, Miss Cameron. And how're we today?"

"Piss off," Camilla muttered from under her muzzle.

"And Miss Austin, how're we today?"

Camilla stared at the man, and then she blabbered under her muzzle, "Who are you talking to? This woman isn't the one I knew as Megan. She is definitely not the one they're calling Ms. Austin."

Damien yanked off Camilla's muzzle and told her to repeat what she had just said. When she did, he suddenly understood why the CF agents had handed over the two females in plain sight. They had wanted him to think the look–alike was PJ Austin. Damien was furious with himself for falling for their ploy.

But Camilla, who was hardly interested in the man's disappointment with the decoy, asked, "Where's my father?"

"Oh, please, young lady. I chopped him up days ago." Then he raised his rifle, aimed it carefully at Camilla's head and shot her point-blank—dead.

He turned to the other woman.

"As for you, Miss Double, the Americans must be paying you a hefty sum to risk your life for that little colored wench. But don't you be fool enough to bank on ever spending any of it. Anyhow, I've got other plans for you. Get in the damn jeep."

As they drove away, the decoy noticed that Damien had left the courier and the other man who accompanied him standing by the roadside. *Sometimes,* she thought, *even reputed assassins make big mistakes.* She was surprised that a cold-blooded killer like this one had stopped short of eliminating all the eyewitnesses.

As soon as Damien disappeared from the two men's sight, the courier contacted the CF and informed them of the incident. He also described the man called Damien.

Meanwhile, the reputed assassin was backtracking as fast as he could make the jeep go. *Something else is happening, and I intend to find out what it is.*

When Damien called his supervisor on his SAT phone, the SANM executive told him, "I'm sure you know the international military unit is on its way here. Their sole purpose is to dismantle our operations."

"And so what's that to do with our arrangement? I've eliminated Camilla Cameron, who wasn't even on my list. But they substituted a double for the American, so I'm heading back to Joburg for her."

"No, oh no! Forget about the American girl. I'm releasing you," Heinreik said. "Besides, we probably won't be here by the time you arrive, anyway."

"Oh, you'll be there all right," Damien insisted and disconnected the call.

Heinreik paled at the reputed assassin's tone. It could be that his own life was now at risk. Yet, he grew much calmer than he had been in recent weeks. He supposed that, like Hans, he could take what others sometimes called "the easy way out." But Heinreik had no desire to take his own life. He would let nature take its course.

In Gaborone, Botswana, Charlie (the manservant) had also listened to the latest news. He figured that the PGs were not going to sit in Johannesburg just waiting for the international military unit to come and get them. He opened up his map and studied it. Musina was a perfect place for the PG to attack. He nodded. He would prepare his troops to prevent precisely that.

Simeon Johannes had also witnessed that televised news story and afterward called an emergency meeting of the Executive Committee, where he declared, "We're in an official state of emergency. Inasmuch as that international military unit intends to destroy us, let's give 'em something to talk about."

Then, he turned to Heinreik and said, "All bets are off for the meeting with the American investor. We've got bigger fish to fry."

Heinreik nodded. "I understand."

Then Simeon shocked them when he said, "I'm sending a battalion up-country to meet those rascals when they enter Musina. Bet that'll show 'em."

Then, one by one, the other committee members weighed in.

"Damn," one of them said.

"I knew I should've cut bait and left with the others," fretted another one.

"Now," said a third, "here we sit."

"We can't even trust our own kind anymore," wailed the same man.

"Well," Simeon said, "did you expect a cakewalk? Heinreik explained the situation to you weeks ago. You should've left with Dawker and the others. Too late now." Then he smirked.

Simeon was correct, but for a reason even he was unaware. Each of the remaining Executive Committee members was already under surveillance by nearly every international intelligence agency in the world.

"So, Simeon, what you're saying is, 'We've no choice but to fight until the end?'" one of the same committee members asked for clarification.

"Yes, that's exactly what I'm saying."

"Well, what's going to happen to the organization, to all our investments?" yet another committee member queried.

"If I know the Americans and the Western Europeans, too, they've already worked that out," Simeon said resolutely.

"So, what'll we do in the meantime?" the same man insisted.

"We command our Patrol Guard as never before, and we hope for the best." Simeon's voice dropped almost to a whisper as he repeated, "And we hope for the best."

The men all sat openly pondering their impending demise, while Simeon continued his prolonged discourse on military strategy. After all those years of Simeon's undaunted leadership, they watched in astonishment as he seemed to unravel before their very eyes. He continued to talk about military tactics and strategy, as if he were commanding the South African Army, instead of a few hundred mercenaries known as the PG. Even so, the six other committee members so feared for their lives that they did not oppose or contradict him.

That evening, when Heinreik arrived at his home, he was greeted by his wife with news that some unexpected guests had arrived. As he walked into his study, he saw three men seated, only one of whom he recognized. Angelo Delgato stood up from his seat and walked over to shake his hand; then he closed the study door behind them.

"By now, you've heard the news about the arrival of the international military unit," Angel said. "So it's time we put our cards on the table."

Completely baffled, Heinreik asked, "And what exactly is it you're talking about, young man?"

"Heinreik, I *am* Angelo Delgato with Delgato Construction Contractors. But I'm more than that, and these two gentlemen are from the CIA and the Mossad."

"And so you already know my story?"

"Yes, Mr. Bernhardt, we've known your story for quite some time," CIA Agent Froley said. "Although, as things stand, we—and be clear now that I'm speaking for the CIA—need to know if we can count on your cooperation."

"I've often wondered whether it would ever come to this. Does my nephew know?"

"No, Carlton has absolutely no idea," Angel said. "But if we're to help you, you must act fast." Then, more emphatically than Agent Froley, he asked, "Can we count on your cooperation?"

Quick-witted, Heinreik sighed. "Aside from the finances, what else is it you want of me?"

"We want you to attend the rally that Mr. Johannes has planned for the PG," said the Mossad agent, who had neither been introduced nor so much as shared a fictitious name. "And we want you to wear a wire. We need to get Simeon Johannes' voice for the record. Can we count on you to do this for us?"

"Do I have a choice? I mean, what's going to happen to my family?"

"Once we have your decision, your family will be immediately taken into protective custody and relocated to a secure site someplace far away," the Mossad agent said. "And depending on how things turn out, you'll be allowed to join them shortly."

"Hardly, fellas. If you figured all this out, don't you think Simeon has too?"

"We can't be sure. That's why we need your help," Agent Froley said. "So, what's it going to be?"

Bargain, Heinreik told himself. *What else can I get?* "And Carlton, does he need to know?"

"We'll only tell him if it becomes a 'need-to-know' issue," Angel said.

Heinreik sank on a sofa and cupped his head in his hands for a moment. "This can't be happening to me. I feel like I'm in my own twilight zone." When he lifted his head finally, there were tears in his eyes. "May I have a drink? Just pour a drink for me. Anything will do."

After Heinreik had drained that drink, he finally consented to the offer. Then he walked out of his study and looked for his wife; when he found her, he told her about his long-held secret.

But she surprised him: "Oh, Heinreik, my Love, I've always known there was a part of your life that you concealed from me. I never understood why, but I trusted it was for a good reason. And still I loved you as I do now. Only now, I love you even more. Just tell me what it is you want me to do."

Heinreik fell to his knees and wept. He now knew that he could do anything. He kissed his wife and said goodbye. Then he watched as several intelligence agents, who accompanied his three unexpected guests, escorted his wife away into protective custody.

Heinreik's children were grown and had families and homes of their own. But they, too, were part of the protective custody and would later link up with Heinreik at a place unknown.

As the evening wore on, the three intelligence agents continued their relentless interrogation of Heinreik. They also secured his fingerprints as well as the passcodes to the penthouse suite of the Executive Committee. Heinreik was now essentially a witness for the prosecution.

A State of Emergency & Reeling in Heinreik Lipponeg

Within hours, information gleaned from the interrogation of Heinreik (Bernhardt) Lipponeg was disseminated to the National Security Agency, the CIA, the Pentagon, the U.S. Secretary of State, Interpol, MI-5, the Mossad, the British foreign secretary, and who knew where else.

All the relevant parties—including the South African prime minister, who was the last to be brought into the loop—collaborated and agreed in principle that the international military unit (the CF and its recruits) could enter South Africa to protect its diamond, gold and platinum industries. Since the South African government was already held in extreme contempt by most nations, its cooperation in this small feat would prove invaluable in the future rebuilding of its political regime.

Nonetheless, the impending demise of the global conglomerate, the SANM Executive Committee, was all but sealed.

30

Battle at the Mwenezi River
&
Breaking News

Dusk settled over the CF encampment near the Mwenezi River. Many of the men—exhausted from building the huge rafts to transport the tanks across this and other barely navigable rivers—had fallen asleep on the very ground where they had been working. A few others lingered aimlessly when, all at once, seemingly from out of nowhere, the thunderous sound of gunfire spread throughout the camp. Patrol Guardsmen stood over the sleeping CF soldiers and emptied their magazines into them until, pierced by a myriad of bullets, thirty-nine of the 200 men were dead. An untold number were wounded, and many others—very nearly dead.

Carlton was reading over some documents when the gunshots blasted through his tent. A bullet pierced his left shoulder. He fell over and pretended to be dead.

But this particular raid focused on killing the CF commander, Tommy Wozniah. There was an unwritten, time-honored tradition among military officers and even some terrorists that officers of the same or similar rank confront, fight, or kill their counterparts, such as commander-to-commander and general-to-general. However, PG Commander Damien Escoffery was not leading the SANM PG; rather, Simeon Johannes was. Thus, the tradition did not apply. As a result, the Patrol Guardsmen fought the Collective Force regardless of tradition.

As some of the PG lifted the flap to the CF commander's tent, he tossed live grenades at them. Calmly, he sat back and watched the men exploding into tiny body parts, scattering over the ground outside his tent. Because Tommy knew he was the PG's prime prey, he was prepared to do what was necessary to defend himself, even if it meant dying. He was as cold-blooded as the men who sought to capture and kill him. But just in case a few of the bad guys lingered, he unloaded two magazines at any signs of movement near his tent.

Onslow, stationed just outside the CF commander's tent, sustained a severe wound to his right thigh. He was deeply distraught at the thought that he would not be with his comrades in what he was sure would be their victory at Johannesburg.

Jordy escaped harm, save for the horrific images of the unconscionable killing of his men. That evening, he had decided to stand guard high up in a tree; to this day, he cannot explain why he did so. Yet that decision alone had saved his life.

When some of the PG entered Priscilla's tent and began firing their rifles, they were met with return fire from the soldiers assigned to protect her. But like almost any bodyguards, they died protecting their charge. Indeed, they fell, one by one, on top of her body and onto the ground, where she pretended to be dead.

As the battle raged, a quiet inner voice cautioned her, "Be still, my child. Be still."

So a frightened Priscilla lay very still under the dead and wounded soldiers piled upon her. She had no idea of the outcome of the raging battle, but she felt the weight of her dead and wounded bodyguards. Blood from their bullet-riddled bodies streamed over her and even spilled into her eyes and her mouth. So covered with blood was she that she herself looked as if she were riddled with multiple gunshot wounds.

Her claustrophobia set in.

Her heart thumped so fast and loud that she thought someone could hear it. So she held her breath and prayed not to move a muscle. Since Priscilla did not like people touching her, she also knew that, if, at this dire moment, she tried to push the dead and wounded soldiers off her, someone might notice.

Therefore, she tried hard to lie still and breathe, quietly, under the dead and wounded soldiers, her protectors.

At first glance, one of the Guardsmen who had killed some of the soldiers on top of Priscilla returned to assess the scene. When he saw portions of her body, he mistook her for a small male soldier. Then, Priscilla heard him saying, "That one underneath is full of holes. No need wasting any more ammo. Let's get out of here." But before he left, he piled three more corpses atop the heap that already covered her body.

Nauseated. Breathless. Terrified. Oh, how she wanted to move. But something inside her would not let her yield to the added weight and the blood flowing from those three additional corpses lying atop her small body.

"Shall we set it aflame?" asked the Guardsman who had just piled three more corpses atop the heap that already covered her body.

"Nah, leave 'em," the other Guardsman said.

That was the last time that Priscilla heard of that pair. Meanwhile, she held her peace—or was that her fear?

As the massacre continued outside her tent, Priscilla continued to heed the quiet, cautious inner voice that had guided her thus far. Then, as other PG looked inside her tent, they also noticed the heap of corpses and called out to one another, "They're all dead."

Every time Priscilla heard someone near her tent, her heart raced and pounded. Since some of the men in the CF had accents similar to those of the PG, she had no way of knowing who was who, so she prayed she would not move a muscle. But oh, how she wanted to move! As she thought about all those dead bodies on top of her, she faded in and out of consciousness. At one point, she realized that the only way she could take a breath was to swallow the blood filling her mouth and her nasal passages. She wondered whether she would vomit as she squeezed her eyes shut and swallowed the blood of her protectors.

Silently, she prayed: *Oh, God, help me.*

Priscilla did not fear for her life because she had always known, *It's easy to die, but damn hard to endure seemingly unbearable circumstances.* Therefore, she decided to endure this unbearable circumstance.

Just as the jubilant PG were preparing to leave the CF camp, a thunderous roar came up from the Mwenezi River. Neither the jubilant PG nor the surviving CF knew what to make of it, but they soon knew what it was.

The CF reinforcements from Gaborone were storming the camp in a kind of stark, raging madness. Having yet to fight a single battle, the men were ready for the vengeful attack. Because the jubilant PG were wholly caught off their guard, the CF reinforcements raised their rifles and picked them off in much the same way as the PG had just killed so many of their men.

One by one, the PG fell to their deaths. Indeed, not a single one of them survived the counterattack by the CF reinforcements from Gaborone.

Meanwhile, Jordy signaled with his flashlight from atop the tree in which he was perched, and Charlie knew that all was well with him. Certain that the PG had been put down, the remaining CF from the caravan joined up with the Gaborone reinforcements to assess the damage and begin cleaning up the area.

From not too far away, Damien watched in amazement as the battles raged and eventually ended. Now he was certain he had finally witnessed the demise of the American, PJ Austin.

As a somber mood spread throughout the encampment, one soldier found what he believed was Priscilla's corpse. Hurriedly, he put what he thought were her remains in a body bag and then discreetly got word to the CF commander that he believed Priscilla and her bodyguards had been killed.

Tommy Wozniah did not say a word. The stunned expression on his face, as he made a brief call on his cellular phone, said it all.

As some of the soldiers erected a makeshift tent to treat the wounded, word spread throughout the camp about Priscilla's presumed death; even the soldiers who had been uneasy about the presence of the females in their midst were suddenly grief-stricken. Jordy selected a team to deliver the remains of the soldiers, including what they all thought were Priscilla's, to the nearby town of Musina for air transport back to the States.

Around the same time, a couple of soldiers carried Onslow on a canvas stretcher past the CF commander, who did his best to conceal his sorrow over what he believed was news of Priscilla's death.

"Sorry, ole fella, but this is it for you. We've had a good run together, but I've got to release you and send you back home to that nagging wife of yours."

Shaking his head in utter disbelief, "All our dead," Onslow said. "It wasn't supposed to happen like this. But tell me, what's the situation with Miss Prissy?"

"Please, Onslow, don't ask me about her." Tommy did not want any of his men to witness his distress, not even his friends.

Onslow's disbelief was glaring. "She's dead! Not after all she's gone through."

The commander nodded and told the soldiers to take Onslow away, who would return home believing his new sassy friend was dead.

But what most troubled the commander was the sight of his friend and CF associate Agent Bernhardt, lying wounded on a stretcher, his face ashen; he looked like he was in pain.

"Do you think you could at least put on your game face?"

"Screw you, Tommy," Carlton rasped as the soldiers carried him away. Since he had overheard the soldiers saying that the commander had called in Priscilla's death to headquarters, he also believed she was dead. Yet he was determined not to leave the field and fly back home before the mission was completed. Carlton would soon see the commander and his other friends and CF associates again—and when they were least expecting it, too.

During his surveillance of the aftermath of the two battles, Jordy came upon the tent where Priscilla was still playing possum. Like the others who had surveyed the scene, he assumed he had found the remains of dead soldiers who had not yet been removed. Just to be sure, he examined some of the bodies. Soon, he felt a warm face wet with blood. Taking a cloth from his pants pocket, he wiped away some of the blood to see if he recognized the man. He was so shocked by the sight of Priscilla's face that he almost screamed.

As he wiped away more blood, he whispered, "Priscilla! Priscilla! Say something. Please, it's me, Jordy."

Priscilla heard the familiar voice and opened her eyes. She coughed up saliva and blood. "I'm still alive."

"Oh, Priscilla, thank God!" Jordy said with tear-filled eyes.

Priscilla could now feel life coursing through her. "Do you think you can help me up from my untimely grave?"

Jordy pulled her up and held her tight. He was happy that this woman, whom he had known back in high school in New York, was still alive. Although she never quite realized her effect on those around her, Priscilla meant so much to him, as with many others.

Yet, even as he realized she was alive, Jordy knew that he had to keep her survival secret. The success of the CF's mission depended on the belief that the whereabouts of PJ Austin were still unknown or that she was, in fact, dead. But with the reliable Onslow wounded and released back to the States, the agent needed another equally reliable confidant to help with Priscilla's safety. *Charlie*, he thought. *Ah, yes. He'll know what to do.* So, Jordy left Priscilla in the tent and went to find Charlie.

When news about the battle at the Mwenezi River reached the nearby city of Mbizi, the international news correspondents picked up the story and ran with it. Public sentiment quickly shifted from sympathy for the right of the Afrikaners to exercise self-determination to sympathy for the massacre of the many "International Peacekeepers." But most of all, there was a tremendous outpouring of grief over the alleged death of the missing American woman, PR executive PJ Austin.

One *BBC World News* broadcast carried the heartrending story as follows:

> Sources close to *BBC World News* say the massacre of over thirty-nine International Peacekeepers at the Mwenezi River in southern Zimbabwe has left the international community aghast. 'Has the South African government lost all sense of civility and international law?' some world leaders ask. The remains of the missing American, PR executive PJ Austin, along with those of the thirty-nine slain Peacekeepers, are being transported back to the United States. But there is no word yet about any reaction from Ms. Austin's family.
>
> *BBC World News* has also learned that the South African National Assembly has consented to allow the International Peacekeepers to provide much-needed security for its diamond, gold and platinum mines as the death toll mounts from a seemingly constant stream of horrific massacres.
>
> Stay tuned to *BBC World News* for information on what began as a mystery in Harare.

In their safehouse at Niagara Falls, New York, Liza, Julia and Germane watched the televised news broadcast in disbelief.

"Is Aunt Priscilla really dead?" Germane cried out.

"Nah," Julia said. "That's not true. Priscilla's not dead. Something just doesn't feel right about that claim. Besides, if they really think she was killed, they'll have to get one of us to identify the body. So, unless and until that happens, let's not give this story any more thought."

"Oh, Grandma, she can't be dead," Germane held Liza tight. "I just don't feel it."

"Me neither, Son." Liza put her arms around him. "Child, we're going to have to wait and see for ourselves. But I agree with you both. Something just doesn't feel right."

It was as if all three felt so connected to Priscilla that they believed they would know if she were dead. Besides, the two women assured each other, surely the FBI's Rothschild and the CIA's Froley would have contacted them if they believed anything dire had happened to Priscilla.

But just then, there came a knock at their door. Julia followed the prescribed security protocols before letting FBI Agent Rothschild into the room. Quickly, he introduced the CIA agent who accompanied him, adding that Agent Froley was in Johannesburg. But the men brought bad news. Priscilla was indeed presumed dead, and Agent Rothschild asked Liza and Julia to accompany them to identify the body. Even as both women began to sob, later they agreed they still did not sense that Priscilla was dead.

Germane ran over to the sofa, hid his face, and cried like the child he was. "Marvin" —the young man and the federal agent had bonded— "why're you doing this to us? My Aunt Priscilla's not dead. She's not, I tell you."

It took exactly twenty-four hours for the remains of the thirty-nine Peacekeepers and those of the PJ Austin decoy to reach Langley, Virginia.

Liza and Julia, along with the family members of the thirty-nine deceased so-called Peacekeepers, waited impatiently to perform the dreaded task of identifying the remains of their loved ones. When Liza and Julia's turn came, the medic slowly unzipped the bag with the remains of the woman presumed to have been Priscilla.

But almost immediately, Liza said, "*That's* not Priscilla. That's not her hair, her face or her complexion." Liza was adamant. "I know my child, and this is not my girl."

The medical examiner was confounded. "You mean to tell me, this woman is *not* your daughter, Priscilla J. Austin?"

"No, Officer. We don't know who 'this' woman is, but she's not my daughter," Liza spoke with undeniable certainty. "Don't you folks ever use medical records? You know, dental and DNA or something?"

"I'm sorry, Ma'am, for putting you through this ordeal. But according to the paperwork, we assumed that these were the remains of your daughter." The medical examiner then zipped the bag back up.

After that disturbing encounter, Liza and Julia once again disguised themselves with shawls and scarves over their heads and around their faces. They were immediately escorted to a nearby hangar where Germane had been sitting impatiently alone in the seat of an empty plane. Finally, emotionally exhausted but at the same time so relieved, they flew back to their safehouse.

Although they felt a measure of relief, they also felt badly because some other unsuspecting family was about to learn of the death of their loved one, the decoy who gave her life in order that Priscilla might live.

The medical records of PJ Austin and her three doubles were eventually retrieved and examined. Shortly thereafter, the medical examiners had conclusive evidence that the remains in that body bag were, in fact, those of one of the three decoys.

But that development created a nagging dilemma for intelligence agency officials, particularly the Americans.

"Then, where the hell is she?" FBI Agent Rothschild asked his CIA colleagues. "And do we want the world to continue thinking she's dead, or just missing?"

To give the real Priscilla an extra measure of security, the intelligence officials decided to try to keep the bad guys in the dark. Agent Rothschild eventually told Liza and Julia to keep the truth to themselves, "at least for the time being."

With much reluctance, Liza, Julia, and even Germane consented.

But the boy was confused. "Grandma, does that mean we have to fake her funeral, too?"

"I don't know, Child," Liza answered. "Let's see what else these crazy people are going to suggest."

31

Another Makeover, Entering South Africa
&
The Prime Minister's Plea

Back at the Mwenezi River, it took Charlie several hours to change Priscilla's appearance and to teach her how to handle and discharge an automatic rifle.

He shaved her head much like a U.S. Marine's. He dressed her in the same type of camouflage uniform that the other soldiers wore. Then, painstakingly, he showed her how to handle the rifle, how to pick it up, how to carry it with ease, how to load and unload it, and, most important, how to aim and fire it. *Her life is at stake as much as the rest of ours,* Charlie thought. *Why shouldn't she have the means to protect herself?*

"It's imperative that as few people as possible hear your voice," he told her. "Missy," he said, "your voice sounds like a woman's. Also, we need a new name for you. How's 'Guy'? I'll try to keep you nearby and give you kitchen detail and miscellaneous tasks, such as placing the levers under tires stuck in the mud. You'll be my little gofer. Try to ignore all the chaffing. Just get the job done. Understand? And if you're discovered, just tell them you're one of the PJ doubles in disguise. Okay?"

When she asked the manservant about Onslow, he simply said, "Onslow's been released back home." But Priscilla thought of him often. She soon missed the bond they had built. Now here she was again, her survival dependent on another new man.

As the two became acquainted, Priscilla observed something amusing about her new protector: Charlie had a habit of pulling at his moustache, especially when he wanted to seem indifferent to her.

Notwithstanding, Priscilla was once again in a seemingly unbearable situation. But at least this time she had a weapon.

Early the next morning, the caravan loaded the rafts with their vehicles and other equipment and prepared to cross the narrow Mwenezi River, one of three waterways they needed to cross. Each river ran perpendicular to the direction the caravan was traveling. Because each river had huge waves like those that beat against the ferry on which Priscilla and her sister Harriet had ridden during that unforgettable crossing of the English Channel, the men faced a more difficult task. Although they had lost many of their comrades and had nearly 300 more miles to travel, the soldiers rallied with much vigor, and so, too, did the PG awaiting them in Johannesburg. Because both the CF and the PG had laid claim to their right to defend their principles, both forces were determined to fight until the end for cause and country.

It did not take long for the caravan to cross the Mwenezi River. Back on land, the men faced the daunting task of hauling the huge rafts onto the shore, but they managed to do so. Then they drove for approximately one-half hour and prepared for passage across the Bubi River.

Again, they launched the rafts for an hour-long trek to the next major crossing at the Umzingwani River, which intersected the city of Bethbridge at the Limpopo River. The river spanned most of South Africa's northern border.

After a tumultuous crossing of the Limpopo River, they entered South Africa, the country of their destination.

As they motored into Musina, the first major city in the country's northwestern section, Priscilla rode in the back seat of another high-riding jeep along a dirt road that paralleled the Great Northern Highway. Jordy and Charlie sat up front, Charlie behind the wheel.

"*Copper* is king in Musina," Charlie said. "There is also iron, graphite and diamonds around here, but the economy is all about copper."

Priscilla shaded her eyes from the bright sun, but she could not make out any mines. Instead, she saw shrubs, thorny bushes, impala lilies, tall grasses, and oddly shaped baobab trees. She stared at the acacia's thorny leaf stalks, the sharp spines at their base, and their fuzzy yellow and white flowers. She was fascinated by the baobabs. *Their trunks must be*, she guessed, *over sixty feet wide*. She loved their smooth grayish-brown bark and their elongated white flowers.

Then, for the first time since their crossing of the Umzingwani River, she saw people. Several women were strolling barefoot along the highway. Some were carrying baskets of fruit atop their heads; others were carrying babies and small children strapped on their backs. Men were picking dates and mangoes from clumps of lush, green orchards.

Occasionally, the caravan halted, allowing a native mother to grab a wandering child who stood in awe of the long caravan. They had to stop sometimes, too, to allow herds of giant elephants and prancing kudus to pass.

Most captivating to Priscilla were the families of white rhinos grazing casually in the tall grass and thorny bushes along the bumpy dirt road. She could not help marveling at the monstrous white beasts grazing in the grass, as if the world belonged to them alone.

As the caravan traveled through the bushveld, Priscilla saw peanut farms, tropical orchards, and wooded plantations. She also saw regal peacocks, proud and unafraid, crossing the roadway in front of the caravan carefree.

Then, as the caravan passed through the Soutpansberg Mountain range, she spotted rock and flat lizards slithering along the roadside, taking care not to dart into the paths of crocodiles and snakes.

From time to time, antelopes romped about freely, slowing the caravan even more. She spotted herds of zebras and stately, elegant giraffes springing into view now and then, as if to spread the message that this territory is theirs, and theirs alone.

In the midst of all of it, Priscilla wondered, *How could a country filled with such greatness be so wretched?*

Even as she continued gazing at God's creation, she pondered the possible ramifications of an incident that had occurred a few hours earlier at one of the rivers. She had been at the mercy of some of the burlier soldiers, who had had great fun teasing her when she jumped up and down on a lever to help anchor one of the rafts. But she had not weighed enough to activate the lever.

Determined to follow Charlie's orders, she had ignored the men and finally succeeded in helping to get the huge rafts afloat. But as she jumped up and down on the lever, one of the men slapped her on the shoulder, as if testing her ability to defend herself. Priscilla had quickly stopped what she was doing, grabbed her rifle, and taken aim at the man directly between his eyes. Immediately, the man and the others close to him backed away. From then on, none of them dared to bother her again.

Charlie had backed her up, shouting out, "Let that be a lesson to you, men. Even the little runts have a role to play in this mission."

From then on, too, Priscilla was accepted as one of "the boys," even though the men started calling her "little runt." But under the circumstances, she did not care one bit.

Because none of the men knew where the little runt came from, they assumed "he" had arrived with the Gaborone reinforcements. So whenever someone asked "Guy" where he came from, Priscilla let them think she had come with the Gaborone reinforcements.

Even Jordy was pleased with her ability to adapt to the situation. Later, when he told the CF commander how Priscilla had come to be known as the little runt, the CF commander would be furious at an incident that had drawn so much memorable attention to her.

The caravan halted for the arrival of additional Gaborone troops.

"All right, fellas," the CF commander said, "We'll rest here a bit."

Priscilla got to work serving their grub. Mostly, she tossed beans and franks into metal dishes, assembly-line style—all while rarely talking.

While they ate their meal, once again the commander spoke. "From here," he said, "we head straight to Joburg with our combined force."

The men shouted jubilantly: "Joburg, Joburg, Joburg!"

The men were eager to reach the climax of the most incredible adventure of their lives. Some of them had joined up because they truly believed in the cause of liberating the Black South Africans to gain their self-determination. Others were pure warriors who had enlisted as mercenaries, fighting not so much for the cause as for pay. Yet all of them—the believers and the mercenaries alike—felt the ensuing battle to the quick of their beings.

The SANM had its mercenaries, too. Simeon Johannes stood before 300 PGs and mercenaries who had come from around the globe to assist in the impending battle to preserve the way of life enjoyed by the Afrikaners. At the crowded rally, Simeon spoke at length:

"Ours is the true cause. Our ancestors crossed the great oceans and liberated these savages. It's a fact that we mined their gold and diamonds and amassed great fortunes, but these people didn't even know what they had."

He continued. "It's a fact that we brought them plumbing, electricity, vehicles, a common language, religion, and much more. It's definitely a fact that we civilized them."

As he rattled on, the level of excitement among the troops escalated.

"But it's also a fact that ours is the superior race, and we will not relinquish our claims to this land and the lifestyles we've developed. Why should we? Did the Americans return their land to the Indian savages? And what of so many other colonialists? Why has the world turned on us? To the victor goes the spoils, I say to you. To the victor goes the spoils!"

The men shouted back: "To the victor goes the spoils!"

As it turned out, Simeon was not on stage alone. Heinreik and the six other committee members were also present at that rally. They had little choice but to demonstrate their loyalty to the cause, so their attendance was required.

Because Heinreik wore a wire, the international intelligence community heard firsthand the voice of Simeon Johannes as he commanded the 300 Patrol Guardsmen and mercenaries to "fight 'til the end."

Just as Simeon was addressing the gathering at the rally in Johannesburg, the South African prime minister was addressing the National Assembly in Cape Town. He said, in part:

> By now, everyone is fully aware that the eyes of the world are on South Africa. People the world over want to know if we, the leaders of this great land, are prepared to do the right thing. Are we prepared to begin the process of liberating the only people in the world who remain outside the folds of democracy within a democracy?

> And even though most of us remain steadfast in our views, we cannot withstand the 'winds of change.' We are being forced off center stage as I speak. The Blacks are no longer afraid of us. They are not afraid to die for a cause so dear to them as the very freedom that you and I take for granted.
>
> And so, I submit to you: At what point will we agree to begin the long-awaited deliberations to grant civil liberties to these people? Will it be by gunpoint and bloodshed? Or will we consent to yield now? I submit to you that the time is nigh.

Outraged, the Nationalists yelled back, "No, Mr. Prime Minister. No! We will not relent."

As the National Assembly met, many people the world over were confounded. Some were even outraged by the prime minister's description of the South African political system as a "democracy". But then again, so many people thought that the Afrikaners possessed a relatively warped view about their presence in the grand scheme of things, anyway.

In spite of the jeers, the prime minister continued his speech. He already knew that his was a lone voice and a lost cause. But he also determined that he wanted to be recorded on "the right side of history."

> Will those of you affiliated with the South African Nationalist Movement leadership stand down, now? Or will you wait on your impending demise? I submit to you to stand down and let us begin anew. For surely there's room for negotiating a new way of life.

The prime minister had already said more than anyone had expected of him. So, eventually, he stopped talking, looked around, and walked out of the South African National Assembly for the last time.

As the South African apartheid era neared its end, the prime minister decided it was best to leave the country and avoid facing the regime's eventual dismantling. Having gone against his own kind, he had little choice but to go into exile. Consequently, he accepted an offer of asylum from a friend in the international community.

Meanwhile, the South African Parliament immediately selected a new leader and decided to uphold the Nationalist position of white supremacy and segregation of the races. Yet the "winds of change" would soon sweep through the land, produce a reform-minded government, and dismantle the apartheid system as it currently existed.

32

More Breaking News, Mistaken Identities
&
The Soweto Blues

Before long, the CF caravan entered the Province of Limpopo, where they came upon the Venetia Diamond Mines, South Africa's largest diamond mines. Nearby, the remainder of the Gaborone troops met with the caravan at the small town of Bela-Bela. Apart from the reinforcements that had just defeated the PG at the Mwenezi River, the Gaborone troops were well-rested and eager for battle. At this point, the Gaborone troops had seen the least action.

CF Commander Wozniah called his unified forces together for an important briefing.

He was well aware that their mission was to rescue the missing American, PJ Austin. But the commander told the troops: "Inasmuch as our primary mission is to aid in securing the diamond, gold, and platinum mines near Pretoria and Johannesburg, some of you will be stationed near here at the Rustenburg site under the command of Charlie and Agent Jordan."

After pausing briefly, he continued. "But the main contingent of our forces will press on to Joburg, where Agent Angelo Delgato, whom you have yet to meet, is already, and where he and I will command the troops there."

Again, he paused, aware not only of what he had just said but also what he had omitted besides failing to mention the authorized mission to rescue PJ Austin, he had not told his troops that the CF had already infiltrated the PG as well as the international news corps, with the help of the CIA, MI-5, and the Mossad. Nor did the CF commander tell the men about the plan to raid the headquarters of the SANM's Executive Committee.

Meanwhile, *BBC World News* issued the following televised report:

> Breaking news out of London: The British Foreign Secretary has tendered his resignation amid reports that his wife, Lady Beryl, is listed among the female assassins, the Judges.
>
> Reaction from the international community has been mixed. The American Secretary of State issued a statement almost immediately after the British Foreign Secretary's, saying, in part: 'I know the Beryls personally and in my official capacity. I offer my heartfelt sympathy to the couple and urge all others to allow this fantastic mystery to play itself out before casting any doubt or blame on Lady Beryl for something she has yet to be convicted of.'
>
> But the Swiss ambassador said, 'More than half the names on that list are women who have established themselves in Swiss society, and we want justice. We eagerly await the findings of the international tribunal on every one of them, and Lady Beryl is no exception. That she managed to situate herself in the lap of the highest foreign office of the British government is precisely why she, too, must undergo the rigors of a treason trial. She must face criminal prosecution.'
>
> Almost every other official has called the matter 'incredible' or 'unconscionable.'

Stay tuned to *BBC World News* for further details as this story, which began as a mystery in Harare, unfolds.

Moments later, another news story swept across the airwaves—from *CBS News* out of New York City:

CBS News has learned that the International Peacekeepers en route to Johannesburg, South Africa, have been approached by officials from the South African Army, the most powerful on the continent due, in part, to the country's sophisticated arms industry. The incident occurred shortly after the Peacekeepers entered the country in the small town of Bela-Bela—situated 160 miles east of Gaborone, Botswana, and nearly ninety miles north of Johannesburg.

When asked by a *CBS* news correspondent about the nature of their meeting, International Peacekeeper Commander Tommy Wozniah said: 'It is customary for the central command to meet with the central command of the country we enter, and for them to acknowledge the presence of any outside military unit. We explained our plans to set up protective units at the diamond, gold, and platinum mines near Pretoria and Johannesburg, and the South African commander informed us of his role in installing corresponding units. While they are not exactly thrilled with our presence, they understand the reason why.'

He expounded. 'Individuals, corporations, and governments the world over have investments in those mines, and we have been commissioned to aid in securing them. Period. Such a plan ensures the uninterrupted operations of the industries and adds protection for the workers, most of whom are poor Blacks from outlying homelands and townships.'

The commander offered no further comment.

CBS News has also learned that the head of the SANM Executive Committee, Simeon Johannes [his photograph shown at the bottom right-hand corner of television screens], has called up 300 Patrol Guardsmen 'to fight 'til the end.' Nonetheless, International Peacekeeper Commander Wozniah did not comment on whether his troops would engage the PG.

In yet other news, *CBS News* has learned that the mother and friend of American PR executive PJ Austin have both emphatically stated, 'the remains shown them at Langley were not hers.' After the medical records for Ms. Austin were produced, there was conclusive evidence that the remains contained in that body bag were, in fact, not hers. So, the questions remain: Where is PJ Austin? And how, if at all, does she fit into this ongoing saga of so much devastation?

Stay tuned to *CBS News* for more on what began as a mystery in Harare, as the story appears to come to a head in Johannesburg.

As he watched and listened to the news report, Carlton sat up in shock in his hospital bed.

"My God," he said, "She's alive! Missy's alive!"

With that stark revelation, he knew what he had to do.

But before he left his bed, he watched in sheer amazement as another news story flashed across the television screen.

The scene was a hall filled with Patrol Guardsmen. A man identified as Simeon Johannes was rallying the troops. Yet there was something peculiar about the scene. Six men in suits and ties flanked Simeon as he spoke on the stage. Carlton stared at the middle-aged man of distinctive Mediterranean features sitting to the right of Simeon Johannes—he was the man wearing a wire around his neck, tiny microphones extending from each end of it. With a start, Carlton knew he was looking at the face of his estranged great uncle, Heinreik (Bernhardt) Lipponeg.

Unbeknownst to Carlton, but he had his suspicions, international intelligence officials had infiltrated the rally of the SANM and its Patrol Guardsmen. They sat among them and filmed them without their knowledge, as the face and voice of Simeon Johannes were validated via the wire that Heinreik wore and by the video taken by one of the CF who sat among them. As it all happened, however, Heinreik had no idea that his own face appeared on the international stage as a member of the SANM Executive Committee.

In a telephone conversation with his Executive Committee supervisor, it suddenly dawned on Damien that the successful completion of his task had become more muddled.

"No, that can't be true," he said to Heinreik. "I saw them put her bloody body in that damn bag—unless, of course, the corpse was another damn double." He winced and said, "I guess I'll meet you in hell, after all."

With that, Damien and his hostage, the PJ double, continued their journey to Johannesburg when, for whatever reason, he stopped the jeep. He looked at his hostage and started talking as if he half expected her to comment.

"Didn't the commander say they were setting up protection units near Pretoria and Joburg?" He paused very briefly since he did not expect an answer. "So I'll have to check out both those camps. That little bitch—the real PJ Austin—has got to be in one of those camps, and I'll bet she's masquerading as one of them, too." He snapped his fingers. "That's it! She'll be one of the smallest soldiers."

Then he stared intensely into the eyes of his hostage: "And I know exactly how I'll use you to catch her."

Meanwhile, en route to Pretoria, the caravan entered the densely populated Gauteng Province, where they veered off to the east and then stopped midway between Brits and Rustenburg. They were in the Bojanala Platinum District Municipality of the Northwest Province. There, at the Rustenburg Platinum Mine, they were met by the South African Army. The soldiers in each force immediately matched up with their counterparts and proceeded to take their respective stations in and around the massive site. One could sense the testosterone rising. The soldiers knew they would soon see action.

The soldiers posted for duty inside the mine suited up with the appropriate gear. Despite the manager's and supervisors' admonitions, they refused to relinquish their weapons. Mining experts know that firing any ammunition or detonating any explosive can cause the delicate walls and floors of mines to cave in, creating enormous devastation. Loud sounds and unusual movements have a similar effect. But the soldiers refused to discard their weapons, causing great anxiety among the miners. Yet the deeper the soldiers went into the mine, the more apparent it became that spontaneous combustion, caused by loud sounds and unusual movements, could, in fact, cause their rifles to fire. Once they realized the error of their ways, they quickly left the mine and stashed their rifles with their comrades at the mine's entrance.

The winter season was ending, and although the temperature was a mild seventy-two degrees Fahrenheit, the soldiers still felt uncomfortable inside the mine, mainly because of the extreme humidity. Despite air conditioning in parts of the mine, it became harder to breathe the further they descended, even with oxygen masks. So the soldiers alternated time in and out of the mine every half hour. Their work was hazardous and labor-intensive, but necessary.

As for the South Africans—that is, the Black miners—they had little understanding of what was happening outside the mines, so they talked among themselves in their various languages.

"Are we at war?"

"Did something happen to Mr. Mandela?"

"Did someone steal some of the platinum?"

Speculation ran rampant because nobody—not the miners, not even the supervisors—had answers to these questions. Soon, rumors spread among the miners about the missing American woman as well as the PG's plan to fight the International Peacekeepers. Eventually, many of the miners also heard that the prime minister had resigned, and that the SANM had called up the PG to fight the CF, who were, in fact, disguised as International Peacekeepers. But the miners were unaware of that last detail.

With that news, several of the miners began to hum a sad tune familiar to all of them. It was called "Soweto Blues." Then, after a while, all the miners began chanting:

> The children got a letter from the master
> No more Xhosa, Sotho, no more Zulu.
> Refusing to comply, they sent an answer
> That's when the policeman came to the rescue.

Children were flying; bullets dying
The mothers screaming and crying
The fathers were working in the cities
The evening news brought out all the publicity.

Just a little atrocity,
Deep in the city.

Benikuphi na madoda xa bedubula abantwana
Benikuphi na?
Abantwana xa bejikijela ezizimbokodo
Benikuphi na?

There was a full moon on the golden city
Knocking at the door was the man without pity
Accusing everyone of conspiracy
Tightening the curfew, charging people with walking
Hmm, the border is where he was waiting
Waiting for the children
Frightened and running

A handful got away, but all the others
Are in the jail without any publicity
Just a little atrocity
Deep in the city

Soweto blues
Soweto blues
Soweto blues…

Before long, the miners were moving in rhythm with the chant, swinging their hammers and jacks, heaving and shoveling the mineral-rich dirt into the hungry carts that sat on the railway. They sang that freedom song made famous by Miriam Makeba and Hugh Masakela because they could sense freedom in the air and knew that such atrocities would soon come to an end. They also knew their supervisors liked it whenever they sang, because then the supervisors believed the miners were happy.

Not far from the mouth of the mine, Charlie and Jordy were assigned a small but comfortable cabin, and they brought the little runt with them. The cabin was an ample open space with a small kitchen off to one side. A shower stall and a toilet were at the back, next to another private space for sleeping.

"This'll do just fine," Charlie said to the South African Army soldier who had escorted them to the cabin. Three CF soldiers were inside the cabin, and three South African Army soldiers were stationed outside.

"Sorry, Guy, but you'll have to make a pallet on the floor," Charlie said to Priscilla. "No one can catch you sleeping in the bed. It's reserved for the commander."

"I understand," she murmured. Although she was concentrating on fitting in with the military mode, part of her yearned to be back in the bush with all those exotic four-footed animals. Too, she was only vaguely aware that she was now near Pretoria, the capital of one of the most notoriously racist territories in the world. And although Charlie had taught her how to use a gun, he had not given her any lessons in being a Black American woman in an apartheid-era society, the need for which would soon come to the fore. At least, she'd acquired the knack for keeping her mouth shut and talking as little as possible. She could never tell when someone else was listening.

"Ever seen platinum being mined?" Jordy asked her somewhat cheerfully. "Do you want to hang out with us for a couple of hours?"

When she nodded, and Charlie approved, they settled into their new quarters and then headed out for a tour of the platinum mine.

33

Setting Up in Joburg & Military Stratagems

Slightly south of Pretoria, the CF commander met up with his friend and compatriot, CF Agent Delgato. The two men would jointly command the CF troops near Johannesburg—known as the City of Gold, or "Egoli." The site of the largest gold reserves was in the Witwatersrand Basin.

"It's hard to believe that we set out on this mission almost two months ago," Angel said. He'd been in Johannesburg for much of the past month. So, he had missed all the action that the caravan had experienced en route. "That's longer than I know, at least Carlton expected." He frowned. "Which reminds me, Tommy, how is Carlton, anyway? How badly was he hurt?"

Tommy shrugged. "A gunshot wound to his left shoulder. But what's really going to bother him is that he's not here with us now, and it's all over the news that it wasn't Miss Prissy who was killed after all." He shook his head. "You know, I could have sworn that was her in that body bag. Carlton will have my head for that faulty ID. I'm sure that really put him through it."

But Angel disagreed and said as much. "What will matter most to him, and to us, too, is that she's *alive*." Then he added, "In the meantime, I believe Carlton has another issue to grapple with."

"Oh-h? Now what?"

"Tommy, man, don't you know? He has an uncle on the goddamn SANM Executive Committee. He's Carlton's father's unc—"

"Liar."

Angel suggested they finish their talk inside their quarters. "Too many eyes and ears out here." In the main military center at the Witwatersrand Basin, South African Army troops also paired their personnel with the International Peacekeepers, as it were. In this case, several were posted right outside the CF's central command center.

Tommy and Angel unpacked their equipment and began scanning for surveillance, wiretapping, and other devices throughout the rooms, including the one housing communications equipment. They waited to continue their conversation until their most trusted aides had installed their own decryption devices and scramblers and had located the South African Army's surveillance devices. They were well aware that both the South African troops and the PG wanted to know their actual plans.

The commander and agent sat silently, considering their situation.

They both knew that Johannesburg, as the center of commerce and finance, was more significant than the capital city of Pretoria. The Witwatersrand mining facility, where they were currently stationed, held voluminous documents pertaining to top-secret government operations, particularly the mining, production, and distribution of diamonds, gold, and platinum used for military research and development. Documents on the construction of commercial and industrial satellites for many governments were stored here, but those records had all been neatly and securely locked up. Still, the communications station had been made available to the Peacekeepers, a remarkable gift for the CF.

What was more remarkable was that they both understood the importance of South Africa's diamond mines and its other minerals. Much of the Western world depended on access to those resources. For many, humanitarian and political concerns were secondary. Many world leaders had made it clear that securing the mines was paramount. So that was what the CF was pretending to do. Indeed, one of their stated missions was to shore up the mines.

Battlefield strategies, however, were more pressing for the CF commander and Angel. They planned to use their vehicles and tanks as a buffer between their forces and the surrounding communities of Pretoria and Johannesburg. Even so, every CF soldier stationed around the makeshift buffer zone was paired with a South African Army soldier. Given the strong sense of nationalism among the Afrikaners, it was difficult to determine whether all, some, or any of the South African Army were PG sympathizers. What truly mattered was on whose side those army troops would fight.

While the CF commander and Angel discussed battlefield strategies, Priscilla, Jordy, and Charlie rode a jeep for some distance before gearing up for their trek on foot inside the Rustenburg Platinum Mine, which stretched for miles of curvilinear carvings into the Earth. They put on oxygen masks to help with breathing in the extreme humidity and entered an elevator shaft. Down, down, deep into the mine they descended until the elevator, which the miners and their supervisors called a "lift," came to a halt.

Priscilla saw thin train tracks throughout a seemingly endless, narrow opening, which reminded her of subway tracks in New York City.

Her attention was caught, too, by the huge metal dumpster carts, some empty and some filled with mineral-rich dirt. Platinum, a lustrous, silver-white, malleable mineral embedded within the dirt, was being transported. As the carts moved along the tracks, a supervisor called out a warning to them: "Lean back against the walls and watch where you put your feet."

As they made their way into the belly of the mine, Priscilla first thought she would lose her stomach, then felt as if she were upside down. She was experiencing claustrophobia and vertigo. Because she had no idea how much more she could endure, she let her limp body take the lead. In her extreme anxiety, she prayed silently, *God, help me. Please get me through this hell.*

Jordy and Charlie seemed intrigued by all that they observed. But Priscilla was already sickened at the sight of all those black arms toiling mercilessly as they hammered and swung heavy jacks against the walls and into the ground. And although mining platinum had developed into an intricate mechanized process, it still required much manual labor. The miners seemed to breathe and move about the enclosed space with ease. But Priscilla saw some of them regarding her as if they were wondering: *Why does the little one seem so interested in us?*

Jordy instinctively knew that when Priscilla moved only a few steps away from him, the little runt was not only a "she" but also a Black American. So he quickly walked back to her and spoke in a low, insistent voice. "This is South Africa, Miss Prissy. Remember where you are."

At that warning, she moved closer to the two men and concentrated on standing up straight and breathing, for her anxiety was telling her that she would surely die down deep in this mine.

The farther they moved, the more heavy machinery they saw. Way down in the depths of the Earth, they watched as more conveyor belts and more tracks carried the platinum-rich soil throughout the curvilinear cavern, up into other cavities until it reached the mine's exterior.

By the time Jordy and Charlie had seen enough of the mining process, it had all but been too late for the claustrophobic and vertigo-stricken Priscilla. Beset with hypertension, she had leveled herself against a wall, where her fingers clawed away at it. She wanted to vomit, but nothing came up. She felt as if she were spinning out of control in an ocean.

When Jordy finally noticed her predicament, he rushed over to her rescue. Charlie quickly followed, and then the two men, like crutches, shouldered her to the lift. They rode up to the main level, where she was finally able to breathe normally again and to stand on her own.

What did the miners do when they saw the little runt all but collapse? They snickered among themselves. They had seen plenty more visitors than this one, all but faint from the close, suffocating quarters of the platinum mine. Not just anybody can withstand the conditions way down deep inside such mines.

Back at Witwatersrand, the Johannesburg site, Tommy and Angel were less concerned with the process of mining diamonds, gold and platinum than they were with the tactics they would employ in capturing or killing the remaining SANM Executive Committee members.

Their discussion on the tactics led to Angel's report on their comrade's uncle.

"This has got to be the most bizarre situation we've ever encountered," Tommy said. "How the hell did Carlton's uncle, who is Lebanese, get involved with the damn SANM?"

"It seems," Angel began, "that at a young age, Carlton's Uncle Heinreik had a bitter dispute with his father, asked for his inheritance, and severed all ties with his family. Then he went as far away from home as possible. He was good at numbers and finance. So he made a small fortune from investing a portion of his inheritance. That caught the attention of Simeon Johannes. The rest is history."

"Amazing, Angel, just damn amazing how small the world is," Tommy said. "Has Uncle Heinreik ever returned home?" (Although Heinreik was Carlton's great uncle, everyone, Carlton included, referred to him as his uncle.)

Angel shook his head and said, "The prodigal's son, he is not. But I suppose that he never imagined he would find himself caught up in a predicament such as this. Tommy, it's my understanding that Uncle Heinreik is worth his weight in gold—and in diamonds, too. We've already gotten his family out of the country, but Heinreik's future depends on how the rest of our mission plays out. For now, though, I really think the less Carlton knows, the more effective we'll be at completing our mission."

"But didn't you say that his uncle was seated among those other guys on stage at that rally? Everybody in the world, probably including Carlton, has already seen his face."

"Yeah, I hear you," Angel said. "We're in a pile of deep doo–doo, for sure. And, what about Miss Prissy? How much of what's transpired does she know?"

The commander nodded. He had already shared much of what he knew about Priscilla with Angel, but he himself was still unaware that she was nearby and under the care of his own manservant. So he said, "We've managed to keep her away from radios and televisions, but I don't know how much longer that will last. We had no choice but to brief her after we rescued her from that cathedral crypt in Harare. But since then, I don't think she's seen or heard any news." Then he expounded, "Although her status is that she may not be dead, she's gone missing again. So, I really don't know what she knows."

"Ah, come on, Tommy. Can the frigging mission get any more complicated?" Angel sighed and then suggested, "Why don't we go over the scenario for the SANM penthouse? That seems a lot easier to grapple with than missing persons, mistaken identities, and notorious uncles."

"Yeah, Angel, man. Better do whatever business we can while we can."

But it was not so much what either man said, but rather, it was what they did not say. Both men knew the only sanctioned part of their mission was the rescue and return of Priscilla; for the rest, however, they were on their own.

34

Something Sinister in the Offing

After the South African Prime Minister's resignation, many international news media representatives gathered in a large media center in Pretoria, where many of them discussed the puzzling scenes and events at the Rustenburg Platinum Mine and at the Witwatersrand Gold Mine, too. Only a few of them were talking about the SANM Executive Committee's announcement that it would establish and fund orphanages and boarding schools for South Africans and Zimbabweans, and about the hue and cry of international humanitarian organizations:

"Why would the SANM devote financial resources to the establishment of orphanages and boarding schools for children of the very people it discriminates against?"

"Doesn't the SANM's mission in this regard plainly contradict the root of nationalism—white supremacy and racial segregation?"

"Besides, since they've already declared war on who knows who, how is all that going to impact their decision to establish those boarding schools and orphanages?"

"And what'll happen to those places if the SANM no longer exists?"

Unbeknownst to the news correspondents, a CF agent, Carlton Elliott Bernhardt, was present—but disguised as an investigative reporter. He sported a mustache and sunglasses, wore a baseball cap, and still kept his ponytail. He was accompanied by another CF officer, disguised as his cameraman and bodyguard, who went by the name "Harry."

Carlton turned toward a small group of reporters and, pointing to his left arm, now in a sling, said, "I'm an American freelancer. Jason Kinard's the name. I took a bullet during the raid at the Anglican Cathedral in Harare, but I wouldn't miss this story for the world," when, in fact, his wound had resulted from a gunshot he sustained during the raid at the Mwenezi River.

Carlton carried a concealed weapon, while his cameraman wore his pistol openly. If other reporters questioned the pistol, they would say that Harry also served as his licensed bodyguard. But any such challenge was unlikely, since nearly all media personnel there carried weapons. That was especially true following the raid at the Anglican Cathedral and the raid at the Hueston Woods Lodge Resort. Still, Carlton and Harry moved carefully through the media center. The last thing they wanted was to attract attention. Otherwise, the other reporters focused mainly on the horrific massacres and the ongoing battles between the CF—whom they believed to be the International Peacekeepers—and the PG. But Carlton focused on finding Priscilla and his estranged Uncle Heinreik.

While Harry stood guard outside a tiny closet in the media center, Carlton spoke through his cell phone to Heinreik Lipponeg's secretary: "Yes, I'm Jason Kinard, freelance writer for several American newspapers. I want to speak with Heinreik Lipponeg about the innovative programs for orphans in Zimbabwe and here in South Africa."

"Hold on a moment, if you please," the secretary said. She buzzed Heinreik, who agreed to make an appointment with the reporter. By now, he no longer cared about what happened to him or, for that matter, what happened to the SANM Executive Committee.

"No problem."

Heinreik's secretary had a favorable answer sooner than Carlton had expected. "Perfect, Mr. Kinard," she said. "We've scheduled you for nine o'clock tomorrow morning."

That was too easy, Carlton thought, *much too easy*. He turned to Harry and said, "Well, Bro, looks like we've landed our first major interview. So let's continue dogging the story."

"Sure," Harry dropped his voice. "But do you want me to continue pretending to be a cameraman or just tag along as your bodyguard?"

"Let's continue to be wannabe media stars. This is almost too much fun."

"For the moment, maybe, but those media guys might not see things the way you do." Harry was familiar with the sometimes-reckless behavior of top CF agents like Carlton Elliott Bernhardt.

The two of them climbed into his jeep. They drove to Wonderboom Airport to catch the two-hour flight to Johannesburg, where they would meet with Tommy and Angel at the Witwatersrand central command outpost.

As members of the international news correspondents' corps, Carlton—a.k.a. Jason Kinard—and his cameraman wore the mandatory press badges hanging from their necks. But when the South African Army soldier who guarded the entrance to the Witwatersrand outpost asked to see their credentials, Carlton almost forgot that he was not a secret agent, but a member of the press corps. Harry quickly stepped forward and pointed to the press credentials hanging around their necks.

Only then did Carlton relax his stiff and commanding demeanor. He pointed out his press badge to the army guard. Then he flashed it in front of the CF soldier, paired with the army soldier, and said with a smirk, "Suppose those fellas comprennent l'Anglais?"

Harry nudged him forward, whispering, "My God, man, what about not creating any unnecessary attention?"

"Was just checking," Carlton whispered back, "to see if one of our own men recognizes me. And he doesn't."

As they progressed through the encampment, Carlton seemed to take delight in the fact that his simple disguise seemed to be working. A South African Army soldier escorted them to the main entrance of the central command center. Upon entering, none of his associates, not even the staffers pecking away at their keyboards in the vibrant office space, recognized him. He saw an old-fashioned PA system, several black touchtone telephones, and electronic and telecommunications equipment.

Soon, their South African Army escort was knocking on the door of the CF commander's office. "There's an American news correspondent, Jason Kinard, asking to see you. His camera guy is here, too. Kinard says you might've heard tell of a man named 'Carlton.'"

Tommy and Angel looked at each other in alarm. "Just what we need, having to deal with someone Carlton sent to find out more about Miss Prissy." Then he said, "Send him in, please, Officer."

Inside the office, Carlton's eyes were drawn to the oversized metal desk at the back wall, where Tommy and Angel were seated. He also noticed a big screen and an IBM desktop computer that displayed images of encrypted data, and what appeared to him to be aerial maps. And, although the temperature was mild, a ceiling fan swirled, a window air conditioner hummed, and there were black-and-white pictures of the big five game hanging on one of the walls.

Carlton walked closer to the commander's desk. He removed his baseball cap and sunglasses, but left the moustache on.

His colleagues stood up and yelled with glee.

After having had fun confusing his friends, he said, "With this shoulder of mine, and anyone who can decorate a room like this, surely you guys could've sent me some damn flowers or a box of candy or something." He grinned.

When his friends stopped hollering in glee, he said, "This here's my cameraman and bodyguard. Just call him Harry."

The men slapped one another's shoulders, exchanged high fives, and boxed one another. They would "have at it" after the mission.

"We thought you were in sickbay," Angel said. "So what gives?"

"Miss Prissy, that's what," Carlton said sternly. "Let's just say for me this is a pressing personal matter."

"We're in the middle of a war, lover boy," Tommy reminded him.

"No time for personal agendas," Angel added.

Carlton lashed back. "Let's get real. I'm not carrying any grudge about Tommy here, apparently not being able to tell the body of one of the decoys from the real deal. Not for scaring me half to death that I'd lost her. No, this is professional as well as personal. What we need to stay on top of is the fact that there's still at least one more PJ double out there, and that I think a man called Damien has her. He's one of Heinreik Lipponeg's best commanders. And a nasty piece of work." Carlton was casually testing his comrades' awareness that he knew of his uncle's affiliation with the very organization they were intent on dismantling.

Like the expert poker players, they all were, neither Tommy nor Angel commented on their associate's remarks. But now they both knew that their friend and associate was aware of his uncle's affiliation with the SANM Executive Committee.

Carlton took a seat and gestured for Harry to do the same.

"So, fellas," he continued, "are you going to share the game plan for the raid on the SANM headquarters? Or are you gonna keep me guessing?"

Tersely, Tommy revealed that the mission was scheduled to take place within the next twenty-four hours, adding that such a tight time limit did not leave much time to find and rescue Priscilla before the fireworks began.

But before long, Carlton and Harry were back in their jeep, speeding up the highway to the Rustenburg Platinum Mine. Something in Carlton's gut told him that Miss Prissy was somewhere in that mine.

As Carlton and Harry made their way to the Rustenburg Platinum Mine, so, too, did Damien, who was now wearing the uniform of a South African Army captain. Beside him, the PJ look–alike was still wearing her CF uniform.

Inside the mine's entrance, they headed toward a large Quonset hut where a contingent of international news correspondents was gathered.

As soon as Damien and the PJ look–alike entered the hut, a crowd of reporters began taking videos and still photographs. The reporters knew it was sensational for a South African Army soldier to have captured a Black person, alive and unharmed. So, they peppered the pair with questions:

"Hey, that prisoner of yours looks like—"

"Aren't you . . . an Afrikaner?"

Damien waved his arms and cut to the quick, "Quiet! I've got a scoop!" As the news correspondents went silent, he continued.

"You're right. This is Miss PJ Austin. I found her wandering around the battlefield near the Mwenezi River after that battle was over. It was only after watching the news that I learned about her true identity."

Donning her CF camouflage uniform, including the military-style helmet, dried mud covering much of her face, the small frame of the look–alike was virtually identical to Priscilla's. Otherwise, none of the news correspondents could see the woman's facial features. On the way here, Damien had told her precisely what she had to do to stay alive. So she pretended to be tired, and occasionally she cracked a slight smile.

Although the news correspondents were stunned, most of them seemed to swallow the story.

Damien concluded, "I was as surprised as you are. But I decided to bring her to the nearest International Peacekeepers' station, which is here at the Rustenburg Platinum Mine."

Moments later, the bulletin about the recovery of PJ Austin was released over the airwaves.

Charlie and Jordy intensely watched the news on the television inside their cabin. But they knew they had the real Priscilla with them, disguised as Guy, the little runt. So, the person in the news story had to be the missing look–alike. The CF agents squinted at the man who had brought in his prisoner. He was wearing the uniform of a South African Army captain. But who was he really? Quickly, Charlie had his men take the woman believed to be Priscilla into custody for interrogation, which was what Damien had expected. Now, he was nearly sure that the real Priscilla was somewhere among them.

But since neither Charlie nor Jordy could verify the news, the CF and the intelligence community remained silent. In that vacuum, onlookers began to believe that the elusive PJ Austin had finally been found alive, which was odd. Why on Earth would a South African Army officer even bother to do anything kind for a Black person? People can be so gullible. Even though Charlie and Jordy knew otherwise, they kept their mouths shut.

Only minutes later did Carlton and his cameraman, Harry, arrive at the Rustenburg Platinum Mine. Then they followed the crowd into the media's Quonset hut, where the reporters quickly apprised Carlton of the recovery of the real PJ Austin. Or so they thought.

But Carlton sensed something sinister in the offing. *In light of the apparent connection between the South African Army and the PG, why would a South African Army captain turn over the missing American woman to the International Peacekeepers, whom even he suspected were the CF, the very force the PG was fighting? Not only that,* Carlton pondered, *but why'd he even bother? Why hadn't he eliminated her?*

Eventually, he spoke, "Harry, I don't believe it."

Intuitively, both Carlton and Harry hurriedly and silently made their way through much tighter security to the CF central command cabin. Their next steps were crucial, particularly since they suspected the South African Army captain was, in fact, Damien.

Meanwhile, Damien quickly spread word among the Nationalist sympathizers in the South African Army that the woman he had just delivered was, in fact, a double and that he believed the real target was embedded somewhere in this very camp.

"She's probably disguised as a CF soldier," he said. "Find the smallest one, and maybe we've found the real PJ Austin."

One of the South African soldiers spoke for his mates. "We *have* seen a small soldier. They call him 'the little runt.'"

"Oh!" Damien flashed an icy smile. "And where might I find that creature?"

"He stays in the central command cabin, and sometimes issues the grub," another army soldier said. "Keeps to himself mostly."

Damien smiled with more warmth. "Well, now, I guess I'll take a closer look around the grounds."

As the news correspondents left the Quonset hut and roamed about the surrounding area like they were looking for something or someone, Priscilla realized with alarm that something new and bad was up—something sinister was more like it. She feared, correctly, that it might have something to do with her. But instead of seeking cover back inside the central command cabin, she headed to the one place that she dreaded most: the black hole of the Rustenburg Platinum Mine.

Meanwhile, Carlton and his cameraman were at the central command cabin, demanding answers from Charlie and Jordy.

However, Jordy was trying to calm his friend and fellow CF associate. "Carlton, my God, man! How were we to know that some South African Army captain would show up with one of our decoys?"

Carlton snapped, "My gut tells me he's PG. Besides, he just showcased," pointing to the PJ decoy, "the double we gave him back during the exchange with the courier at Gweru."

But Carlton could not help noticing the two men seemed unusually tense, and so he asked them, point-blank, "Do either of you have *any* idea where Miss Prissy is?"

Sweat beaded on Charlie's face. He pulled at his moustache. Eventually, he spoke. "There's no need keeping it secret any longer. We've had her with us disguised as a soldier since the raid at Mwenezi River. And if she got wind of that little media episode, I believe I know just where she went."

Carlton whistled and said, "And so, she *is* here. Hell, fellas, out with it."

"We've had her with us in protective custody," Jordy said.

Then Charlie suggested, "She's probably gone back inside the mine." He shrugged and then continued, though reluctantly. "We were there together not long ago. And she seems to have bonded with the miners. That girl has really been put through it. So much deception, so many lies upon lies. Maybe those miners are the only people she feels comfortable with."

While Charlie and Jordy confided their secrets, Carlton did his best to control his temper. He could not believe what he was hearing. But before he could speak again, Jordy shared more.

"Okay, Carlton, here's all we know. We'd just come back from touring the platinum mine, and Miss Prissy said something about needing a cup of coffee and a smoke. You know her ways, man." Jordy was trying to reassure him that Priscilla was indeed safe.

Carlton's blood rushed. "That's how you care for someone in protective custody? You let her roam off whenever and wherever she wants?" His famous temper was building.

Charlie came to Jordy's defense. "Easy now," he said. "After all, we were dealing with the media report of her rescue by that South African Army captain. But no, we haven't seen high or low of our girl since she went for a smoke. But that was only a few minutes ago."

Carlton's better judgment told him to work through the mess and "have at it" with his boys later. Right now, he needed to find and rescue his Miss Prissy.

Suddenly, the PJ look–alike spoke up: "I believe Damien's passing word amongst the South African Army troops to help him find 'the smallest among the soldiers.' He suspects Ms. Austin is in this camp posing as a CF soldier."

The men continued arguing among themselves, only more vehemently, until, once again, the PJ look–alike suggested: "Why not all of us just walk out into the open and head over to the mine? If I know that bastard Damien, he will follow us there. That is, if he hasn't already gone inside himself."

A delayed reaction or what? But all of a sudden, the men stopped arguing—as if they had thought of or stumbled onto something remarkable.

Then Jordy exclaimed, "Let's go! No time to waste!"

But before they left, Carlton walked over to the panel at the communications station.

"Now what?" asked Jordy.

"'Now,' we sound the alert for 'a man on the run' and post the photo of 'Damien Escoffery, the most wanted terrorist the world over.' That's 'what.'"

At once, the full-alert siren sounded throughout the camp. Carlton's message, "Man on the run!" reverberated over the loudspeaker, and Damien Escoffery's photograph appeared on a large screen erected on the grounds.

It was then that the news correspondents realized they had been duped by the man who had masqueraded as a South African Army captain. It took only moments for the news cameramen to light up most of the grounds. They panned the surroundings and periodically zoomed in on the mouth of the mine to enable viewers the world over to witness firsthand the most recent episode in this incredible mystery, which seemed to be coming to a head at a platinum mine in South Africa, of all places.

Charlie ordered his troops to "Seal off the entrance to the mine." Likewise, did the South African Army. Then he, Carlton, Jordy, and the PJ decoy headed into the depths of the platinum mine.

However, unknowingly to them, not far behind, Damien—now wearing a CF officer's uniform—successfully slipped past the barricade and into the mine.

Inside the platinum mine, Priscilla looked up in panic as the siren shrieked, and the loudspeaker shouted words that she could not quite make out. But she knew the sound of panic when she heard it. She knew she could not outrun the man who she sensed was already following her. Nor could she breathe with any ease, too far down in this immense cavern. She'd already walked past a few soldiers without any problem, but the sound of the siren had put them on full alert. Had they mistakenly allowed her to pass? She knew the next group of soldiers would stop her.

She used her lighted helmet to search the mine's walls for any cavity she thought she could reach. Finally, she found one. She struggled but failed to climb the steep wall. But when it seemed as if she would have to continue walking along the path, she heard the sound of rapidly approaching footsteps.

All right now, she reasoned, *before I completely lose my mind, think.*

Her eyes caught sight of a pile of tools on one of the carts on the tracks, many of which were unfamiliar to her, and some looked too big to carry. Still, she picked up a couple of familiar tools, a small hammer and a stake, and put them in her back pants pockets. "Never know when these'll come in handy," she said to herself. "Might have to dig myself out of here." She felt better with a weapon. This time, she was in self-defense mode. So when she mused about digging herself out of there, she was really thinking about doing battle with the man whom she thought was a South African Army captain. She already suspected that the vicious villain probably would get the better of her. But she was acutely aware of her own trademark: none of the people she fought ever came back for seconds. Her hands trembled as she patted the hammer and stake in her back pocket. Then she remembered the time she took a butcher's knife to a street fight back during her high school years in Prendergast. She breathed faster with each thought and each step.

Frightened nearly out of her wits, Priscilla kept talking to herself to muster her courage. Then she remembered someone shouting at them during their tour to "Lean against the wall." She hobbled sideways against the wall until, at long last, she reached the lift. She was sweating profusely. She felt her heart beating fast, too. She steadied herself near the lift, leaning as hard as she could against the wall, because she feared the footsteps she'd been hearing were those of someone looking to do her harm, and she did not want him to hear her moving or panting either.

But soon she saw that those footsteps she had been hearing belonged to the miners—either walking towards the lift or getting off it and heading out of the mine. Priscilla was caught between the miners' changing shifts.

Since she was clearly visible near the lift, some of the miners stopped and stared at her.

Suddenly, she whispered, "Help me. Please help me. Hide me." Then she pointed to a place high up the steep wall.

Certain words, expressions, and symbols are universal, and the image of someone in distress is one such expression. And one never knows when the kindness of strangers will come to the rescue. The simple, compassionate interest that she'd shown in the miners during her earlier tour was just about to pay off. By the expressions on their faces, it seemed that several of the men recognized Priscilla from her earlier trip inside the mine that day. Obviously, too, they were making an effort to understand what this mysterious little soldier, who was noticeably panting, was saying. It did not take them long to determine both that "he" was in distress and what "he" was asking of them.

A few of them nodded and then escorted the little soldier a short distance away from the lift before hoisting "him" up.

The little soldier—Priscilla—was now able to feel cracks and crevices in the wall. "He" hung on tight and lifted "himself" even higher.

As the little soldier was settling "himself" in "his" hideout, a large crevice, a few other miners wisely created a diversion by noisily loading one of the huge carts with dirt.

Their timing was perfect because Priscilla's stalker was not far away.

Damien walked up to the same group of men who had just aided the little soldier (Priscilla) and showed them a picture of the little runt.

"Have you seen this soldier?" he asked in Afrikaans, his native tongue.

The miners had no great love for Afrikaners, so they immediately pointed to the lift.

Damien walked to the lift and waited for it to return. As soon as the lift arrived, he pushed the miners who had been waiting out of the way and got onto it alone.

For what seemed like a long time, the miners waited for the lift to disappear safely out of their sight. Then they walked back over to the part of the wall, the large crevice high up, where the little soldier was hiding to see if "he" was all right. And when the little soldier gave the miners a thumbs-up that "he" was indeed all right, they grinned and went their way.

The shift change seemed endless, but it did not take as long as Priscilla had been imagining. All of a sudden, the clanking of the changing shifts was interrupted by the sound of English-speaking voices. She heard voices she recognized—Carlton, Jordy, Charlie—and two she did not—her look–alike and the cameraman. Yet Priscilla did not budge from her hiding place. Instead, she allowed the group to stand among the miners and wait for their turn to climb onto the lift and descend further down into the mine.

But something seemed to be happening to prevent them from leaving.

"Something's not right, I tell you," Carlton said. "If Miss Prissy is here and being hunted by a PG agent, do you really think that monster would let us prowl around without a fight? And Miss Prissy has more phobias than a dog has fleas. She'd never go down deeper in this mine unless she were with someone she trusted, or she felt she had no other choice but to do so."

Since Charlie and Jordy had already suffered some of Carlton's wrath, they were not about to tell him about their earlier experience with Priscilla's anxiety attack. So Jordy calmly asked, "So, Carlton, what do you suggest?"

"I suggest we split up," Carlton said as he looked into the faces of some of the miners. "A couple of you go down, and a couple of us remain up here. Something tells me there's more happening than meets our eyes."

"OK, Carlton." Jordy nodded. But he knew Priscilla better than any of the others did. So he added, as he, Charlie, and the look–alike waited for the next ride on the lift, "If we don't find her in the next few minutes, we're heading back up here. Deal?"

"Deal," Carlton said. Then he and Harry began pacing about the main level. But since it never occurred to them to look up, they walked past Priscilla's hideaway without even knowing it.

After they passed by again, Priscilla psyched herself up to try to move about the steep wall. As she commanded her hands to find cracks and crevices to cling to, inwardly she prayed: *Please don't let any rats and bats and snakes be in here. I don't know what I'd do if I felt one!* She managed to hoist the fullness of her body even higher up the wall. She did not dare to use the light on her helmet because she did not want to be discovered. She told herself that she needed to be so high on the wall that the tallest man could not see her or her shadow as he flashed his lights about the narrow space. So she crawled and climbed as high as she could, until there was no more space above her.

Along the hard way up, she thought: *Have I wet my pants? Or was that sweat?* Perspiration dripped down her face, through her short hair, behind her ears, underneath her bosom and underarms, and her private parts.

Finally, she found a cavity deep enough to conceal her body. There she crouched, high above the ground. Priscilla was more afraid than she had been when she confronted Moses Cameron in the cathedral crypt in Harare, or even when she had played possum on the floor of her tent during the battle at the Mwenezi River. This time, she had only glimpsed her stalker for a few seconds while she was smoking her cigarette behind the central command cabin when the so-called South African Army captain had delivered her look–alike.

As she crouched high up on the wall on the main level of the Rustenburg Platinum Mine, she felt nausea in her gut. She knew her life was in danger. She had to stay where she was, forever if necessary.

"I'll be damned if I'm going back down into that hellhole of a miner's tunnel," she said to herself. Then she continued in a silent, albeit deep and fervent prayer: *And, oh yeah, lest I forget, I wanna thank you for those thoughtful miners.* Even she knew a little empathy from those miners had just saved her life—at least for the time being. And she prayed that her legs would not start cramping, too.

Then she tried to center herself by recalling memories of other times of fear and danger that she had transcended somehow. She remembered some dire times with her family decades ago in Mississippi and then in upstate New York. But most of all, she followed the quiet, still voice that said to her: *Stay strong and focused.*

While Priscilla hid inside the mine, outside, several news correspondents, including those from *BBC World News*, reported to television viewers around the globe:

> Something strange is happening here at the Rustenburg camp of the International Peacekeepers. A short while ago, a man believed to be a South African Army captain arrived with a woman, whom he identified as the missing American PR executive, PJ Austin. Then, without further comment, one of the South African soldiers escorted the woman to the central command station.
>
> Shortly after, the full-alert siren sounded, and we saw a group—including the woman believed to be PJ Austin—International Peacekeeper soldiers, and two members of the media heading to the Rustenburg Platinum Mine.
>
> At the same time, someone announced over the public address system that Damien Escoffery, a SANM PG Commander and international terrorist, was 'a man on the run,' and that every intelligence agency in the

world wanted him. [A photo of Damien Escoffery appeared at the bottom of the television screen, along with a caption containing the above quotation.] As it turned out, he was the man posing as a South African Army captain who'd brought the woman believed to be PJ Austin here.

Meanwhile, Interpol has confirmed that Damien Escoffery is, in fact, a Patrol Guard assassin whose primary target is PJ Austin.

It could, therefore, be somewhere inside the deep darkness of this mine that 'the mystery in Harare' may finally be solved.

Stay tuned to *BBC World News* as this riveting story continues to unfurl before our very eyes.

Back in Johannesburg, Tommy and Angel found it hard to believe this latest news bulletin.

"My God, man, what's next?" the CF commander asked. "This crap has gotten way out of hand."

"I sure hope they rescue Miss Prissy this time," Angel said. "And Lord, I hope they take out that bastard Damien. Think we should join them?"

"We've got our hands full getting ready to take out the Patrol Guard," said the commander, as he prayed things would work out in their favor. "Besides, Carlton said he wanted more adventure. And it looks like he's getting it."

35

Showdown at Witwatersrand Basin

It was not long before Tommy and Angel had second thoughts.

Angel poured himself a Scotch, poured another for Tommy, and came to grips with his feeling that something was not quite right in the Witwatersrand Basin, where they found themselves.

"What if we've overlooked the obvious?"

"Meaning what, Angel?"

"Doesn't it seem strange that the PG held that massive rally and then everything died down so quickly? Something's not right."

"Maybe." The commander gulped a swig of his Scotch whiskey. "So what do you think is going on?"

"I suggest we put our men on full alert and prepare to do battle right here. I think those blokes are countering our plan. They're bringing the fight to *us* right here and in plain sight of the world."

"Oh shit!" Tommy leapt to his feet. "Angel, I think you're right. We've misread everything."

There was an unexpected knock on the door. A South African Army soldier entered and said, "Someone here to see you, Commander."

A CF soldier stumbled into the commander's office. Red-faced and drenched in sweat, he was panting and struggling to stand. He gasped, "PG, Boss. Lots of 'em all 'round the place." He collapsed. The blade of a large hunting knife protruded from his back, driven into his flesh almost to the hilt.

Grimly, Tommy and Angel exchanged a silent, knowing look.

Perhaps because it was night, no one had apparently noticed the blade as the man approached the main office. Did a South African Army guard knife him to thwart him from delivering his message? No one ever knew for sure, but someone did know that the man had succeeded in informing his commander of the impending raid by the PG.

"Whatever we do," Angel said in a whisper, "we mustn't sound the alarm and let the bastards know we're onto them."

Tommy nodded. "Word of mouth, then." He walked outside and whispered something to a CF soldier, who then sauntered to the next station.

The commander came back inside.

But Angel dashed toward the periphery of the camp, where he commanded the troops there.

What seemed only moments later, CF troops were raising their rifles against the South African Army troops who'd been paired with them. Each CF soldier shouted, "You're either with us or against us."

Although the battle between the International Peacekeepers, that is, the CF, and the PG was on, the news correspondents at the Witwatersrand site were slow to comprehend what was happening; mostly, they concentrated on taking cover as gunshots rained everywhere.

Mercenaries, professional soldiers, and special ops were all firing in the darkness of the night. CF soldiers who patrolled the periphery of the site raised their rifles toward their South African Army counterparts, which included many PG sympathizers. Other CF soldiers dived underneath and behind vehicles and tanks, all while firing and reloading.

To the surprise of the South African Army soldiers—many of whom were PG sympathizers—one of the CF soldiers yelled, "OK, men, drop your rifles in front of you. That would be *now!*"

But a South African Army soldier shouted: "What the bloody hell!"

The same CF soldier then pointed his rifle at the army soldier's forehead and yelled, "Don't make me ask you again!"

At once, the South African Army soldiers, to the man, began dropping their rifles and tossing them to the ground. Because television cameras were rolling, the world watched as one of the most powerful military forces in the world surrendered its weapons to what they believed was an International Peacekeeping unit.

After the CF soldiers quickly collected the rifles of their South African Army counterparts, they just as quickly raised and pointed those rifles at their former owners. Then, a CF soldier shouted to his own men, "If anyone moves, shoot him!"

When the PG soldiers stationed on the periphery of the outpost saw that the CF soldiers had readied for battle, they knew that word of their surprise attack had fatally leaked. So they ran back into the thickets that surrounded much of the outpost.

And when Angel arrived on the periphery, he immediately assessed the locations of his troops and observed they were well-stationed underneath and behind vehicles and tanks. He shouted, "OK, now, men, the folks we've been waiting for are all out there in those thickets! Raise your weapons! If anyone moves, even sneezes, *shoot* them!"

At the same time, the CF commander put his men on alert inside the central command center. Then, he ran back outside, where, standing tall, he bent over, took a deep breath, and blew on his whistle as loud as he could. He shouted to his men standing around him, "Tell those guys in the gold mine it's time to come out—like yesterday!"

In short order, every CF soldier on the mine's main level raced out of the expansive, curvilinear cavern and grabbed hold of a rifle from a pile of weapons in the center of the camp.

As the CF and the PG prepared to fight, the news correspondents continued to scurry about for safety. Some ran inside the tent that had been assigned to them. Others huddled underneath the grub station. Some even huddled near groups of CF and South African Army soldiers or tried to enter the central command office.

That night, the world watched the streaming live news reports as the battle ensued at the Witwatersrand Gold Mine.

At his home in Johannesburg, not far away from the battle, Heinreik asked CIA Agent Froley, "Why are they calling him Jason Kinard? And he's no reporter. Now, what is he up to? Can you believe he contrived a story to interview me in the morning?"

"Oh, so you do recognize your nephew after all?" Agent Froley said as they continued watching the news coming out of Pretoria. The news about the battle at the Witwatersrand Gold Mine followed.

"I certainly do."

"Any idea why he'd endure such danger in this godforsaken hellhole?"

"You forget, Agent Froley, my nephew and I don't exactly share strong family ties. But I pray he comes through this without further harm. I can see he's already suffered a wound to his arm. Or is that his shoulder?"

At CIA Headquarters at Langley, federal agents moved about as if they themselves were dodging bullets. None of them wanted to say much for fear of having to take the blame if the mission were to fail—and in plain sight of the world, at that. It is certainly not easy to launch a surprise invasion or even to attempt a rescue, but all bets are off if the international media are broadcasting it all live.

"Remember the Iranian hostage debacle?" one of the agents fretted. "Just blew up in our bloody faces. But I have to tell you, even though I'm not much on prayer, I'm sending up some heavy timber on this one. *God, please do something to save the day.*"

In their undisclosed location in America—which was still Niagara Falls, New York—Liza and Julia were watching the same breaking news.

"Again, I say, that girl they keep showing us is *not* Priscilla," Julia said. "Besides, the body language is off."

"Not only that, but our Miss Prissy is afraid of heights—and low places, too, for that matter," Liza said. "I can't see her strutting voluntarily down into a doggone mine, of all places."

"You're telling me, Girlfriend," Julia said, and then she laughed. "Right now, though, I'm hoping this comes out right, and we—Priscilla included—get to go home. I still can't believe we've been isolated for nearly two months." But just then, Julia noticed that Liza seemed distracted. "Something in particular bothering you?"

Liza nodded. "I'm not sure how much longer I can control Germane. He's a child, but he's not stupid. I'm beginning to have trouble putting him off."

"Well, we have some consolation ahead," Julia said with a grin. "School starts soon."

But Liza only looked more anxious. "What if I have to homeschool him?" With a sigh, she rose and put another popcorn pack in the microwave oven.

Then, together, they continued watching the live broadcasts coming out of South Africa.

Back at the Witwatersrand Basin at Johannesburg, televised reports worldwide revealed the International Peacekeepers (the CF) rounding up all the South African Army soldiers—many of whom were Nationalist sympathizers—corralling them mid-camp, and then encircling them with armed guards. Each CF soldier now wore his own rifle on his shoulder and held a South African Army rifle at the ready.

Just as the CF troops completed their takeover of the Witwatersrand Gold Mine, the PG contingency—hiding out in the darkness of the thickets—suddenly advanced in what seemed like a suicide mission. Like the teenage Judges back in Harare, the Patrol Guardsmen had taken oaths that they would never willingly be taken hostage.

The PG contingent that Simeon had dispatched charged the CF camp, fully aware that they were doing so at their own peril. From the darkness of the thickets into the light, groups of twenty to thirty PG at a time—300 men in all—raced out from their hiding places behind the thickets and trees, holding their rifles at the ready. As a consequence, the CF had little choice but to defend themselves.

Angel turned to his men underneath the tanks and trucks and yelled, "Fire!" His men gunned down the PG soldiers until there were no more. Most of them never even made it to the camp's center.

Later, when a curious reporter asked Commander Wozniah why the PG did not use grenades or even try to bomb the place, he told them, "There were too many of their own kind being held at gunpoint by the International Peacekeepers. So maybe they did what was, for them, the next best thing: They willingly gave their lives for their cause."

While it all happened, news correspondents kept their cameras rolling as the PG, to the man, fell dead, and while their South African Army comrades stood helpless at gunpoint and witnessed the massacre.

As one of the cameramen taped the battle, he yelled at the CF commander, "Say, Commander, why didn't you just take them captive?"

Still standing tall amid the center of the command outpost, Tommy raised his voice and answered: "Would that have been before, during, or after their attempted raid of our camp?" adding, "The Patrol Guard could have surrendered, but that was not their mission or their MO. They came to fight until the end, and that was what they did."

"Suicidal!" bellowed someone else among the news correspondents of the PG's charge. "The sheer madness of it all…."

Although the massacre ended within a few minutes, it was hardly what the CF troops and mercenaries had signed on for.

Simeon Johannes watched the massacre of his Patrol Guardsmen and mercenaries at the Witwatersrand Gold Mine at Johannesburg from his opulent office at the SANM headquarters. He cursed the TV screen: "God-damn wimps. All that training, all those years, and all that damn money too—and for what?"

"Simeon, let's face it," said a committee member sitting in front of him at his desk. "It's all over. They're coming for us next."

Infuriated by the man's remarks, Simeon took a revolver from his desk drawer, aimed it at the man's forehead, and pulled the trigger. The man slumped forward onto the desk, blood gushing from the bullet hole in his forehead.

Then Simeon walked over to the bar and poured himself a drink of bourbon. He went back to his desk, sat back down, and gulped his drink with an air of satisfaction as if he'd just successfully completed a significant feat. Five minutes later, he strolled casually out of his office, leaving his dead colleague and pretending his body was not even there.

With Simeon having just killed that colleague of his, only five others remained. However, unbeknownst to Simeon, helicopters hovered over each of their palatial properties in gated communities outside Johannesburg. No helicopters were needed at the miniature mansion of Heinreik (Bernhardt) Lipponeg, who was already in custody, well, sort of.

As the helicopters landed, the international intelligence agents entered the homes of the remaining Executive Committee members and escorted them for transport to the nearby Johannesburg International Airport. Each member was then flown to CIA headquarters in Langley, Virginia, for interrogation before being referred to the federal criminal court system, not to mention facing charges and trials from other countries in the international criminal court.

And so it was that the highly anticipated takeover of the SANM Executive Committee occurred out of plain sight and with no fanfare or "farting" —not exactly the climax the CF agents, troops, and mercenaries had anticipated.

Before long, a battalion of the South African Army arrived at the CF central command outpost at the Witwatersrand Gold Mine. The soldiers removed the bodies of their fallen PG comrades. They also escorted their own troops away from the scene because there was not a single casualty among them. The South African government was reasonably satisfied that the International Peacekeepers had kept their word. The only loss they sustained was the public debasement of their troops in reports televised worldwide.

36

Matching Wits with

The Man Called Damien

Not too far away, in the depths of the Rustenburg Platinum Mine, where Priscilla was hiding in a crevice high up a wall, Charlie suddenly remembered that the South African Army possessed sophisticated war weaponry and technology—including devices that could track a person's movements.

"Wait a minute," he said to Jordy and the PJ decoy. For a moment, he studied the young woman and then asked her to remove one of her boots. When she complied, he took the boot and examined it closely. He tried to turn the heel one way and then the other. When he attempted to slide the heel backward, it snapped open. It was then that he saw the small tracking device that Damien had inserted inside the heel of the boot.

Jordy nodded as he stared at the device. "OK, so now what?"

"Now we plant it on someone else. Or we could just toss it."

"Nah," Jordy said, "then the bloody bastard will know that we found it."

But someone else had been watching and listening to the exchange.

There emerged from the gathering of miners near the lift a tall, well-built South African dressed much like the miners. He was, in fact, a Pan-Africanist

Congress (PAC) sympathizer. The man walked over to the CF entourage with the pomp of a commanding officer. He stomped his foot on the ground, removed one of his boots, and offered to install the tracker in its heel.

Jordy asked the man why he had stepped forward.

The PAC sympathizer looked the CF agent in his eyes and proclaimed, "I believe my people must fight for our freedom, and we want all of you out of here. Let them track me. At least if I die, it will be for *my* people."

Charlie took the boot and planted the tracking device in its heel.

"And let that be a lesson to us all," Jordy said, as all three of them thanked the noble volunteer. "Maybe Carlton was onto something after all. Things really aren't what they seem. But now we have another problem to solve. We have to face the fact that we have no idea where Priscilla's stalker is. So where do we go from here?"

Once again, the PJ decoy used her common sense. "Let us start by showing Damien's photo to these miners."

Charlie first showed the PAC sympathizer Damien's picture. He nodded and said he had seen the fellow. He pointed up. Several other miners nodded in agreement.

Immediately, Charlie, Jordy, the look–alike, and the PAC sympathizer all set out together to find Damien, whom they now believed was back on the main level above them.

Not far away, the object of their search was meanwhile realizing he must have been misled by the miners who had told him they did not recognize the photo of the little runt. So he gave the area where he was a final look-over and then returned to the main level.

Up one level, yet still not to the main level, he used his helmet light to examine the multitude of footprints. He also examined any peculiar smudges or markings on the walls. As he walked among the miners on that level, they parted the way for him. Even out of the public sphere, South African people were conditioned to step aside and allow white people unimpeded passage. But even the miners seemed to realize that the strange white man was on the prowl for the little soldier that some of their fellow workers had aided earlier. Word travels fast among the miners.

By the time that Jordy, Charlie, the PJ decoy, and the PAC sympathizer arrived at a level closer to the main level, they encountered the same miners who had just parted the way for Damien. When they showed his picture to the miners, they pointed in the direction he had just gone.

"Damn it, we've just missed him," Jordy said.

Utterly baffled, the entourage asked one another how they could have lost him so quickly, whereas Damien, so sure of himself, felt his heart race as he made his way through the tunnel to the mine's main level. He knew he would soon confront his target. He felt for the knife he would use to end her life. He laughed aloud, thinking no one could hear him way down deep in the Earth. Yet his laughter reverberated throughout the fabric of the platinum mine.

Not so far away, the PAC sympathizer, now with the tracking device in his boot, realized the laughter had come from the tunnels. He told the CF entourage about the tunnels and said he suspected the laughter of the man they were searching for came from within them. Then he led them to the main level, where he was pretty sure they would find their man.

Around the same time that Charlie, Jordy, the PJ decoy, and the PAC sympathizer were heading to the main level of the mine, Tommy and Angel had just arrived at the site. However, they decided to wait out of sight inside the central command cabin for a resolution to the final confrontation between Priscilla and the notorious Damien Escoffery. It was also well into the night, and they knew that it would be tough to maneuver throughout the area, especially inside the mine. Nor did they wish to interfere with the command that was already underway.

So, impatiently, they waited, and waited and waited.

As events unfolded inside the platinum mine, Tommy and Angel dodged the crowd of news correspondents gathered outside their headquarters. The media pressed them about the identity of a reporter who called himself Jason Kinard, whom they had learned was actually a military attaché for one of the fighting forces. They also sought details about the recent massacre of approximately 300 Guardsmen and mercenaries at the Witwatersrand Gold Mine in Johannesburg.

"No comment," Tommy kept saying. "No comment."

When the reporters realized that the CF commander was not going to give them any statement, they returned to their respective stations. There they waited for something, anything, to happen inside the Rustenburg mine.

While they waited, the lights from their cameras created an eerie backdrop for what almost all the reporters hoped would be the end to the horrific episode that had begun as a mystery in Harare.

Back inside the platinum mine, Carlton and his cameraman, Harry, continued to sniff out Damien on the same level of the mine where Priscilla was crouched in her crevice. However, they were at a total loss for any signs that Priscilla was even anywhere near them.

But they were acutely aware of Damien's skill at tracking his prey. They knew that he had a nose, eyes, and ears matched only by American Indians and the local tribe members here. So they knew he would easily sense Priscilla's presence, especially in the close quarters of the mine.

"We have got to find her first," Carlton said with urgency.

"Should we split up?" Harry asked.

"Maybe so. And search high and low. Watch out for holes in the walls, even for tunnels. I'm told the miners often dig tunnels in case of cave-ins." He looked all around in frustration. "Damn it, Missy, where are you?"

Just as Carlton and Harry were moving off in opposite directions, Damien was making gradual headway inside a tunnel in the darkness of the mine.

Priscilla, perched high above all of them, kept psyching herself that up was down and down was up. She did not know how much longer she could crouch in her small space. But since she had already chosen life over death, she had to stay put, at least until that quiet, still voice inside her told her otherwise. Once again, she heard Carlton and whoever he had with him walking and talking below her. Yet still she did not budge.

Then, after an absolute stillness, she heard the clanking sound of the lift. From what she guessed was only a few yards away came the sound of more familiar voices, but one of them she could not identify. It was the voice of the PAC sympathizer who had volunteered to put the tracking device in his boot. She did not know it for sure, but Jordy, Charlie, and one of her look–alikes were with that miner.

As it all happened, Damien thought he heard something or someone. He lowered his helmet light to a portable electronic tracking device that he had pulled out of one of his vest pockets.

"Ah, they're on the main level, too," he said as he neared what he assumed to be his prey. "And so we will meet again." He thought that the PJ decoy still wore the tracking device.

As he drew nearer to the tunnel's entrance to the main level, he remained still and listened more carefully. He sensed a strong scent of fear. As Priscilla's body released a pungent odor, Damien's nostrils flared as if he were sniffing out one of the big five game. But his sense of hearing was keener.

He counted. *There are four of 'em.*

But then he heard crumbling sounds coming from some other place nearby.

High above him, Priscilla was getting more uncomfortable by the minute. She struggled to stretch her aching legs. But as she moved about her small space, debris crumbled and rolled down the wall onto the ground.

Damien smiled and looked up. *Ah, ha! Unless that's a mighty big rat, I believe I've located the little runt.* He crawled quickly through the tunnel.

Carlton had meanwhile walked nearly half a mile away from the place where Priscilla had hidden herself; and Harry had walked a similar distance in the opposite direction. Although the cavern covered several miles in diameter, Carlton doubted Priscilla would venture too far away from the main entrance. *This is crazy*, he thought.

But around the same time, soon after they had gotten off the lift, Jordy and his cohorts had also split up to continue their search. None of the CF members was aware where any of the others had wandered off to. But Charlie and the PJ decoy had gone in one direction, which was in fact away from Priscilla, Damien, and Carlton. As for the others, Jordy and the PAC sympathizer had walked toward Priscilla, Damien, and Carlton.

Priscilla heard movements in the wall beneath her. She watched from her catbird seat as the man whom she thought was a South African Army captain slid out from a tunnel beneath her on to the main level. He stood still, his back tight against the wall.

Then she saw one, no two, men approaching. By the time she recognized Jordy, the man she thought was a South African Army captain raised his right fist and knocked Jordy to the ground unconscious. Never mind Jordy was not wearing the tracking device; Damien wanted to put as many men out of commission as possible, after which he could more easily capture his prey.

Priscilla had no way of knowing it, but he was hoping to disable the decoy, but she was no longer wearing the tracking device. Right behind Jordy was a noble Black man wearing the uniform of a miner, but he did not seem as such to Priscilla, and she was right. He was, in fact, a PAC sympathizer. Otherwise, Priscilla did not know about the tracking device that the decoy had worn. Nor did she know that the miner (the PAC sympathizer) was now wearing it. Although Priscilla was frightened, she somehow found solace at the sight of the noble man.

She then watched in amazement as the miner valiantly sprang forward, and then as he and the man whom Priscilla now perceived as the vicious villain wrestled. The vicious villain wrapped his right arm around the valiant miner's shoulder and threw him to the ground. The miner clawed at the villain's knuckles but could not escape his hold on him. After nearly being choked unconscious, the miner somehow managed to escape the other man's hold on him. But the villain put him into other holds, and they continued to fight. All the while, Priscilla watched the two men fighting ferociously.

Although they were at opposite ends of the main level, both Carlton and Harry heard the noise from the scuffle and hurried in its direction. Priscilla remained still, hoping the miner was winning the fight. But then the villain pulled out a sharp hunting knife and stabbed as close to the miner's heart as he could get. Still, the miner did not relent; he kept on fighting.

When she thought the fight was over, Priscilla was surprised when, miraculously, the miner rose to his feet. She was even more surprised when, somehow, he held the villain by his throat up against the wall. Then she watched as he clutched the adversary's throat and held on. Both men seemed doomed. The adversary choked, and the miner bled profusely. Yet it seemed to Priscilla that some mystical force was empowering the miner, despite his impending demise, to hold onto the adversary's throat.

All at once, the CF entourage converged on the scene of the fight.

But Priscilla ignored the converging entourage and gathered the courage to come out of the cavity where she had hidden herself. Her mind raced. For whatever reason, she thought about the biblical Jael, wife of Heber the Kenite. *But Jael had a rug to cover Sisera. All I have is a big, dirty, checkered handkerchief.* Because she knew she did not have the stomach to witness what she was about to do, she felt for the handkerchief in her vest pocket, pulled it out, and tossed it over the villain's head (the adversary). Then, quite methodically, she removed the hammer and the stake from her pants pocket and leaned forward. She needed to reach the two men struggling beneath her.

Then, quite unexpectedly, she heard a familiar voice ringing out frantically, "No, Missy, no!" It was Carlton, but his plea was to no avail.

Priscilla looked instead into the agonized face of the miner, the PAC sympathizer, who had spotted her from below. It was as if he had been holding onto the villain's throat—Damien—just long enough for Priscilla to react.

Priscilla and the miner caught each other's eyes. She saw a man who knew who he was and the significance of his actions. But he looked into the eyes of a woman who was not yet sure of who she was or, rather, her purpose in life. Even so, there was something infinitely reassuring in the man's eyes that gave Priscilla the strength of her conviction.

She raised her hammer as far back as she could and brought it down onto the stake, which rammed into the villain's temple. Priscilla heard the stake crack through the man's skull. Then she heard the stake penetrate the wall. She used all her might to hammer down on the stake again. She watched Damien tremble frantically against the wall. She saw blood spilling from the hole in the checkered handkerchief covering his head. She saw blood and brain matter spew onto the wall and onto the floor beneath him. She heard him gasp.

Then she whispered, "Three times to make it holy and to avenge the lives of so many of my people, the likes of you and your kind have killed. God, please forgive me for this awful deed." For the final time, she hammered down on the stake. More blood and gore.

With Damien Escoffery nailed against the wall inside the Rustenburg Platinum Mine, the PAC sympathizer released his grip from around the man's throat, let out a final gasping breath, and fell to the ground—dead.

Ironically, Priscilla's journey into southern Africa ended as it had begun two months ago, halfway around the globe at First Church in Columbus, Ohio. Oh, the blood and the gore! At her ill-fated wedding, she had witnessed it from afar. But here, in Rustenburg, South Africa, inside this dark and eerie platinum mine, blood stained her face and her hands. Adept at compartmentalizing her thoughts and her actions, too, Priscilla likened her awful deed to that of the biblical Jael, who hammered the tent peg into Sisera's temple. But no matter how much she washed her face and her hands, she was never able to erase from her mind all that blood and gore, or the fact that she had killed someone.

Priscilla—along with the rest of the entourage inside the mine—later wondered how she was able to lean down without growing dizzy, and herself falling. What she explained to the others was that she had already convinced herself that up was down and down was up. So, she had reasoned, it must have been easier for her to believe that she was looking up than it was for her to look down—into the face of the PAC sympathizer and at Damien's forehead.

But it had been more than that. No longer the self-centered, self-absorbed "Daddy's girl," she'd chosen to risk her life for someone else. Besides, she knew instinctively that she could not live with herself if she did not do what needed to be done for that valiant miner to go to his grave in peace. In so doing, she had become an unwitting participant in the South African people's struggle for freedom, something that even her father would have been pleased to know.

Meanwhile, because Priscilla was awkwardly positioned—she had planted her knees and feet into holes in the wall to secure her balance to lean forward in the first place—Carlton and Harry struggled to pull her up and out and then down from the cavity where she had crouched.

After she regained her bearings, she knelt to examine the face of the dead miner, the PAC sympathizer, who had been her savior. She kissed his cheek and whispered in his ear a word of thanks. After all, the PAC sympathizer had just saved her life. For if Damien had gotten to her first, surely, he would have killed her, or so she had thought.

When Priscilla got back up to her feet, trembling, she looked into the face of her double.

For a moment, all the others remained silent and still. They understood that they needed to give her a moment to reflect on what she had just done as the final act of her long trauma since being abducted from the church where she had thought she was about to be married.

When finally she spoke to her look–alike, Priscilla's voice was very gentle.

"Here in South Africa," she said, "both of us are considered 'Coloureds.' And here, even the Coloureds and the Blacks aren't supposed to interact. Oh, the irony of it all! Back home in the States, I'd be offended being called 'coloured,' but here, well, it's likened to a badge of honor."

Once she started talking, Priscilla did not seem to be able to stop. She was still distressed, afraid, and was overcome with much guilt.

"But in both societies, for a Black person to kill a white person is most assuredly a capital offense," she noted. "Nonetheless, I just killed someone, and I feel so sick." Her stomach churned. A sour substance funneled up her throat. She welled up, leaned over, and vomited.

When she was finished, her look–alike embraced her, and Priscilla cried like a wailing baby.

As she continued to hold Priscilla, the look–alike murmured, "What does one say about someone who wanted to kill someone else simply because of skin color? And what does one say to someone who has just killed someone to save another person's life *and* her own? In my line of work, it's called a 'first kill.' But it's still someone's life."

Instinctively, Carlton stepped forward and warmly embraced the two women. Charlie and Harry joined in. The whole lot of them had their arms around one another in a huge hug. They all so desperately wanted to console Priscilla.

Then suddenly they heard a groaning sound. They sprang apart.

Jordy was still on the ground, but now he was stirring.

"Oh-h, my head aches," he groaned. "Feels like someone hit me with a sledgehammer."

As one, they all let out a peal of hearty laughter.

Then they helped Jordy to his feet and turned to leave the mine.

But Priscilla insisted that they take the valiant miner to his people down below. "They must know of his courage," she said, "and that he saved my life."

As the CF entourage did as she requested, Jordy pulled Carlton aside. They agreed, in whispers, about what they would tell the media, who surely would be waiting for them outside the mine. Carlton would acknowledge "the real American woman, PR executive PJ Austin, has been safely rescued, PG Commander Damien Escoffery has been killed; and we will have no further comment until after we have reported to our respective headquarters."

When the South African miners saw the CF entourage coming with the dead body of their comrade, they all began singing "the Soweto Blues." For them, now the song was an indication or validation that their freedom was imminent:

> Children were flying; bullets dying
> The mothers screaming and crying

The fathers were working in the cities
The evening news brought out all the publicity.

Just a little atrocity,
Deep in the city.
Soweto blues
Soweto blues
Soweto blues
Soweto Blues….

37

Debriefing & Dismantling

Soon, television viewers worldwide watched live shots of the weary but victorious International Peacekeepers (the CF entourage)—Carlton, Jordy, and Charlie, along with the real PJ Austin (still posing as the little runt), one of her decoys, and Harry emerging from the depths of the Rustenburg Platinum Mine near Pretoria.

As the reporters surrounded them with eager questions, the only statement came from the man who had pretended to be one of them himself.

"By now," CF Agent Carlton Elliott Bernhardt (a.k.a. Jason Kinard) said, "you're fully aware of my cover as a reporter. Oh well, it was fun while it lasted." He chuckled. Although he still wore his moustache and baseball cap, he did not reveal his real name or his affiliation with the Collective Force. But he did tell the reporters that he was affiliated with the International Peacekeepers.

"We've concluded a successful mission here," he continued, noting that "and following the usual debriefing, I'm sure the relevant agencies will conduct an official press conference and fill you in on all the details. For now, however, we can tell you that the villainous Damien Escoffery was killed in a scuffle with one of our burly little soldiers."

He pointed to the little runt, whose face was so dirty that no one could make out her features, and the reporters all cheered.

"And yes," he rolled on, "we've finally located the elusive PJ Austin, and she is well. Now, if you will allow me a point of personal privilege . . .. I have a message for a young man named Germane, Ms. Austin's beloved nephew: 'Your Aunt Priscilla is just fine, and you will be together soon.'"

Throughout the agent's remarks, none of the international news correspondents asked him where the missing PJ Austin was. They simply took him at his word that she had been rescued.

The entourage then moved swiftly to the central command cabin, where Tommy and Angel were ecstatic to see them, especially Miss Prissy. Almost immediately, both Angel and Tommy recognized something familiar in the relaxed demeanor of the little runt, who no longer carried herself like a male soldier. Still, it was Angel who picked her up and planted an affectionate kiss on her smudged cheeks.

As he stood in the midst of the entourage, Tommy looked from one to the other. "What a motley crew we make. But Miss Prissy," warmly he said, rubbing her shoulders, "we're sure glad to see you."

Charlie wiped moisture from his forehead and looked at his boss. He sighed. Then, apologetically, "Sorry, Boss," he mumbled as he tugged at his moustache. "But it was a matter of expediency." That he said because he had kept the commander outside the loop of Priscilla's whereabouts; she had been right under his nose in her disguise as the smallest among them.

After a moment of laughter, the commander listened as his team briefed him on what had happened inside the mine. Then he nodded and said, "Okay, folks," as he peered intensely into Priscilla's eyes, "anybody else have anything I should know?"

No one uttered a word, although all eyes were now on Priscilla.

Still trembling from having killed Damien Escoffery, Priscilla just wanted to be left alone. She was tired, and she wanted to go home. She longed for her familiar surroundings and the relatively serene life that she had taken for granted. Yet she sensed her life would never be the same again.

At last, she spoke: "Now what? What on Earth do you want from me now?"

"First, little one," Tommy said, "you're going to have to undergo a debriefing. Much of what you've experienced these past several weeks will have to be kept under wraps."

Jordy moved closer to her. He smiled. "And even if you were to reveal some of what has happened, people will be hard-pressed to believe it anyway."

Then, much to the surprise of everyone, Priscilla raised her voice.

"Oh, I get it. This was some sort of god–awful unauthorized mission. And my rescue was the only part that was government-sanctioned?"

Then, just as quickly, wearily, she lowered her voice, twisted her foot, and asked, as if she felt there would be more to these men's game plan, "How soon before *I* can go home and be with my family?"

The commander and the others shared a quick frown, stunned by her accurate description of their mission. Then the commander said, somewhat haphazardly, "Let me call headquarters first. Then I can answer your question."

"Just a minute," Priscilla said. She remembered something. "And I want to see Onslow. He's the reason I've made it this far in the first place. He taught me survival skills, and he was the first among you to accept me for who I am. Where's Onslow?" she demanded to know.

Carlton spoke soothingly, as to a child, or was that she thought, as if her request had been insignificant. "Oh, Missy, Onslow's fine. He took a hit during the raid at the Mwenezi camp. By now, he's back home in the States with his family."

"But when can I *see* him?" she asked. "I don't much care what else you ask of me. But I must thank Onslow. He needs to know I appreciate him."

"I'm sure," Tommy said, "Miss Prissy, that we can arrange for that later, but not right now," in much the same condescending tone as Carlton.

Priscilla looked as if she were about to explode. "But *when,* then?" She felt they had all taken Onslow for granted. But she was not about to forget this man who had rescued her from so much devastation and who, towards the end of her horrible journey, showed the humanity for which she would be eternally grateful.

"Once we return to the States," Tommy said with some finality. "But we've got quite a bit more to do here first," which answered her earlier concern about what else was in the works.

"Maybe you do," she said. "But all bets are off as far as I'm concerned, until you do as I ask." Maybe she did not fully understand it at the time, but

Priscilla had come to realize her role in the mission. She also realized something else: that these four men, these pretentious high-powered Ohio lobbyists, were, in fact, special operatives for some clandestine unit of American intelligence. And she did not really care which intelligence agency that was, only that she now knew they knew she knew more than they had ever intended for her to know. And so she was hardly going to back down now.

Yet it was Angel who interceded in the little debate.

"All right, already. I'll set something into motion with Onslow. I'm thinking, considering all Miss Prissy's been through, that this is a small order. Don't you think, everybody?" Angel discerned an element of chutzpah in Priscilla that had not been there before her African adventure. The once pompous, maybe even cocky, legislative aide turned PR executive—known for her stylish high heels, her black woolen pinstripe suits, and her silk blouses— stood comfortably before him, donning the camouflage uniform of a CF soldier. *Who would've thought?*

Shortly after Angel negotiated a simple but effective way to appease Priscilla, Carlton stood before her and said, "OK, now, Missy, can you and I at least talk? I've got some explaining to do."

She raised her eyebrows. "Gee, Carlton, to think I shared my all with you. Did you ever think to give me some little hint that you guys were involved in something as grand as this… crap?"

"But Missy," he pleaded. "That's not something any of us are at liberty to—"

"And to think you subjected me to something as treacherous as the SANM, and, hell, the PG, too, and even those damn wenches, the Judges! My goodness, Carlton! And now you bloody bastards want me to pretend that none of it ever even happened?"

Crestfallen. "Oh, Missy, I am so sorry," said the once suave, intrepid CF Agent Bernhardt.

"Yeah, well, I'll bet you are." She did not crack a smile. "And why the devil is it I suspect there's even more to this sad story?"

Carlton's beseeching voice rose. "Why won't you let me explain? I'm not asking to be forgiven, but I would like to explain."

"Not right now, Carlton. Right now, I need some time to myself. All right? Not right now."

Carlton turned his back and walked away. He sat down in a chair in one of the corners of the room. He was humiliated enough over the situation involving his uncle—and now by the woman whom everyone knew he still loved. He sulked.

Then Jordy approached her ever so cautiously. "Say, Miss Prissy, don't you think you're being a little hard on our boy? It's not as if he brought on all this. Why won't you give him a chance to explain?"

"Oh, Jordy, I hear you, but I can't understand why you guys *all* misled me. Why couldn't you have just told me enough to prepare me for some of this crap? My God, fellas, I *killed* a man. Can you believe that? I actually took someone's life. It's as if I don't even know you, like you've been living double lives."

"But we *have* been living double lives." There now, Jordy finally said it. "That's what Carlton is trying to tell you. None of us can ever tell our families and friends the truth about this part of our lives. That's why we couldn't tell you, either—that is, until now."

"What of it all now, anyway, Jordy?" Priscilla was being rhetorical.

"We'll work that out later," he said to his former high schoolmate. "But first, why not give Carlton a chance to talk to you?"

"Oh, all right, Jordy." Then she turned to Carlton and said, "Later, Carlton. We can talk later." But Priscilla had no more "make nice" energy. She wanted to be left alone. "When can I get out of here?" she asked. "I need a bath, a cup of coffee, and a cigarette."

Her look–alike met her eyes and nodded with the understanding that Priscilla desperately needed to make sense of some of her African experience. She asked her CF associates to find another place to debrief and leave the two of them alone for a while. When they trooped away, she escorted her model-ward to the back of the cabin and then to a shower stall.

The double had a gin and tonic and a pack of cigarettes ready for Priscilla when she emerged squeaky clean and wrapped in a robe.

Priscilla lit up. "You know something, Ms. Double? I have never thanked you for helping to save my life. Lord knows, I'm more than grateful."

"All in a day's work, Missy." She called Priscilla by the familiar name that Carlton sometimes used because she felt she had bonded with her model-ward, and she had.

"And I suppose you can't tell me your real name and other actual stuff about your life?"

"Nah, but you can call me 'Sally.' That's what all the fellas call me."

"Okay, Sally sounds better than 'Hey, you.'" They grinned at each other. Then Priscilla asked Sally, "Was it difficult pretending to be me?"

"I could never quite master your mannerisms. And now that I've spent some time with you, I don't think I ever would be able to acquire your passion."

"Ah, come on, now. 'Mannerisms?' 'Passion?'"

"Miss Prissy, when they train us, they're cautious to let us know there will always be some idiosyncrasies in our model that we'll never master. Do you know why that is?"

"No."

"Mother Nature and God imbued each of us with certain qualities that no matter how we try, we can never impersonate, mimic, or replicate," Sally said. "That's what makes you, Priscilla, and me, Sally. I'll bet your mom was watching all of this on television, and she never once believed that I was really her daughter. That's because she, more than anybody else, knows her child."

"I think I get it."

"Now, I have a question for you," Sally said. "Do you understand why it's important that you never divulge to your family and friends the details of our experiences? The less that people know, the more effective our work is. That's what Jordy and Carlton were trying to tell you."

"I see. I really do." Priscilla yawned.

Before long, Sally left her to retire.

Priscilla slept uninterrupted through much of the night, perhaps because she was in a real bed for the first time in a long while. When she awoke the next morning, it was after ten o'clock. She felt as if she had awakened to an entirely new and different world, and, well, she had.

As it turned out, Heinreik (Bernhardt) Lipponeg spent much of that same night under continuously rigorous interrogation by the CIA, the Mossad, and the CF agents. When they were satisfied that he had told them what they needed to hear, he asked for some private time with his great-nephew.

"You're my nephew's son," Heinreik began. Carlton was the only member of his family whom Heinreik had seen or spoken to since his departure from home in Lebanon nearly forty years ago. "And here you are, so handsome and,

350

I think, so stubborn. I'd have known you anywhere! You look like your father did at your age. You know, growing up, I was always the quiet one. No one expected me to take the course that I did. They always assumed I'd stay behind and take over the family business, but that wasn't for me. I wanted to find my own way. But, Carlton, you must believe me." At this point, he'd become animated. "I never imagined anything turning out like this." Remorse was evident all over his handsome face.

But Carlton said, "In our age of telecommunications and advanced technology, there's hardly a darn thing anyone can do without someone else knowing about it."

Briefly, Heinreik smiled and then said, "Anyway, back when you were posing as a reporter… You asked about the SANM's plans to establish those orphanages and boarding schools. So, what exactly is it you wanted to know?"

"Have you put anything in place yet?"

"We have, and I believe the success of the foundation will depend on you. I've named *you* CEO of the new foundation that funds the program."

"Hell, no!"

"Hell, yes! It's already done. Agent Froley and the others have cleared the program with the blessing of your superiors at Langley. So now you may do with me whatever you wish. At least I can go knowing I've done some small measure of good to rectify the wrong I've done."

"Oh, no you don't!" Carlton lashed out at his estranged great-uncle. "You don't get off that easy. There's at least one other person you need to face."

Charlie, Priscilla, and Sally had taken an early afternoon commuter flight to Johannesburg, where they'd rented an SUV and driven to the outskirts of the city. At this very moment, they were turning into the gated community where Heinreik lived. His two-story mansion was like an oasis in the midst of a large forest. Jacarandas flanked the winding road leading up to it. Tall Italian marble columns welcomed visitors at its main entrance, where they were greeted by an ebony-complexioned butler wearing tails. Upon entering through massive wooden French doors, Priscilla noticed more Italian marble on the floor and circling columns around the impressive foyer. An eye-catching staircase welcomed them for a second time.

While the butler escorted Priscilla to Heinreik's study, she noticed the absence of stuffed animal heads on the walls or animal skins on the floor.

Instead, she saw much artwork carefully displayed. On the floor were wooden carvings and glass, too. And the walls displayed a modest array of Cezanne, Renoir, and Toulouse-Lautrec, along with some local art.

As she entered Heinreik's study, Carlton and his great-uncle were engaged in what seemed to be an intimate discussion. But immediately they fell silent. Carlton was standing beside his uncle, who sat in a simple leather chair behind a neatly organized mahogany desk. Despite his display of wealth, he seemed a man of simple taste and ways.

Carlton beckoned to her. "Come over here, Missy, and meet our host, my great-uncle, Heinreik Bernhardt. But he's used the name Lipponeg for over forty years."

Eager to meet someone—anyone—who was far removed from her recent escapades, Priscilla smiled and happily shook the man's hand while he held onto hers.

"Hello, Mr. Bernhardt," she chirped.

Then she turned to Carlton and said in a much kinder voice than she had the night before, "Gee, Carlton, he looks exactly like you, only a lot more distinguished."

It was hard for Carlton to say his next words.

"Missy, my great-uncle is a member of the Executive Committee of the South African Nationalists Movement, the organization that assigned the assassin to take out Senator Callahan and who mistakenly shot and killed your groom, Jonathan." There, now, he said it.

Stunned, Priscilla attempted to pull her hand from Heinreik's grip.

But Heinreik held onto her hand and pleaded with her, "I am so sorry, truly I am."

While Heinreik spoke, Priscilla's mind raced. She remembered the day of her ill-fated wedding, her stay at the safehouse in Prospect, her days as a housekeeper at the Anglican Cathedral in Harare, her captivity in the crypt of and her encounter with Moses Cameron, her near-death experience under those dead and wounded soldiers during the battle at the Mwenezi River, and her own horrible killing of Damien Escoffery.

No, he can't be behind all that, she thought. She trembled noticeably. She pulled at Heinreik's fingers to unclasp her hand. "You don't seem to be an evil person. Besides, you're Carlton's kin. Why would you want to hurt Jonathan or the senator or *me? Why?*"

"Oh, young lady, I am so-o sorry. I declare I am."

Copious tears streamed down both of their cheeks. Neither could believe their overwhelming situation, Heinreik because he saw the love his nephew had for this young woman, and Priscilla because she saw the strong resemblance between her lover and the first relative of his that she'd ever met.

But there was nothing Heinreik could do or say to assuage the pain that Priscilla felt—as if someone had removed the stake from Damien's forehead and pierced her heart. But she very much feared that—if what was happening under the surface between Carlton and her was as precious to her as she thought it might be—she might have to live through her pain and agony over Heinreik's familial ties with Carlton for some time to come. *Could Heinreik's role in the SANM have been the reason why Carlton wanted to talk to me last night?* Even as she ran out of the room, she could not stop asking herself: *Why?*

Carlton waited until Priscilla was gone and the door was securely closed behind her. He turned to his uncle and said, "So you see, dear Uncle Heinreik, just as you've spent a lifetime turning a deaf ear and a blind eye to the atrocities perpetrated on so many people, it will take you another lifetime to reconcile the harm such benign neglect has caused. And so, no amount of money infused in some doggone orphanages and boarding schools will ever fix any of that, either."

Then CF Agent Carlton Bernhardt walked out of the room—and out of his great-uncle's life, or so he thought.

After that final order of business was completed, the CIA and the "unauthorized" CF agents took Heinreik away from his palatial estate to a place where he and the other surviving members of the SANM Executive Committee would be detained for a while. But unlike the others, eventually, Heinreik would be granted a reprieve and allowed to reconnect with his family in an undisclosed location and under a new identity, too.

Much earlier, in the still of the night, the CF commander and his comrades had entered the opulent headquarters of the SANM Executive Committee. There, they found two corpses: the man Simeon Johannes had shot the day before, and Simeon himself.

Simeon's body slumped over his desk, amid a pile of money. He appeared to have died by his own hand. Also on the desk was an empty medicine bottle. Simeon had taken his cyanide pill and who knew what else.

Simeon had a piece of paper clenched in his hand, which read, "Bury me with my money."

The intelligence agents had then systematically ransacked the place, taking care to empty the file cabinets and collect the electronic devices and equipment.

Then Tommy doused the place—including the remains of the two men—with kerosene from a large bucket that he had brought with him. Angel removed a box of large matches from his vest pocket, struck a match, and threw it flaming onto the kerosene that permeated the conglomerate's once opulent headquarters. Then the men watched as flames and smoke erupted from the floor, engulfing the expensive furniture and everything else inside that suite.

At the last moment, they ran out of the place as quickly as they could, leaving behind the kerosene bucket and the box of matches.

In the interim, the CF's so-called International Peacekeeping forces disbanded, and the many mercenaries dispersed to their respective countries to resume their other lives. Among them were CF Commander Tommy Wozniah, CF Agent Bartholomew Jordan, CF Agent Angelo Delgato, the agent known as Charlie—the manservant, the PJ Austin look–alike Sally, and the cameraman who answered to the name of Harry.

Only CF Agent Carlton Elliott Bernhardt remained behind.

With the destruction of the conglomerate's opulent headquarters, coupled with all the other news about the battles that had ensued, as well as the rescue of the American PR executive PJ Austin, news correspondents blanketed the world with news of how deeply the SANM and its PG had penetrated South African society—especially its financial and political realms. Eventually, several highly esteemed members of the National Assembly were forced to resign. Soon, too, the United States would possess secrets the authorities in the South African government, not to mention the SANM conglomerate, never imagined anyone but themselves ever possessing.

But that's not all that happened; there was one more debriefing essential to Priscilla's time in southern Africa, one that she would never forget.

38

Now, She's the Real Priscilla!

After Priscilla got dressed the following morning, she walked into the principal office of the CF central command cabin at the Rustenburg Platinum Mine near Pretoria. An unfamiliar man, who identified himself as a liaison from the U.S. Department of State, waited for her and began speaking.

Yet, as she looked around the otherwise empty office that once served as the CF's headquarters at the Rustenburg Platinum Mine, she initially ignored the man. Eventually, though, she asked the obvious question, "Where is everybody?" She didn't know that all but one of her rescuers had already left. She had been told she was scheduled to fly to West Germany before returning to the States, but that was all she had been told.

Then, the only other person in the room spoke.

"Ms. Austin, as I mentioned a moment ago, I am Wendell Rogers, representing the United States Department of State. I'm here to brief you on what is about to happen."

"That's all well and good," she said, "but where did the others go?"

"The first thing I need to tell you is, 'There are no others.' From this point on, Ms. Austin, you must completely forget everything you know about the people you've interacted with over the past few weeks."

"Oh, I see. But surely I can admit that I was abducted. And what exactly is the party line for the span of those missing two months in my life?"

"For starters, you *were* abducted, but you're still not sure by whom. In fact, you never even saw the faces of your kidnappers. Now, did you?"

Priscilla shook her head. "No, I did not," she said.

"Good, now we're getting somewhere. That's precisely what you are to say to your family, your friends, the media, and everyone else."

"And the two-month gap in my life?"

"You were held hostage by persons unknown at the Anglican Cathedral in Harare. From there, you were moved to a mine near Pretoria, again by persons unknown. They spoke English or a South African dialect. They shaved your head as a form of intimidation. They subjected you to intense interrogation, sometimes depriving you of sleep and food—"

"Okay," Priscilla said, interrupting the man, "but what kind of interrogation? What exactly did my abductors want to know?"

"They wanted to know the role of your former boss, Senator Daniel P. Callahan, in plotting to overthrow the apartheid regime in South Africa."

For the first time in a long time, she almost laughed. "Oh, come on. This is ridiculous," a distraught Priscilla eventually said. "It would be more credible if I'd been raped and mutilated or otherwise tortured."

Mr. Rogers came back at her with, "Not funny, Ms. Austin. You'd be surprised at the mindset of some of the Afrikaners and their sympathizers."

Yet, she held her own when she retorted not-so-subtly, "And you might be surprised at what those fools can actually do to a human body. Anyway, I think I understand where you're headed. I don't look like someone who's been violated, so we'll need to approach this differently. Does that mean you're going to bombard me with such foolishness on our flight to Germany?"

"Yes, well, you know . . . They did tell me you were bright. But I wasn't exactly expecting you to be so forthright."

"Well now, Mr. Rogers," she said in jest, as she tried her darn best not to laugh at the likeness of his last name and that of the television personality, "Mister Rogers."

"Welcome to my world. But I need a few moments to myself."

"Sure, take your time."

Priscilla milled about the office of the abandoned central command outpost until it finally occurred to her that she had not seen Tommy, Jordy,

Angel, or Charlie, the manservant, not even Carlton. Deeply saddened, she suddenly understood what it would mean as they said, to "forget about everything and everybody." After reflecting, she gathered up her meager belongings and headed to the front door of the cabin.

At that moment, the door swung open, and to her surprise, Carlton stepped across the threshold.

"I see I'm just in time. Missy, I *had* to see you before we were separated again."

"Carlton, I don't believe this." She shook her head.

"I want you to know how sorry I am about the role of my estranged uncle in all that has happened to you," her former lover said. "I also want to ask a *really big* favor." He was panting, pretty much out of breath.

Although she frowned, he continued: "I'm quite serious." Then he glanced over at the liaison. "We need a minute. I won't be long. Just give us a minute or two."

"No problem, Agent B." The liaison said and stepped outside.

"Miss Prissy, my uncle named me CEO of a foundation that the SANM created," he said. "Its mission is to foster good relations among the races and ethnic groups in South Africa and Zimbabwe. One of the avenues to achieve that goal is to build and operate orphanages and boarding schools for mixed-race girls. And…well, I was kind of hoping that you mi—"

"You've got to be kidding me!" The shocked expression on her face was priceless.

"No, Miss Prissy, I'm quite serious." The serious expression on his face was equally priceless. "Which is precisely my point. You see, Missy, I figure one way for you to deal with all that tragedy would be to engage in the type of work this project involves."

Priscilla stood dumbfounded. "My God, Carlton, when will my life be as it once was?"

Just then, Mr. Rogers knocked softly on the door and came back inside without waiting for an answer. "I'm afraid," he said, "I've got to get her aboard that flight. We've got to wrap this up."

"Miss Prissy," Carlton pleaded, "promise me that you'll at least think over my offer. And whatever else you might think of me, always know that I've never stopped loving you." He did not care that the State Department official heard him, either.

Tears streamed down Priscilla's cheeks. She already knew how Carlton felt. But she was hardly ready to yield her enduring love to anyone else, not even to him. She might be ready someday, maybe even tomorrow or the next day. Or maybe not ever. But for now, too much has happened. Love was not what she wanted. She wanted time and space; she wanted to go home.

"Please, Carlton," she said tearfully but gently. "Not now. Not yet."

At that, Carlton Elliott Bernhardt hung on to what he deduced as being hope. *She did not say 'no,'* he surmised. And so, he stepped aside and held the door as Priscilla and U.S. State Department Liaison Wendell Rogers walked out of the abandoned CF central command cabin at the Rustenburg Platinum Mine near Pretoria for the last time.

Priscilla and the U.S. State Department liaison boarded a flight en route to West Germany, where at a military intelligence facility near Bonn, Priscilla was debriefed for the umpteenth time and underwent extensive psychological and medical examinations.

Once she was cleared for release, a short press conference was arranged in a large conference room for television viewers worldwide to see the real American PR executive, PJ Austin, for the first time since her abduction over two months ago.

Liza, Germane, and Julia had arrived ahead of her. They were all seated in the front row of that large room.

Earlier, they'd experienced a momentary reunion with Priscilla. They had also been briefed on the protocols of the press conference. But Liza, Germane, and Julia only wanted to reunite with their beloved Priscilla for a much more extended period of time than that earlier, very brief reunion. They did not even want to talk to the reporters.

Dressed in the loose, casual garments that she wore when her African adventures first began in that suburb of Harare, Priscilla appeared healthy, but somewhat stoic. Her experiences over the past two months had hardened her spirit, but she herself was not yet aware of that.

Liza kept saying, "Now, she's the real Priscilla! You got anything else to add, Julia?"

Julia just shook her head.

Priscilla sat near the middle of the conference table. She was flanked by the CIA director, a deputy secretary of state, two American congressmen, and several diplomats from countries in Western Europe and southern Africa.

As the press conference began, the most astute observers among the news correspondents understood that Priscilla's triumph belonged to those officials flanking her as much as it did to her. In fact, the CIA director and the deputy secretary of state talked on and on about the various tragic episodes, although each put their own spin on the stories. When they referred to the episode at the Anglican Cathedral, they did not mention that Priscilla had been stashed away in that crypt, and they did not mention that it was she who had all but whacked off Moses Cameron's private parts either. For sure, no one mentioned that she'd killed Damien Escoffery.

The CIA director and the deputy director of the State Department instead preferred to say, "We still find it hard to believe that the South African Nationalist sympathizers actually groomed teenagers to become spies and assassins, young women at that. And we certainly can't fathom the European connection to the Judges."

The West German press conference was intended to focus on the rescue of Ms. Austin, whereas all matters pertaining to the SANM Executive Committee and its PG and the foiled assassination of Senator Callahan would be addressed at the Langley press conference. Even federal officials have a pecking order.

Yet, one time too many, the deputy secretary of state referred to Priscilla as "an unfortunate victim of circumstance."

Priscilla abruptly stood up from her seat, turned to the deputy secretary of state, and said, "On that note, I will not be silent. I'm *nobody's* victim. A victim is someone who loses hope and gives up. I never did."

That reaction from Priscilla created a bit of intrigue among the news corps. For at that point, the reporters and their audience the world over could see that PJ Austin was indeed a force to be reckoned with. They also readily discerned there was more to Priscilla's story than what they were being told.

As for Priscilla's favorite nephew, Germane, the young man milled impatiently about the space throughout the press conference. As such, the cameramen filmed him because he manifested so much joy. Or perhaps they were filming him because Priscilla's remarks were so terse.

"I just want to go home," she kept saying. "Please, let me go home."

During one part of the press conference, reporters broadcast photographs and footage of Priscilla, members of the Patrol Guard, including Claus Fokker, Leonard Genn, Alistair Longworth, and Damien Escoffery, and the teenage Judges, including Camilla Cameron and her two friends, Joyce and Anna.

All the while, Germane moved about the room and fidgeted with camera equipment. At one point, he even walked onto the stage and hugged his aunt, a scene that the cameramen showed repeatedly.

But the scene that most captured the viewers' attention was the young man running his hands through his aunt's hair.

"Aunt Priscilla, they cut your hair. I don't care, though. You're still my Aunt Priscilla."

And so it was that amid the orchestrated stories about the sensational chain of events that stemmed from what came to be called "Mystery in Harare," this simple act of a child made the press conference seem authentic and persuasive.

Gleeful, Germane said over and over again, "My Aunt Priscilla has come back home. I knew she would."

As for Julia, she did not say much. When she did speak, she referred the reporters to Liza. Even the reporters began to repeat the women's constant chant: "Now, she's the real Priscilla! You got anything else to add, Ms. Liza?" And "Now, she's the real Priscilla! You got anything else to add, Julia?"

A few hours later, the Austin delegation boarded their return flight to the States, now en route to Langley, Virginia, where the official welcome home was scheduled to take place.

"Ah, yes," Priscilla said hours later, as she stared out the window of the giant airliner at the countryside below, "now that's what I'm talking about."

Priscilla would be thrilled to see her siblings: Nelson, Jr., Ellen, Harriet, Helen, and Camille, all of whom eagerly stood on the tarmac at the foot of the metal staircase that she, along with Liza, Germane, and Julia, descended. The siblings had not seen Priscilla or their mother or Germane since the carnage at First Church on that ill-fated day of Priscilla's wedding. Moreover, although her mother and nephew had been in protective custody, the authorities had figured it best that there be no contact between them and the siblings, either. As it turned out, a small family union was in order for the Austin clan. They all embraced one another and laughed and cried at the same time.

Also, as he had promised Priscilla, Angel held true to his word. In Virginia, Priscilla was allowed to see Onslow. She learned that he was indeed married to a remarkable woman—a tenured professor in antiquities at Columbia University—and that the couple had three teenage sons. She discovered Onslow's facade was indeed just that—his cover. In his day job, Onslow was a stockbroker on Wall Street, and he was not at all the macho adventurer he projected during her time in Africa. Nonetheless, Onslow was overwhelmed with the news that Priscilla had insisted on seeing him before witnessing any of the official welcome celebrations at Langley.

"Once a friend, always a friend," he said to her, and they embraced.

Still, after she had insisted on seeing Onslow to thank him, all Priscilla could do was cry.

But soon CIA Agent Froley and FBI Agent Rothschild appeared. After they greeted her and introduced themselves, they, too, reminded her to forget all about her recent adventures in Africa, including Onslow.

"Yeah, yeah," she said. "I know."

Then, the two federal intelligence agents escorted her to a private room and shut the door behind them when they told her that they had something important to discuss with her.

Oh, no! She took a deep breath and understood that whatever it was, she was not prepared in the least for it.

But when CIA Agent Froley and FBI Agent Rothschild waved her to take a seat, she sat down and cracked a smile.

As it turned out, Angel—and Tommy, too, for that matter—were not the only ones to have noticed Priscilla's changed demeanor. So too had a couple of other fellows above their pay grade. Whether Priscilla knew it or not, this time the "plum offer" was coming from above the ranks of the high-powered Ohio lobbyists. But would she recognize it for what it was?

Oh, well, she thought. *Welcome to the big league, Girlfriend.*

There was that smirk, again.

Mystery in
HARARE

About the Author

Indie author M. J. Simms-Maddox, Ph.D., is the creator of 'The Priscilla Series,' a distinctive novel series that chronicles the coming-of-age journey and adventures of a modern-day, self-assured Black American heroine of diverse ancestry.

- The series' storylines center on politics, and the fictional Priscilla shares many traits with the author.

- The South Carolina native grew up in the Snowbelt of western New York, where she loved the cold weather and snow. She earned her Ph.D. in political science from *The* Ohio State University, served as a legislative aide in the Ohio Senate, ran a PR firm, and taught in her field before retiring.

- She has also published *A Handbook for Emerging and Seasoned Authors: An Insider's Step-by-Step Approach to Becoming a Successful Indie Author.*

- The author enjoys public speaking, reading, traveling, watching culinary, travel, and mystery shows, doing yard work, and, of course, writing.

Political affiliations include the African Literature Association, the Chanticleer Authors' Conference, and the Surrey International Writers' Conference.

To learn about the author and her literary works, visit: www.novelsbymj.com.